Autoerotic Fatalities

Autoerotic Fatalities

Robert R. Hazelwood
FBI Academy
Park Elliott Dietz
Schools of Law and Medicine
University of Virginia
Ann Wolbert Burgess
School of Nursing
University of Pennsylvania

LexingtonBooks
D.C. Heath and Company
Lexington, Massachusetts
Toronto

Library of Congress Cataloging in Publication Data
Hazelwood, Robert R.
   Autoerotic fatalities.

   Bibliography: p.
   Includes indexes.
   1. Autoerotic asphyxia.   2. Autoerotic death.
I. Dietz, Park Elliott.   II. Burgess, Ann Wolbert.
III. Title. [DNLM: 1. Asphyxia—Complications.
2. Erotica.   3. Death, Sudden—Etiology.   4. Paraphilias.
WM 610 H429a]
RA1002.H39 1982   616.85'83   81-47692
ISBN 0-669-04716-3

Copyright © 1983 by D.C. Heath and Company

All rights reserved. No part of this publication may be reproduced or transmitted in any form or by any means, electronic or mechanical, including photocopy, recording, or any information storage or retrieval system, without permission in writing from the publisher.

Second printing, November 1984

Published simultaneously in Canada

Printed in the United States of America on acid-free paper

International Standard Book Number: 0-669-04716-3

Library of Congress Catalog Card Number: 81-47692

To our families

Contents

	Preface	ix
	Acknowledgments	xiii
Chapter 1	Autoeroticism and the Public Visibility of Autoerotic Asphyxia *Robert R. Hazelwood, Park Elliott Dietz, Ann Wolbert Burgess,* and *Kenneth V. Lanning*	1
Chapter 2	Recurrent Discovery of Autoerotic Asphyxia *Park Elliott Dietz*	13
Chapter 3	Study Design and Sample Characteristics *Ann Wolbert Burgess, Park Elliott Dietz,* and *Robert R. Hazelwood*	45
Chapter 4	Asphyxial Autoerotic Fatalities *Robert R. Hazelwood, Park Elliott Dietz,* and *Ann Wolbert Burgess*	55
Chapter 5	Autoerotic Asphyxia, the Paraphilias, and Mental Disorder *Park Elliott Dietz, Ann Wolbert Burgess,* and *Robert R. Hazelwood*	77
Chapter 6	Atypical Autoerotic Fatalities *Park Elliott Dietz* and *Robert R. Hazelwood*	101
Chapter 7	Investigation of Autoerotic Fatalities *Robert R. Hazelwood, Park Elliott Dietz,* and *Ann Wolbert Burgess*	121
Chapter 8	Equivocal Deaths: Accident, Suicide, or Homicide? *Robert R. Hazelwood, Park Elliott Dietz,* and *Ann Wolbert Burgess*	139
Chapter 9	Judicial Decisions Regarding Insurance Benefits in Autoerotic Fatalities *Park Elliott Dietz* and *Robert R. Hazelwood*	155

References	189
Index	201
About the Authors	207

Preface

This book concerns deaths occurring in the course of autoerotic activities in which a potentially injurious agent was used to heighten sexual arousal. Such seemingly obscure deaths affect not only the victims, but also their survivors and those whose professional roles demand knowledge of these matters.

The autoerotic practices that sometimes result in death come to the attention of clinicians of all disciplines, law-enforcement personnel, medical examiners, and coroners. These various disciplines are structured such that there is no sharing of observations in any systematic way. We hope that this work will help to inform concerned representatives of each of these disciplines about the knowledge that has accumulated through their separate efforts.

Our efforts to explore autoerotic fatalities and the practices that underlie them are, of necessity, more descriptive than analytic and more analytic than quantitative. The phenomena we describe are not typical of everyday experience. Thus we have provided more graphic descriptions than would be necessary in a work about familiar phenomena. The unfamiliarity of these phenomena also underlies errors in the recognition and classification of cases, requiring that we develop diagnostic criteria and a workable typology. Too often cases have gone unrecognized or have been misclassified through ignorance, mistaken belief, and the absence of a readily accessible source of information.

The empirical study of autoerotic fatalities based on submitted cases was initiated by Roy Hazelwood in the Behavioral Science Unit of the FBI Academy at about the same time as Park Dietz was tracing the history of the subject while at Johns Hopkins and the University of Pennsylvania. Ann Burgess, who had been conducting studies of victims of sexual assault, proposed that we collaborate. This book is the product of that collaboration.

Writing on this subject presented unique problems. One major concern was whether there was a risk of propagating this dangerous behavior by writing about it. As our investigation unfolded, we found that these behaviors are already visible to the public through literature, films, and the mass media. Thus we believe that the time has come for a careful scientific presentation of the facts.

Other behavioral scientists and clinicians have faced similar problems. For many years physicians studying sexual behavior published their observations in Latin in order to prevent the undereducated classes from learning of such matters, under the theory that discussions of sexual behavior would incite lust and lead to depravity. Less than a century ago, Havelock Ellis's monumental *Studies in the Psychology of Sex* was the subject of obscenity proceedings when first translated into English. (Ellis summarized the attempt to suppress his work in the foreword he wrote to the 1936 Random House edition [Ellis 1936].)

More recently, in studying drug abuse during the 1960s, there were times when it was considered preferable not to write about the effects of certain drugs in order not to encourage their use. Once a drug was widely known within the drug subculture and already subject to much abuse, the responsibility of professionals shifted to become that of providing accurate information rather than withholding it from the public.

One major encouragement we found for bringing this problem to the attention of the professions came from parents of young victims who had been shocked at the sudden death of a child and who had known nothing about the manner in which their son had died. We know from parents whom we have interviewed and from parents who have been interviewed by newspaper reporters following the death of a child by autoerotic asphyxia that they feel it would be helpful for other parents to have access to accurate information. Surviving parents who have addressed the question of whether the public should know about such deaths have unanimously expressed the opinion that such information should be available.

Structure of the Book

We attempt in nine chapters to lend order to a scattered and often contradictory professional literature, drawing on a series of 150 autoerotic fatality cases we have studied. The result is therefore something of a hybrid between a text with case materials and a research monograph. For reasons outlined in chapter 3, the sample we have had the opportunity to study, while the largest on record, is not statistically representative. Thus we have made quantitative generalizations cautiously. In those instances in which we have used descriptive statistics to characterize our sample, the reader should recognize that the findings may not be generalizable. At present, however, there are no other sources of data to which these findings could reasonably be compared. We have not tabulated data from published case reports because we are aware that the selective biases that influence the publication of case reports are strong (Dietz 1979).

Although this book does not follow the traditional structure of study design, results, discussion, and conclusions, each of these is to be found within its covers. Unless otherwise cited, all case examples and data refer to the series of 150 cases that we have studied. Names, dates, and

Preface

other potentially identifying facts have been changed to maintain the anonymity of the subjects.

Chapter 1 provides overviews of sexual arousal, autoerotic behavior, erotic risk-taking, and the public visibility of autoerotic asphyxia.

Chapter 2 traces the historical development of knowledge about asphyxiation for sexual purposes. This is done through a chronological presentation (chiefly of English-language reports) that demonstrates the problems inherent in the development of information about a phenomenon that can only be understood when more than one discipline is brought to bear on its elucidation.

Chapter 3 describes the conception of the study initiated at the FBI Academy in 1978 and the nature of the sample. The characteristics and limitations of the sample are discussed here.

Chapter 4 reviews the pathophysiology of asphyxiation and describes asphyxial autoerotic fatalities, the most frequently recognized form of autoerotic fatality.

Chapter 5 examines the relationship between autoerotic asphyxia, sexual orientation, psychosexual disorders, and other mental disorders. Particular attention is devoted to the evidence linking autoerotic asphyxia with sexual bondage behavior, sexual masochism, sexual sadism, fetishism, and transvestism.

Chapter 6 considers autoerotic fatalities that did not result directly from the use of asphyxia to improve sexual arousal. These atypical autoerotic fatalities include those in which the cause of death was electrocution, chemicals other than anesthetics, natural disease, and other causes.

Chapter 7 focuses on the investigation of autoerotic fatalities, stressing the importance of thorough death-scene investigation. It should be of particular interest to law-enforcement and medicolegal investigators.

Chapter 8 concerns itself with equivocal cases, those in which another person may have been present or in which the manner of death remains elusive even after investigation. The process of behavioral analysis and reconstruction is described, with particular emphasis on scene investigation and interviews with survivors.

Finally, in chapter 9, we reprint cases and provide commentary on judicial decisions regarding death benefits.

Expectations

The stigma associated with autoerotic fatalities results not only in attempts at concealment on the part of both professionals and surviving family members but also in untoward emotional responses among survivors and others who learn about such deaths. Responses characterized by shame, guilt, puzzlement, and even cruelty have prevented some survivors from satisfactorily resolving their grief. Although it would be unrealistic to expect this book to decrease the prevalence of autoerotic fatalities, we hope that it will at least provide the helping professions with tools through which they can help alleviate the suffering of those whose lives are touched by such deaths.

We expect that as dangerous autoerotic activities and the resultant fatalities become better known to professionals, more cases will be identified through improved recognition and classification. Thus we expect that the reported incidence will increase. Although there is no evidence that the behaviors that become identified as, for example, rape and incest are being committed more often than in the past, increased reporting due to destigmatization causes alarm among those who view the apparent increases in incidence as a growing epidemic. This phenomenon may be occurring already with respect to autoerotic fatalities as a result of several widely publicized cases.

We anticipate a greater willingness on the part of people to recognize the problem and to reveal the facts. Secrecy, shame, and stigma surrounding dangerous autoerotic practices and the resulting deaths prevent many people from seeking help for their concerns about themselves or others. We hope that frank and responsible discussion about these matters will encourage those who are troubled to seek appropriate assistance.

We have written this book primarily for mental-health, medical, and law-enforcement audiences, though we hope that it will prove useful to attorneys, insurance adjusters, educators, and the clergy. Most importantly, we hope that this publication will result, however indirectly, in benefits for those persons who are troubled by the sexual preferences of themselves, their loved ones, or their lost one.

Do not attempt any of the autoerotic activities described or depicted in this monograph. These activities are inherently dangerous and carry a risk of death. There is no reason to believe that these activities are pleasurable to the average person, and there is every reason to believe that they may prove fatal.

Acknowledgments

This book was made possible through the efforts of those law-enforcement professionals who contributed the cases on which the study is based. They deserve much more than a passing acknowledgment, yet their number precludes individual mention.

Others deserving of special thanks are Special Agent Roger Depue (FBI) for encouragement and administrative support; Allen Burgess for data analysis; Dr. A. Nicholas Groth for his role in formulating the original plan of the study; Renee Gould for research assistance; Laura Dietz and Peggy Driver-Hazelwood for support, encouragement, and managing preparation of the manuscript; Sgt. Jack Barrie (RCMP) and Dr. William Adrion for their kind contribution of multiple cases to the study; Special Agent (FBI) Ken Lanning for his contribution to chapter 1 and many helpful discussions; Dr. Daryl Matthews for his criticism of chapters 1 and 2; Special Agent (FBI) Charles Riley and Carl Winner, Esq., for their legal research; Professor Jeffrey O'Connell and Willis Spaulding, J.D., for their criticism of chapter 9; Drs. Patrick E. Besant-Matthews, Lewis M. Bloomingdale, Lawrence B. Erlich, and Alan Usher for helpful correspondence; and Susan Efimenco, Cindy Lent, Kathy Meadows, Linda Woodson, and Susan Zamperini for typing.

Insofar as we have succeeded in advancing the understanding of autoerotic fatalities, we have benefitted by the views and writings of others. We owe intellectual debt to: Dr. Halbert Fillinger, Jr., Dr. Stephen J. Hucker, and Mr. Frank Sass (FBI, retired), whose expertise influenced our interests and views; Dr. Joseph Rupp for catalyzing interest in sexual fatalities among forensic scientists; and Drs. Richard von Krafft-Ebing, Wilhelm Stekel, Havelock Ellis, John Money, Robert Litman, Harvey Resnik, and Robert Stoller for pioneering works spanning a century.

Many of the materials covered in this book are drawn from the knowledge base of forensic pathology, requiring a note of explanation as to how it is that nonpathologists step beyond their traditional disciplinary boundaries. Roy Hazelwood spent a year as a Fellow in Forensic Medicine at the Armed Forces Institute of Pathology. Park Dietz was provided laboratory and other resources for several years by Dr. Russell S. Fisher and the Maryland Medical-Legal Foundation at the Office of the Chief Medical Examiner for the State of Maryland. Subsequently, Dr. Marvin E. Aronson made it possible for Dietz to attend conferences at the Philadelphia Medical Examiner's Office. Dietz's views of forensic pathology have also been broadened by visits to the forensic-medicine museums at the University of Edinburgh and New York University, the

Department of Forensic Medicine at Guy's Hospital with Professors Keith Simpson and A. Keith Mant, and the San Francisco Chief Medical Examiner-Coroner Office with Dr. Boyd G. Stephens. These experiences have all contributed to our appreciation for and knowledge of forensic pathology.

All errors and shortcomings in the text are, of course, ours.

1

Autoeroticism and the Public Visibility of Autoerotic Asphyxia

*Robert R. Hazelwood,
Park Elliott Dietz,
Ann Wolbert Burgess,* and
Kenneth V. Lanning

Autoerotic fatalities are deaths that occur as the result of or in association with masturbation or other autoerotic activity. Masturbation, of course, is as universal as marriage or religion. Manual masturbation, once viewed with alarm, condemnation, and shame, is now viewed as natural and harmless.

Certain embellishments of masturbation sometimes result in death. These embellishments and the resulting deaths are the subject of this book. For reasons put forth in chapter 4, we can only speculate about the number of such deaths each year: five hundred to one thousand deaths annually in the United States and Canada.

Once the secret lore of crime investigators and forensic pathologists, autoerotic fatalities became known among the intelligentsia through literature, film, and serious erotica, and today are openly discussed in the mass media.

In keeping with our purpose of informing a multidisciplinary readership, this chapter provides brief introductions to the subjects of sexual arousal, masturbation and autoeroticism, and erotic risk-taking, and reviews the public visibility of autoerotic asphyxia.

Sexual Arousal

Sexual arousal is that internal state in which the probability of orgasm is increased. Major studies of the last forty years have measured the circumstances under which such arousal occurs for men (Kinsey et al. 1948) and women (Kinsey et al. 1953) in the general population and the anatomic and physiological bases of arousal and orgasm (Masters and Johnson 1966). The former studies show the who, what, where, and when of human sexuality; the latter shows the how of orgasm. Between these two charted territories, however, lies an area where measurement is even more difficult: the processes in the brain through which sensory stimulation and fantasy combine to heighten arousal and carry it forward to the point at which orgasm is inevitable. Each of the major theories of human behavior can be invoked, with greater or lesser success, in an attempt to understand this evasive linkage.

From whatever theoretical vantage point we view it, sexual arousal has both universal and individual features. Direct tactile stimulation of sexually significant parts of the body is a universal feature of sexual arousal, though the most effective forms of tactile stimulation and the specific areas of the body that hold sexual significance vary among individuals. Likewise, fantasy—the mental representation of sights, feelings, and other sensations—is a universal component of sexual arousal, though the specific mental imagery that is most effective varies widely among individuals.

Available evidence is consistent with the widely shared view that individual variations in the effectiveness of and preference for specific types of sensory stimulation and fantasy originate in the life histories of individuals. This view, however, does not take us very far in understanding sexual arousal, for individual life-history experiences range from the prenatal environment (Money and Ehrhardt 1972), through early childhood experiences, to learning that continues through adolescence and adulthood by the repeated pairing of stimulation and fantasy with pleasure and orgasm.

We are at an even greater loss when we attempt to understand unconventional forms of stimulation and fantasy that produce sexual arousal for only a relatively small segment of the population. Even for homosexuality—the most thoroughly studied unconventional sexual preference—the origins of the preferred behaviors and fantasies are unknown (Bell et al. 1981).

Our level of analysis, due both to our own backgrounds and the nature of our data sources, ends at the level of phenomenology and descriptive psychopathology. The reader seeking a psychodynamic understanding of sexual arousal ought to consult Stoller's superb writings on perversion (1975) and sexual excitement (1979). The essence of Stoller's view, as it applies to autoerotic risk-taking and death, is summed up in his observation that " 'excitement' implies anticipation in which one alternates with extreme rapidity between expectation of danger and just about equal expectation of avoidance of danger, and in some cases, such as in erotism, of replacing danger with pleasure" (Stoller 1979, p. 4).

Masturbation and Autoeroticism

The terms *masturbation* and *autoeroticism* have been given a host of technical definitions, some of them mutually contradictory. (For a selection of some of these definitions, see Francis and Marcus 1975.) The term *masturbation* probably derives from the Latin word *masturbatio*, meaning disturbance or agitation of the male genital. (See Spitz, 1952, who cites a 1928 paper by Landauer on this point.) The term *autoeroticism* derives from the Greek words *auto* (same or self) and *eros* (to love or desire). Despite these dissimilar derivations, these terms are often used interchangeably.

For our purposes, it will be helpful to distinguish between masturbation and autoeroticism. We will use the term *masturbation* in those instances in which we are referring to the tactile stimulation of the genitals with rhythmic movements. This stimulation may be applied directly with the hand or may be applied indirectly through clothing and other materials. Individuals masturbate alone and in the company of sexual partners. In order to have some readily understandable term to describe sexual activity carried out alone—regardless of whether the genitals are stimulated with rhythmic movement—we will reserve the terms *autoeroticism* and *autoerotic* for this meaning. The term *monoerotic*, from the Greek word *monos* (alone or single) would be more precise, but we will resist this neologism on the grounds that the term *autoerotic* is commonly known. Thus individuals who stimulate their own genitals during the course of lovemaking with a partner are masturbating but not engaging in autoerotic behavior, whereas individuals who engage in solitary sexual fantasy and achieve sexual arousal without tactile stimulation of the genitals are engaging in autoerotic behavior but not masturbating.

Though generally clear, this distinction becomes subtle in those instances in which an individual's sexual arousal is self-centered despite the presence of a partner. Thus the individual who fantasizes about other partners or other circumstances while having intercourse with a partner is psychologically engaging in autoerotic behavior. At the extreme, the partner may be no more than a prop in the individual's autoerotic dramatic production. In such instances, the partner used as a prop may be assigned a particular script to follow, including both behavior and lines, and may be asked or required to wear a particular costume. These are not rare events, as can be seen from any serious study of prostitution, all of which mention clients' requests for these scripts and costumes.

Masturbation has been the subject of hundreds of articles and scores of books, which reflect the views of their authors and the prevailing societal norms (Spitz 1952). Religious and other efforts to suppress sexual intercourse for pleasure have been doomed from the start by the inherently reinforcing properties of orgasm for most people. Although efforts to suppress sexual activity can never achieve that goal, they do result in shame and guilt among those many members of the population who continue to engage in such activities, and naivete and ignorance among those few members of the population who fully internalize the suppressive beliefs.

Although supported only by anecdotal evidence, it is a common observation among clinicians who work with sexual offenders or patients with sexual deviations that these individuals are, more often than others, inhibited from sexual expression through masturbation and intercourse with consenting partners. Likewise, the observation that a Catholic religious background is somewhat overrepresented among sexual offenders (Dietz 1978c) could be interpreted as suggesting that the sexually inhibited teachings of Catholic schools and churches spawn the development of unconventional forms of sexual expression.

Eighteenth-century treatises on masturbation attributed all manner of physical and mental disease to excessive masturbation. According to Spitz (1952), the first moralistic publication devoted exclusively to masturbation was an anonymous publication of approximately 1700 entitled: *Onania or the Heinous Sin of Self-Pollution and All Its Frightful Consequences, in Both Sexes, Considered with Spiritual and Physical Advice to Those Who Have Already Injur'd Themselves by this Abominable Practice, to which Is Subjoin'd a Letter from a Lady to the Author, Concerning the Use and Abuse of the Marriage Bed, with the Author's Answer*. The author of this pamphlet apparently coined the term *onanism* through an erroneous interpretation of a biblical passage (Genesis 38:7–10) in which God punished Onan for spilling his semen on the ground (probably through withdrawal from intercourse, rather than masturbation). Although the author of *Onania* blamed masturbation for shortness, fainting fits, epilepsy, tuberculosis, infertility, and impotence, these were mild effects compared to those proposed by Tissot in an influential work published later in the eighteenth century that blamed masturbation not only for the previously mentioned ills, but also for blindness, imbecility, insanity, rheumatism, tumors, and eventually death (see Spitz 1952, from whom this discussion is derived).

Despite the eagerness of religious and medical authorities to condemn masturbation during the eighteenth and nineteenth centuries, cases in which autoerotic activities led directly to death are nowhere mentioned in the early writings on masturbation. Even two recent compilations on masturbation (Marcus and Francis 1975; DeMartino 1979) make no mention of autoerotic fatalities. Although justified on the ground that the more universal forms of autoerotic activity are not inherently dangerous, this omission also reflects ignorance of autoerotic fatalities, the misperception that they are rare, and the mistaken classification of autoerotic fatalities as suicides (see chapter 2).

It would be erroneous to believe that masturbation was suppressed only in past centuries, as shown in these excerpts from the 1934 and 1944 editions of the Boy Scouts of America *Handbook for Boys:*

> . . . In the body of every boy in his 'teens, a very important fluid is produced. This fluid is important to the whole body. Some parts of it

Public Visibility of Autoerotic Asphyxia 5

find their way into the blood, and through the blood give tone to the muscles, power to the brain, and strength to the nerves. This is the sex fluid and is formed by the testicles. . . .
(Boy Scouts of America 1935, p. 522)

. . . Boys need not and should not worry about these experiences [nocturnal emissions]. They are natural, but no steps should be taken to excite seminal emissions. That is masturbation. It's a bad habit. It should be fought against. It's something to keep away from. Keep control in sex matters. It's manly to do so. It's important for one's life, happiness, efficiency and the whole human race as well. Keep in training. A cold hip bath will help (water temperature 56 to 60° F., sitting in a tub, feet out, fifteen minutes at night before going to bed).
(Boy Scouts of America 1944, pp. 418–419)

The erroneous belief that loss of semen would sap the vital energies is said to derive from Tissot's claim that the loss of 1 ounce of semen would infeeble one more than the loss of 40 ounces of blood (Dearborn 1963). Belief in the magical properties of semen, however, predates Tissot. Bourke (1934) cites a description by Flemming in 1738 of the use of semen in love potions and a description by Beckherius in 1660 of the use of semen to break down ligatures placed by witches or the devil and in curing impotence.

Apart from autoerotic fatalities and the dangerous behaviors from which they result, concern about masturbation is today limited to the concern of parents that their children may be masturbating excessively and the concern of adults that their sexual partners may prefer masturbation or autoerotic activity to sexual intercourse. Masturbation is excessive only when it interferes with other aspects of the individual's life. Professional intervention is warranted if a child masturbates so frequently that play and peer relationships are neglected, if an adolescent or adult masturbates publicly, if a marital relationship is threatened by one partner's autoerotic activities, or if an individual engages in life-threatening autoerotic activities. On the whole, however, discouragement of masturbation is more likely to lead to larger problems than is masturbation itself.

Even in the 1940s, approximately 90 percent of men reported a history of masturbation (Ramsey 1943; Hohman and Schaffner 1947; Kinsey et al. 1948). Although genital self-stimulation is observed in infancy, the Kinsey (1948) data indicate that not more than 10 percent of men recall true masturbation before the age of nine, and most begin at age ten, eleven, or twelve.

The Kinsey data (1953) regarding women indicate that 58 percent were masturbating to orgasm during some period of their lives. By age seven, 4 percent were masturbating; by age twelve, 12 percent; and by age thirteen, 15 percent. For both women and men, the techniques used for manual masturbation are highly individualized (Masters and Johnson 1966).

Erotic Risk-Taking

The individuality of sexual preferences is such that activities abhorrent to most people are sexually arousing to some. Among the activities that some individuals find arousing are procedures that carry an inherent risk to life. In the broadest sense, no human activity is without risk, but we refer here to activity in which the inherent risk of death is greater than that associated with such everyday activities as crossing a busy street or driving in heavy traffic.

The recognized forms of erotic risk-taking that result in death are discussed throughout this book but may represent only a small fraction of the total number of fatalities resulting from erotic risk-taking. Based on what we know of the recognized forms, we suspect that there may be many individuals who engage in risk-taking behavior at least in part because it arouses sexual feelings. Such individuals do not necessarily suffer from any form of psychosexual disorder. The brain centers involved in sexual behavior are closely linked with those involved in aggressive behavior, and this proximity may underlie part of the association between sexuality and aggression. The biochemical and hormonal linkages between sexual arousal, risk-taking, and aggression are only now being investigated. Studies showing the production of an amphetamine-like substance in the body during parachute jumps (Paulos and Tessel 1982) and elevations of a hormone involved in male sexuality among men behaving violently when they died (Mendelson et al. 1982), to cite just two examples, are fertile sources for speculation about these as-yet-uncharted linkages.

Of all the currently recognized forms of erotic risk-taking, none results in death more frequently than asphyxia. The term *asphyxia* has a variety of meanings (see chapter 4), but in this book is used synonymously with hypoxia, a decrease in the availability of oxygen to the tissues of the body, particularly the brain. The asphyxial techniques most commonly recognized in autoerotic fatalities are compression of the neck through hanging or strangulation, exclusion of oxygen with a plastic bag or other material covering the head, obstruction of the airway through suffocation or choking, compression of the chest preventing respiratory movements, and replacement of oxygen with anesthetic agents.

A mild degree of asphyxia results in the familiar feeling of being out of breath, causing an increase in the frequency and depth of respiration in an unconsciously controlled effort to restore the normal levels of oxygen and carbon dioxide in the blood. Greater degrees of asphyxia produce cyanosis (a blue appearance of the skin caused by a lack of oxygen in the underlying blood, which is no longer bright red), loss of consciousness, convulsions, brain damage, and death. Relief from asphyxia and prompt intervention may interrupt this process at any stage prior to death and may be life-saving.

Other recognized forms of erotic risk-taking less frequently result in death. These are taken up in chapter 6 and do not require consideration here.

Public Visibility of Autoerotic Asphyxia

Autoerotic Asphyxia in the Arts

The concept of death for love has a long history in romantic literature. We leave it to authorities on literature to determine whether hanging is overrepresented in the imagery of death for love, but there is no mistaking its use in the following poem by the seventeenth-century poet and preacher Robert Herrick entitled "Upon Love."

> Love brought me to a silent Grove,
>   And shew'd me there a Tree,
> Where some had hang'd themselves for love,
>   And gave a Twist to me.
>
> The Halter was of silk, and gold,
>   That he reacht forth unto me:
> No otherwise, then if he would
>   By dainty things undo me.
>
> He bade me then that Neck-lace use;
>   And told me too, he maketh
> A glorious end by such a Noose,
>   His Death for Love that taketh.
>
> 'Twas but a dream; but had I been
>   There really alone;
> My desp'rate feares, in love, had seen
>   Mine Execution.
>   (Herrick 1648)

In 1710, writing about techniques for inducing altered states of consciousness, Jonathan Swift wrote about "Swinging by Session upon a Cord, in order to raise artificial Extasies" but appears to have been referring to the exhilarating feeling produced by nonasphyxial swinging (see Note 2, p. 272, in Guthkelch and Smith 1958).

Probably the most famous sexual asphyxia in literature is Roland's hanging, assisted by Thérèse, in the Marquis de Sade's *Justine* (see p. 101 of the 1964 edition or pp. 686–688 of the 1965 edition), which suggests that sexual pleasure accompanies hanging and choking. The first publication of *Justine* was an anonymous edition issued in Paris in 1791 (Bloch 1931), and it has been repeatedly reissued in many languages throughout the world.

At a time when hanging was a familiar public event, many people were aware that hanged men sometimes developed an erection. Although the mechanism of such erections is probably a spinal reflex occurring when the spinal cord is severed (as occurs in judicial hangings, which involve a drop of 6 to 10 feet), onlookers sometimes mistook this response for a sign of sexual arousal. Thus nonerotic literary works sometimes allude to the presumed erotic effects of hanging. One such allusion occurs in Beckett's *Waiting for Godot* (1954). As we shall see in chapter 2, this reflex erection during judicial hangings has led in at least one instance to experimentation with autoerotic asphyxia.

Fans of novelist P.D. James will recall that one of her mystery novels, *An Unsuitable Job for a Woman* (1972), includes alteration of a death scene to make it appear like an autoerotic fatality. With her forensic-science background, James is able to provide realistic details.

John Leonard's review of Kohout's *The Hangwoman* (1980) indicates that the book provides instructions on the relationship between death and sex. A young woman in the book is "taught to strangle, chop, impale, gas and electrocute. 'Violent death,' we are advised, 'is the sex of the timid.' More than once, an analogy is made between the noose and female genitalia" (Leonard 1981).

No one, however, is more graphic in his descriptions of sexual hanging than William S. Burroughs. His book, *Naked Lunch* (1966), widely read since its first publication in 1959, provides explicit descriptions of sexual hangings. A later work by Burroughs, *Cities of the Red Night* (1981), is so replete with descriptions of sexual hangings that the reviewer for the *New York Times Book Review* entitled his review "Pleasures of Hanging" and wrote: "What Mr. Burroughs offered the rubes back in 1959 and what he offers them today, in somewhat wearier condition, is entrance to a side show where they can view his curious id capering and making faces and confessing to bizarre inclinations" (Disch 1981). Burroughs makes frequent reference to "Ix Tab" [sic], Mayan goddess of the hanged (discussed in chapter 2) and suggests some of the subjective experiences that accompany sexual hangings (discussed in chapter 4).

A popular 1972 English film, *The Ruling Class* (directed by Peter Medek and starring Peter O'Toole) opens with a scene in which the Earl of Gurney dons the upper half of a military uniform and a ballet tutu, swings ecstatically by the neck, loses his footing, and is hanged to death, discovered too late by the butler. If memory serves, an autoerotic asphyxia is also depicted in *The Damned,* a film about decadence among the munitions manufacturers in wartime Germany. A Japanese film released in the United States in 1978, *In the Realm of the Senses* (directed by Nagisa Oshima), said to be based on a true story from 1936, depicts a couple who strangle one another during intercourse, eventuating in the woman's fatally strangling her male partner. After his death, she amputates his penis and in an epilogue is said to have been found days later wandering the streets of Tokyo, still carrying the amputated penis.

Autoerotic Asphyxia in the Sexual Advice Literature

The Joy of Sex, the longest-running trade-paperback bestseller on the *New York Times Book Review* list (as of March 1982), contains warnings against several forms of potentially injurious autoerotic and sexual activity. This advice includes prohibitions against constriction of the neck or blockage of the airways (Comfort 1972), though the fact that some individuals practice such acts is implied rather than stated.

Hustler magazine's "Advise & Consent" column, which purports to answer reader-submitted questions, has included two items about sexual asphyxia. In one item, a woman wrote to say that her lover taught her to apply pressure to his neck with her knees until he loses consciousness as an interlude between oral and genital intercourse. The editorial response stated that this practice is "extremely dangerous," is known as "terminal sex," and "kills 200 to 300 people a year in the U.S." The reponse also mentioned the autoerotic use of asphyxia and stated that asphyxia is no less dangerous with a partner. It concluded: "You should start looking for a different turn-on before it's too late." The other question was submitted by a woman who asked what to do about her boyfriend who had been strangling her with increasing intensity during intercourse just prior to his orgasm. The editorial response stated that her boyfriend might not even be aware that he was strangling her or might be under the impression that she would find strangulation arousing. Emphasizing the danger, the response concluded: "Don't be afraid to take this up with him or your silence could make your boyfriend a murderer."

Hustler also published a two-page article entitled "Orgasm of Death." The article described autoerotic asphyxia and stated: "As many as 1000 youngsters—mostly males—die every year in this country by hanging themselves while masturbating."[1] The basis of this assertion is not stated, though Chicago medical examiner Dr. Robert Stein is quoted as saying that there are fifteen to twenty fatalities each year in the Chicago area. The article also quotes Litman and Swearingen (1972) and Rosenblum and Faber (1979). According to this piece, cartoonist Vaughn Bode died at age thirty-three of an autoerotic asphyxia. More than one-hundred empty bottles of butyl nitrite (covered in chapter 6) were said to have been found in Bode's room, and a friend is quoted as saying that Bode "did anything that would get him higher. . . . it was a form of spiritual Russian roulette." The article concludes: "Auto-asphyxiation is one form of sex play you try only if you're anxious to wind up in cold storage, with a coroner's tag on your big toe" (Milner 1981).

Newspaper Reports of Autoerotic Asphyxias

The frequency with which newspapers report autoerotic asphyxias is unknown. We cite a few such reports here to illustrate the variability between newspapers in their approach to this topic and in the accuracy of their information. The newspaper clippings that have crossed our desks most often suggest that the autoerotic nature of the fatality went unrecognized or was being withheld from publication. One clipping, for example, reported that a scuba-diving enthusiast was found dead in his apartment "apparently the victim of suffocation while experimenting with his diving gear." He was found on his bedroom floor dressed in a black-rubber diving suit and rubber gloves, with a surgical glove stretched over his head. Another newspaper reported that a man was found wearing a woman's slip and black-silk skirt and was tied to a tree by a rope around his neck. His feet were bound, and his hands were tied behind his back with a pair of rubber-like handcuffs. According to the newspaper account, the prosecutor's office was investigating whether the death was a murder or a suicide.

Newspaper headlines about autoerotic fatalities are, of course, designed to attract attention: "Macabre Experiment Led to Teen's Death"[2] (Schneider 1978), "Hanging Game Proves Head-Long Rush to Death"[3] (Associated Press 1981), and "A Deadly Experiment" (Miller 1981). A United Press (1981) story based on the Texas Supreme Court's holding in *Connecticut General Life Insurance Co.* v. *Tommie* (described in chapter 9) was entitled "Sex-Hanging Insurance."

A newspaper report concerning an autoerotic asphyxial fatality at a prison farm indicated that when the nude and bound body was first discovered, "everyone thought at first it was a murder." The detective who investigated the hanging said that he recognized it as an autoerotic asphyxia because he had read a chapter on that subject in a homicide-investigation manual. The reporter wrote: "three psychiatrists said that they had never heard of such a sexual act" (Honick 1976).

An Associated Press story reported that preadolescents had coined the term *head rushing* to describe hanging-induced euphoria. Four deaths were said to have occurred during thirteen months in Fort Collins, Colorado. A junior-high-school teacher was quoted as saying that in the aftermath of one student's death the other students were saying: "It's okay to do it if you've got someone to cut you down." A staff member of the local mental-health center was quoted as saying: "It's imperative that everyone—schools, churches, professionals, parents—get some education." The mother of one victim said: "If this information can make just one person discontinue any notion of trying this most dangerous game, perhaps my son's death won't seem such a senseless waste of young life. If one parent, teacher, or counselor will discuss the game and its dangers, it may deter that child from trying" (Associated Press 1981).

Another newspaper report based on a local death asserted that the teenager was "another sudden victim of a bizarre sexual practice that has claimed thousands of lives in America during the past few years." The young man's parents told the reporter that they had noticed rope burns on their son's neck, but that he had told them that he had injured his neck playing football. At death, a protective towel was found under the noose. The boy's father was willing to discuss his son's death, saying, "If it would save even one life, it would be worth it. . . . I don't really understand what happened, but I've accepted it. . . . it actually helped me to find out that it was an accident and not suicide. . . . I would have had a harder time understanding why he would've wanted to kill himself deliberately." The coroner was quoted as saying that another family who had recently lost a son were unwilling to accept the coroner's opinion that the death was autoerotic in nature (Miller 1981).

Elsewhere, a thirteen-year-old boy was awarded a posthumous blue ribbon for a short story that he wrote about two youngsters in a roller-coaster car destined to crash. His parents approached the local newspaper because their "anger and anguish" were overridden by their belief that the public must be informed of what they feared was a dangerous and insidious trend. The boy's mother had heard about two other local deaths that sounded similar to her son's, leading her to contact the families involved, who confirmed her suspicions. She told the reporter that "information about the dangers of this must be communicated to our youth. Somebody had to say something." The parents, the article concluded, were left "with a thousand questions that are still begging answers" (Schneider 1978). In the following chapters, we seek to provide some of these answers.

Notes

1. Milner, R. Orgasm of death. *Hustler* 8:33–34, August 1981.

2. Associated Press. Hanging game proves headlong rush to death. *Colorado Springs Gazette Telegraph* (Colorado Springs, Colo.), April 3, 1981.

3. Miller, J. A deadly experiment. *Chronicle-Tribune* (Marion, Ind.), April 26, 1981.

2

Recurrent Discovery of Autoerotic Asphyxia

Park Elliott Dietz

It has been my experience that people learning of autoerotic asphyxia and autoerotic fatalities through a lecture or readings respond with initial disbelief and, as belief takes hold, wonder how it is that there could be such an aspect of human behavior that they had previously not known. These are not matters of everyday conversation, and each individual who learns of them feels a sense of discovery. More than a few individuals, sensing that discovery, have written about autoerotic asphyxia as though no one else had ever heard of it.

It may facilitate the reader's appreciation of the gradual unfolding of knowledge about autoerotic asphyxia to set forth at the outset two propositions about this behavior that can be tested against the disparate observations reported here (and in subsequent chapters).

1. For certain individuals the preferred or exclusive mode of producing sexual excitement is to be mechanically or chemically asphyxiated to or beyond the point at which consciousness or perception is altered by cerebral hypoxia (diminished availability of oxygen to the brain).
2. Other individuals for whom these are not the preferred or exclusive mode of producing sexual excitement nonetheless repeatedly, intentionally induce their own cerebral hypoxia to or beyond the point at which consciousness or perception is altered in order to produce sexual excitement.

These postulates, which I believe are supported by the evidence reviewed in this chapter (and in chapters 4 and 5), are the basis for my proposing that a new diagnostic category be formulated to recognize these behaviors, which are in many instances life-threatening and in some instances fatal. For those individuals whose behavior corresponds to the descriptions in either of the preceding postulates I propose the labels of *hypoxyphilia*[1] and *Kotzwarraism*.[2] This condition is one of the paraphilias (formerly known as sexual deviations) (see chapter 5 for a detailed description of the paraphilias) and is a nonpsychotic mental disorder. (A description of the physiological processes in asphyxiation is provided in chapter 4, and the evidence for other mental disorders among those dying of autoerotic asphyxia is presented in chapter 5.)

It should be understood that reflex erection and ejaculation such as occur in a proportion of judicial hangings bear no relationship to the erotic uses of asphyxia except as an instigator of the idea that hanging might be sexually arousing. In judicial hangings, which involve a drop of 6 to 10 feet, death results from damage to the spinal cord; it is rare for the victim to survive long enough to die of asphyxia (Moritz 1954, p. 187). Even if an executed man were conscious at the moment of erection and ejaculation, the typical tearing of the spinal cord from its junction with the brain stem (Simpson 1965, Vol. 1, p. 400) would make it impossible for him to perceive these effects.

This chapter presents a chronological history of the development of knowledge about autoerotic asphyxia, from ancient origins to the present. Such an ambitious undertaking has its risks, and there can be no doubt that many sources, particularly ancient ones, have been neglected. Nonetheless, the history is substantial as it stands and documents that autoerotic asphyxia has been recurrently discovered.

Ancient Origins

A stone sculpture in the *Museo de Antropológia* in Mexico City depicts a naked man with a rope looped around his neck. Scars are visible on his cheeks and forehead, and his penis, once erect, has been fractured from the sculpture. The museum sign beneath the statue states that it is a Mayan relic from the late classic or early postclassic period depicting an adolescent from a phallic cult. The scars on his face are said to be facial decorations. The sculpture was apparently done c. 1000 A.D., the approximate date of the transition between the late classic and early postclassic periods (Willey 1982). A museum guidebook incorrectly identifies the sculpture as a god of death, whereas Bennett (1974) identifies the same sculpture as a phallic figure and notes that Mayan phallic cult figures ''were destroyed or hidden by the Mexican authorities in reaction to a complaint by some American women tourists to their pastor back home. The pastor wrote the Mexican tourist bureau protesting the 'obscenity' and the offending figures were removed'' (p. 89).

Whether the ancient Maya had discovered autoerotic asphyxia, as the sculpture so strongly suggests, will perhaps never be known with certainty. It is known, however, that the Maya believed that the souls of individuals who hang themselves go directly to paradise, where they are received by Ixtab, goddess of the hanged (Alexander 1964). The representation of Ixtab in a Mayan manuscript drawing shows her in a kneeling posture, her one visible nipple erect, suspended by a noose around her neck; her ankles appear to be bound together (see the Dresden Codex on p. 316 of Anders 1963).

Frazer (1959) described ritual and religious hangings among the Greeks and other ancient cultures. Many of these rituals appear to have been closely related to human sacrifice and self-mutilation, but a hint of sexuality appears in the myth that the skin of the dead satyr, Marsyas, would "thrill" at the sound of his native melodies while he hung in his cave (p. 317).

European Artifacts

As noted in chapter 1, literary accounts of sexual hanging date at least to 1791, and the first documented description of an erotic asphyxial fatality is of the same vintage. An engraving attributed to Dürer (c. 1520), however, depicts a man ejaculating while being hanged in a torture chamber amidst chained skeletons while another prisoner is flogged. Thus the observation that ejaculation may accompany hanging had become known to laymen at least by the early sixteenth century.

An anonymous London publication from the end of the eighteenth century was entitled *Modern Propensities: Or an Essay on the Art of Strangling*. The author describes examples of men who died from taking aphrodisiac agents and points out that flagellation was an improvement over dangerous "internal nostrums." The pamphlet details the deaths of two men through sexual asphyxia: the musician Kotzwarra, and the Reverend Parson Manacle. In view of their historic importance and the rarity of the pamphlet (a microfilm is available at Yale University), these cases are described in detail here.

Francis Kotzwarra was born in Prague in approximately 1750. His name at birth appears to have been František Koczwara (or Kočvara), but he is known in German as Franz Kočžwara, Franz Kotzware, or Franz Kotzwara; in French as Francois Kotzwara; and in English as Francis Kotzwarra. Kotzwarra became known as an exceptional double bassist and a minor composer. Although his best-known original composition was the *Battle of Prague,* he was also well known for his forgeries of Hadyn, Mozart, and Pleyel (see Parke 1830; Newman 1963). Kotzwarra was said to have been poor due to his "habit of gratifying his sensual appetites to excess," and was described as having been "a genius and like many of that class, as uncertain as the climate or the stock exchange" (Parke 1830). According to *Modern Propensities,* a country girl named Susannah Hill went to London in search of the boyfriend who had abandoned her and turned to prostitution for financial support. She had the misfortune of receiving Francis Kotzwarra among her clients and found herself on trial for murder as a result of her dealings with him. We reprint here the description of her trial from *Modern Propensities*.

THE TRIAL OF SUSANNAH HILL FOR THE MURDER OF FRANCIS KOTZWARRA

Before the RECORDER of LONDON.
And JUDGE GOULD.
At the *Sessions House, Old Bailey*, Sept. 16, 1791.

Mr. Garrow appeared as counsel for the prosecution; and, previous to his stating of the case, he began lamenting the melancholy truth, that there were men who, to gratify the most unwarrantable species of lust, resorted to methods at which reason and morality revolted. The present instance had, he feared, excited a dangerous curiosity, which by no means tended to advance the morals or the welfare of society. It therefore, he told the Jury, became necessary to check the evil—if such men were yet left behind—by deterring those women who prostitute their persons for hire—from becoming accessory to such shameful, such disgraceful purposes. And though he had doubts of being able to convict the Prisoner of *Murder*, he would insist that her crime came under the description of Manslaughter.

Suicide, by the laws of this country, was not held to be legal, a punishment followed deliberate acts of so criminal a nature: And a second person assisting towards the completion of such a purpose, was equally culpable, although aiding at the express desire of the person attempting to destroy himself, and must inevitably incur the crime of Manslaughter.

The present case was an aggravated instance; it was an immoral act, it was grossly immoral. The Prisoner could not be a stranger to the probable consequences that might ensue from such a mode of suspension; and, being aware, cannot be supposed ignorant of the enormity of the transaction in which she took so decisive a part.

The Prisoner, indeed, did not conduct herself like a murderer, who had acted from deliberation; she treated it in a manner perfectly consistent with her abandoned way of life; she ran out of the house, exclaiming to the neighbors, "that she had hanged a Man, but feared she had hung him too long!"

This was an attrocious case of Manslaughter, to say the least of it; and he hoped it would have a proper influence upon the minds of the Jury, that by holding forth a severe example, it might deter the depraved part of mankind from seeking indecent stimulatives, to pervert the ordinary course of nature; that it might also deter the abandoned part of the female sex from lending themselves for hire, to purposes so vile, so unnatural and so detestable.

After this exordium, which reflected great credit on him as a man, Mr. Garrow proceeded to state the catastrophe, as it occurred on the 2nd of September, the day on which the melancholy circumstance happened. He apologized for the use of expressions which the nature of the case demanded; and, after having gone through the whole with admirable precision, called the first witness; who was one of the officers belonging to Bow Street. He said, he went to the prisoner's lodgings on the second of September; that she lived in Vine Street, at No. 5; that she rented a front parlour; and that she had lived there about nine months.

That, on being taken into custody and brought before the magistrate, she delivered her evidence to the following effect. That in the afternoon of the 2d of September, between one and two o'clock, a man whom she had never seen before, and who was deceased, came past the house where she lived—That he came into the house, the street door being open (as usual, it was observed by the counsel) and asked her if she would have any thing to drink. That she replied, if she chose any thing, it should be a little porter. The deceased said he should like some brandy and water: and gave her money to buy both porter and brandy— with two shillings for some ham and beef, which she accordingly bought.

Some time after this, they went into a back room, where several acts of the grossest indecency passed; in particular, he pressed her to cut off the means of generation, and expressly wished to have it cut in two. But this she refused. He then said he should like to be *hanged* for *five* minutes; and while he gave her money to buy a cord, observed, that *hanging* would *raise* his passions—that it would produce all he wanted. But as a cord large enough could not be immediately procured, she brought two small ones, and put them round his neck. He then tied himself up to the back parlour door, a place where he hung very low, and bending down his knees.

Court: Did she say how the cord was fastened?

Ans: No.

After hanging five minutes, she cut him down; he immediately fell to the ground: she thought he was in a fit, and called to an opposite neighbor for help. She then went to a publican where she used, and he ran for a surgeon, who came and attempted to bleed him.

Garrow: You went afterwards to the place?

Officer: Yes, about nine in the evening; and then saw the deceased lying on a bed in the back room: he had a bruise on the bridge of his nose and two above each of his eyes, probably occasioned by the fall, after suspension. The witness observed that by his arm, there had been previous attempts to bleed him; he was covered with large and small old scars, and several fresh scratches, seemingly inflicted by an instrument.

Court: Saw you a cord?

Officer: Not then, but afterwards at the house of the constable. (Here a long consultation took place between the Judge, the Recorder, and Mr. Garrow.)

Court to the Officer: How did she tell her story before the magistrate?

Ans: Very deliberately—more so than I could have imagined.

Elizabeth Dalton sworn.

Mr. Garrow: You lived opposite the house where the prisoner lodged?

Ans: Yes.

Garrow: Did she call to you on the 2d of September?

Ans: Yes, she called to me, and said she was in a very great fright. I went to her apartment: she said, "I have hanged a man! and I am afraid he is dead."

Garrow: Were those the very words?"

Ans: Yes.

Garrow: You then went into the back room?

Ans: Yes.

(Here another consultation of the Court took place, the result of which was, that Judge Gould declined giving the Jury any further trouble, and immediately dismissed the prisoner.)

She was neatly dressed in common apparel; and, on her countenance we could discover nothing that seemed to indicate a rooted depravity; nor was there any thing in her person particularly attractive: from which it may be inferred, that the unfortunate—if not lamented Kotzwarra—trusted more to the charms of the cord, than to those of his *fair one*. When she first came into Court, she appeared intimidated; but on her dismission, the signs of excessive joy were visible; and if in that joy, there should have been any mixture of compunction we hope that the rigidity of female abhorrence will relax so as to receive in, some subordinate station, this mis-guided young woman, that she may be timely rescued from daily prostitution, and its dreadful concomitants.

FINIS.

I became aware of Kotzwarra's death through reference to it in Hirschfeld (1948), who quotes (without citation) an account by Von Archenholtz which indicated that a coroner's jury deliberated for nine hours before Susannah Hill was remanded for trial on the murder charge and which confirms that the Court regarded her action as accidental manslaughter and released her.

In keeping with the origin of the word *sadism* after the Marquis de

Sade and the origin of *masochism* after Leopold von Sacher-Masoch, I proposed the word *Kotzwarraism* to describe a paraphilia characterized by "the induction of cerebral hypoxia to enhance the sexual arousal or gratification of the hypoxic individual" in a paper (Dietz 1978*b*) that has been expanded into the present historical review. I suggested there that Kotzwarra may have learned of the erotic use of hanging by reading the Marquis de Sade's *Justine,* which was first published in Paris in 1791 (Bloch 1931), the year in which Kotzwarra died, and in which it is suggested that sexual pleasure accompanies hanging. Alternatively, Kotzwarra, whose old scars and request for penile mutilation suggest long-standing sexual masochism, may have independently discovered the technique (see chapter 4 for a discussion of the means of individual discovery). The subsequent analysis by Wolfe (1980) of an original manuscript from the late eighteenth century suggests yet another possible source of Kotzwarra's information (see the following).

The other death detailed by the author of *Modern Propensities* is also of considerable historical interest, not only because it may have antedated Kotzwarra's death, but also because it provides the most detailed description on record of the means by which an individual discovered that his own response to hanging was pleasurable enough that he wished to repeat it. This was the case of the Reverend Parson Manacle (possibly a pseudonym, if the case is genuine at all) who ministered to condemned men and women at Newgate Prison.

Reverend Manacle had personally observed that hanged criminals developed erections (see chapter 1). He contracted a venereal disease from a woman prisoner who was condemned to death for infanticide, and the nature of his illness was apparently such as to cause him to become impotent. Having noticed the effect of hanging on prisoners, he consulted an anatomist at Surgeons Hall and was told that irritation in the lungs and thorax produced "titulation in the generative organs" because blood impeded from upward circulation rushed to the genitals. The anatomist cited as illustrations "the well known powers of consumptive and asthmatic men, and the effects of *tickling* and *long kissing,* when the natural valves of respiration are so far deranged as to produce *short breathings, pantings, faintings,* and other *amorous* symptoms in the human frame."

Reverend Manacle, seeking relief from his impotence, turned to a condemned woman, Mrs. Birdlime (ordered for execution because of shoplifting) as he had previously turned to other prisoners to fulfill his more straightforward sexual needs. The original account of what followed is reprinted here.

. . . Doctor Manacle visited her often, and always found her under more terrifying apprehension respecting the pain of her passage, than place of her destination.

From this trifling fear he had often, but in vain, endeavoured to dissuade her; and now it suddenly occurred to him, that, by his own example, he might possibly alleviate at least the horrors under which she laboured. Accordingly, the evening before the fatal day, he provided himself with a good strong rope, and went as usual, full, no doubt, of the spirit, to give her spiritual comfort.

Finding her greatly agitated by the feelings above mentioned, he informed her, that in order to draw her mind from such earthly considerations, and to shew by occular demonstration the folly of her fears, he was determined to give her indisputable proofs, that there was little or nothing painful in the act of hanging; that for that purpose he had prepared a rope; and, that his intentions were to suspend himself from the upper part of the bed, for a short time; and he directed her to be careful in cutting the rope the moment she saw any appearance of actual danger. The first moments, he observed, of strangulation, must, of course, be the moments of pain, and she would find, by the composure with which he would endure them, that her apprehensions were ill-founded.

Mrs. Birdlime listened to her ghostly visitor with ineffable astonishment: she knew both *men* and *things* as well as most women, yet had not the most remote idea of his real inducement: she begged to decline the criterion, but the Doctor was peremptory; assuring her there could be no danger, and shewing that, by the position in which he meant to suspend himself, he could at any time, by extending his legs, relieve himself from extremity of danger.

There was something so extremely whimsical in this new species of consolation, that Mrs. Birdlime, though under circumstances so doleful, could scarcely refrain herself from a smile. However, after repeated requisitions, she consented; and when the Doctor had fixed the noose properly about his neck, actually fastened the other end agreeably to his desire.

Every thing being now prepared, the Rev. Doctor Manacle raised his feet from the floor, and to the incredible astonishment of his fair assistant, actually hung for one or two minutes with infinite composure. At length, observing his breast begin to heave, and that he still made no effort to relieve himself, she readily performed the remainder of the agreement, and cut the instrument which might otherwise have proved fatal.

For a few moments after his release, the Doctor lay upon the bed in a kind of stupor; but Mrs. Birdlime, by rubbing his temples and other blandishments, soon brought him to himself; he clasped her in his arms, and in a transport of extacy demanded a return for the distinguished proof he had given her of his regard.

There is nothing more certain than that every thing which Doctor Manacle promised himself, was performed by this operation; but whether the effects were observed by Mrs. Birdlime or not, is a matter which never came to light. It is however natural enough to suppose the affirmative, and that her occular sensations had prepared her for that vigorous rencontre which succeeded. In short, Mrs. Birdlime made little or no resistance, and her reverend comforter was made happy.

Before they parted, the lady acknowledged that her ideas of hanging were greatly dissipated, and that she believed a few repetitions, which she lamented it was then too late for the enjoyment of, would entirely remove her terrors. Thus relieved by the extraordinary kindness of the *tenderhearted* parson, the next morning she mounted the cart, and, followed by her reverend comforter, proceeded to Tyburn; where, in the presence of many thousands, she confessed that the cause of her death was not altogether *accidental,* and openly avowed the *good effects* of *hanging*.

Having thus physically accounted for *one* of the extraordinary productions of strangling, it becomes necessary to take some notice of *another*, which, though not altogether so wonderful, is yet equally certain, if the utmost care be not taken to prevent it.

Poor Parson Manacle, in one or two subsequent instances, was lucky enough to escape this fatal consequence; but he became at length so extremely fond of the practice and the sensations which accompanied it, that, spending one evening in a situation exactly similar to that with Mrs. Birdlime, he indulged himself a little too long, and fairly expired in the process. The thing was kept a profound secret, lest the gaoler should suffer blame, his body was privately conveyed to his lodging in a shell, and he was reported to have died suddenly of the gaol distemper.

It were therefore to be wished that *gentlemen* who are obliged to acquire the powers of procreation through the physical medium of strangling, would devise some certain means of watching its progress, and checking an inordinate indulgence of its paregoric influence; and for this purpose there is no medical or surgical artist better calculated than the celebrated Patent Inventor of Spring Bands, in Mount-Street, who, from his wonderful improvements in surgery and mechanics, could very probably invent not only a safe but an agreeable and graceful mode of suspension, in which the gentle undulations of the body vibrating with reciprocal motion to the actions and reactions of elastic powers, might communicate a softer degree of pressure to the jugular muscles, and prevent any future appearance in that part which might betray a practice that ignorance would probably endeavor to turn into ridicule and contempt.

Indeed it is not at all improbable but that the advantages of such an invention might accumulate and extend to new discoveries in the sublime science of strangulation; as, by means of such gentle undulations, the whole of the nervous system and every part capable of irritation, might experience effects at present unknown, and of course undescribable.

The author of *Modern Propensities* foreshadowed a great deal of what was later to be learned of autoerotic asphyxia. He charted one individual's discovery of the technique more convincingly than has since been achieved, he recognized that the practice was likely to be continued, and he satirically suggested that improvements in the apparatus used could provide both a greater margin of safety and concealment of physical marks that others might recognize. Although I regard these latter points as satirical, Wolfe (1980) interpreted them as advertisements for Martin Vanbutchell, a famous London quack of the day. Vanbutchell is referred to in the reprinted passage as "the celebrated Patent Inventor of Spring Bands, in Mount-Street," and he is named in the succeeding pages of *Modern Propensities*. There, the author recommends "Vanbutchell's Balsam of Life" and, until a safe mode of suspension is available, the use of "elastic garters" such as Vanbutchell had custom-made for famous patrons.

Wolfe's (1980) historical analysis is based on an examination of an original manuscript at the Francis A. Countway Library of Medicine in Boston and publications from the 1790s. The Countway manuscript provides a more detailed record of Susannah Hill's trial than that reprinted previously from *Modern Propensities* or that published in newspapers of the time. It indicates that Judge Gould ordered the shorthand reporter to tear up the notes he had taken of the proceedings and that this was accomplished, suggesting that the manuscript was written by someone else in attendance at the trial. It includes a proof impression of the same copperplate engraving used to print the frontispiece to *Modern Propensities,* and this illustration in the manuscript bears a caption used for the title of *Modern Propensities*. Wolfe also identified an imprint of the same engraving in an article in *Bon Ton Magazine* in September 1793. Based on references to Martin Vanbutchell in both *Modern Propensities* and *Bon Ton Magazine* and on other historical evidence, Wolfe postulated that Vanbutchell authored both of these, was promoting erotic asphyxia as a sexual aid (for his own profit), and may have been the source of Kotzwarra's knowledge of the practice.

The Twentieth Century

The state of knowledge in the medical jurisprudence literature at the turn of the century is reflected in the advice of a standard text of the time concerning the evaluation of hanging fatalities: "[E]ven if the hands and feet are found tied, the inference is not warranted that the act was homicidal since determined suicides have been known to perform this very act previous to hanging themselves. . . . Cases of accidental hanging are of occasional occurrence, especially among children, who have, while swinging or otherwise playing, accidentally become entangled in a noose or loop of cord, which was then drawn tightly enough around the neck to strangle them'' (Reese 1906). Statements to the effect that accidental hangings, rare though they are, most often involve young boys are found in many of the writings about hanging in the late nineteenth and early twentieth centuries. Robertson (1925) noted that "Boys 'playing at hanging' have died without giving any evidence of distress, as have also public exhibitors of hanging."

The first case report that I have identified in the psychiatric literature in English was published under the title "An Unusual Form of Suicide." The case was that of a 24-year-old man said to have been normal in mental capacity, behavior, and social relationships, who was found dead with a complicated arrangement of weights and counterbalances that provided asphyxial compression to his neck. The direct transmission of pressure was through a woman's high-heeled shoe laced onto a bootmaker's iron boot last, over which he had placed a woman's stocking. The weight resting on these consisted of the bottom end of a heavy double bed. The author observed that the choice of a woman's clothing for this use "seems undoubtedly to point to a masochistic impulse" with the apparatus representing a woman's foot and leg. The careful arrangement of the apparatus and the accuracy with which the bed had been balanced were observed to "point to previous experiment or use to induce some pleasurable gratification." The author concluded that although the verdict returned at the inquest had been "suicide during temporary insanity," if his analysis were correct, "it is open to question whether death may not have been due to misadventure rather than to an impulse to self-destruction'' (Auden 1927).

In his classic work, *Sadism and Masochism*, Stekel (1929) described hanging and choking as the means by which an epileptic seizure may be induced. Apparently a diagnostic procedure of the day, used to elicit what was known as Tsiminaki's sign, consisted of compression of the carotid artery in order to determine whether an epileptic seizure would be elicited. In Stekel's view, epilepsy was a mental disorder, the unconscious source of which could be revealed through psychoanalysis. He described one patient who had witnessed his mother's hanging and run for his father rather than cutting her down. Subsequently, he would have seizures when reminded of the dead, graveyards, hearses, hanging, or choking. In the context of this discussion, Stekel introduced "the fact which many physicians do not know, that choking sets free in certain individuals feelings of pleasure and even an orgasm. These are evidently persons for whom choking represents their adequate satisfaction (lust murderers)." He cited the erection and ejaculation of hanged criminals as evidence for this but also referred to "onanists who make use of choking and self-strangulation for their onanism. Such cases are according to my experience not so rare" (Vol. 2, p. 357).

Stekel reviewed a case originally published by Runge in German of a 20-year-old who attempted to strangle himself while suicidal regarding his health and an unfortunate love affair. During the strangulation attempt, he noticed a feeling of pleasure, after which, "there was very frequent impulsive repetition of the attempts at strangling, in which a sort of orgasm appeared." The patient continued to strangle himself for more than a year but stopped doing so after repeated hypnoses. The sensation the patient had experienced with strangling was described as "a voluptuous sense of giddiness, like the feeling that overcomes one on a height," and he found the "most beautiful moment" to be that just before he discontinued the strangling. Although the patient denied any sexual feeling, Runge had considered the case to be one of "masked onanism" (Vol. 2, pp. 357–358).

Stekel also reviewed two cases that had been reported earlier in German by Hass. One of these was a man who made holes in both ends of a towel, twisted the towel around his neck, slipped his feet into the holes, and stretched his legs so as to bring about strangulation and orgasm. He was discovered choked to death from this practice. The other case was that of a twelve-year-old girl who, soon after her mother's death from tuberculosis with suffocation, began to compulsively strangle herself with both hands. Although she most often hid herself when doing so, she eventually did so even during classes at school. Her self-strangulation became as frequent as thirty times a day, damaging the skin of her neck. Attempts to prevent her from doing so through discipline, threats, punishment, and a plaster collar all failed. She was placed in a restraining jacket for several months but began strangling herself as soon as it was removed. Under hypnosis she said that on the day of her mother's death, she had become ill from eating too much, had pressed her throat in order to induce vomiting, and had noticed that "such pleasant sensation arose from her stomach upward that she almost lost her senses." Finally, Stekel mentioned that he knew of "men who must slightly choke their love objects to have an orgasm. Onanists usually enact the strangling on their own penis" (Vol. 2, pp. 358–359).

In an Austrian encyclopedia of sexuality published from 1928 to 1931, entire sections are devoted to strangulation and to "penis strangulation." The strangulation section refers to autoerotic practices involving self-strangulation or self-hanging, and two photographs, one of a man and one of a woman (or an exceptionally well-dressed and well-made-up transvestite) are shown. The text indicates that a student of Charcot had observed the sexually arousing effects of compression of the carotid artery as this was used in the diagnosis of neurologic disorders (the same phenomenon referred to by Stekel). Elaborate bondage and strangulation were said to have been practiced in harems and, until an accidental death led to untoward publicity, in Paris brothels (Institut für Sexualforschung 1931).

The 1935 edition of one of Bloch's books describes "sadistic accompaniments of coitus," including the choking of women during intercourse which was said to play a role in folk songs of "the Southern Slavs" (Bloch 1935).

The fact that the sexual uses of asphyxia had largely escaped notice by experts in medical jurisprudence and criminal investigation prior to 1940 would not be surprising if references to it were limited to the rather obscure sources cited earlier. It is, however, remarkable that the monumental work of Havelock Ellis, which created such a stir at the time, was not noticed by these audiences. Ellis devoted several pages to strangulation and its relationships to sexuality, including requests that men make of prostitutes to be strangled, sexual excitement accompanying suspension for the treatment of spinal-cord disorders, and the pleasurable effects of swinging, suspension, and restraints that affect respiration. Ellis refers to "the impulse to strangle the object of sexual desire" and "the corresponding craving to be strangled." A symbolic form of this impulse, he wrote, "is seen in the desire to strangle birds with the object of stimulating or even satisfying sexual desire. Prostitutes are sometimes acquainted with men who bring a live pigeon with them to be strangled just before intercourse." In keeping with the view of the day that sexual masochism was more common among women than men, Ellis suggested that "the pleasurable connection of the thought of being strangled with sexual emotion" might be particularly common among women (1936, Vol. 1, p. 151).

Ellis also mentioned sexual excitement occurring during the administration of anesthesia. He quotes a colleague, Dr. J.F.W. Silk: "Sexual emotions may apparently be aroused during this stage of excitement preceding or following the administration of any anaesthetic; these emotions may take the form of mere delirious utterances, or may be associated with what is apparently a sexual orgasm." Silk also stated that sexual responses "are more frequently observed with a weak anaesthetic like nitrous oxide than with chloroform" (Ellis 1936, Vol. 3, p. 156).

Sexual asphyxia was introduced to modern English-language literature in medical jurisprudence, legal medicine, and forensic pathology through a single sentence in the text by Gonzales et al. (1940): "A few accidental hangings are self-inflicted where the deceased has attempted constriction of the neck for the purpose of inciting sexual sensations" (p. 262). A subsequent edition of the same work makes no mention of autoerotic hangings but does mention autoerotic strangulations (p. 464) and includes a photograph of a naked woman with the caption: "Suicidal, Ligature Strangulation. Cloth dress belt around neck and tied tightly in front with a single knot. Body found nude in prone position on bed" (Gonzales et al. 1954, p. 467).

In a 1942 paper on sudden death, Gardner mentioned the case of a boy "who had died from hanging during a masochistic experiment." Although the boy had passed his head through a noose and suspended himself from a beam, Gardner inferred that he had not intended to kill himself, for "he had arranged an ingenious quick release device by which he could slacken the rope whenever he decided to do so; but as the rope took the weight of his body, unconsciousness and death took place too quickly for him to have time to use it" (Gardner 1942). Gardner suggested two likely mechanisms for the rapidity of such deaths: pressure upon the vagus nerve or upon the carotid sinus. Both are consistent with current knowledge of the physiology of hanging, and in either case, death is mediated through vagal stimulation (see chapter 4). In the discussion of Gardner's paper, Sir Bernard Spilsbury urged that coroners be made aware that deaths during "masochistic rites" are accidents and not suicides and cited as evidence for this view the case of a young chemist found hanged in a staircase in such a position that he could readily have halted the suspension. Eight folds of bath towel were wrapped around his neck, in Spilsbury's opinion, "to relieve the pressure on his neck." The more likely explanation of the towel was that it was to prevent rope abrasions.

In the meantime, psychoanalysts continued to study the origins of sadomasochism, occasionally describing cases in which asphyxia was used sexually. For example, a sadomasochist psychoanalyzed by Boss (1949) had early masturbation fantasies of being beaten on the buttocks, and in his later relationships with women derived pleasure from mistreating them: "He tied them up, pulled them up with a rope so that they wriggled defensively in the air. He liked to tie up their wrists with iron chains or bind them to the bedposts with leather straps, or to lace them up in a corset until they had difficulty in breathing. He was most strongly stimulated when he choked them until they turned blue; then he experienced the fullest sexual excitement" (pp. 83–84). Later, he sometimes let women beat, chain, or choke him. In his words, "Then the pleasure was almost greater than when I lashed them myself. But it is rather dangerous to let myself be beaten. . . . I might give myself away and get lost. . . . I am like a small boy who has no responsibilities. However, when I do the beating, I retain control over everything" (p. 85). (The issue of control is also prominent in the minds of many rapists [Dietz 1978a; Rada 1978; Groth 1979].) The patient described the importance of choking to him, saying it made no difference whether he did the choking or was choked, and he associated his excitement from choking with the excitement he imagined would accompany lust murder.

The majority of authors in the last thirty years who have referred to original publications at all have dated the "discovery" of erotic hangings to a widely misquoted paper by Stearns (1953). In tabulating data on 4,891 deaths ruled as suicides in Massachusetts from 1941 through 1950, Stearns found one female and thirty-one males from ages 11 to 20 who died by self-hanging. Apparently the female and six of the males had "obvious motivation" for suicide, leaving twenty-five cases that Stearns called "probable suicide in young persons without obvious motivation." Stearns knew that it was the opinion of Keith Simpson at Guy's Hospital and of Richard Ford at Harvard that autoerotic-hanging deaths occur that are sexually motivated, with death being accidental. He also knew that Simpson believed such cases to be "masochistic deaths" and that cases are occasionally seen in adults with cross-dressing and bondage. Finally, he had heard of a presumably sexual self-hanging game among Eskimo children (see Freuchen 1961) and the Yahgan custom of tying something tightly around the neck to induce stupefaction and colorful visions.

Stearns did not group his cases according to the presence or absence of evidence of sexual activity or binding of the body. The twenty-five cases he reported included four characterized by nudity, four by cross-dressing in female attire, one by binding of the hands and feet and the presence of mirror glass near the body, and one by binding of one hand and the use of a towel around the neck that was tied to the rope from which the young man was partially suspended. Each of these ten cases has a least one of the stigmata that have since come to be interpreted as evidence of autoerotic asphyxia: namely, nudity, cross-dressing, bondage, use of mirrors, and protection of the skin of the neck.

Exactly one year after Stearns presented his paper in Boston, Gutheil (1954) presented a paper in New York as part of a symposium on transsexualism and transvestism. In it, he mentioned "cases of strangulation masochism which invariably is accompanied by transvestism." Gutheil referred to individuals who masturbate by dressing and making up as women and then engaging in self-strangulation, sometimes by imitation hanging. Gutheil recognized that constriction of the neck was used as a sexual stimulant and that the constriction is relaxed after orgasm unless there is an accidental loss of consciousness and death ensues.

In the same year, the first edition of *Gradwohl's Legal Medicine* contained a photograph, in Strassmann's (1954) chapter on mechanical asphyxia, that depicted a naked man suspended by the neck with his ankles bound together, his left arm bound to the wall, and a rope (perhaps the neck ligature) running down between his legs and around his waist. It appears that there was padding underneath the neck ligature. Despite the now-obvious signs of autoerotic asphyxia, the caption reads: "Mental case: Suicidal in standing position, peculiar arrangement of the ligature, tying of feet and left hand, protrusion of tongue visible" (p. 270).

At about the same time, Stearns (1955) published a second paper to refute the pathologists who had told him that they believed the cases he had described to be accidental deaths (see chapter 9). Stearns based his opinion that such deaths were suicides on the cases that he chose to group together. These cases were all males age 34 or younger who had died by hanging, and he included in his consideration victims who had been fully dressed as well as those who had been naked or cross-dressed. Among the seventeen cases Stearns reported in his second paper (some of which had been included in his 1953 paper) was one in which there was no evidence of autoerotic asphyxia and a detailed suicide note had been left. The remaining cases had features consistent with accidental autoerotic asphyxias, and Stearns gave no explanation for his view that they were suicides. Stearns mentioned, without specifying details, that several cases had come to his attention that were "in every way comparable except for the fact that a cellophane or plastic bag was put over the head to cause suffocation" (1955).

Shankel and Carr (1956) were aware of Gutheil's paper when they presented a detailed case history of a seventeen-year-old boy who began self-hanging at age ten or eleven when he was thinking of killing himself because of family and school difficulties: "I wasn't really trying to kill myself, but was thinking about it, and wondered what hanging would be like, so I tried it out." He found the initial hanging episode exhilarating and developed an erection. He denied any suicidal intent in the many hanging episodes that followed, uniformly accompanied by cross-dressing and masturbation. The patient reported that he had begun wearing female clothing at the same age at which he discovered self-hanging. During a sodium-amytal interview he apparently was asked leading questions, in response to which he acknowledged that he would like to be surgically converted into a woman. He said that for sexual gratification it was his practice to dress in women's clothes, strut in front of a mirror, and then hang himself by kicking books out from under him so that he would be suspended from a rope hung over a door and tied to the doorknob on the other side: "Then, after it had choked me for a while, I would grab hold of the rope and get loose. . . . It always gave me a nice erection, and then I would masturbate. Sometimes the hanging would give me a bad headache that lasted days."[3] For years this patient's mother had been aware of his stealing clothes and cross-dressing, and on several occasions she had observed rope burns on his neck and a knotted rope over the door or among her dishevelled clothing. She had also noticed that when they visited friends he would sometimes put on soiled female clothes from the laundry hamper and emerge from a long session in the bathroom with a scarlet or ashen face and enlarged eyes.

Shankel and Carr suggested that the patient's use of hanging "might be symbolic of an acting out of fears of castration, in which he masochistically tortures himself with the threat of genital loss, over which he nevertheless has control, being able to avert the threat by terminating the hanging short of physical harm." This formulation presupposes an unconscious equation of the phallus with the body, a phenomenon described previously by other psychoanalysts (see, for example, Stekel's comment on penis-strangulation, cited earlier). On another level, the authors suggested that self-hanging may be an acting out of lust murder in which the patient plays the part of both aggressor and victim (a suggestion also made by Stekel, as cited previously). Shankel and Carr do cite one of Stekel's works on another point but not the work (1929) in which he made these observations.

During the following years (from 1956 to 1972), a number of observations appeared in the literature with no cited cross-linkages between the reports of fatalities on the part of forensic pathologists and the reports of repetitive, nonfatal, autoerotic hangings by Stekel, Gutheil, and Shankel and Carr.

Writing about suicide in children, Schechter (1957) noted the phenomenon of cross-dressing episodes with binding of the body and neck among boys and reported a case in which the subject was rescued from a semiconscious state when discovered by his parents. The subject continued to cross-dress after this episode, but the outcome after a year of intensive psychotherapy was not reported. Schechter emphasized the elements of transvestism and sadomasochism in such cases and postulated that deaths occur while struggling against the bonds as part of the acting out of a fantasy that includes identification with the female and passive submission to an aggressor in a sexual act. He took issue with the ruling of such deaths as accidental and suggested that these deaths be seen as suicides in which "the act itself represents the final submission to the all-powerful male figure."

In the same year as Schechter's commentary, Ford (1957) reported six hangings in which there was evidence of genital activity but no cross-dressing. He concluded from evidence that the practice is repetitive that death is not the purpose of the noose. In one of Ford's cases, the decedent had constructed an effigy that was discovered in the same condition as his body, with a rubberized cloth hood held about the neck with a noose. In another the decedent had smeared feces on his cheeks.

Apparently relying on newspaper accounts, Reinhardt (1957) emphasized narcissism as an explanation of the deaths because all three cases known to him involved the use of mirrors. In one, an elaborate suicide note was found (this case was subsequently reported in detail by Litman and Swearingen [1972] and is reviewed in the following section). Other texts of the same time mentioned accidental hangings among children and adolescents without mentioning autoerotic asphyxia (Merkley 1957; Kerr 1957).

Professor Thomas and Senior Assistant Van Hecke (1959), both in forensic medicine at the University of Ghent, mentioned in connection with a case report that they were aware of only four autoerotic asphyxias in Belgium during the previous quarter-century. Their paper includes a photograph of a case in which the hands were bound to a cross-beam in a manner resembling crucifixion (see Case #3 in chapter 7, involving a pillory).

In a case reported by Strauss and Mann (1960) a bath towel was found between the rope and the neck, leading to the suggestion that such padding is an important diagnostic finding. The authors also mention that families, in their experience, are better able to accept being told that the death is accidental, despite the circumstances, than that the death was suicidal.

Making no mention of the previously published descriptions of autoerotic hangings, Johnstone et al. (1960) reported four accidental asphyxial deaths of adult males who had covered their heads with plastic bags. Two wore items of female apparel, a third had been masturbating into a handkerchief, and the fourth, whose clothed body was entirely encased in a large garment bag, was found in a public lavatory known to be frequented by homosexuals. The authors (all pathologists) speculated that an unconscious desire to return to the womb may have motivated the enclosure in plastic, although they admitted that the decedents may have been seeking excitement from hypoxia (see chapter 4 for further discussion of this hypothesis). Holzhausen and Hunger (1960) reported autoerotic asphyxias with plastic bags in Germany and mentioned that volatile agents such as ether or cleaning fluid had been used in some cases. Other cases involving the use of plastic bags were soon depicted by Simpson (1965) and Polson (1965). Litman et al. (1963) mentioned the accidental death of a man who habitually inhaled chloroform while masturbating. This appears to have been the first anesthetic-related autoerotic asphyxia reported in the United States.

Polson (1961) emphasized the importance of distinguishing between hanging and strangulation as an important element in determining manner of death. He emphasized that as many as 90 percent of hangings were suicidal, the remainder being accidental, ''of which not a few are a consequence of sexual deviation.''

Mant (1962) showed that spermatozoa can be found in the urethra of 75 percent of all males dying under age eighty-one regardless of the cause of death. This observation has been widely ignored, and police and autopsy reports continue to make reference to the presence of spermatozoa in the urethra as though it were evidence of a sexually related death. Mant's observation was emphasized by Usher (1963) in a discussion of autoerotic asphyxias. Although there had been by this time several case reports of women dying through autoerotic asphyxia in Germany, Usher nonetheless stated that "the victim is always male." Usher distinguished between sexually related hangings among adolescents and adults on the one hand and hangings among older children "in the course of adventurous games or experiments in self-suspension with a variety of ligatures" on the other.

In a popularized book on suicide, McCormick (1964) mentioned two cases that he apparently regarded as unusual suicides. One was that of an overweight fifteen-year-old who "was so worried about his 15 stone weight that he wore his mother's corsets to make him look slimmer. He hanged himself in his bedroom" (p. 66). The other case was that of a well-known actor who was found dead in a sewage-inspection pit. Twice previously he had been found chained up, once to railings in a basement and once to a bedstead. On the third occasion, his manacled skeleton was discovered two years after his disappearance. The coroner told the jury that the actor, "though normal in the ordinary way had at times some sudden urge to chain himself up."

Simpson (1965) and Polson (1965) each described a twenty-five-year-old who asphyxiated in a shallow bath wearing a wetsuit and a mechanical breathing apparatus. It is not clear whether both authors described the same case, but it is noteworthy that Polson mentioned that a twenty-seven-year-old neighbor of the decedent reported by him had died similarly four months earlier. The possibility that they had communicated about an autoerotic technique must remain speculative, for there was no physical evidence that their deaths occurred in the course of sexual activity.

The extent to which the psychiatric literature remained isolated from the forensic-pathology literature as knowledge of sexual arousal through cerebral hypoxia unfolded is well illustrated by two mid-1960s publications. On the one hand, Weisman (1965), writing of the relationship between self-destruction and sexual perversion, made no mention of the cumulative knowledge of these cases, even in describing a woman who experienced an orgasm during a suicide attempt by hanging at age twenty (and had earlier used suffocation with a pillow to induce orgasm or a state of mind in which masturbation was permissible). Thereafter the woman used hanging autoerotically, experiencing gratification while simultaneously being punished for it and preferred for her paid male sexual partners to threaten, degrade, and partially suffocate her. On the other hand, Snyder (1967) claimed that "There is no record of anyone ever being discovered in the situation before death occurred . . ." (p. 207). Snyder suggested that accidental autoerotic asphyxias were "a result of some sexual maladjustment associated with puberty" (p. 208).

In an Australian report, Rogers (1966) mentioned that he had seen three cases in a period of twenty-seven months in Sydney (population approximately 2 million) though, as far as he could ascertain, none had ever been recognized there before. Rogers suggested that cases had been overlooked in the past because friends or relatives would be likely to remove evidence of sexual activity before reporting the death to the police, as occurred with one of the three cases that he reported. Luke (1967), in a study of asphyxial deaths by hanging in Manhattan from 1964 through 1965, mentioned 1 asphyxial autoerotic fatality out of 106 hangings.

The following year, Brittain (1968) provided the first summary of psychiatric knowledge and physical findings regarding asphyxial autoerotic fatalities and introduced the term *sexual asphyxias*. Although Brittain provided no documentation, he made several original generalizations that were consistent with the cumulative evidence at the time: First, fatal cases had usually come as a surprise to everyone, there being no previously known history of psychiatric or sexual disorder. Second, the complicated preparations and apparatus in some cases suggested a gradual elaboration of technique. Third, similar cases had occurred in which death was due to drowning, inhalation of asphyxiant gases, anesthetics, or the fumes of volatile liquids, the use of an anesthetic mask, or electrocution. Fourth, the incidence appeared to be higher in Anglo-Saxon and Germanic than in Latin populations, higher among whites than among nonwhites, and higher among the more intelligent than among the less intelligent. Finally, Brittain wrote that he knew of two cases in which men who engaged in autoerotic hanging or strangulation committed sadistic murders. Thus Stekel's (1929) hypothetical suggestion of a connection between self-hanging and lust murder received empirical support for the first time, nearly forty years later. In the interim, Boss (1949) had described a patient whose thoughts reinforced the hypothesis, and Shankel and Carr (1956) had suggested the same hypothesis.

Hunt (1968) mentioned that some autoerotic asphyxias occur among individuals who shut themselves in confined spaces but did not describe or cite any such cases. Chapman and Matthews (1970) reported the case of a thirty-year-old man who died of an autoerotic asphyxia after having enclosed himself within a homemade vinyl pouch that was constructed so as to permit opening and closing from the inside. Unlike most victims, he had been under psychiatric treatment at some time in the past and had been diagnosed as suffering from an "anxiety reaction with hysterical features."

Wecht (1970) described two autoerotic hangings and stated that in various Oriental societies partners commonly squeeze each other's necks during intercourse to induce cerebral "anoxia." As noted in chapter 1, the Japanese film entitled *In the Realm of the Senses* depicts a couple employing this practice, which eventuated in the death of the male partner. Gwozdz (1970) reported an additional seven fatalities.

An autoerotic-asphyxiation case in Mexico (Quiroz-Cuaron and Reyes-Castillo 1971) was given a most unusual interpretation. The case showed complex bondage and infibulation of the nose and tongue, both of which had been pierced by rings (see chapter 5 for detailed discussion of these features), and the authors suggested that there was some foreign body in the mouth although they did not identify it. Their interpretation of the death emphasized that the decedent had been a religious man:

> His death occurred on the fifth day of Lent, thus appearing as a sacrifice, penance or expiation. Secondly, there were 7 knots in the cord of the window blind [not part of his bondage] which could symbolise the crown of thorns connected with the seven mysteries in honour of the Virgin. Thirdly, we are reminded of the penance of St. Anthony and especially that of St. Xavier who whipped his flesh with cords full of knots: are we not in the presence of what Altavilla described as an ill-defined polymorphous passion? which overrides the instinct of self-preservation and ends in "self-mutilation" or its close relative "suicide," or even in other disturbances of the instincts—such as the possession instinct, which under the effect of this type of passion, can degenerate as easily into avarice as it can to prodigality . . . .[4]

The authors cite several sources on the subjects of sexual masochism and autoerotic asphyxias yet conclude that "we are faced with a case of compulsive psycho-neurosis with masochistic and mystico-religious overtones."

Henry (1971) described the death of a woman who had suspended herself with a window-sash cord wrapped around her chest and crotch and who died as a result of having inadvertently caught a belt used as a blindfold and gag in the sash cord used for suspension in such a way that hanging resulted. Although the facts of the case are such as to suggest that she had not intended to induce asphyxia, this case is often cited as the first autoerotic asphyxia ever reported in a woman. As noted earlier, even if it were an example of autoerotic asphyxiation resulting in death by asphyxia, it would not be the first reported case in a woman.

In their book on suicide, Lester and Lester (1971) mentioned autoerotic fatalities, citing Stearns (1953), and stated that the motives in such cases are "undoubtedly very complex and perhaps should not be classified simply as suicidal" (p. 7).

Resnik (1972) reviewed "erotized repetitive hangings" because they had "to date not been considered as a psychologic entity." He provided several examples of literary works that referred to the association between hanging and erection, ejaculation, or sexual pleasure. The sources Resnik cited have served as the basis for most subsequent reviews, though few authors credit him as the source of their citations. His paper marked a turning point in the literature on autoerotic asphyxia, through its integration of evidence from multiple disciplines and from literature and through his efforts to fathom the psychodynamics of sexual hangings. To earlier psychodynamic formulations about autoerotic hangings, Resnik added the interpretation that immobilization and asphyxia contribute to fantasies of feeding, reunion, and rebirth, and are thus related to conflict over separation from the mother. Resnik also noted that he had observed games in which children "choke" each other by compressing the neck or chest, and that Shoshone-Bannock Indian children are said to engage in risk-taking and suffocation games.

In another seminal paper that has become a standard citation, Litman and Swearingen (1972) reported two fatalities with unusually elaborate features of bondage and masochism that are particularly enlightening because of the long handwritten notes left by the decedents. One had written a list of sexual paraphernalia and fantasies. The other had left an impersonal note explaining that he had used autoerotic asphyxia in the past, that he was aware of several persons who had died unexpectedly through self-strangulation, and that he intended on this occasion to effect his own death. He also left a descriptive note that is unique in the history of autoerotic fatalities and for that reason is reprinted here in its entirety:

> To all who are interested—please be tender when you cut me down. My panty girdles are fastened to my brassieres with safety pins. There are no hooks on the garter belts so you will have to pull them off. I am going to stand on the telephone books on a chair and use 50 feet of rope, truss myself as tightly as possible. I'm putting one pair of panties in my mouth, pulling a nylon over my face, and placing two false rubber breast pads wet over my nose and mouth—two or three turns of rope around my neck over the bar, back around my neck, closing the closet door. I'm going to set fire to the hems of the slips and then bind my hands behind me, then I will kick the phone books away and madly await the end. My body is carefully perfumed and powdered. The nylon slip I stole from the clothes line zippers down and caresses me lovingly. Now I slip the taffeta dress over my head and pull it down over my body. The base makeup starts to change my face into feminine softness, no sign of a beard. It takes ten minutes to put the lipstick on right. Now emerald rings, more jewelry. Now my blond wig transforms me into a woman completely. Now in utter passion I walk about the room, feeling the bite, pull, stretching of bras, garters, panties, all working me up to torture. Standing a chair in the clothes closet, I screw two hook-eyes into the door molding. Next I tie

the keys to three padlocks on a string and hang them on a clothes pole at eye level. I put a pair of panties in my mouth that have been soaked in water. Now I pull a stocking down over my head and secure it around my neck with a choker replacing the wig. It certainly makes me look fiendish. I feel fiendish. Now I stand on the chair and deliberately and tightly padlock one end of the chain around my knees. The free end I pull through one hook and pass it around my neck and snap the padlock shut back under the wig. Now I pass the rest of the chain through the other hook and down to my wrists. Because I am just experimenting this time I only wrap the chain but do not padlock it here; reaching back I pull the door closed and hear the lock snap. It is totally black and my blood pounds fiercely. Carefully I work my feet to the edge of the chair and ever so slowly I let my feet slide off. The effect is thrilling. I can't tell where the keys are. I can't find the chair. I can't call for help, and I'm hanging controlled. I can free my hands this time and pull myself up on the chair again. Standing there in the inky darkness I know my next move. Measuring very carefully, I make ready the open lock and end of the chain. I stand on the very top of the chair. Now I strike a match but I'm so nervous it goes out. The next one will do the job though. Quivering with excitement, I just stand and swish the lovely skirts about my legs. I know what I'm going to do next. I'm really terrified by sadistic thrill. It is 9:35 Sunday night and in three minutes I will be dead. I strike the match, reach down and set fire to the gossamer edge of the black nylon slip. Quickly I wrap the chain around my wrists and snap the padlock firmly. In a frenzy of passion, I kick the chair over and my body is spasming at the end of the chain noose. I come wildly, madly. The pain is intense as my clothes start burning my legs. My eyes bulge and I try and reach the keys, knowing I have finally found the courage to end a horrible nightmare life dangerously.[5]

This suicide note (which is also the suicide note mentioned by Reinhardt 1957) provides an unequaled subjective account of an experience encompassing bondage, cross-dressing, masochism, risk-taking, and the sexual excitement that accompanied these. This case (Litman and Swearingen's Case B) is referred to again in subsequent chapters. The case is so vivid and detailed that it tends to stick in the mind and distort one's perception of the proportion of cases in which the previously listed features, particularly that of suicidal intent, occur. Thus it is easy to lose sight of the fact that this is one of the very few examples ever recorded of demonstrable suicidal intent accompanying an autoerotic-asphyxial fatality.

With the cooperation of the editors of the *Los Angeles Free Press,* Litman and Swearingen (1972) announced their interest in interviewing bondage practitioners and received thirty replies resulting in interviews with nine male practitioners and three women who had participated transiently or in order to please men. Of the nine men, six employed hanging or strangulation in their sexual practices. The authors concluded that all of these men were isolated, depressed, and oriented toward death, and suggested that where such men seek treatment, they usually present with depression and minimize the importance of their sexual activities.

Another nonfatal case was described by Edmondson (1972), whose patient was a fourteen-year-old whose mother had found him blue in the face, masturbating, with a rope looped around his neck and around the end of the bed where he was lying on his back. During the preceding three years he had developed increasing guilt feelings about masturbation. According to Edmondson, these guilt feelings led him to punish himself, initially by forcing something into his rectum, later by threatening himself with knives while masturbating and burying his head in his pillow during orgasm, and finally by fixing a rope around his neck. Unlike other cases described, this boy had low intelligence.

One of the most unusual recorded fatalities was that reported by Rupp (1973). A forty-year-old airline pilot had had a chain harness custom-made that included a loop to be worn around the neck, bolted in front, and strands of chain that passed through the gluteal fold. He had rigged his Volkswagen to run in concentric circles in low gear and had chained himself to the rear bumper, nude except for his chain harness. The chain by which he was attached to the bumper had become entwined around the left rear axle of the car, and when found he had been asphyxiated by compression against the left rear fender.

By this time, writings of pathologists nearly all reflected a recognition of the major features of autoerotic asphyxial fatalities. Some misconceptions continued to be propagated, such as those about the age range (Enos and Beyer 1973; Fatteh 1973), the belief that Henry (1971) had reported the only case in a woman (Fatteh 1973; Spitz 1973), overestimation of the proportion of cases in which a mirror (Enos and Beyer 1973) or cross-dressing, ligature padding, and pornography (Fatteh 1973) are present. (Enos and Beyer [1980] had revised their material in this respect for a subsequent edition of the book in which it appeared, though Spitz [1980] had not; also see Burton [1977] for additional misconceptions.)

A possible exception to the growing sophistication concerning asphyxial autoerotic fatalities was a Greek case report (Adjutantis et al. 1974) of a sixty-year-old woman found naked in a flooded bathroom with a ligature about her neck to which had been attached a heavy iron. The authors reported the case as an unusual suicide and, despite a reference to the 1968 edition of *Gradwohl's Legal Medicine* in which Brittain's review of sexual asphyxias appeared, made no mention of that possibility.

Coe (1974) reported another unusual asphyxial autoerotic fatality: a hospital orderly had hooked a padded rope to a motorized lift in the cast room such that he had manual control of the up-and-down motion of the lift. Coe reported that there had been twelve autoerotic hangings and 1 autoerotic plastic-bag asphyxia during a ten-year period in Hennepin County, Minnesota, during which time there were 110 suicidal hangings and 9 suicidal asphyxias with plastic materials.

Curvey (1974) reported the findings of a survey of twenty-five medical examiners and sixteen insurance companies asked about the manner of death and payment of double-indemnity benefits in five hypothetical cases. One of the cases is an obvious autoerotic hanging with evidence of repetition and with padding of the neck, and all twenty of the medical examiners who responded said that they would certify the death as accidental. Of the ten insurance companies that responded, eight said that if the death were certified as natural, accidental, or undetermined, they would not honor the double-indemnity clause; one would consider the death accidental and would honor the double-indemnity clause even if the death were certified as natural or undetermined; and one would honor the double-indemnity clause only if the death were certified as accidental, and even then with some reservations (see chapter 9).

The authors of a paper reporting two French cases (Petit et al. 1974) were apparently impressed by the mystico-religious explanation offered by Quiroz-Cuaron and Reyes-Castillo (1971), though they did not invoke it to explain their own cases. They offered the comment that during the eighteenth century, members of the medical profession argued whether hanging was a source of sexual pleasure and summarized the opinion of some leading figures of the eighteenth and nineteenth centuries to the effect that "Guyon favored such a point of view, countenanced by Devergie, that Tardieu, Casper, Marchka, and Hoffmann did not, and that Thoinot had an open mind about it." Petit et al. nonetheless concluded: "We do not believe that hanging is valued for that reason nowadays, but more probably for the extreme pain caused by the rope or cord on the neck."

In 1975, Sass, who had collected a large series of cases through his work at the FBI Academy, published the first case report of an asphyxial autoerotic fatality of a woman in the United States. A thirty-five-year-old woman had been found naked in a closet with clothespins clamped on her nipples, a towel around her neck for padding, and a loop of nylon stocking around her neck. An electric vibrator, the head of which was in contact with her vulva, was still running when her body was discovered.

In 1975, Stoller emphasized that the sexual excitement of some people is heightened when they perform sexual acts in which they might be caught breaking a custom, taboo, or statute. In a footnote, he noted that such risk-taking is not always used simply "to add sauce to a dish":

"sometimes it can be a major element in the sexual act, as in sadomasochistic sexual rituals or in those persons who hang or anesthetize themselves to produce orgasm" (p. 117).

Knight (1976) noted that some autoerotic asphyxias were still being misclassified, particularly those among young boys. Knight said that the explanations that the boy had been "experimenting with ropes" or that he had been "reenacting some cowboy film on television" were almost always erroneous and that the true explanation was sexual.

Wright and Davis (1976) reported the death of a man last seen in the company of two women later identified as prostitutes. He was found hanged and bound in the bathroom and was considered possibly to have died through an autoerotic hanging, but some valuables had been stolen, and interrogation of the two women led to a statement to the effect that they had tied up their intoxicated client in order to rob him. The death was ruled to be a homicide.

The first report based on a sizable sample of cases ("by far the largest study of its kind ever accomplished," in the words of the editor of the volume in which it appeared [Wecht 1977]) was a 1977 paper by Walsh and co-workers presenting data on forty-three autoerotic hangings, strangulations, and asphyxiations. The cases were selected from the Armed Forces Institute of Pathology (AFIP) Registry of Forensic Pathology and reflect the sampling biases that would therefore be expected, such as the fact that all but one of the decedents were men aged twenty-nine or older. The results of toxicologic studies had not been included in most previously published cases, and Walsh et al. reported that of twenty-one cases in which some toxicologic analysis had been done, two showed significant blood-alcohol concentrations and one showed a toxic level of barbiturates. Evidence of painful self stimulation in several of their cases included one with metal clamps attached to the axillae, one with a wooden table leg inserted in his rectum, and one with cigarette-type burns on the scrotum and thighs and broken swizzle sticks piercing the nipples. In another of their cases, the decedent possessed sketches of women with bleeding wounds and photographs he had taken of himself, including one in which he is lying prone in a wooded area with simulated, bleeding wounds on his naked back and left buttock.

Walsh et al. (1977) also provided the results of an unpublished test case presented to a group of pathologists attending a seminar at the 1962 meeting of the American Society of Clinical Pathologists. In response to an obvious autoerotic fatality, 35 percent of the pathologists who reviewed the case were of the opinion that the manner of death was suicide, 32 percent saw it as an accident, 20 percent viewed it as strangulation (not a manner of death), and 7 percent classified it as homicide (6 percent did not respond). These responses stand in marked contrast to the unanimous opinion rendered by medical examiners a decade later (Curvey 1974), as described earlier, that such deaths were accidental.

Smith and Braun (1978) provided the first complete report of an individual who had engaged in autoerotic asphyxia and also committed a sexual homicide. The case also furthers the evidence suggesting an association between erotic self-hanging and strangulation of others. Their patient had a history of homosexual prostitution, sadism, promiscuity, exhibitionism, incestual fantasy and sexual molesting of one of his sisters, voyeurism, and necrophilia, in addition to episodes of erotic self-hanging. His masturbation fantasies were sadistic, and he preferred that women be unconscious or remain motionless during intercourse. He reported having partially strangled at least twenty different women, and he was remarkably successful in finding women who tolerated or requested his abuse. He claimed that three different women had asked him to kill them and that only eight of the twenty women he had assaulted were assaulted against their will and without forewarning. The onset of his necrophiliac activities is particularly illuminating:

> The patient's necrophiliac activities began in earnest with his first wife when he choked her with his legs during oral-genital intercourse and fantasized that she was under his complete control and that he was free to perform lecherous acts upon her body without resistance or awareness on her part. Eventually, he demanded that his wife "play dead" during intercourse. If she refused, he would forcibly strangle her until she lost consciousness. He would then, according to his wife's account, perform sexual deeds upon her body like a furious animal. Interestingly, he never forced himself upon any woman unless intoxicated with alcohol.[6]

The twentieth woman whom the patient strangled died as a result, and he was convicted of manslaughter. Smith and Braun suggested a psychodynamic interaction between erotic self-hanging or lust-suicide, on the one hand, and necrophilia or lust murder, on the other.

McDowell (1978) attempted to distinguish between "accidental masochistic deaths," by which he apparently meant autoerotic hangings and strangulations, and "accidental anoxic deaths," by which he meant autoerotic fatalities involving the use of a plastic bag over the head or the inhalation of volatile compounds. According to McDowell, these latter cases had not yet been reported and "appear to be a somewhat new phenomenon" (but see earlier). McDowell also perpetuated the myth that the victims of autoerotic hangings and strangulations tend to be "homosexually oriented."

Knight (1979), fully aware of the usual varieties of asphyxial autoerotic fatalities, published four uncharacteristic cases to remind readers that an occasional autoerotic asphyxia is suicidal. The first of these cases was a twenty-five-year-old man who hanged himself from a tree while naked, with his wrists, ankles, and waist bound. He had apparently jumped from a branch of the tree, and his feet were three to four feet above the ground when he was found so there had been no possibility of his escaping. The second case was that of a twenty-nine-year-old man hanged by the neck with tight bondage of the wrists and ankles and complete covering of his mouth with surgical adhesive plaster. He had left notes indicating that he intended to commit suicide. The third and fourth cases are less convincing. One was that of a fifty-six-year-old man found naked within a homemade airtight bag from which he could have escaped merely by crawling out. The last was a fifty-two-year-old man found naked with his nose and mouth covered by a plastic mackintosh and his head jammed inextricably in a hole between the floorboards. (Though rare in the United States, mackintosh fetishism is well known in England [Gosselin and Wilson 1980].) Knight also suggested the "faint though real" possibility "that some cases may not be solo operations and that there might be some other party involved," foreshadowing some of the cases we describe in chapter 8.

Rosenblum and Faber (1979) added another case report of a survivor of autoerotic asphyxiation. Their patient was a 15-year-old male, referred by the police after he told them of his practice while being interrogated about another matter. At age twelve, he and a male cousin had masturbated together while looking at *Playboy,* and his cousin had taught him to ejaculate into the cousin's sister's bras and panties. Subsequently, the cousin showed him how to suspend himself from a door and ejaculate while hanging. The boy tried these activities himself and managed to steal underwear from his sister and from shops. He hanged himself from the clothes rod in his closet by lifting his feet from the ground and learned to place a towel around his neck under the ligature to prevent marks or bruises. He reported that he hanged for one-half to two minutes and nearly always ejaculated while suspended. The frequency of his self-hanging episodes had increased from once every two weeks to as often as four times a week. The boy's mother was described as "a very dominant punitive, demeaning individual" who knew about her son's masturbatory practices for some time, often listened at his door, but never intervened or confronted him about his behavior; she even washed his female clothing for him. The boy's father once repaired a broken clothes rod in the boy's closet without asking any questions. Even as a child, the boy had been preoccupied with ropes, and at age fifteen, he wore two neck chains and a wrist chain and constantly worked on fan belts and bike chains. The boy described intermittent depression, especially when his mother was angry toward him, and said that he engaged in self-hanging because he wanted to get his mother angry; because it relieved his depression, at least temporarily; because it made him feel good; and because he wanted to provoke his family into doing more things together. The boy agreed to stop hanging himself when the examiner agreed to arrange psychotherapy and foster-care placement. A year after these had been accomplished, no further hanging episodes were known.

Rosenblum and Faber interpreted Litman and Swearingen's (1972) observations concerning depression and partner activities among nine interviewees as representative of adults who engage in autoerotic asphyxia. Contrasting their patient with the men interviewed by Litman and Swearingen, Rosenblum and Faber suggested a developmental sequence progressing from childhood interest in ropes, through adolescent sexual asphyxia, to an adult bondage syndrome in which death would be suicidal. As shown in subsequent chapters, however, there is no evidence to suggest that the proportion of cases with demonstrable suicidal intent is sizable at any age.

Rosenblum and Faber commented, in passing, that "it would seem reasonable to estimate that at least 250 deaths occur per year in the U.S. alone." As so often happens, this statement was transmogrified for the abstract, which stated: "The syndrome accounts for at least 250 deaths per year in the United States alone." This figure was apparently the unacknowledged source of *Hustler* magazine's statement that "terminal sex" (another phrase taken from Rosenblum and Faber) "kills 200 to 300 people a year in the U.S." (see chapter 1).

Another example of an erroneous abstract was that associated with Danto's (1980) case report of a black woman dying through autoerotic asphyxia. Danto's statement that "Female case reports have been too rare and infrequent to help us see what might be involved when a woman practices this lethal sexual perversion" is transmogrified in the abstract to the statement: "As cases involving females have never been reported, this presentation offers some opportunity to see how psychiatric insight assisted police investigation of an autoerotic death." Danto overestimated the proportion of victims of autoerotic asphyxias who were viewing themselves in mirrors at approximately 50 percent (see chapter 7). He offered the interpretation that "this perversion reenacts the victim's feelings of emasculation by his mother. . . . If when he dies he is wearing panty hose or other female attire, symbolically and on a fantasy level, it is his mother who dies. In this fantasied homicide, the fantasy creator identifies with the victim." This interpretation resembles those made by several authors since Stekel (1929), none of whom is cited. Danto concluded that what men who engage in lethal autoerotic behavior have in common is that "Each seeks being totally in power to reach a fantasied wish to control life and death. They engaged in such a struggle while alone, narcissistically carrying out the battle for mastery of their inner conflict by eroticizing their helplessness, weakness, and threat to life.'' (Contrast this statement with Litman and Swearingen's [1972] statement, not cited by Danto, that ''The essential element that these men had in common was the erotization of a situation of helplessness, weakness, and threat to life which was then overcome in survival, and there was eventual triumph. Some of the subjects consciously and overtly emphasized the theme of strength and endurance.'')

In a chapter on ''Sex-Related Deaths'' in an important recent text, Rupp (1980), a well-known expert on autoerotic fatalities, repeated the persistent belief that ''To date there have been only two well-documented cases reported in females.'' He suggested that self-mutilation is commonly found but that ''the quick escape mechanism is the exception rather than the rule.'' Rupp, like Brittain (1968) and Rosenblum and Faber (1979), suggests that there is a developmental sequence with progressive elaboration and embellishment of technique, with increasing proportions of cases displaying ''bondage, mutilation, transvestism,'' and other features with advancing age. (To the extent that this hypothesis could be tested from the present study, it was not confirmed; see chapter 5.)

Rupp (1980) stated that ''no large, well-documented series has ever been compiled or thoroughly investigated.'' Rupp concluded:

> Autoerotic asphyxia is carried on by thousands of individuals who arrive at this practice independently of one another. It represents an as yet unexplored, almost unknown, aspect of human behavior. There is every indication that what might be learned from a thorough scientific study of autoerotic asphyxia might prove a significant contribution to our understanding of human sexuality.[7]

Lest the reader believe, on the basis of the foregoing review, that autoerotic asphyxia is thoroughly familiar to all who should know about it, I quote the following cryptic paragraph on autoerotic fatalities from a leading textbook of criminal investigation:

> A suicidal hanging is frequently associated with sexual homicide. The victim may, for example, be dressed in the clothing of the opposite sex (typically a man in women's clothing) or have pornographic literature present. Other signs such as loosely binding the hands or legs and binding the genitals may be noted. (Svensson et al. 1981, p. 463.)

Conclusions

The history of the development of knowledge about autoerotic asphyxia illustrates several problems in the transmission of information. Perhaps the most important of these is the general tendency to neglect history and its lessons. Time and again, authors have reflected unawareness of all that had gone on before their contributions were made. Though this might have been understandable in previous centuries when there were no periodical indexes or telephone networks, it appears to be more characteristic of the twentieth century.

A second point to be made about the history of these ideas is the widespread neglect of languages other than our own. In the areas of criminology, sexual deviations, and legal medicine, observations by German authors seem to antedate those in English by decades or longer. This has certainly been true with respect to autoerotic asphyxia, about which there may be a rich nineteenth-century literature which has been neglected here.

A third observation to be made in concluding this chapter is that the history of the development of knowledge about autoerotic asphyxia underscores the hazards of disciplinary specialization. Most notably, the long lag between psychiatric observations of nonfatal autoerotic asphyxia and recognition of the sexual nature of autoerotic fatalities by pathologists demonstrates that the separation between psychiatry and pathology weakens medicolegal practice. The point has been made elsewhere that this separation weakens medicolegal teaching (Dietz 1976) and research (Dietz 1977). The fact that self-conscious multidisciplinary efforts can overcome this handicap is evidenced by the fact that two of the most important contributions reviewed in this chapter (Litman and Swearingen 1972; Resnik 1972) grew out of collaboration between psychiatrists and medical examiners, and another was written by a physician with training in both psychiatry and forensic pathology (Brittain 1968).

Notes

1. The Greek word *hypo* (under) is used as a prefix in many medical terms to denote "lack of." The word *oxygen* derives from the Greek word *oxys* (sour or acid). The Greek words *philein* (to regard with affection, to love) and *philos* (dear) are the roots of the suffix *-philia*, used in medical terms to denote "tendency toward" or "attraction to."

2. Eponymic names of pathological conditions typically derive from the names of the discoverers, literary and mythological characters, or patients (Jablonski 1969, p. iii). As detailed later in this chapter, Kotzwarra was an eighteenth-century musician who died in an erotic asphyxial episode.

3. Shankel, L.W. and Carr, A.C. Transvestism and hanging episodes in a male adolescent. *Psychiatric Quarterly* 30:478–493, 1956.

4. Quiroz-Cuaron, A., and Reyes-Castillo, R. Auto-eroticism and accidental strangulation. *International Criminal Police Review* 250:171–178, 1971.

5. Litman, R.E., and Swearingen, C. Bondage and suicide. *Archives of General Psychiatry* 27:80–85, 1972. Copyright 1972, American Medical Association.

6. Smith, S.M. and Braun, C. Necrophilia and lust murder: Report of a rare occurrence. *Bulletin of the American Academy of Psychiatry and the Law* 6:259–268, 1978.

7. Rupp, J.C. Sex-related deaths. In Curran, W.J., McGarry, A.L., and Petty, C.S. (eds.). *Modern Legal Medicine, Psychiatry, and Forensic Science*. Philadelphia: F.A. Davis, 1980, pp. 575–587.

3

Study Design and Sample Characteristics

*Ann Wolbert Burgess,
Park Elliott Dietz,* and
Robert R. Hazelwood

In this chapter we briefly review the history of the autoerotic-fatalities study, point out limitations inherent in the type of sample that was gathered, describe the other sources of information available, and present some descriptive information concerning the sample, including the types of cases that were studied and basic demographic information about the study cases.

Initiation of the Study

In the spring of 1978, the Federal Bureau of Investigation (FBI) issued a mandate that original in-depth research be conducted on matters relevant to the law-enforcement community. In response to this mandate, Robert Hazelwood requested that students at the Academy submit cases representing autoerotic fatalities that had occurred since 1970. One-hundred and fifty-seven suspected cases were submitted to the Behavioral Science Unit at the FBI Academy in the three years following this request. Cases were submitted primarily by law-enforcement officers who had been students at the Academy or who had heard lectures on the subject by one or more of the authors. The students and audiences familiar with the Academy's interest in collecting such materials were drawn from the local, state, provincial, and federal law-enforcement communities throughout the United States and Canada. Cases were submitted from persons throughout these jurisdictions.

Materials Submitted

Materials submitted varied somewhat between cases. In all instances, investigative reports were submitted along with either a description or photographs of the scene of death. The investigative reports generally made reference to information provided by the person who had discovered the body and statements made by relatives or others who knew the victim. In some cases, the individual submitting the case had conducted additional interviews in order to gather information that had been omitted from the original investigation. In other cases, the individual submitting a case had first investigated it after receiving specialized training, and in these instances the investigative reports tended to be extremely thorough. Writings, drawings, photographs, or notes that had been made by the victim were submitted in a number of cases. Many of the individuals submitting cases were contacted with requests for additional information or questions regarding unresolved issues.

This study was not entirely prospective, and not all cases were recorded and submitted in the recommended format. Data were missing for some variables and it is quite likely that important sources of information—for example, writings by the victim or knowledge concerning his previous sexual preferences—were lost from an unknown number of cases. Despite these shortcomings, virtually all of the cases included in the sample were described at least as thoroughly as any of the published case reports of autoerotic fatalities.

Limitations of the Sample

Although this collection of cases cannot be said to be a probability sample, it appears to be the largest collection of thoroughly investigated cases anywhere and reflects no demonstrable sampling bias. Nonetheless, we would expect that the cases submitted reflect a few reporting biases. First among these is that only those cases that come to the attention of investigators could have been detected for reporting. Thus we would expect our series to underrepresent cases in which attempts were made by survivors to conceal the nature of the death. Second, in some urban areas with well-established medical-examiner systems, such cases are so well known and common that interest in extensive investigation culminating in submission to the Academy is probably limited, resulting in underrepresentation of cases from such areas. Third, because the Academy offers analysis and opinion in difficult or equivocal cases, it is likely that there is an overrepresentation of difficult or equivocal cases. Fourth, because the Academy's research interest in such cases is known to the potential contributors, it is likely that the more bizarre and complex cases have a higher probability of submission than the more typical cases.

Despite our recognition of these potential sources of reporting bias and our recognition that the cases available do not constitute a probability sample, we have sometimes calculated percentage distributions of variables in order to give the reader some sense of the proportion of cases in which certain features occur. Taking account of the earlier-noted biases, the reader should bear in mind that the percentage of cases demonstrating a particular attention-fixing feature—for example, transvestism, elaborate bondage, or expensive pornography collections—is probably a maximum estimate of the true proportion of cases in which such features occur. Contrariwise, the fact that some information may have been lost from cases that were not investigated by the individual submitting the materials means that the percentage of cases demonstrating a particular feature that is easily missed—for example, writings, drawings, subtle evidence of previous activity, or a history of sexual preferences known only to intimates—is probably a minimum estimate of the true proportion of cases in which such features occur.

Another limitation of the data stems from the tendency of all concerned to be secretive about the behaviors of interest. We are familiar with a few cases in which asphyxial autoerotic fatalities were camouflaged by family members or others to appear as suicides, and the frequency with which such efforts are successful is unknown. Even when the true nature of the death is ascertained, as in the cases reported here, it is possible that family members or others may have removed certain materials, such as pornography, writings, or photographs, from the scene of death or may be less than fully forthcoming about their knowledge of the decedents' sexual preferences. Finally, the greatest threat to the validity of our findings is that the decedents themselves may have been secretive about their sexual thoughts and preferences to the extent that homosexuality or a psychosexual disorder was neither revealed to intimates nor discernible from their possessions or circumstances of death. Thus the proportions of cases in which homosexuality or a psychosexual disorder is identified must be regarded as minimum estimates.

Additional Sources of Information

In addition to collecting and reviewing the case reports, we have spoken with families and associates of victims, investigating officers, medical examiners, and other researchers in this area, and with living practitioners of autoerotic asphyxia and their physicians. These interviews have focused on the questions we regard as unanswered by previous sources of information but have not been standardized interviews.

The strategy followed for the literature-review component of our study consisted of identification of all original journal articles in English that could be identified as containing information on autoerotic fatalities or potentially injurious sexual practices. Textbooks and treatises in medical jurisprudence, forensic pathology, and forensic medicine, and monographs on sexual deviations, sadism, masochism, and fetishism were also reviewed. In reviewing all of these sources of published information, all references to other writings in English that could provide additional information were also consulted. We have found with this topic, as with others, that the quest for a comprehensive bibliography seems endless. We will no doubt continue to discover additional writings that we have missed, and we invite readers aware of such information to share it with us. An extensive literature in German, a minor literature in French, and a small literature in other languages have been neglected largely due to our linguistic and budgetary shortcomings.

Sample Characteristics

Data were systematically abstracted from 157 suspected autoerotic fatalities submitted. The cases submitted included accidental sexual deaths attributable to the use of ligatures compressing the neck, airway obstruction, chest compression, chemicals or gases, and electrical stimulation. Cases have been received in which the victim died of natural causes (for example, myocardial infarction) or exposure while engaged in autoerotic activity. Investigative agencies have also submitted equivocal deaths for evaluation, soliciting opinions as to the manner of death and/or the possibility of second-party involvement.

After analysis and review, we classified 132 of these cases as asphyxial autoerotic deaths, 18 as atypical autoerotic deaths (mostly non-asphyxial), 5 as deaths occurring during sexual activity with a partner, and 2 as autoerotic suicides. The types of cases submitted are shown in Table 3-1.

The fact that the cases most often submitted were asphyxial autoerotic fatalities conforms to the relative frequencies of the various types of cases as expected on the basis of case reports and other observations published in the professional literature (contrast chapter 4 with chapter 6). Reports of asphyxial autoerotic fatalities greatly outnumber reports of other types of autoerotic fatalities. We separate the four types of cases

Table 3-1
Final Classification of 157 Suspected Autoerotic Fatalities

Classification	N	(%)
Asphyxial autoerotic fatality	132	(84.1)
Atypical autoerotic fatality	18	(11.5)
Sexual-asphyxial fatality involving a partner	5	(3.2)
Autoerotic suicide	2	(1.3)
Total	157	(100.1)

Study Design and Sample Characteristics 49

in our analysis in order to avoid introducing unnecessary variance by lumping dissimilar events. Information about living practitioners of autoerotic asphyxia is provided chiefly in chapter 2. Nonasphyxial and other atypical autoerotic deaths are covered in chapter 6, and sexual asphyxial deaths possibly involving partners are discussed primarily in chapter 8.

Asphyxial Autoerotic Fatalities

The most common form of dangerous autoerotic activity involves the use of some technique for reducing oxygen to the brain to achieve an altered state of consciousness.

As noted in chapter 1 and reviewed in detail in chapter 4, some authors reserve the term *asphyxia* for conditions resulting from interference with respiratory exchange within the lungs whereas others use the term more generally to include all conditions resulting in decreases in the level of oxygen within the blood. We use the term *asphyxia* in the broader sense here, and would, therefore, consider strangulation (including hanging, ligature strangulation, and throttling), suffocation (including smothering and choking), chest compression interfering with the ability to breathe, exclusion of oxygen from ambient air, and inhalation of asphyxiating gases to be asphyxial mechanisms.

Four basic methods of inducing asphyxia are encountered in asphyxial autoerotic fatalities: (1) neck compression, (2) oxygen exclusion, (3) airway obstruction, and (4) chest compression. If any of these four methods of asphyxia is not terminated in time, death will result. The most common cause of death in autoerotic fatalities is asphyxiation.

It is important to note the distinction between autoerotic or sexual asphyxia on the one hand and asphyxia as a cause of death on the other. Autoerotic or sexual asphyxia refers to the use of asphyxia to heighten sexual arousal, more often than not with a nonfatal outcome. Although not necessarily fatal, sexual asphyxial practices are clearly dangerous. The autoerotic-asphyxia practitioner who dies while engaged in autoerotic asphyxiation most often dies from an unexpected overdose of asphyxiation when, for one reason or another, he becomes unable to terminate his means of enjoyment. From time to time, however, someone engaged in autoerotic asphyxia may die a nonasphyxial death (for example, from a heart attack, stroke, or exposure) during this activity. Conversely, it is theoretically possible that someone engaged in nonasphyxial autoerotic activity might die an asphyxial death (for example, carbon-monoxide poisoning from a faulty heater or automobile-exhaust system).

The overwhelming majority of decedents were male. Of 132 dece-

Table 3-2
Age of Decedents by Type of Fatality, Sex, and Race

	Asphyxial Autoerotic (N = 132)				Atypical Autoerotic (N = 18)	
	Male		Female		Male	Female
Age Group	White	Black	White	Black	White	Black
9–12	3	1			1	
13–19	37				2	
20–29	41	1	3*	1	2	2
30–39	26**	2			4	
40–49	8*				1	
50–59	6				1	
60–69	1		1		3	
70–79	1				2	
Total	123	4	4	1	16	2

*Includes one Native American.
**Includes one Hispanic.

dents, 5 were female. The mean age of decedents was 26.5 years. Four victims were preadolescent, 37 were teenagers, 46 were in their twenties, 28 in their thirties, 8 in their forties, 6 in their fifties, 2 in their sixties, and 1 in his seventies. The distributions by age, sex, and race are shown in Table 3–2.

Table 3–3 shows the distribution by marital status. Although 76 (67.9 percent) of 112 decedents for whom marital status was known were single, 41 of the 132 decedents from whom they were drawn were under age twenty, some of them too young to have been married.

Available data on social class suggest that the decedents were more often middle class than upper, working, or lower class. This is an unusual

Table 3-3
Marital Status of Decedents by Type of Fatality

	Asphyxial Autoerotic		Atypical Autoerotic	
Marital Status	N	(%)	N	(%)
Single	76	(67.9)	13	(72.2)
Married	30	(26.8)	4	(22.2)
Separated	3	(2.7)		
Divorced	1	(1.0)	1	(5.6)
Widowed	2	(2.0)		
Total	112*	(100.4)	18	(100.0)

*Marital status data were missing for twenty cases, and these have not been included in the percentages for this table.

observation for cases coming to the attention of medical examiners and law-enforcement agencies, for members of the lowest social strata usually are disproportionately represented among traumatic deaths.

Atypical Autoerotic Fatalities

As previously mentioned, there are forms of dangerous autoerotic activity that do not involve the purposeful use of asphyxia. These activities involve a wide variety of potentially dangerous practices, such as the use of nonasphyxial sexual bondage, infibulation, electricity, insertion of foreign bodies in the urethra, vagina, or rectum, and life-threatening games.

Although it cannot be said with certainty whether these nonasphyxial dangerous practices are more widely practiced than sexual asphyxia, with the exception of electricity they seem less likely to result in death. Deaths from such activities are less prevalent than deaths during autoerotic asphyxia, and they are therefore referred to as atypical autoerotic fatalities.

Nonasphyxial autoerotic practices can result in a variety of causes of death, as illustrated in chapter 6. There were sixteen such cases submitted, including deaths by electrocution (six), heart attack (four), poisoning (four), exposure (one), and undetermined (one). In two other atypical cases, autoerotic asphyxia resulted indirectly in an asphyxial death due to aspiration of vomitus. These eighteen decedents comprised sixteen white males and two black females. Their age, sex, and race distributions are shown in Table 3–2 and their distribution by marital status in Table 3–3.

Sexual Asphyxial Fatalities Including a Partner

Sexual asphyxia deaths also occur in the presence of a partner. Most often, these are homicides in which a male assailant strangles, smothers, or otherwise asphyxiates a rape victim (female or male). Cases in which it was obvious that this was what had occurred were not requested for this study, and none was submitted. A less common occurrence is the death by asphyxia of an individual who apparently consented to engage in sexual activity. In such instances, it is likely that there will be considerable difficulty in differentiating willful murder from negligent manslaughter. In addition, under certain circumstances, there may be difficulty in determining whether a sexual partner was present at the time of death. To assist in the discrimination of such cases from autoerotic fatalities they are discussed in chapter 8.

It is also possible that a person engaged in autoerotic activity may incidentally become a homicide victim. The autoerotic activity may have nothing to do with the homicide. For example, an individual may be engaged in autoerotic activity when a burglar enters his home and kills him. The autoerotic activity may also have some bearing on the homicide. In one case (not from the study sample) a wife shot and killed her husband in his bed, believing him to be her husband's female lover. What she did not know at the time of the shooting was that her husband was a transvestite and had fallen asleep dressed in his female clothing after engaging in autoerotic activity.

A remote possibility that must always be borne in mind is that of a homicide scene deliberately altered to appear to be an accidental autoerotic death. P.D. James (1972) describes a fictional example of this phenomenon, but we are unaware of a single published account of a murder being camouflaged in this manner. We do know of one case in which it was suspected that a police officer, who may have been the murderer, altered a crime scene to make it appear like an autoerotic asphyxia but failed to include an escape mechanism in the scene that he designed. In one published case (Wright and Davis 1976) the possibility that a homicide had been deliberately concealed as an autoerotic asphyxia was considered but seems not to have been the case. Thus we are unable to point to any documented cases in which a crime scene was deliberately altered to appear to be an accidental autoerotic death. The possibility exists that such cases have occurred and that the individual who altered the scene succeeded in masking the true manner of death.

In one unusual case from the study sample, the decedent's wife, who had previously observed him engaging in autoerotic asphyxia, altered the death scene to make it appear like a homicide. Her effort was singularly unsuccessful, for she left the noose within sight and inflicted a minor stab wound that was readily shown to have been inflicted after death by asphyxia.

Autoerotic Suicides

In our opinion, true autoerotic suicides are rare. Over the years, many autoerotic fatalities have been mistaken for suicide, largely because the investigators were unaware of the phenomenon of autoerotic asphyxia. Thus cases described as a suicide by unusual methods or a bizarre form of suicide are scattered throughout the literature.

In addition, some cases are factitious suicides in which family members or others have removed evidence of sexual activity in order to make the manner of death appear to be suicide. In one study case, for example, the decedent's wife removed the female clothing he had been wearing at death and dressed his body in a suit before calling the police.

Two of our study cases were autoerotic suicides that could be documented as such on the basis of antemortem behavioral indicators, such as a suicide note (see Case #4 in chapter 8). There is no possible means by which to determine with certainty how often other cases may have involved clear suicidal intent. It is certainly feasible, as we know from the rare cases in which antemortem behavioral indicators documented the intent (see the suicide note reprinted in chapter 2 from Litman and Swearingen 1972), that an individual fond of dangerous autoerotic activity will include that behavior in a purposeful suicide. It is conceivable that a suicidal individual, having heard of sexual asphyxia, might choose an asphyxial method of suicide over other options in order to lessen discomfort, but this possibility remains highly speculative. Also, an individual who repetitively engages in dangerous autoerotic practices might decide in the course of such activity to end his or her life, though here too there is no proof of this ever having occurred. More likely, individuals fond of sexual risk-taking might escalate the risk to their lives purposefully with full knowledge that death might ensue, but without formulating a conscious intent to die on one particular occasion. As shown in chapter 9, courts deciding whether to award accidental-death benefits in asphyxial autoerotic fatalities have presumed the intent of the decedent, ruling that the fact of the insured's having engaged in an obviously life-threatening act is sufficient evidence of the intent to bring about "the natural and probable consequences of the act," quite apart from whether any particular consequence was consciously intended in a given instance.

4 Asphyxial Autoerotic Fatalities

*Robert R. Hazelwood,
Park Elliott Dietz, and
Ann Wolbert Burgess*

Asphyxial autoerotic fatalities are deaths resulting directly from the excessive application of an asphyxial mechanism employed for the purpose of increasing sexual excitement. Various other types of autoerotic fatalities occur (discussed in chapter 6), requiring that the definition of asphyxial autoerotic fatalities take account of the form of self-stimulation (asphyxiation), the cause of death (asphyxia), and the relationships between these two.

Whether death from natural disease during manual masturbation is more common than asphyxial autoerotic fatalities is unknown (described in chapter 6), but there can be no doubt that asphyxial autoerotic deaths are the most prevalent recognized traumatic-autoerotic fatalities. The literature on asphyxial autoerotic deaths (refer to chapter 2) is far more extensive than the literature on other traumatic-autoerotic fatalities (see chapter 6). Of 150 autoerotic fatalities submitted for this project, 132 (88.0 percent) were autoerotic asphyxias.

Individual Discovery of Autoerotic Asphyxia

Among the more challenging questions concerning autoerotic asphyxia is the issue of how those who use these techniques first learn about them. Based on the limited evidence available about the processes by which individuals discover the method, we suspect that the most common process is fortuitous discovery, that another sizable group of individuals learn about the method by word of mouth, that a few learn about the method from descriptions in literature and the media, and that rare individuals, on the basis of some other observation, postulate that asphyxia would be sexually exciting and then conduct experiments in order to test their hypothesis.

Fortuitous discovery is indicated in the cases reported by Stekel (1929, after Runge), Shankel and Carr (1956), and Weisman (1965) of individuals who found themselves aroused in the course of asphyxial suicide attempts and thereafter employed asphyxiation sexually (see chapter 2). More often, we suspect, individuals notice that they become sexually excited through sexual bondage, activities affecting respiration (for example, breath-holding games or recreational inhalation of nitrous oxide), or risk-taking behavior (for example, fast driving, roller-coaster rides, or standing near the edge at the top of a cliff or tall building). It is noteworthy that this last group of high-risk activities is often described as breathtaking. It is not unreasonable to postulate that individuals noticing sexual excitement in association with any of these activities might subsequently attempt to recreate the sensation through autoerotic asphyxia.

A suggestive example is the case of one twenty-year-old victim whose fifteen-year-old neighbor reported that the decedent had been in the habit of getting his "kicks" by purposely inducing unconsciousness. He was said to have hyperventilated until becoming dizzy, then requesting that someone give him a bear hug until he passed out. He lost his life when he engaged in autoerotic neck compression to produce a similar sensation.

Discovery by word of mouth is illustrated by Rosenblum and Faber's (1979) patient, who was taught by his cousin, and is suggested by cases in which people who have known one another have died through autoerotic asphyxia. This was suspected in one high school in which two deaths occurred within a short period of time and at a university in which three students died within a few years. Simpson (1965) mentions two neighbors who died a few months apart through asphyxiation with diving gear. In our sample, the death of a schoolteacher thought to have been sexually abusing adolescents (see chapter 5, Pedophilia) was suspected of being related to the death of a student at his school shortly thereafter. On the basis of available historical evidence, Wolfe (1980) suggested that Kotzwarra may have learned of erotic asphyxia from Martin Vanbutchell, a quack doctor in London.

Evidence that individuals learn about autoerotic asphyxia from literature or the media is scanty, though a few cases are suggestive. In one case (not in the sample), a newspaper clipping describing an autoerotic-hanging fatality was found near an adult male who died in this manner. Whether he first learned of the practice from the newspaper is unknown. As indicated in chapter 2, it has also been suggested (Dietz 1978*b*) that Kotzwarra may first have learned of sexual asphyxiation by reading the Marquis de Sade's *Justine,* since Kotzwarra died in 1791, the year in which Justine was first published (Bloch 1931). *Justine* is well known within the contemporary sadomasochism subculture.

Bondage pornography is found in the possession of a sizable proportion of autoerotic-asphyxia decedents, leading more than a few commentators to suggest that the practice was learned from the pornography. Schneider (1978) quotes a police officer as saying that his department had investigated one case in which a magazine had been found in the boy's room that "detailed exactly how to perform the act that killed him." In the course of conducting a study of contemporary pornography (Dietz and Evans 1982), the researchers noted many bondage illustrations depicting ligatures or collars about the neck but no direct recommendations of asphyxial techniques. One publisher (H.O.M., Inc.) of several bondage magazines routinely prints certain rules for the so-called bondage game inside the front cover of its magazines. These rules include the advice to "avoid positions where someone may be injured if they slip or fall, especially ropes or straps around the neck. . . . Carelessness could allow fun and games to turn into lawsuits, a jail sentence, or even a human life on your conscience! A WILLING PARTNER IS TOO PRECIOUS TO HURT WITH A THOUGHTLESSLY PLACED ROPE."

The Joy of Sex (Comfort 1972) also warns against asphyxial sexual techniques. If individuals do, in fact, learn of asphyxial techniques from literature and pornography, it remains true that those individuals are more likely than not to have sought out such literature or pornography as a result of sexual preferences that antedated their discovery of sexual asphyxiation.

The fourth suggested route by which an individual may come to engage in autoerotic asphyxia—that of hypothesis-testing—is illustrated in the case of the Reverend Doctor Manacle which was presented in detail in chapter 2. Observations of penile erection during judicial hangings may have led others to experiment with autoerotic asphyxiation.

These observations on the processes through which individuals discover autoerotic asphyxiation, though based on scanty evidence, are sufficient to refute the claims of Rupp (1980) on this point. Rupp states:

> . . . the evidence indicates that the practice of producing partial anoxia while engaged in sexual activity is not learned from any printed source or by word of mouth. . . . In the absence of any evidence to the contrary, one must accept the idea that each of the persons involved comes to this practice by individual experimentation at a very early age and that the idea of constricting the neck with the production of partial anoxia while engaged in sexual activity is instinctual.

In support of this theory, Rupp describes a young man who committed suicide by gunshot wound and left a note saying that he had been engaging in autoerotic asphyxiation with cross-dressing, had never heard of this practice, and, thinking his behavior unique, believed that he was going mad and decided to kill himself. Although this case argues toward the importance of providing accurate information about autoerotic asphyxia, it certainly is not evidence that the behavior is instinctual.

Incidence of Asphyxial Autoerotic Fatalities

The true incidence of asphyxial autoerotic fatalities is unknown. Apart from sheer guesswork, there are three approaches to estimating how often they occur. The first is to assume that all true cases within some jurisdiction are being detected and to simply report this frequency. It is doubtful that anyone seriously believes that all cases are detected and reported. Nonetheless, some authors do mention the number of cases detected within the jurisdiction in which they work. For example, Thomas and Van Hecke (1959) mention four cases in Belgium during the preceding quarter of a century. This figure is not useful in the absence of knowledge of the population at risk. An improvement is the statement by Rogers (1966) that Sydney, Australia, had three such deaths during twenty-seven months and that the population of the city was approximately two million. Yet even a statement of this sort is inclined to mislead, since the fact that three cases had recently come to attention is likely to have been an impetus to Rogers to prepare a manuscript on the subject. Papers describing cases are not written unless cases have been encountered, so there is an expected bias toward the publication of papers overestimating the frequency of detected and reported cases.

The second technique for estimating frequency is to calculate the proportion of some broader class of deaths that represented asphyxial autoerotic fatalities and then extrapolate from that ratio. Data from Luke's (1967) paper on asphyxial hangings in New York City can be used for this purpose, although it was not a point that Luke attempted to make. Thus of 106 asphyxial hangings in Manhattan during 1964 and 1965, 1 was an autoerotic asphyxia. Similarly, Gwozdz (1970) reported that there had been an average of 1 autoerotic asphyxia for every 200 violent deaths (excluding vehicular crashes) in Houston, Texas. Coe (1974) indicated that he had encountered 13 autoerotic asphyxias in a ten-year period in Hennepin County, Minnesota, and that 12 of these had been by hanging (as compared with 110 suicidal hangings) and 1 by use of a plastic bag (as compared with 9 suicidal asphyxias from plastic materials). Figures of this sort, while seemingly providing a means by which one could compute the number of asphyxial autoerotic fatalities from the known number of hangings, violent deaths, or asphyxial suicides, cannot be so used without taking into account the wide variations among jurisdictions in the population-based incidence of each type of violent death.

The third and best approach uses population-based incidence data to extrapolate from one population to another. In a paper with another focus, Litman and Swearingen used the number (twenty-five) of detected and reported cases in Los Angeles from 1958 through 1970 and, apparently, the known populations of Los Angeles and the United States during that period, to "estimate that there are about 50 bondage deaths in the United States yearly."

Sir David Paul, coroner for the City of London, estimated that there were 4 deaths per year in a population at risk of over 2 million (cited in Hazelwood et al. 1981*a*). Unpublished data from Ontario, Canada, suggest an incidence of approximately 1 death per million population per year (courtesy of Dr. S. Hucker, Clarke Institute, University of Toronto). If the incidence of detected and reported cases is, in fact, 1 to 2 deaths per million population per year, and if we assume that approximately half of cases are detected and reported, the actual number of cases occurring in the United States could be estimated at 500 to 1,000 per year. Such estimates, however, are highly speculative because both the reported incidence and the percentage of cases detected are unknown.

Types of Asphyxia

The Greek origins of the term *asphyxia* imply a stopping of the pulse. This, of course, occurs in every death. Multiple definitions and classifications for asphyxia have been proposed (Davis 1980), leading to some confusion for anyone who consults more than a single reference on this subject. We have attempted to be consistent in this book in using the term *asphyxia* to mean a decrease in oxygen available to the brain. When we describe asphyxial methods, we refer to all those techniques by which the supply of oxygen to the brain is diminished (that is, cerebral hypoxia). When we discuss asphyxia as a cause of death, we refer to death resulting from some asphyxial process.

As we use the term, *asphyxiation* refers to any process that interferes with the availability of oxygen for the brain. This includes obstruction of the breathing passages, obstruction of the blood vessels leading to and from the brain, interference with the movement of muscles necessary for respiration, and the breathing of gases containing insufficient oxygen to sustain life.

Strictly speaking, asphyxiation also includes a decrease in the availability of oxygen to the brain due to changes in the oxygen-carrying capacity of hemoglobin, as occurs with cyanide or carbon-monoxide poisoning or poisoning with certain nitrites (refer to chapter 6). These were not encountered among true autoerotic asphyxias in our sample (but see chapter 6 for an example of an atypical autoerotic fatality from nitrite ingestion). These various methods of asphyxiation do not all produce death through the same mechanism. In the following sections, the relationships between asphyxial methods and mechanisms of death are briefly reviewed.

Hanging and Strangulation

In both hanging and strangulation asphyxia results from compression of the neck by a ligature. In hanging, some or all of the weight of the body pulls upon a ligature attached to a suspension point; in strangulation, the force pulling on the ligature is not the weight of the body (Polson 1965). Hanging may occur in any position (Spitz 1980), and both suicidal and autoerotic hangings have occurred with the victim standing, kneeling, sitting, and even lying down, the weight of the head and neck being sufficient to result in fatal asphyxia.

It is a common misconception that hanging and strangulation cause death by compressing the airway (trachea). The degree of force necessary to compress the trachea is considerably greater than what usually occurs during hanging or strangulation. In the majority of cases, compression of the neck kills through effects on the blood vessels of the neck rather than interference with respiratory exchange through the trachea. An extraordinary illustration is the case of a woman who committed suicide by hanging despite the presence of a tracheostomy located below the level of the noose through which she would have been able to continue breathing (Spitz 1980).

The effects of neck compression on the blood vessels of the neck include interference with the return of blood through the veins to the chest, interference with the supply of fresh blood through the major arteries to the head, and effects not widely known to laymen that involve pressure-sensitive areas in the neck (see the following).

Experiments conducted in Europe in the late nineteenth century and replicated several times since (see Polson 1965, pp. 293–294) have shown that the degree of tension necessary to achieve these effects varies in a predictable sequence. With slight force (less than 5 lbs.) the jugular veins are closed; with somewhat higher force (7 to 11 lbs.) blood flow through the carotid arteries is reduced to a trickle, and then eliminated; and at forces greater than 30 lbs., the trachea and vertebral arteries are closed. Detailed accounts of other effects of neck compression and the signs of death from hanging and strangulation are available in standard textbooks of forensic pathology, though perhaps the best is that in Polson and Gee (1973).

Some unknown proportion of deaths from neck compression occur not as a result of obstruction of blood flow in the blood vessels of the neck but rather from the effects of the neck compression on a pressure-sensitive organ in the neck known as the carotid baroreceptor. Just above the division of the common carotid artery into the internal and external carotid arteries, there is a widening of the internal carotid artery known as the carotid sinus. This sinus includes pressure-sensitive cells and chemically sensitive cells. The pressure-sensitive carotid baroreceptors respond to pressure by slowing the heart. Forceful pressure upon this area is believed to result in a precipitous fall in heart rate and blood pressure, causing unconsciousness. The chemically sensitive carotid body responds to changes in the oxygen tension in the blood (as well as changes in hemoglobin concentration, carbon dioxide tension, and pH). Under conditions of decreased oxygen (hypoxia), the carotid body generates nerve impulses that increase respiration.

According to Adelson (1974), pressure to the neck overlying the carotid sinuses can cause practically instantaneous death "in the predisposed victim" (p. 526). Although we are unaware of solid evidence that individuals differ in their pressure sensitivity, there is evidence suggesting that normal individuals differ in chemical sensitivity and that biological responses to hypoxia may be controlled genetically (Hudgel and Weil 1974; Moore et al. 1976; Mountain et al. 1978). Since the carotid bodies apparently have evolved from our reptilian ancestors (Anonymous 1978), there has been ample opportunity for genetic diversity to develop.

Sudden death resulting from pressure on the carotid sinuses occurs through changes in nerve impulses conveyed by the vagus nerve, one of the major actions of which is to slow the heart. Sudden death conveyed through these vagal impulses is variously known as "death from inhibition," "reflex cardiac death," "instantaneous physiologic death" (Adelson 1974, pp. 526–527), and death from vagal inhibition.

Death from vagal inhibition has been proposed as a mechanism of sudden death in autoerotic asphyxias for at least thirty years (Gardner 1942). Gardner suggested that the contributory role of carotid-sinus pressure in sudden death was better recognized in North America than England, though writings of the time do not seem to support that greener-grass view. In any case, Gardner had noticed occasional tears across the carotid sinus in cases of hanging. This observation led him to consult a Japanese instructor of jujitsu in London about the "knockout holds" in jujitsu exercises.

> . . . He told me he could render anyone unconscious in 3 seconds or kill him in 20 by pressure on the sinus, and he passed a silk belt about two inches wide across the back of my neck and brought the ends in front; then holding one he pressed the other against the side of my neck high up under the angle of the jaw, and as far as unconsciousness went he spoke truly, but I think it happened in under the 3 seconds[1]

Suffocation

The term *suffocation* is sometimes used synonymously with asphyxia, though many pathologists use the former to describe a broad range of asphyxias other than those involving neck compression. We restrict the use of the term *suffocation* to those cases in which asphyxia results from the exhaustion of a limited supply of oxygen, that is, cases in which the victim ran out of air. Generally, suffocation occurs when the head or the entire body is enclosed in an airtight space. In autoerotic asphyxias, the airtight space is usually a plastic bag (see Chapman and Matthews 1970 for an example of a case involving an airtight vinyl pouch and Knight 1979 for another pouch case).

Death from suffocation occurs more slowly than death from hanging or strangulation, often taking two to five minutes from the time that the oxygen supply has been exhausted (Polson 1965). Although certain reliable signs of suffocation are recognized by forensic pathologists, death due to suffocation may be considerably more difficult to prove than death due to neck compression, in which ligature marks and other obvious signs more often occur. Thus in cases in which a plastic bag or other suffocating agent has been removed, the cause of death may remain undetermined or death may be erroneously attributed to some incidental natural disease.

Airway Obstruction (Choking)

Although the term *choking* is sometimes used to describe manual strangulation (throttling), we restrict the usage to cases in which the breathing passages have been internally blocked. Although familiar in the form of the café coronary, in which an individual's airway is obstructed by food, and among infants and young children, choking is unusual among autoerotic asphyxias. Quiroz-Cuaron and Reyes-Castillo (1971) suggest that the case they reported may have involved obstruction of the airway with a foreign body; they are unclear on this point.

The usual mechanism of death by choking is inability of the victim to take in oxygen or expire carbon dioxide. Thus death takes two to five minutes if the airway obstruction is complete and longer if the obstruction is partial. Occasionally, however, choking results in sudden death from cardiac inhibition (Simpson 1965; Polson 1965) since the vagus nerve has sensitive branches around the airways.

Anesthetic Agents

Agents used for general anesthesia cause loss of consciousness. The difference between the dose necessary to produce loss of consciousness and the dose necessary to cause death varies widely between anesthetics.

Some anesthetic agents, such as ether and chloroform, have a low margin of safety and can produce death in doses not much greater than necessary to cause loss of consciousness. Such agents have been largely abandoned from medical use. Other agents—for example, nitrous oxide and halothane—have wider margins of safety and are used routinely in surgical anesthesia. In addition to whatever direct toxicity an anesthetic agent has, anesthetic agents are commonly administered in a manner that reduces available oxygen. Thus a low concentration of an anesthetic such as nitrous oxide mixed with oxygen rich air can be safely administered for many minutes as dental patients who have received nitrous oxide (or laughing gas) know. When nitrous oxide is administered without sufficient oxygen, loss of consciousness is followed by cessation of respiration and death results. Deaths resulting from inhalation of anesthetic gases without sufficient oxygen are similar to deaths from suffocation except that the anesthetic speeds loss of consciousness.

Chest Compression

Asphyxia produced through compression of the chest (also known as *traumatic asphyxia)* is an unusual cause of death in general and is also an unusual form of autoerotic asphyxia. Asphyxia through chest compression may be a slow form of death, depending on the force of the compression. Since there is no complete blockage of the airways, but rather restriction in the movements of the muscles controlling respiration and expansion of the chest wall, the victim may be able to sustain life for a time through shallow respirations. Efforts to struggle will hasten death through increased use of oxygen and failure to employ whatever respiratory movements remain available.

Effects of Hypoxia

Subjective Experiences

The subjective effects of hypoxia can only be viewed through the statements of individuals who have experienced hypoxia. As with other altered physiological states, the subjective experience of hypoxia is likely to be affected profoundly by both individual and situational factors. Some years ago there was a debate in the field now known as physiological psychology as to whether altered physiological states carried with them inherent subjective experiences or whether the subjective experience was learned. This debate has been largely resolved by recognition that physiological stimuli become interpreted through an individual's prior learning experiences as well as the situational factors present. Thus we cannot hope for consistency between individuals who report their subjective experiences with hypoxia. Moreover, we should not hope to be able to successfully extrapolate from the experiences of individuals suffering from adverse conditions creating hypoxia (for example, individuals with respiratory disturbance or in oxygen-poor environments) to the experience of willfully induced hypoxia for sexual excitement.

One individual who had engaged in autoerotic asphyxia for many years told Dr. Dietz in an interview that he enjoyed the feeling as he lost consciousness and perceived his body going limp. Although he had difficulty expressing the exact nature of the sensation, it appeared that numbness and possibly tingling were part of what he sought, and that a dissociative feeling of watching his body go limp may have played a major role for him. His habit was to use asphyxia as a prelude to masturbation, and he reported that he never ejaculated during asphyxiation. When rushed for time, instead of cross-dressing and hanging himself, he would "give myself a quickie" by applying pressure to both sides of his neck with one hand until losing consciousness. The only previous medical accounts of the sensations accompanying autoerotic asphyxia appear to be those of the patients seen by Runge and by Haas. Stekel (1929) wrote that Runge's patient had described "a voluptuous sense of giddiness, like the feeling that overcomes one on a height," and stated: "I need that sense of giddiness; I must have it!" (p. 358). Stekel wrote that the girl treated by Haas noted upon pressing her throat "that such pleasant sensation arose from her stomach upward that she almost lost her senses" (p. 259). (Additional details of these cases are reviewed in chapter 2.)

Although there is a variety of sources indicating that individuals are sexually aroused during autoerotic asphyxiation, there seem to be individual differences in the timing of orgasm. Like the patient mentioned previously, the patient reported by Shankel and Carr (1956) indicated that he would masturbate after asphyxia, whereas the patients reported by Weisman (1965) and by Rosenblum and Faber (1979) each indicated that orgasm accompanied asphyxia.

Fictional accounts by Burroughs suggest something of the subjective experience. *Naked Lunch* (1966) describes the experience of a boy who was being hanged while sexually stimulated: "Green sparks explode behind his eyes and sweet toothache pain shoots through his neck down the spine to the groin, contracting the body in spasms of delight" (p. 76). In *Cities of the Red Night,* a passage in which the characters prepare for sexual activity involving hanging mentions that "the magical inten-

Asphyxial Autoerotic Fatalities

tion is projected in the moment of orgasm and visualized as an outpouring of liquid gold'' (p. 77). In the passage that follows it is not clear whether anyone is actually being hanged, but one character describes his sensation as: "Shadowy figures rise beyond the candlelight; the Goddess Ix Tab, patroness of those who hang themselves . . . a vista of gallows and burning cities from Bosch . . . set . . . Osiris . . . smell of the sea . . . Jerry hanging naked from the beam. A sweet rotten red musky metal smell swirls round our bodies palpable as a haze, and as I start to ejaculate, the room gets lighter'' (p. 77; ellipses in original). These suggestions of an odor and visualized colors may be related to the true subjective experience of autoerotic asphyxia. Prior to having read Burroughs's description, we regarded a coded note (see figure 4–1) left by one decedent, a foot fetishist (described as Case #7 in chapter 5), as a series of notes he had taken about his subjective experiences. Some items in his notes appear to be about color: "no flor," "bright gold flor,"

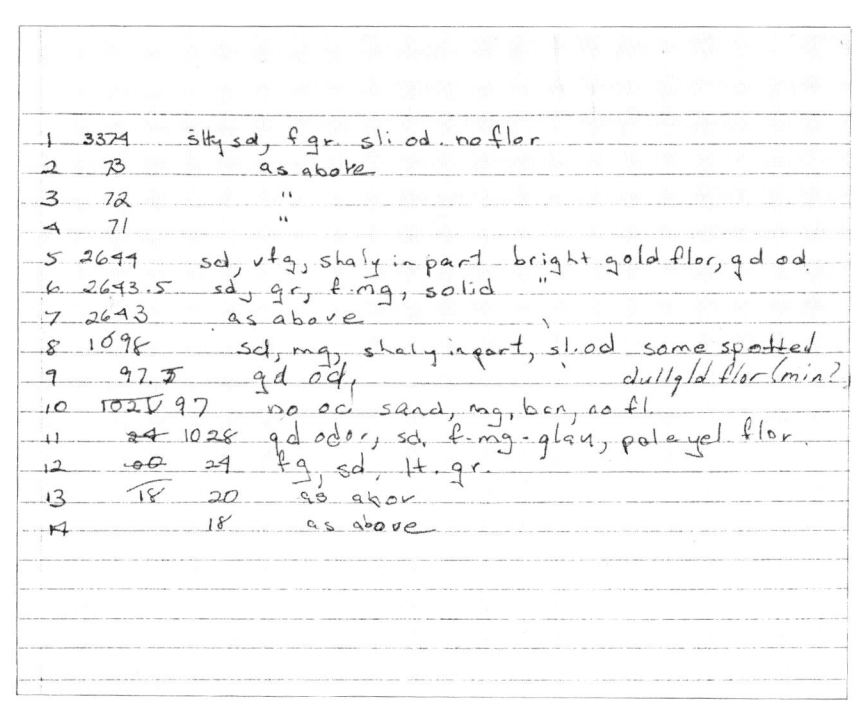

Figure 4–1. Handwritten, Coded Notes Describing Subjective Sensations of Repeated Autoerotic Hangings, Discovered Postmortem.

"dull gld flor," "no fl.," "pale yel flor," and "lt. gr." Others appear to be about odor—possibly related specifically to his foot fetish—since a story he wrote also mentions odors. Burroughs's descriptions lend support to our interpretation that visual imagery may change with autoerotic asphyxia.

Physiological Effects

The predictable sequence of events that occurs with advanced and continued hypoxia includes cyanosis (blue discoloration of the skin), increasingly strenuous efforts at respiration, fading of consciousness, convulsive movements, fading of respiratory effort, irregularity of the pulse, a dramatic fall in blood pressure, and death (Adelson 1974).

Not all parts of the body respond to hypoxia at the same rate. Brain cells are particularly vulnerable, but different regions of the brain are damaged at varying rates. Studies of the effects on the brain of nonfatal hanging (Berlyne and Strachan 1968) and fatal hypoxia from a variety of mechanisms (Lindenberg 1968) suggest that the brain centers controlling memory are among the most vulnerable, that higher brain centers controlling abstract-thinking abilities are also quite vulnerable, and that the basic brain centers sustaining life are among the least vulnerable. For this reason, interruption of hypoxia at an advanced stage but prior to death may leave an individual brain-damaged. In several cases in the sample, relatives recalled that decedents had sometimes seemed confused or to have memory impairment. In one case in the sample, an individual was believed to have suffered some loss in intellect through repeated autoerotic asphyxia. In still another case, rescue occurred only after extensive brain damage had taken place; the individual remained comatose for some time and eventually died when life-support measures were removed.

Types of Autoerotic Asphyxia

Each of the forms of asphyxia described earlier was encountered among the asphyxial autoerotic fatalities in the sample. All 5 of the women had induced asphyxia through neck compression by hanging. Of the 127 men, 113 (89.0 percent) had induced asphyxia through neck compression; 100 (78.7 percent) by hanging; and 13 (10.2 percent) by strangulation. Other techniques for inducing asphyxiation were less frequently encountered. These included suffocation with a plastic bag in 5 cases, and obstruction of the airway (choking) in 2.

Nine other cases challenge our definition of asphyxial autoerotic fatalities as deaths resulting from the excessive application of an asphyxial method employed for the purpose of increasing sexual excitement. Two of these cases in which the cause of death was aspiration of vomitus are reported in chapter 6 as atypical autoerotic fatalities since aspiration of vomitus was certainly not the decedents' goal in producing asphyxiation through hanging in one case and strangulation in the other. The other seven cases that challenge our definition are reported here, though their inclusion here rather than in chapter 6 is somewhat arbitrary. These included five cases in which anesthetic agents had been inhaled (nitrous oxide in four; chloroform in one), and two cases in which chest compression interfered with movement of the muscles of respiration.

In this chapter we provide descriptions of cases exemplifying hanging, strangulation, suffocation, choking, inhalation of anesthetics, and chest compression.

Hanging

All 5 of the women and 100 of the men who died of autoerotic asphyxia had used some type of ligature (rope, belt, cord, chain, or whip) to suspend themselves by the neck from some point within their reach. In many cases, padding of some type (for example, towels, scarves, or sweaters) was used under the ligature to prevent development of abrasions or other marks on the neck that might leave visible evidence of the self-hanging.

Indoor hangings were most often in a secluded location, such as the decedent's own room, closet, basement, or attic:

Case #1

A twenty-year-old single man was found dead in the attic of his home. He was lying on his back beneath the A-frame rafters. The center of a long piece of rope was nailed to the rafters; one free end bound his ankles and knees; the other encircled his neck. He wore only a pair of jockey shorts. His eyeglasses were lying on the floor near his head, his trousers were beneath his knees, and his shirt was nearby. A search of his room revealed a facial tissue, later determined to contain semen, and a long ace bandage wrapped with cotton cloth. Also found were bondage magazines depicting the use of complex bindings such as he had used.

Autoerotic self-hangings outdoors, like those indoors, are usually conducted in private or secluded locations. Outdoors, the suspension point is most often a tree limb. One sixteen-year-old was found hanging by a rope tied to a tree branch. The tree was on a steep incline, and only his feet touched the ground. Markings on the ground indicated that his feet had begun to slide out from under him and that he had attempted to dig his toes into the earth to halt this slide. In another case a man was found face down in a drainage ditch with a rope around his neck and attached to a fence in the ditch. Secluded outdoor locations are not necessarily remote from other people.

Case #2

Police responded to a mother's frantic call that her son was dead. She directed them to a sliding board in the backyard. The slide was located behind the garage and could not be seen from the neighboring houses on the west and north. A tree and shrubs blocked the view from neighbors to the east. The boy was lying on his back on the slide, with his head near the top. He was fully clothed, including a jacket, the collar of which had been pulled up over his neck. A clothesline encircling his neck (protected by the collar) was attached to the top of the slide. His hands were tied in front of him in handcuff fashion approximately 14 inches apart. The wrist binding was the nylon drawstring from his jacket. No signs of struggle were apparent on the victim or in the surrounding area, and he was not gagged. He could have relieved the pressure around his neck by rolling off the slide or by placing one leg on the ground. He also could have placed his feet flat on the slide's surface and pushed himself upwards, as he wore climbing shoes with slip resistant soles, or he could have reached over his head and grasped the top of the slide, as his arms were not bound. A search of his room revealed an electrical cord in which two loops had been formed, with slip knots in each. The loops were such that if placed over the wrists, they would have been approximately 10 inches apart.

Strangulation

Thirteen men induced asphyxia with a ligature about the neck that was not affixed to a suspension point. In each of these cases, the ligature was attached to another portion of the decedent's body, most often to the ankles. (See Case #2 in chapter 6 for an example of ligature strangulation in which the ligature was not attached to another part of the victim's body and was not the proximate cause of the asphyxia that resulted in death.)

Case #3

A nineteen-year-old was visiting his fiancé at her parents' home on the evening of his death. They had finished eating dinner when the parents decided to go shopping and invited the young couple along. The young man declined to accompany the girl and her parents but agreed to remain at the residence to await them. Upon their return two hours later, they found the television set on but could not locate him in the home. They walked to the backyard swimming pool. Checking the bathhouse, they found his clothing and droplets of blood leading toward the rear of the property. They discovered the victim dead beneath a rail fence that surrounded their property. He was naked, with his buttocks on the ground. A rope tied around his neck at one end passed over the top of the fence and was attached to his ankles at the other. In his rectum was a corn cob, the insertion of which was later determined to have caused the bleeding that had led them to his body. He was covered entirely in dried, caked mud. A freshly dug hole near his body contained water. A garden hose lay nearby and was connected to a faucet at the rear of the house. The reconstruction of what had occurred was that his fiancé and her parents had departed, the young man had gone to the bathhouse, disrobed, inserted the corn cob in his rectum (causing the bleeding), and, taking the garden hose with him, walked to the rear of the property where he dug a hole and made mud. After covering himself with the mud, he engaged in autoerotic asphyxia, using the rope as the injurious agent. The unusual feature of this case is the victim's use of mud to cover himself. Possible explanations for the use of mud include mysophilia (attraction to filth), symbolic coprophilia (attraction to feces), and sexual bondage (discussed in chapter 5). As mud dries on the skin, it constricts and causes sensations of increased surface pressure, restraint, and enclosure.

In another strangulation case, the victim died in his home while his parents and siblings were asleep.

Case #4

The deceased, fourteen years of age, was a good student and had no specific problems at home. According to his parents, his room was his own domain, which they never entered to examine or clean. On the night of his death, the family retired to their beds at the usual time. Sometime during the night the mother heard a noise that she thought came from the son's room. It soon stopped, and she did not investigate further. The family arose in the morning, and after she had been up for some time, the mother noticed there had been no activity from her son's room. She investigated but was unable to open the door. With assistance, it was opened. The body of her son was found face down dressed only in shorts. Bright silver-colored steel braces approximately 1 to 1½ inches wide were locked around his neck and each ankle. His lower limbs were flexed at the knees, with both feet pulled up to the base of his spine. Each ankle brace was held toward the neck with a ¼-inch chain. His left hand was free and under him; his right hand was above his head as if he were reaching for the keys found just inside the door, near the corner of his room. The bed was disturbed in a manner indicating that he was initially on the bed and then threw himself or fell from the bed onto the floor and against the door (accounting for the noise during the night) as he attempted to reach the keys. Then his head fell forward, with the anterior aspect of his neck pressing against the steel clamp, causing him to asphyxiate. The room contained neither a suicide note nor any writings that would indicate depression. Some poetry and fiction (of a happy note) were found, as was a tape recording of a fictional story about the twenty-first century. The room also contained a number of knives.

Plastic-Bag Suffocation

As noted in chapter 2, autoerotic fatalities through plastic-bag suffocation have been reported since 1955 (Stearns), not long after plastic wrapping materials came into widespread use. This fact, like the early sexual abuses of anesthetic agents, the automotive autoerotic fatality case (Rupp 1973), and the current use of bondage restraints with Velcro fastenings, reflects the incorporation of whatever technologies are available into ancient sexual practices.

Of the five cases in which death resulted from suffocation with a plastic bag placed over the head, three of the men were both cross-dressed and bound, one was cross-dressed but not bound (Case #5) and one was bound but not cross-dressed (Case #6).

Case #5

An eighteen-year-old white male was discovered by his mother in what she believed to be an unconscious state. She drove him to a local hospital

Asphyxial Autoerotic Fatalities

where he was pronounced dead. Upon arrival at the hospital, he wore only a pair of red, women's panties. Markings around his chest led to further questioning of his mother who then stated that when she found her son, there had been a plastic bag around his head that was secured around his neck with a rubber band, and he had been wearing a brassiere and a slip. She had removed all of these before taking him to the hospital. A search of his room at home disclosed an extensive collection of women's clothing and several other plastic bags. The plastic bag he had used during the fatal episode had holes in it that had been repaired with masking tape.

Case #6

A twenty-three-year-old single man was found dead on the floor of his home. He wore only a beach robe tied around his waist. His buttocks were against a chair, and his feet were on the chair seat. The body was intricately bound with what appeared to be sash cord. He had placed a plastic garbage bag over his head. A piece of the cord secured the bag snugly around his neck and was tied in a slip knot. The other end of this cord was attached to a radiator in the room. To the side of the chair he had stacked three pillows and a cylindrical piece of furniture (shaped like a drum), on top of which he had balanced a barbell. A separate piece of cord was tied to the barbell with a slip knot and ran to his ankles, where another slip knot had been tied, and from there ran up to his calves, wound around his thighs three times, travelled between his thighs, where it was pulled tightly through his crotch, encircled his waist, and ended at his wrists which it bound with another slip knot. Just above his knees he had tied another plastic bag around his legs and attached it to the cord connected to the barbell. When he was found, the cylindrical stand was overturned and the barbell was behind the chair, with its attached cords stretched over the back of the chair and leading to the victim. Apparently the barbell had toppled and fallen behind the chair. In the process, it increased the tension on the rope, tightening the various slip knots. Unable to loosen himself from the bindings, the victim suffocated by rebreathing the carbon dioxide he was exhaling.

Airway Obstruction (Choking)

Mechanical obstruction of the airway with foreign materials stuffed deeply into the throat is an unusual mechanism for autoerotic asphyxiation. Although gags are commonly used in sexual bondage activities, they are more often used to cover the mouth (where the risk is that of suffocation, not choking) than inserted in the mouth. (See Case #6 in chapter 8 for an example of a death by choking due to insertion of a gag into the mouth by a partner.) In two asphyxial autoerotic fatalities, the asphyxial mechanism was mechanical obstruction of the airways, and both of these cases are reported here.

Case #7

A thirty-two-year-old father of three was discovered dead by his eleven-year-old daughter. He had gone to his bedroom to nap, and the young girl had later attempted to awaken him by knocking on the door. Unable to arouse him, she entered the room and found him lying face down on the bed. He wore pantyhose, a brassiere (stuffed with stockings), and a sweater, all of which belonged to his wife. His hands were interconnected with a cloth belt (from his wife's robe) and were tied with slip knots. A pink brassiere covered his nose and mouth. In his mouth was a sanitary pad. The cause of death was determined to be accidental asphyxiation due to mechanical obstruction of the nasopharynx and oral cavity. He had practiced genital masochism, as indicated by the fact that his scrotum was swollen and exhibited two small burns resembling cigarette burns. A similar burn was observed on the inner aspect of the left thigh near the scrotum. Investigation revealed that the victim had been discovered by his younger son in the same position one month earlier. In that instance, the son thought his father was dead and began crying, whereupon the father sat up, released his hands (via the slip knots), removed the materials from his face, and told the boy that he was playing a game. In the fatal episode, he had apparently misjudged the time available to extricate himself or lost consciousness, for it would otherwise have been possible for him to have released himself as he had previously.

Case #8

A twenty-year-old college student was discovered dead in his dormitory room by his roommate who was returning from a weekend at home. The roommate found the body on a bed after unlocking the door to the room. The deceased was lying face up and wore jeans, socks, underwear, and a black-leather motorcycle jacket. Over his head was a clear plastic bag, the front of which he had inhaled. A small diameter rope loosely encircled his neck. The rope was tied as a modified hangman's noose (nine loops rather than thirteen). The rope passed from his neck over his chest and down his left side, where it was attached to his wrists. Each wrist had been wrapped once, and they were approximately 4 inches apart. The ends of the rope were tied in a slip knot around his left wrist. His roommate, classmates, and instructors had never seen him wearing the black leather jacket socially or privately. He apparently reserved the jacket for asphyxial autoerotic rituals.

Although Case #8 is quite similar to other plastic-bag asphyxias in which the mechanism is technically suffocation, it is classified as an example of airway obstruction because the portion of the plastic bag that he had aspirated provided mechanical obstruction of the airway. Note also that two cases involving aspiration of vomitus (Cases #1 and 2 in chapter 6) were classified as atypical autoerotic fatalities despite their similarity to the preceding Case #8. These cases underscore the somewhat arbitrary distinctions inherent in any simple classification of complex behaviors.

Anesthetic Agents

In five cases, anesthetic agents had been inhaled during autoerotic activities, and death had resulted from failure to terminate their inhalation. In three of these, nitrous oxide was inhaled from a plastic bag placed over the head. In the fourth, nitrous oxide was inhaled through a mouth mask designed for the medical administration of nitrous oxide. None of the nitrous-oxide cases involved sexual bondage apart from the means used to secure the inhalation apparatus, and none involved cross-dressing. In the fifth, chloroform was inhaled through a gas mask (see Case #3 in chapter 7 for a full description).

Case #9

A thirty-one-year-old single man was found dead in his room by his mother and brother. He was lying on his bed nude except for an undershirt and socks. Several pornographic magazines were found in the room, and a copy of Our Bodies, Ourselves *opened to a section on sexual intercourse and orgasm was near him. Over his head was a large-sized plastic garbage bag which was not fastened to his body. A metal tube in the bag was connected to a cylinder on the floor containing nitrous oxide. The cause of death was ruled to be asphyxiation due to inhalation of nitrous oxide.*

Case #10

A forty-seven-year-old divorced dentist was found on the floor of his office by the janitor. He was lying face down on the floor with an anesthesia mask held in place over his mouth and nose by the weight of his head. His shirt was open and his trousers unzipped. He was alleged to have taken sexual advantage of his patients while they were under anesthesia in his office.

Chest Compression

Like airway obstruction, chest compression is an unusual mechanism for self-induced asphyxiation. Even when it is clear that chest compression was purposely used to heighten sexual arousal, it is not necessarily the case that the chest compression was applied for the purpose of inducing hypoxia. Many forms of sexual bondage and restraint are not designed to affect respiration. It is therefore possible that the effects of chest compression on the muscles of respiration are unanticipated and unintended by those who engage in autoerotic chest compression. Our knowledge of chest compression cases is limited by their rarity, and both cases from the sample are reported here.

Case #11

An eighteen-year-old white male who lived with his parents was discovered dead in their garage. His parents were away on vacation at the time of his death. When they were unable to reach him by telephone, they became concerned and called neighbors, who then discovered the body. His body was found in a 30-pound garbage can from which only his head and neck protruded. A roll of chicken wire lay beside the container, and a portion of the wire extended partially over the mouth of the can. Blood, later determined to be of the same type as the victim's, was found on that portion of the wire near the victim's mouth. In order to extricate the body from the can, the police found it necessary to use a hammer and chisel. When the can had been opened, he was found to be wearing a T-shirt, a pair of jockey shorts, and sneakers. His arms extended down his sides, and his hands were between his feet and buttocks. His knees were pressed tightly against his chest. His wrists were loosely bound with leather roller-skate straps. No other bindings were present. His knees, elbows, and knuckles were abraded, and there were scratches around his mouth. No other injuries were present, and the toxicology report revealed no trace of alcohol or other drugs. The cause of death was ruled to be suffocation. His parents refused to accept his death as accidental and were of the opinion that it was murder in connection with a robbery. The investigating agency reenacted the occurrence on two occasions, having an officer of the same build and weight insert himself into a similar garbage can by placing the heels of his feet on one lip of the can and his buttocks on the opposite lip, then pulling his knees to his chest, causing him to slip into the can. The officers accounted for the victim's knee, elbow, and knuckle abrasions as being caused when the victim slipped into the can or during his futile attempt to extricate himself. The scratches around his mouth and the blood on the wire were accounted for as being caused by the victim's having grasped the wire in his mouth in an attempt to tip over the can. The injurious agent in this instance was the garbage can used for self-immobilization. The victim had apparently intended for the roll of wire to serve as a self-rescue mechanism but failed to take account of the can's low center of gravity, as a result of which the roll of wire fell over instead. A search of the victim's room disclosed several additional roller-skate straps tied in various ways and numerous pieces of knotted rope.

The second case of autoerotic asphyxia through chest compression was less complex and more readily demonstrable as sexually related.

Case #12

Early one morning a motorist noted a body suspended by a rope from the bridge he was about to cross. He notified the police who arrived to find a naked young man dangling over the river that passed beneath the bridge. His arms and feet pointed toward the water. A rope encircled his chest below his arms and was attached to the bridge railing approximately 12 feet above his body. After the body was removed, it was determined that the rope was secured to his body with a slip knot. Abrasions on his back extended from below his shoulder blades to the upper portion of his back where the rope rested. The deceased had obviously lowered himself from the bridge intending to later release the slip knot by reaching behind and pulling on it. The weight of his body, however, caused the rope to slide up his back beyond his reach. Consequently, the rope compressed his chest so tightly that he was unable to breath and died before he could free himself.

The cases just described provide a sampling of the types of autoerotic asphyxias that comprise the 132 cases studied. Other cases are presented in detail in chapters 5, 7, and 8. In the next chapter, we consider the evidence concerning psychosexual disorders among individuals dying through autoerotic asphyxia.

Notes

1. Gardner, E. Mechanism of certain forms of sudden death in medico-legal practice. *Medico-Legal Review* 10:120–133, 1942.

5 Autoerotic Asphyxia, the Paraphilias, and Mental Disorder

*Park Elliott Dietz,
Ann Wolbert Burgess,* and
Robert R. Hazelwood

The often-unconventional circumstances of death by autoerotic asphyxia have led more than a few commentators to suggest the presence of psychiatric disorder among those who so die. More importantly, survivors of those who die by autoerotic asphyxia are puzzled and troubled by what must seem to them bizarre behavior on the part of individuals whom they believed to be free of serious psychiatric disturbance.

As we cannot hope to provide an overview of psychopathology in the course of one chapter, we refer the reader interested in learning more about psychopathology and the diagnosis of mental disorder to the third editions of the *Diagnostic and Statistical Manual of Mental Disorders* (DSM-III) (American Psychiatric Association 1980) and the *Comprehensive Textbook of Psychiatry* (Kaplan et al. 1980).

None of the accounts in the psychiatric literature has provided so much as a trace of evidence to suggest the occurrence of psychotic disorders among those who practice autoerotic asphyxia. Those individuals who come to the attention of psychiatrists, as we know from studies in other areas, would be more likely than those not seeing psychiatrists to suffer from mental disorder. Despite this bias toward the discovery of mental disorder, no evidence of an association between psychotic disorders and autoerotic asphyxia has been garnered. Even Litman and Swearingen (1972), whose interview subjects probably evidenced the same bias and who actively sought evidence of mental disorder through psychiatric interviews, found only a history of nonpsychotic depression. Their observation has been perpetuated in the later writings of others who, by emphasizing the dynamic of depression, might mislead those unfamiliar with the psychiatric literature to believe that depression is a cause of autoerotic asphyxia. Although it is true that depressed individuals are more likely than others to take risks with their lives, the choice of a sexual form of risk-taking reflects the operation of factors other than depression.

The postmortem diagnosis of mental disorder, despite the introduction of psychological autopsies (see chapter 9), is controversial at best.

The best efforts to render diagnostic opinions after death would include psychiatric interviews with as many survivors as possible, a review of as many records about the decedent as possible, and detailed inquiry into the behavior and social relations of the decedent throughout his life. This was not the goal of this study, and the sources available for classifying decedents according to psychiatric diagnosis fall far short of this ideal. In an effort to take advantage of those sources of information that were available, however, we have devised criteria for the postmortem diagnosis of several mental disorders that we believe were represented among the decedents. These diagnostic criteria have not been independently validated, but we have used so conservative an approach and have adhered so closely to DSM-III (except where otherwise noted) that we hope our criteria have sufficient face validity to persuade the reader as to their applicability.

It need hardly be stated that we could only find evidence that was findable and that we risk severely underestimating the prevalence of mental disorders for which physical evidence does not exist. Thus we have no evidence worth presenting of the prevalence of personality disorders, affective illness, or schizophrenia. It should nonetheless be noted that in nearly all cases, survivors stressed their observation that the decedent had been in good spirits, actively participating in life, and looking forward to the future. We doubt very much that psychotic disorders could have gone unnoticed in more than a few cases. The anecdotal evidence available regarding the occurrence of nonpsychosexual disorders among a few of the decedents is reviewed toward the end of this chapter under the heading Other Mental Disorders.

The primary focus of this chapter is on the evidence for psychosexual disorders among the 132 individuals who died through autoerotic asphyxia. These individuals were 127 men (mean age 26.3 years) and 5 women (mean age 32.2 years).

Sexual Orientation

Clear evidence of homosexual orientation was identified among eight of the men (6.3 percent) and none of the women. The best evidence of homosexuality consisted of a clear history provided by intimates of exclusively homosexual orientation (6 cases), a collection of homosexual pornography (1), and writings by the decedent documenting homosexual fantasies (1). Among these eight men, four were known to have made public their homosexuality, three were known to have kept their homosexuality secret, and in one case the degree of secrecy could not be determined.

It was not possible to determine which, if any, of the cases met diagnostic criteria for Ego-dystonic Homosexuality (see DSM-III). Thus no diagnoses related to homosexuality were made, for homosexual orientation in and of itself is no longer considered to represent a mental disorder.

Even when the decedent's family was aware of his homosexual orientation, the family was not necessarily aware of the practice of autoerotic asphyxia. One father had known that his twenty-nine-year old son was homosexual, but he was unable to understand the police officer's explanation of accidental autoerotic death.

We believe that our sample is sufficiently large that the low prevalence of recognized homosexuality among decedents may be properly interpreted as evidence that autoerotic asphyxia is not disproportionately associated with homosexuality. It could be the case, of course, that homosexuals are no more likely than heterosexuals to engage in autoerotic asphyxia. Alternatively, it might be argued that homosexuals are more likely to be able to find partners with whom to engage in sexual asphyxia and that they do so more frequently but die equally often because the partner can intervene if life-threatening hypoxia develops. Litman and Swearingen (1972) suggested that some men turn toward homosexual relations in order to find partners to assist them in bondage behavior, but if this were widely true, we would expect to find a higher proportion of cases in which there was a history of homosexual associations.

The presence of a partner does not provide absolute protection against loss of life, as evidenced by deaths occurring in the presence of a partner (see chapters 2, 3, 7, and 8). Of five partner cases submitted for this study, three of the decedents were homosexuals.

Newly Defined Paraphilias

The concept of the paraphilias is central to our understanding of autoerotic fatalities. The introduction of this topic in DSM-III is so lucid and precise that we reprint it here.

> The essential feature of disorders in this subclass is that unusual or bizarre imagery or acts are necessary for sexual excitement. Such imagery or acts tend to be insistently and involuntarily repetitive and generally involve either: (1) preference for use of a nonhuman object for sexual arousal, (2) repetitive sexual activity with humans involving real or simulated suffering or humiliation, or (3) repetitive sexual activity with nonconsenting partners. In other classifications these disorders are referred to as Sexual Deviations. The term Paraphilia is preferable because it correctly emphasizes that the deviation (para) is in that to which the individual is attracted (philia).

This imagery in a Paraphilia, such as simulated bondage, may be playful and harmless and acted out with a mutually consenting partner. More likely it is not reciprocated by the partner, who consequently feels erotically excluded or superfluous to some degree. In more extreme form, paraphiliac imagery is acted out with a nonconsenting partner, and is noxious and injurious to the partner (as in severe Sexual Sadism) or to the self (as in Sexual Masochism).

Since paraphiliac imagery is necessary for erotic arousal, it must be included in masturbatory or coital fantasies, if not actually acted out alone or with a partner and supporting cast or paraphernalia. In the absence of paraphiliac imagery there is no relief from nonerotic tension, and sexual excitement or orgasm is not attained.

The imagery in a paraphiliac fantasy or the object of sexual excitement in a Paraphilia is frequently the stimulus for sexual excitement in individuals without a Psychosexual Disorder. For example, women's undergarments and imagery of sexual coercion are sexually exciting for many men; they are paraphiliac only when they become necessary for sexual excitement.[1]

Readers interested in learning more about the paraphilias in general should consult Money (1977), Meyer (1980), or Money (1981).

We believe that the DSM-III definition of sexual masochism is overly inclusive. Although it may simplify matters to lump together a variety of behaviors under the label *sexual masochism,* several distinct patterns of behavior can be recognized within that broader rubric. Just as the differentiation of subtypes of affective illness has been an important corollary of the elucidation of their biological bases and the development of treatment techniques, the differentiation of patterns of sexual preference from the broader class of sexual masochism may be critical to furthering knowledge of these behaviors.

Kotzwarraism (Hypoxyphilia)

We believe that there is a paraphilia distinguishable from sexual masochism in which the induction of cerebral hypoxia plays a key role and for which the names Kotzwarraism or hypoxyphilia have been suggested (see chapter 2). The proposed diagnostic criteria for this paraphilia are (1) a preferred or exclusive mode of producing sexual excitement is to be mechanically or chemically asphyxiated to or beyond the point at which consciousness or perception is altered by cerebral hypoxia, or (2) the individual has repeatedly, intentionally induced his or her own cerebral hypoxia in order to produce sexual excitement. The term *Kotzwarraism* has been proposed for this paraphilia, after the musician Francis Kotzwarra (see chapter 2). An alternative term with a Greek derivation is *hypoxyphilia,* a desire for the state of oxygen deficiency. The variety of techniques employed to induce this state, the repetitiveness with which this is done, the independent adoption of this behavior by people throughout the world, and the lack of any other feature common to all cases are strong evidence that this desire is sufficiently distinctive to be considered a paraphilia in its own right. Definitive evidence that this paraphilia occurs in the absence of other signs or symptoms of sexual masochism would consist of a showing that there are individuals who meet these criteria and have no other signs or symptoms of sexual masochism. Such evidence cannot, of course, be provided from postmortem analysis, and we must therefore rely on information obtained from living individuals. Chapters 2 and 4 each include descriptions of cases in which the preceding criteria for Kotzwarraism (hypoxyphilia) appear to be met and in which no other evidence of sexual masochism was known. We recognize the possibility that other evidence of sexual masochism was overlooked or that the individuals studied have been so well defended against masochistic impulses that such evidence was unavailable. These same critiques apply to paraphilias that gained recognition in the past, and the delineation of new paraphilias should not be held to a standard that could not be met by those already recognized. The observation that the proposed paraphilia of Kotzwarraism frequently co-exists with other recognized paraphilias is not determinative of the legitimacy of this paraphilia, for it is unusual to see any paraphilia in isolation.

Except for chapter 6, this book is largely devoted to hypoxyphilic behaviors, though not all of the individuals described were dependent on hypoxia for sexual arousal. Thus the material presented about the 132 cases of fatal autoerotic asphyxia represents knowledge about both terminal cases of Kotzwarraism and deaths among individuals engaging in similar behavior without necessarily being dependent on this behavior for sexual excitement. By all indications, Kotzwarraism has a higher case-fatality ratio than any other nonorganic mental disorder.

Sexual Bondage: Ligottism (Cordophilia)

DSM-III does not provide for the diagnosis of sexual bondage as a paraphilia. According to DSM-III, an individual whose preferred or exclusive mode of producing sexual excitement is to be bound should be diagnosed as evidencing sexual masochism, on the assumption that a preference for being bound indicates a preference for being made to suffer. This assumption has been questioned, however, and awaits resolution. Dietz has described the widespread use of sexual bondage between consenting partners (ligottage) and has suggested the possibility that for some individuals without other features of sexual sadism or sexual masochism, physical restraint of others or themselves may be the preferred or exclusive mode of producing sexual excitement. For those individuals dependent on bondage imagery or action for sexual arousal, the terms *ligottism* or *cordophilia* have been proposed (Dietz, in press).

The proposed diagnostic criteria for ligottism or cordophilia are (1) a preferred or exclusive mode of producing sexual excitement is to be physically bound or restrained, or (2) the individual has repeatedly, intentionally bound himself or herself or allowed others to bind him or her in order to produce sexual excitement, or (3) a preferred or exclusive mode of producing sexual excitement is to physically bind or restrain another, or (4) the individual has repeatedly, intentionally bound another in order to produce his or her own sexual excitement (Dietz, in press).

In keeping with our effort to diagnose paraphilias independently of the asphyxial mechanism that led to death and inclusion in the sample, we do not include the use of a ligature about the neck in the postmortem diagnosis of cordophilia. As noted in chapter 4, ligatures about the neck resulted in hanging in 100 cases and strangulation in 13. In some of the hangings and all 13 of the strangulation fatalities, the ligature was also used to bind another part of the body. If another part of the body was bound, cordophilia was diagnosed. Cordophilia was also diagnosed in cases in which asphyxia had been the result of suffocation, choking, inhalation of anesthetics, or chest compression if some part of the body other than the neck was bound. Materials used in binding the body included ropes, leather straps, chains, hoods, ace bandages, blindfolds, and gags. Although constrictive garments are also used in binding the body, these were excluded from the defining characteristics for cordophilia since garments may also have fetishistic or cross-dressing significance. (As noted in the following section on fetishism, certain binding materials such as leather may have fetishistic significance to the individual. Nonetheless, we believe that if their use is such as to bind and constrict the body, they are better classified as signs of cordophilia than fetishism.)

Despite an absence of bondage at death, a diagnosis of cordophilia was made on the basis of an extensive collection of bondage paraphernalia (3), the presence of six knotted pieces of rope (1), a history of previous bondage activities (1), and a diary devoted to bondage fantasies (1). In one case a diagnosis of cordophilia was made on the basis of the decedent having tied his fingers to his penis.

By these criteria, 65 (51.2 percent) of the men and none of the women were diagnosed as cordophiliacs (but see Case #2 in chapter 6 for an example of a woman cordophiliac). Although we expected that the proportion of cases showing cordophilia would be higher among older decedents than among younger, this hypothesis received no support.

The parts of the body bound included the wrists (37), ankles (27), thighs (10), head (6), chest (5), and mouth (5). Cordophilia was so prevalent in the sample that many of the cases presented throughout this monograph demonstrate its features. Two cases are presented here to illustrate the repetitiveness of the behavior.

Case #1

Police responding to a call for assistance discovered the body of a white male in his early thirties slumped over a chair. A belt was around his neck, and a length of rope was tied to the belt. Believing a suicide had occurred, the responding officers called for a detective unit. The detectives arrived and observed an open bondage magazine on the coffee table near the victim. A desk drawer was opened, and rope, more bondage books, and polaroid photos of the victim engaging in bondage activity were found. The detectives interviewed the wife, who initially contended that her husband had committed suicide. When she was confronted with the bondage magazine and photos, she brought from the bedroom a box full of photos depicting her husband and her engaging in bondage activity. She then conveyed the history of their bondage activity. Her husband had been talking about bondage for about four years before he asked her to join him. She participated to please her husband. The bondage magazine on the table was his favorite and was open to his favorite picture. Whenever possible, he wanted to be tied exactly like the person in the photo, duplicating every twist, knot, and wrapping of the rope to the most minute detail. Metal eyelet hooks had been installed in the roof and walls of the trailer to facilitate bondage activity. The couple had had an argument the previous day, and the wife had left to spend the night at a motel, not wishing to further anger her husband. When she returned in the morning, she found him hanging. She had cut him down before calling the police.

Case #2

A woman neighbor heard someone screaming for help. She went to the door of the apartment and asked the man if he needed help, to which he stated "yes, break the door down." She then asked, "Is this a joke?", to which he replied, "No." The woman then got two young boys to kick the door in, and they found the man lying prone on the floor in the front room. *His hands were tied behind him, and his ankles pulled up and tied to his hands. A mop handle had been passed behind his knees. He was quite upset, and his hands were starting to turn blue from loss of circulation. The woman found a knife in the kitchen and cut the bonds. A police officer arrived and questioned the man, who stated that he had returned home around 3:45 P.M. and took a nap on the couch. When he awakened at about 5:15 P.M., he said, he found himself tied up on the floor. The apartment had been completely locked with no signs of forced entry. The man went on to say that he had no known enemies and no friends who would pull this type of prank on him. When he was asked where the rope came from, he stated that he had been thinking about moving and had had a sack of rope in his bedroom. In the front room by the couch were a torn sack and a large quantity of thin rope, most of it in short lengths. A steak knife was also noted on the floor near where he had been found. The officers observed the man to be perspiring profusely and short of breath. He had defecated in his pants, and the front portion of his pants was stained as if he had urinated in them. The officer's report stated that "this could possibly be a sexual deviation act." During an interview the following day, the man admitted that this was a self-inflicted act. One month later, an officer was dispatched to the same apartment. The housemanager had found the man lying face down on the floor. He had a satin gag in his mouth and rope tied around his head and his mouth. He had rope tied around his chest, several strands of rope around his waist, and several strands of rope tied from his back to his crotch. He was also tied at the ankles, where deep indentations were observed. His elbows were pinned behind his back with a broom handle. A paper bag was over his head and nose, and he was hyperventilating when found. The man stated that he had been doing some isometric exercises and had gotten tied up in the rope. After the second incident, the police talked with the dean of the school where the man worked and requested that some action be taken. The school had advised the man to contact the school's counseling department. He agreed and was referred to a private psychiatrist. The dean stated that this was just a "one-time thing" and that after the man received help there would be no reason to think it would recur. Two years later, he had moved and was similarly employed elsewhere. When he failed to report to work one Monday, an assistant was sent to his home and discovered him dead. Investigation and reenactment suggested that on the preceding Friday he had tied himself up in a complex fashion requiring the following steps: He sat on the bed and crossed his left leg over his right at the ankles and tied them together with twine. He placed a tie around his neck with a slip knot at the back and secured the free ends to an 86-inch pole. He placed the pole along his left side, with the upper end abutting the front of his left* shoulder. He then placed his hands behind his still-bent legs and tied his wrists with a piece of rope, leaving approximately 4 inches between his wrists. He tied the rope binding his wrists to the pole and to an electric cord worn around his waist. He than laid down on the bed, flat on his back, and straightened his legs. This action caused the pole to pull on the tie from his neck, strangling him. To lessen the tension, he could have rolled onto his side and bent his legs, but for the fact that the upper end of the pole was against the wall and prevented his rolling.

Recognized Paraphilias

None of the 5 women who died by autoerotic asphyxia evidenced any recognized paraphilia. The following material on paraphilias is therefore based on 127 male decedents.

Sexual Masochism

DSM-III criteria (American Psychiatric Association 1980) for sexual masochism are either "(1) a preferred or exclusive mode of producing sexual excitement is to be humiliated, bound, beaten, or otherwise made to suffer," or "(2) the individual has intentionally participated in an activity in which he or she was physically harmed or his or her life was threatened, in order to produce sexual excitement." By these criteria, every one of the decedents in our sample would carry an antemortem diagnosis of sexual masochism, with the possible exception of four pre-pubertal males (all age thirteen or younger) whose sexual arousal might be questioned.

As noted earlier, however, we differentiate Kotzwarraism (hypoxyphilia) and ligottism (cordophilia) from sexual masochism. In addition to the reasons set forth previously, it should be noted that asphyxia and, to a lesser extent, bondage, are the index behaviors that, having resulted in death, led to the decedents being included in this sample of asphyxial autoerotic fatalities. In order to determine how frequently sexual masochism occurs in such cases, the diagnosis should be based on findings other than these index behaviors. For this reason, we apply the same conservative diagnostic approach in the postmortem diagnosis of sexual masochism as we have applied in the postmortem diagnosis of other paraphilias.

Sexual masochism was diagnosed only when there was evidence apart from asphyxia and bondage that the individual's preferred or exclusive mode of producing sexual excitement was to be humiliated, beaten, or otherwise made to suffer, or that the individual had intentionally participated in nonasphyxial and nonbondage activities in which he or she was physically harmed or his or her life was threatened in order to produce sexual excitement.

By these criteria, 15 (11.8 percent) of the 127 male decedents were diagnosed as sexual masochists. The evidence for sexual masochism consisted of writings or photographs documenting masochistic fantasies (5), cigarette burns to the scrotum and/or inner thighs (3) (see Case #7, chapter 4, for an example), clothespins or metal clips attached to the nipples (3), infibulation (2), puncture wounds of the thighs (1), and mutilation of the penis (1). Infibulation, the piercing of the skin with separate entrance and exit sites, consisted of piercings with needles in both cases (and does not include the one cross-dresser who had his ears pierced). One was a twenty-nine-year-old white homosexual male found naked and hanging from the ceiling in his room. Suture thread ran through each of his nipples and a blood-stained plastic bag on the bed contained additional suture thread, a suture needle, and a pair of scissors. A metal ring encircled his penis and scrotum. On the floor were a box of Band-Aids, a jar of petroleum jelly, an 11-inch vibrator, and a bottle of nasal spray. The other individual evidencing infibulation had passed a needle transversely through a fold of skin near the umbilicus. A piece of string tied loosely around his penis was also looped about the needle.

The sole example of mutilation of the penis was a man who had an old, healed scar about the circumference of his penis. A metal washer encircled his penis and was found in this groove. His wife reported in an interview that he had asked her to pass needles through his nipples or to allow him to do so to her (for a full description of the circumstances of his death, see Case #3 in chapter 8).

Sexual Sadism

The DSM-III criteria for sexual sadism are that one of the following applies: "(1) on a non-consenting partner, the individual has repeatedly, intentionally inflicted physical or psychological suffering in order to produce sexual excitement," "(2) with a consenting partner, the preferred or exclusive mode of achieving sexual excitement combines humiliation with simulated or mildly injurious bodily suffering," or "(3) on a consenting partner, bodily injury that is extensive, permanent or possibly mortal is inflicted in order to achieve sexual excitement."

By these criteria (assuming that the partner cannot be oneself), only 1 of the 127 men was diagnosed as a sexual sadist. He had run advertisements in an underground newspaper indicating that he was a sexual sadist, and he was known as a "leather master" among the members of his "S & M" network.

In an additional five cases, the decedents' writings or sketches documented sadistic sexual fantasies. The most dramatic evidence of sadistic fantasies encountered were the sketches.

Case #3

A thirty-six-year-old black male was discovered dead suspended from a belt around his neck. A towel protected his neck from chafing. He wore only his underwear. His wife reported that they had not had intercourse for the past two years. Instead, his practice was to manually manipulate her vulva while fondling himself, and then leave the bed. While she watched, he placed a wet towel around his neck, looped a belt over the towel, affixed the belt to the bedroom door, and leaned away from the door while masturbating. His wife provided his sketchbook, drawings from which are shown in Figure 5–1. His wife remained troubled a year after his death. Her most terrible moments, she said, were memories of finding his body: "The human brain records and when the eye sees tragedy, one cannot forget. I can still see him hanging there. You don't know how terrible it was to see him hanging there." She indicated that her children were being treated badly by their peers, who "tortured them" by saying that their father had committed suicide by hanging himself. She had turned increasingly to religion since her husband's death and regarded his actions as unnatural and abnormal, "like a man having relations with an animal. It's beyond homosexuality." As a result of their declining sexual relationship and her view that his self-asphyxiation was "homosexual," she had once gone to a physician to see if there was anything wrong with her and had asked her husband to see him too in order to see if there was anything wrong with him. She thought that her husband had gone to the physician, but whatever had transpired with the doctor was never disclosed to her.

Case #4

A twenty-five-year-old white man was found hanging by a belt dressed in a skirt and sweater. Open on the bed nearby were photographs of women in sweaters. A search of the room disclosed many more sweater photographs and drawings the decedent had made of women being stabbed. Many of his sketches depicted a man embracing and kissing a woman

Figure 5–1. Sketches by an Autoerotic Fatality Victim Depicting Sadistic Sexual Fantasies.

Figure 5–1 continued

wearing a sweater, while he stabbed her in the abdomen. Splashes of blood in the sketch were surrounded by the printed word orgasm.

The observation by Stekel (1929) and subsequent authors (see chapter 2) that the individual who engages in self-strangulation may be acting out on himself what he fantasizes doing to others is consistent with the psychoanalytic view of sadomasochism and suggests a possible link between autoerotic asphyxia and certain sexual homicides. This hypothesis cannot be properly tested from postmortem behavioral analysis but is consistent with several observations from this study.

For example, one young man had drawn a sketch of a hanged woman with needles passed through her nipples. His own fatal hanging was in an unusual position precisely like that of the woman in his drawing. His possessions included a photograph of himself prepared from a negative in which he had pierced the image of his own nipples (see Case #9, chapter 7, for additional description of this case). Another illustrative case follows.

Case #5

A sixteen-year-old student was found hanging in a secluded, wooded area. His hands were tied behind his back with a plaid cloth bathrobe belt. His ankles were tied together with a cord. He wore a plaid long-sleeved shirt, trousers, and a brassiere stuffed with plastic cups. At the base of the tree were a belt with a holster containing an air pistol resembling a revolver, a Bowie knife with scabbard, and a pair of women's sandals. His mother permitted a search of his room, where two dolls were found under his bed. The first was a Barbie doll with a strip of cloth around the breast imitating a brassiere, a strip of cloth representing a skirt, and a jacket. The arms of the jacket were tied together with string at the level of the wrists. The doll's wrists were also tied together with a piece of string. One end of a 10-inch piece of red yarn was wrapped around the doll's neck. The other doll, dressed to imitate a male, wore a plaid jacket and jeans. Attached to a belt around its waist was a cloth holster with a revolver. The same type of red yarn that was around the neck of the first doll extended over the second doll's shoulder and was tied to a scabbard containing what represented a Bowie knife.

Ford (1957) reported another case in which an effigy was discovered in the same condition as the body of a young man, with a rubberized cloth hood held about the neck with a noose. In each of these effigy cases, the decedent had done to a human representation what he subsequently did to himself. Case #5 is not among those in which we consider the evidence diagnostic of either sexual sadism or sexual masochism but rather is suggestive of the close relationship between sadism and masochism embodied in the psychodynamic concept of sadomasochism.

Fetishism

Excluding restraining devices from the category of fetish objects, there were few documented fetishists in the sample. Definitive diagnosis of fetishism was based on either (1) the discovery of a collection of the presumed fetish item that could not be accounted for in any other way, or (2) writings by the decedent that indisputably document the sexual arousal occasioned by the fetish item. Statements by a sexual partner that the presumed fetish item was a repeatedly preferred or exclusive accompaniment to sexual excitement would be an equally good criterion, but in every case in which such statements were made, a collection of the fetish was found.

Objects designed to be used for mechanical sexual stimulation (for example, vibrator, dildo, or rectal plug) and single articles of female clothing present or worn at death were not included as fetish items.

By these criteria, fetishism was definitively diagnosed in 12 cases. The fetish items included leather (3), panties (3), rubber (1), brassieres

(1), women's scarves (1), women's sweaters (1), breasts (1), and feet (1). These last two fetishes (technically *partialism,* since the fetish object is a portion of the human anatomy) were diagnosed on the basis of collections of photographs in one case and the decedent's writings in the other. One of the men with a leather fetish also had a collection of women's boots and was found wearing thigh-high rubber hip boots at death.

Two cases illustrating the role that a fetish may play in the sexual fantasies enacted during autoerotic asphyxia are presented here (also see Case #10 in chapter 7).

Case #6

A thirty-three-year-old separated man was found hanging by a clothesline from a doorway in his home. He wore white jockey shorts, a woman's brassiere, black men's socks, and his glasses. A phonograph was in the on position, and the first song of the album on the turntable had the same name as his wife. Directly in front of him, propped up against a stand, was a detective magazine with a cover illustration depicting the strangulation murder of a young woman wearing only a brassiere. On the wall across from him, within his view, he had hung a brassiere advertisement and a record album cover depicting two women wearing halter tops similar in style to the brassiere he wore.

Case #7

A thirty-two-year-old white man was found suspended from a belt which encircled his neck over a pullover sweater. The belt was attached to a rafter in the attic. He was normally dressed but was not wearing shoes or socks. Although most of his body was in the attic, his calves and feet extended through the staircase opening into the room below. On the floor beneath his feet was a portable mirror, situated so as to allow him to view his lower body.

A book on sadism and two notebooks were found among his possessions. One of the notebooks contained a coded list (see figure 4–1 in chapter 4) and a story containing the following passages:

> His bare feet were doing the hangman's dance a foot from the floor. His heels kicked and his toes stretched as his feet arched trying to reach the floor. His hands grasped the noose around his neck to prevent it from tightening enough to strangle him. As his body twisted with the

rope he would kick out blindly trying to find some piece of furniture to climb onto. The black hood over his head prevented him from seeing that everything had been moved back out of his reach. The smaller of the two men witnessing the spectacle lay on the floor, his face just inches from the bare feet dangling before him. The only odor he could smell was a slightly sweet sweaty smell. He stared at the outstretched toes with glazed eyes. He felt a quiver run through his groin when, from time to time, the toes would wriggle and spread before, once again stretching downward. . . . The foot fetishist . . . buried his nose in the bunched toes of the right foot. He was grasping both feet by the ankles holding the feet together. He quickly slipped the small rope around his victim's legs and tied the kicking feet together. . . . He began kissing the bare feet before him, beginning at the heels and working his way down to the toes. He started with a little toe, frenching it where it joined the foot, then between it and the next toe. He did this with all ten toes before he began sucking them. . . . He leaned up and hugged Don's ankles and began pulling with all his weight. He heard the rope groan as it tightened around Don's neck. He heard the gurgling from the hanged man's throat. The feet against his chest which had been rigid began to relax. . . . He was vaguely aware of Don's hands falling limply to his side and of his feet and legs separating as he lapsed into unconsciousness. The little man grabbed the feet and spun the dangling man around. He lay back and enjoyed the sight of Don's feet and the sound of the creaking rope as he spun slowly one way and then the other. . . . The two then performed CPR on their victim. After several minutes he began to revive. They had bound his hands and removed his hood. He regained consciousness gagging and choking. He collapsed to the floor and the two dragged him to the four-poster bed in the corner and spread-eagled his legs to the foot posts.

In one other case, fetishism was suspected but not confirmed: A seventeen-year-old boy was found lying on his mother's sandals at death in a location other than where she had left them.

The distinction between bondage equipment and a fetish collection may be difficult to make, in part because unfamiliarity with sexual bondage behavior leads investigators to overlook collections of materials that could be used for sexual bondage unless the materials are unusual. Most importantly, ropes may be overlooked, particularly if the death occurred in a garage, attic, or storeroom. In 7 cases, collections of materials that could be used for sexual bondage and/or could also have fetishistic significance were found; these cases do not overlap with the confirmed fetishism cases described earlier. These collections included leather restraint devices (3), knotted scarves (1), heavy link chain (1), and ropes (2). There were undoubtedly many more cases in which collections of rope were present but overlooked, but in each of the two cases with documented rope collections the decedent was young and a parent commented that the boy seemed fascinated with ropes and knots.

Two of the confirmed panty fetishists and the confirmed sweater fetishist were wearing one or more items of their fetish at death. The man with a collection of chains was wearing a dress at death. Although there is little doubt that many of the cross-dressers (see the following) were fetishistic, postmortem discrimination between fetishistic and non-fetishistic cross-dressing is extremely difficult.

Relying on the conservative criterion of fetishism, only 12 (9.4 percent) of the male decedents were fetishists. If, in addition, the probable cases and those in which bondage equipment of possible fetishistic significance are included, the number rises to 20 (15.8 percent) of the males.

Transvestism

Transvestism was definitively diagnosed only when intimates confirmed recurrent and persistent cross-dressing by a heterosexual male for whom there was no explanation other than sexual excitement for the cross-dressing behavior. For example, one wife said: "When we would start to have sex, he would want to wear my clothes or put makeup or a wig on." By these criteria, five (3.9 percent) of the presumably heterosexual men in the sample were diagnosed as transvestites. Each of these men was cross-dressed at death, wearing clothing identified by his wife as transvestite apparel she had known him to wear in the past.

In an additional five cases, the decedent possessed a collection of women's clothing that was judged to be cross-dressing apparel on the basis of size, variety of articles, or the presence of makeup as well as clothing. In all but one of these, the decedent was cross-dressed at death.

In addition to the 10 cases mentioned earlier, 17 other men were cross-dressed at death. Thus 26 (20.5 percent) of the 127 male decedents were cross-dressed at death. None of the 8 homosexual men was a known or suspected cross-dresser or cross-dressed at death. Thus of 119 presumably heterosexual men, 5 (4.2 percent) were diagnosed transvestites, a total of 10 (8.4 percent) were diagnosed or suspected transvestites, and 26 (21.8 percent) were cross-dressed at death.

In order of decreasing frequency, items worn at the time of death included: brassieres, panties, stockings, slips, blouses, skirts, pantyhose, women's shoes, garter belts, girdles, sweaters, women's wigs, women's makeup, and one nightgown. Of those wearing brassieres, approximately half had stuffed them with such materials as socks, nylon stockings, rubber pads, washcloths, plastic cups, and water-filled balloons. Two cross-dressed men had taped or strapped their penises into their gluteal folds, and two had shaved their bodies. Although we had expected that the proportion of decedents who were cross-dressed would be higher among older men than among younger decedents, no evidence was found to support this hypothesis.

In many cases, the women's clothing worn at the time of death was identified as belonging to the decedent's wife, daughter, or girlfriend. In still other cases, the men independently had obtained the women's clothing. For example, a married man employed at a women's-apparel store was found hanging in his garage wearing a woman's brown blouse, green skirt, black-and-red bra-and-panties set, black women's boots, and a gold choker necklace.

Pedophilia

Pedophilia was diagnosed only if there was incontrovertible evidence of repeated actions or fantasies of engaging in sexual activity with prepubertal children and the decedent was an adult at least ten years older than the prepubertal children. Only one of the men met these criteria for pedophilia. A second man had a sexual preference for postpubescent adolescents, and a third was suspected to have a sexual preference for children.

The one man diagnosable as a pedophile was thirty years old. His body was found under a chest of drawers about two weeks after his death. Bottles of medication were found in his room, but his body was too badly decomposed to determine whether any drugs were present. The investigative report mentioned "drugs used to treat schizophrenia and psychoneuroses" but did not identify them. The man had recently broken up with a woman after she learned that he had molested her nine-year-old daughter. The police investigation determined that he had made sexual advances to many neighborhood children.

The second case was that of a thirty-one-year-old homosexual male who died by placing a plastic bag over his head and inhaling nitrous oxide. He worked as a junior-high-school teacher and, in the summer, as a camp counselor. The parents of a thirteen-year-old boy at the camp had filed a complaint charging that the decedent had made sexual advances to their son. One month prior to the teacher's death, a fifteen-year-old student at his school had died of autoerotic asphyxia using a plastic bag. Evidence was also found that suggested the teacher had held nitrous-oxide parties for students from his school.

In the third case, police suspected a twenty-year-old single man of being sexually attracted to young children because film developed from his camera showed that he had taken many pictures of children playing outside his window.

Atypical Paraphilias

Two of the seven atypical paraphilias recognized in DSM-III were apparently represented in the sample. There was suggestive evidence for coprophilia in six cases, two in which men had wrapped feces in a towel or in paper, and four in which feces were noted in the unflushed toilet in the room in which the victim was found. In one of these, feces were also present in the bathtub and on the rug. No men were known to eat feces.

Other evidence of anorectal eroticism consisted of the insertion of foreign bodies into the rectum. Several men had dildos inserted in the rectum at death. Two had pencils inserted into the rectum, and one had a tampon, still wrapped, in his rectum. These behaviors lack diagnostic specificity since anorectal stimulation is a recognized component of both heterosexual and homosexual relations and has not been studied as an autoerotic practice.

One man (Case #3, chapter 4) had covered his body with mud, suggesting the possibility of mysophilia. As the mud dried and caked, it would have generated a sense of restriction due to the increased surface pressure on his body so his use of mud possibly represented sexual bondage rather than or in addition to mysophilia. Another man repeatedly jumped into a mudhole he dug, pulled himself out with a cable suspended from above, and then hanged himself by the neck.

None of the individuals in the sample was known to have engaged in frotteurism, klismaphilia, necrophilia, telephone scatologia, or urophilia.

Voyeurism

One twenty-year-old may have been a voyeur, as the police suspected after his death. He lived near a young woman whose apartment had recently been forcibly entered. Although nothing had been taken, her underwear drawer was disheveled, and fashion magazines she owned had been moved and left on her bed. After his death, the police found that his tennis shoes matched shoe prints left in the young woman's apartment. He was known to ride his bicycle around the city late at night.

Zoophilia and Exhibitionism

No cases of zoophilia or exhibitionism were documented in the sample. These, like voyeurism, are less subject to documentation through physical evidence than those paraphilias identified among the study cases.

Gender-Identity Disorders

None of the cases had clear evidence for transsexualism. Five men had expressed fantasies of sex change or other surgical procedures to intimates or through their writings, as sometimes occurs in sexual masochism without gender-identity disorder. For example, a girlfriend of a college student volunteered that he had told her of his fantasies of having a vasectomy and being castrated. A thirty-one-year-old man, married for five years, had previously been found by his wife wearing her clothes. He had told her that this reflected a problem he had had since he was a small child and that he should have been a woman.

No studied individual was known to have sought sex-change surgery, to have taken feminizing hormones, or to have systematically collected materials on transsexualism or sex reassignment. As noted earlier, two men who cross-dressed had shaved their arm and leg hair. One wife reported that her husband had told her when they married that he liked to wear women's clothes but had thrown them away. Two years later, he began to come home early from work and dress in women's clothes in the attic. Three months before he died, he began shaving his underarms and legs and had his ears pierced (see Case #1 in chapter 8).

Other Mental Disorders

For the reasons set forth in the introduction to this chapter, we do not believe that our data can be used to make quantitative statements about the prevalence, among these decedents, of nonpsychosexual mental disorders. Anecdotal evidence about mental disorder was provided in a small number of cases.

A sixty-eight-year-old widow had a history of psychiatric hospitalizations and had been diagnosed as suffering from paranoid schizophrenia. Her psychiatrist indicated that she had spoken to him about her sexual fears and fantasies, but he indicated that he had known nothing about her autoerotic practices. Underscoring the difficulties in rendering postmortem diagnostic opinions about nonpsychosexual disorders from the types of information available to us, information obtained from her daughter would not have suggested a diagnosis of schizophrenia. The daughter said that her mother had been forgetful, confused, disoriented, and lightheaded, and had been lonely since her husband's death a year previously and her brother's even-more-recent death. Although this history and her age were markedly unusual for the sample as a whole, repeated autoerotic asphyxia was suggested by the fact that she had carefully padded the ligature with her nightgown and had knelt on a pillow, apparently to prevent discomfort and abrasions of her knees.

Three individuals in the sample were known to have been depressed during the months preceding death, including one man in his fifties whose depression began after his mother's death and who was cross-dressed in his mother's old-fashioned clothes at the time of his own death. Another individual had seen a psychiatrist for three weeks following a drug overdose sometime in the past. Although he was initially thought to have committed suicide, he had used padding under the ligature, and rope abrasions on the rafter from which he suspended himself indicated that he had employed autoerotic asphyxia repeatedly in the past.

One decedent was reported to have been mentally retarded and visually handicapped. Another man had been the victim of an assault of an unspecified nature and was said to have had physical and emotional problems as a result.

The lack of criminal histories among the decedents is particularly noteworthy. The only evidence of past criminal behavior ascertained for any decedent was a misdemeanor charge for setting a fire with friends during college in one case. Interestingly enough, this same man had come to police attention two more times before his death on occasions when he had been unable to extricate himself from bondage restraints; in each instance they freed him and no charges were brought against him (see Case #2).

Psychodynamics

Our postmortem data are an unsatisfactory source of psychodynamic information. Our knowledge of psychodynamic processes is limited to accounts provided by living practitioners of autoerotic asphyxia and to inferences drawn from decedents' writings, sketches, and death scenarios.

From these, we believe that the most common psychological processes underlying autoerotic asphyxia are a desire for the subjective experience of hypoxia, the acting out of a masochistic fantasy that includes being abused, tortured, or executed, and the desire to be sexually aroused through risk-taking.

To the accounts of living practitioners cited in chapter 2, we would add the explanation offered by one patient interviewed in connection with the present study. He indicated that his autoerotic asphyxiation began at age twelve, though he could not recall how he first came to use it. Even in the early years of his practice, he enjoyed the subjective experience of hypoxia and passing out, which was always associated with a fantasy that powerful women were doing this to him. Often he tied himself up or cross-dressed and fantasized that women had done this to him as well. His history illustrates the elements of hypoxia-seeking and masochistic fantasies.

For an illustration of the risk-taking aspect of the behavior we return to the patient described by Boss (1949), previously mentioned in chapter 2, who said: "My pleasure is closely connected with fear, the fear of strangling, chaining, the fear of actual choking. . . . Choking and tying up cause terrible fear. In a state of fear, life and lust are compressed into a very narrow space. The more pressure is exerted by fear, the more vivid gets the pleasure inside." (Boss 1949, pp. 88-89.)

Two specific theories of autoerotic asphyxia have been proposed by others that we believe deserve comment. Both of these theories concern unconscious phenomena and for that reason are immune from disproof. Nonetheless, there are several indications that they are incorrect.

One of these is the suggestion by Resnik (1972) that repetitive, erotic, self-hangings might reflect repressed oral sadism in which the ligature represents a spider web since spiders are a symbol of oral sadism. This hypothesis could only be supported by psychoanalytic studies of living practitioners in which they were shown to have unconscious associations between self-hanging and spiders more often than other individuals have unconscious sexual associations with spiders. We are aware of no clues suggesting such an association. Moreover, this theory would not account for the autoerotic use of suffocation, choking, or inhalation of anesthetics.

The second hypothesis deserving of comment has been the suggestion by several pathologists that autoerotic asphyxia reflects a desire to return to the womb. Johnstone et al. (1960) suggested this as an explanation for plastic-bag asphyxias, and Rupp (1980) resurrected the hypothesis and extended it to apply to hangings and ligature strangulations. In Rupp's words: "Might it not be that the blindfolds, gags, ligatures, and anoxia are merely the acting out of the fetal memory, for certainly there are parallels in uterine life." There are three indications that this is incorrect. First, there is no suggestion among any of the psychiatric reports of individuals who engage in autoerotic asphyxia that any of them had stronger conscious or unconscious wishes to return to the womb than anyone else, nor are there such suggestions in the scant psychiatric literature regarding sexual bondage behavior (see Dietz, in press). Second, the return-to-the-womb hypothesis would not account for the use of choking, inhalation of anesthetics, or chest compression. Third, unlike the repressed-oral-sadism hypothesis, this theory cannot account for the observed association between autoerotic asphyxia and other paraphilias, some of which have been extensively studied with psychoanalytic techniques and none of which has been connected with an unconscious desire to return to the womb. If a psychodynamic theory is to account for autoerotic asphyxiation, it must also account for the association of autoerotic asphyxia with other paraphilias. Stoller's views of perversion (1975) and sexual excitement (1979) come closer to achieving that goal than the return-to-the-womb hypothesis.

Conclusions

Rather than assuming the presence of psychosexual or other mental disorders among the decedents studied, we have sought evidence of disorder independent of the behavior causing death. Applying conservative postmortem diagnostic criteria, we found independent evidence of paraphilias among some of the 127 men and none of the 5 women. Among the men, diagnoses included a sexual-bondage paraphilia (cordophilia) in 65 (51.2 percent), sexual masochism in 15 (11.8 percent), fetishism in 12 (9.4 percent), transvestism in 5 (3.9 percent), and sexual sadism and pedophilia in 1 case each. A few cases presented suggestive evidence of voyeurism, coprophilia, and mysophilia.

These conservative, minimum estimates reflect our effort to avoid diagnosing a paraphilia on the basis of behaviors that may not be repetitive or habitual. In restricting diagnosis to cases in which there is no explanation for the observed signs other than repetitive and habitual sexual behavior, we maximize diagnostic specificity at the expense of sensitivity. The chances of falsely diagnosing a paraphilia when none is present (false positives) are very low with these criteria. Conversely, the chances of not diagnosing a paraphilia when one is present (false negatives) are quite high with these criteria. This issue has greatest relevance in our diagnosis of sexual masochism.

Undoubtedly the act of inducing life-threatening asphyxia to improve sexual excitement is more often a reflection of a sexually masochistic trait than a careless or casual experiment. When this is done repeatedly, diagnosis of sexual masochism and hypoxyphilia would be justified. Our available data, however, did not always include reliable indicators of repetition. We suspect, but cannot prove, that all but a few of the youngest decedents were habitual self-asphyxiators, that is, hypoxyphiliac sexual masochists.

This view of the high prevalence of sexually masochistic behavior—if not diagnosable sexual masochism—in the study population underlies our careful differentiation between transvestism and cross-dressing. Although many authors in the past have used the term *transvestism* rather casually in labeling decedents wearing one or more articles of female attire at death, we think this usage is unjustified. The wearing of female attire is a frequent element in the sexual fantasies of sexual masochists, and reflects a desire to be humiliated and subjugated. In our view, individuals found cross-dressed at death are more likely to have worn female clothes for their masochistic value than as a reflection of transvestism.

Similar arguments could be made with regard to self-imposed bondage and the few cases suggesting coprophilia and mysophilia, all of which are masochistic behaviors. Just as coprophilia and mysophilia are recognized as independent (albeit atypical) paraphilias, we believe cordophilia should be recognized independently of sexual masochism and sadism.

In our opinion, autoerotic asphyxia is primarily associated with a hypoxyphiliac variety of sexual masochism. Autoerotic asphyxia is associated with cordophilia (in approximately one-half of cases) and masochistic cross-dressing (in approximately one-fifth of cases), but fetishism, transvestism, and other paraphilias are evidenced in only some 10 percent or fewer cases.

We found no evidence to suggest that autoerotic asphyxia is disproportionately associated with homosexuality, for the prevalence of identifiable homosexuality among decedents was of the same order of magnitude as that in the general population.

Although we do not have proper data on the occurrence of nonpsychosexual mental disorders among decedents, we do have sufficient information to conclude that there is no basis for believing that psychotic disorders are any more prevalent in this population than in the general population.

Note

1. American Psychiatric Association. *Diagnostic and Statistical Manual of Mental Disorders,* 3rd ed. Washington, D.C.: American Psychiatric Association, 1980.

6 Atypical Autoerotic Fatalities

Park Elliott Dietz and
Robert R. Hazelwood

This chapter describes autoerotic fatalities different from those considered elsewhere in this book. They are distinguished in part by the causes of death, which for the 18 cases studied were electrocution (6), cardiovascular disease (4), Freon inhalation (3), aspiration (2), volatile nitrites (1), exposure (1), and undetermined (1).

In the "typical" autoerotic fatality, the autoerotic behavior includes intentional asphyxiation and the cause of death is asphyxia resulting from the excessive application of whatever means was employed for asphyxiation. In this chapter, we turn to the consideration of cases in which the cause of death is not asphyxia or, if asphyxia, is produced indirectly through a mechanism other than excessive application of the purposefully applied mechanism. Thus some atypical cases involve no purposive use of asphyxia whereas others do.

We have defined cases as atypical on the basis of three factors: the nature of the autoerotic activity, the cause of death, and the relationship between these two. A classification system that takes account of only one of these factors will not suffice in distinguishing between the types of atypical cases observed.

Death associated with autoerotic asphyxiation is not necessarily a direct result of the asphyxiation. The asphyxiation may result in a complication that is the proximal cause of death. This occurred in two cases in which asphyxiation was complicated by the blocking of the airway with vomitus (Cases #1 and 2).

We are unaware of any case in which autoerotic asphyxiation resulted in death from a nonasphyxial cause. Such a death is nonetheless theoretically possible: for example, autoerotic choking resulting in collapse and fatal head injury.

Death sometimes occurs during nonasphyxial autoerotic activities, as illustrated by the other 16 cases reported in this chapter. In such cases, the degree to which an injurious agent used for sexual arousal is the direct cause of death varies along a broad spectrum. At one extreme,

---

Adapted from: Atypical autoerotic fatalities. *Medicine and Law* 1:307–319, 1982.

excessive application of an injurious agent may directly cause death, as in some electrocutions (see Cases #4 to 6). At the other extreme, death may be largely incidental to the autoerotic activity, as in some heart attacks (see Cases #15 to 17).

Nonasphyxial autoerotic activities may result in asphyxial death (Cases #11 and 12 in chapter 4 and some anesthetic deaths might be viewed as examples of this). Rupp (1973) described a case in which a man rigged his car to run in concentric circles after he had attached himself to it with a heavy chain connected to a harness which was his only garb. Whether he jogged after the moving car or allowed himself to be dragged is unknown, but he died of asphyxiation after the heavy chain became entangled around an axle. Henry (1971) reported the death of a woman who suspended herself from a door hinge by a rope wrapped around her crotch and breasts in a complicated manner. She wore a "harem-girl" costume at death, and a story about a harem in which women were "stored" by hanging them around the walls had been read so many times that the pages were loosened from the book's binding. In the final episode, she inadvertently tied a gag around her mouth and neck in such a manner that it encompassed the rope used for suspension. When she kicked a chair out from under herself, the tension on the rope caused the gag to constrict her neck with the effect of hanging. In each of these cases, nonasphyxial autoerotic activity led indirectly to death by asphyxia (also see chapter 2 for further detail on these cases).

Every case should be approached with attention to the injurious agent used for sexual arousal, the cause of death, and the relationship between these two.

Aspiration

Aspiration refers to the taking of foreign matter into the airway. The experience of having food go down the wrong way is a familiar form of aspiration. Aspiration may prove fatal if the foreign material blocks or severely narrows the airway. Fatal aspiration is a form of choking, which in turn is a type of asphyxia. Aspiration of vomitus most often occurs in individuals who are unconscious or partly conscious and has been observed to be particularly likely to occur in the presence of alcohol or other drugs (Moritz 1954; Spitz 1980). Aspiration of vomitus is a recognized complication of suffocation (Simpson 1965), hanging (Strassman 1954; Spitz 1973), and indeed, any variety of asphyxia (Moritz 1954). Medical authorities certified the cause of death in two study cases as aspiration of vomitus.

Case #1

A twelve-year-old white boy who resided with his parents was discovered dead in a storage room of the family residence. He was suspended by the neck with a pair of leotards attached to a wood beam in the room. The door was closed but had no locking device. He wore a dress, panties, and a brassiere which belonged to his mother and had been taken from bags stored in the room. Although totally suspended above the floor, evidence at the scene indicated that he had originally stood on a nearby shelf to affix the ligature and then had slipped off the shelf after losing consciousness. Investigation determined that the young boy had evidenced no depression and was considered to be well-adjusted. Toxicological analysis showed a high blood-alcohol concentration. The cause of death was determined to be aspiration of vomitus.

Case #2

The decedent, a twenty-three-year-old single black woman, resided with her parents, who were on vacation out of the country at the time of her death. She was discovered in her bathroom by a male friend who had stopped by to see her. She was nude and resting on her knees with the upper portion of her body over the top of the tub and her head submerged in water. Her hands were snugly tied in front, and a 9½-inch bolt rested on the floor beneath her buttocks. Vomitus was present in the tub. Another piece of rope was looped around her neck with the free ends draped over her right shoulder, indicating that she had been pulling on the rope with her right hand (she was right-handed). She is thought to have been engaging in a masochistic fantasy (hence, the bound wrists), inducing hypoxia with the neck ligature, when she lost consciousness, falling across the tub and into the water. After autopsy, death was attributed to aspiration, but the manner of death was left open at the time. (See chapters 2 and 8 for additional information about this case, which was also reported by Danto [1980].)

In both of the preceding cases, the individual was apparently engaging in autoerotic asphyxia just prior to death, and the death would not have occurred had this not been so. While it is possible that the young man would not have died had he not been intoxicated, and while his intoxication may have been a contributing factor to the aspiration of vomitus, his death is not very distinct from the typical asphyxial autoerotic fatalities described in the remainder of this book. The other case, however, is different in that the tension on the ligature about her neck was relaxed after she lost consciousness. Had she not aspirated vomitus, death would not have occurred. In each of these cases, the ultimate cause of death was asphyxial. These cases illustrate the fine shading between typical cases and atypical cases.

It should also be noted, without prejudice toward the medical investigation of the previous two cases, that death is sometimes spuriously attributed to aspiration. Fatteh (1972) studied the aspiration of gastric contents in 140 cases with other documentable causes of death such as coronary-artery disease, automobile-crash injuries, pneumonia, and gunshot wounds. Cases in which aspiration was thought to be a precipitating cause of death were excluded. In 33 (23.5 percent) of these cases, aspiration of gastric contents could be demonstrated. Fatteh concluded that regurgitation and aspiration of gastric contents are common agonal artefacts and warned that pathologists and other physicians too often erroneously attribute death to aspiration of gastric contents. It is likely that aspiration of gastric contents was noted at autopsy in other cases in this study but was not listed as a cause of death or contributory cause of death.

Electrocution

The dangers of excessive electrical stimulation are known to all thinking members of industrial societies. Direct electrical stimulation of the human body is used in a variety of diagnostic and therapeutic procedures. Geddes and Baker (1971) observed that even for many medical procedures in which current is passed through the body, the safe levels of current have not been determined. It is therefore not surprising that individuals who purposely use electrical stimulation for sexual purposes may miscalculate the level of current to be applied.

In 1779, not long after the advent of electricity, James Graham's Temple of Health opened in London and became famous for its perfumed, musical, celestial bed, which Graham claimed had electric currents that varied according to the amorous vigor of those upon it (Marti-Ibañez 1961; Bloch 1964). Today the use of electrical current for sexual stimulation is a part of some so-called healing practices of quacks but is also known within the sexual underground.

Some items of underground literature directed toward sexual masochists provide instructions for the construction of electrically stimulating devices from household materials. Descriptions of the use of electricity for sexual stimulation during intercourse have also appeared in the letter-to-the-editor sections of several mass-circulation erotic men's magazines. It can therefore be assumed that the sexually stimulating possibilities of electricity are widely known among those individuals most likely to make use of such techniques for they are particularly likely to seek out and read such materials. Nonetheless the frequency with which electricity is used for sexual purposes is unknown, and there are few published reports of resultant electrocution (see the following).

Multiple factors influence the effect of electric shock on the body, including the site of application, moistness of the skin, and characteristics of the current itself; detailed accounts of these factors are available elsewhere (Polson 1959; Fisher 1980).

According to Mant (1968), electrocution can result in death from any of three mechanisms. The first and most frequent is cardiac fibrillation, which is rapid electrical activity in the heart muscle that results in a cessation of blood flow and eventual death. The second mechanism is muscular spasm which paralyzes the muscles necessary for breathing, resulting in death by asphyxiation while the heart continues to beat. The third and rarest mechanism involves the passage of electric current through the brain with paralysis of those centers in the nervous system that control respiration. In each of these forms of electrocution, prompt intervention can be lifesaving.

Case #3

A nineteen-year-old white man was discovered dead in his room by his friends. He wore an undershirt, cut-off shorts, and socks, and an electrical floor buffer was turning slowly between his thighs when he was originally discovered. He was in an oblique, reclining position with his left shoulder and upper left arm touching a metal steam radiator and his buttocks partially resting on a folded quilt, a pillow, and canvas material. The buffer's electrical plug was originally of the three-pronged variety, but the ground prong had been removed. The buffer's switch was held in the on position by a piece of electrical wire. The man's inner thighs and left shoulder were badly burned. A subsequent examination of the buffer disclosed that it was electrically deficient. Current had passed from the buffer through the victim's thighs, exiting his left shoulder on contact with the metal radiator.

Case #4

A fifteen-year-old white boy was found dead, lying on his back on the stairs leading to the basement of the family residence. His left leg was chained to the first step, and another chain was draped over his left arm. An additional length of chain was found lying over one of the steps. A transformer was plugged into an extension cord which was connected to an electrical outlet in the ceiling. One wire interconnected the transformer and a piece of copper pipe found in the boy's rectum. A second wire from the transformer led to a plastic tripod which supported a metal rod. A third wire ran from the tripod to an alligator clip fastened on the boy's lower lip.

Case #5

A forty-nine-year-old white man was discovered lying dead on a tile floor in his home. He was wearing only a T-shirt. A bare wire ran from an electrical transformer near his body into his urethra. Semen was on his left thigh and had flowed to his buttock where it made contact with the tile floor causing a ground effect. A large burn mark was present on his left buttock. Autopsy disclosed cauterization of the foreskin on his penis and burns of the distal inch of the urethra, the distance to which the wire had been inserted.

Case #6

Police were summoned to an apartment where they discovered a sixty-three-year-old man lying on a bed naked except for a brassiere, stockings, and high-heeled shoes. He was lying on a narrow board. A piece of rope surrounded the board and his waist and was tied at his left side. It then traversed his left leg, ran beneath the board, and affixed his calves to the board. A lamp was lying on the bed to his left, and its cord was plugged into a wall outlet. Two electrical wires extended from the lamp: one entered his rectum, the other led beneath the brassiere. The female attire belonged to his daughter, in whose apartment he died. He had been divorced, and his former wife stated that she had never known him to dress in women's clothes.

Case #7

A twenty-four-year-old computer operator was found dead in his apartment. He was naked except for a brassiere and a gold necklace. A rope tied around his waist also extended about his groin, binding his genitalia down into the gluteal fold. He was lying on his right side with both hands grasping magazines depicting females in various stages of undress. Newspaper advertising supplements showing similar photographs were scattered about his body. An electrode spliced into speaker wire was taped to each nipple. These wires ran behind his back, where they were joined, *traversed his left leg, where they were taped to his body, and were connected to a stereo amplifier (120 to 180 watts, 120 volts, 3 amperes). The amplifier had been on when he was found.*

Case #8

A thirty-year-old single, white man was found dead in his bedroom after he failed to join his family for dinner. His door had to be forced open because he had secured it with a dead-bolt lock. He was lying on the floor wearing only a long-line brassiere. Wires led from the brassiere to a motorized rotisserie which every three to four seconds forced a metal bar into contact with the wires for one and one-half seconds. Two small transformers connected the rotisserie to a small motor plugged into a wall outlet. Investigators determined that he had placed tin foil around the wires leading to his body, wrapped them in wet terrycloth towels, and then placed a wire so wrapped in each cup of the brassiere. A third wire which had been similarly treated was beneath his back on the left side. Testing of the device showed that it was producing 52 volts and less than 1 ampere of current to the body. His family indicated that they had observed similar devices in his room over the past four to five years and that the victim was considered an electrical expert. Several magazines depicting undressed women were around his body, as were pages from catalogues advertising lingerie. Beneath his left leg was a girdle. A small box in the room contained more brassieres and girdles. He had also positioned a wall mirror so as to allow him to view himself while lying on the floor. (See chapter 7 for further details on this case.)

The first of these six electrocution deaths (Case #3) was that of a young man who was accidentally electrocuted through an electrical deficiency in a floor buffer he had been using to masturbate. There is no indication that he was purposely applying electrical stimulation for sexual arousal. In another case (Case #17) an individual died naturally while using a household appliance (a vacuum cleaner) during masturbation, but in that instance there was neither electrical stimulation nor electrocution. The use of household appliances for masturbation or other sexual activities is well known in some quarters, and warnings against their use have been issued in a best-selling book (Comfort 1972).

The other five electrocution cases were the result of the use of electricity for sexual stimulation. Such cases are alluded to by Brittain (1968), and Polson and Gee (1973) cite several European case reports. A preliminary report on the first seventy cases acquired for the present study tabulated five electrocutions (Hazelwood et al. 1981). Sivaloganathan

(1981) reported an English case of a thirty-six-year-old male who had removed the back of a television set and connected wires from the speaker terminal to his body. One wire formed a loop that surrounded his scrotum; the other wire was looped and inserted in his anal canal, which had been lubricated with petroleum jelly. One of the wires connected to the loudspeaker had become disconnected, and the decedent apparently made contact with an electrically live piece of metal inside the television when he investigated the source of his disconnection. Cairns and Rainer (1981) reported two New Zealand cases that greatly resemble one another. In each, the decedent had attached wire from an electrical source controlled by a rheostat to coins taped over each nipple and to his anus. Both victims died of electrocution, though mechanical failure of the apparatus was apparent in neither case, and one of the decedents was a radio repairman known for his electrical knowledge.

In each of the cases just reviewed in which electrical stimulation resulted in electrocution, the decedent had attached wires to one or more sexually significant parts of the body. Of eight cases (Cases #4 to 8 and the three case reports previously published in English), five victims had inserted wires into the anal canal, five had attached wires on or near the nipples, one had encircled his scrotum with a wire, and one had inserted a wire into his urethra. Bondage played a part in Cases #4, 6, and 7, and in one of the cases reported by Cairns and Rainer (1981). The victims in Cases #6, 7, and 8 wore articles of women's clothing, and one of the cases reported by Cairns and Rainer had items of female clothing near him when he died. The only independent evidence of sexual masochism (apart from the electrical stimulation itself and bondage) is the fact that Cairns's and Rainer's case who possessed women's clothing had clamped his chest so that the tissue protruded to mimic breasts.

The postmortem burn suffered by the decedent in Case #5 when his semen flowed to the floor is reminiscent of cases in which urine has conducted electricity. Simpson (1965) reported one case in which a man was electrocuted when he urinated on a live electrical conduit and fell onto the conduit after having been shocked through the stream of urine. Burchell (1970) mentioned a case in which a patient's urine immersed the controlling switch of an electrically powered bed and caused cardiac fibrillation, a case in which a mentally retarded child underwent cardiac fibrillation when the pulse generator of a cardiac pacemaker became saturated with urine, and a practice among New Zealand soccer pranksters of connecting batteries to metal urinal troughs.

Freon Inhalation

Voluntary inhalation of gases for their euphoric or intoxicating effect has been sporadically reported in the scientific literature for over a century

(Hayden and Comstock 1976). Anesthetic gases such as nitrous oxide and ether were not only among the first to be abused for their euphoric properties but were also among the first to be associated with autoerotic fatalities (see chapter 2). Although we have classified the inhalation of anesthetic gases as an asphyxial mechanism (in part because a major effect of certain anesthetics, such as nitrous oxide, is oxygen replacement), the inclusion of anesthetics with typical cases and the relegation of other chemicals to atypical status is somewhat arbitrary. A wide variety of chemicals is used for their supposed stimulating properties, and a few acquire reputations as aphrodisiacs. The search for effective aphrodisiacs is among mankind's oldest quests, proof that the quest has been fruitless. To this day, popular men's magazines contain advertisements for alleged aphrodisiacs which are worthless, dangerous, or at best, inert. The particular chemical agents associated with autoerotic fatalities can be expected to correspond to the chemical fashions of the day and do not, therefore, bear extensive discussion here.

Case #9

Police responded to a missing-persons report at a trailer park and discovered the body of the thirty-year-old missing man completely encased in a large plastic bag. The opening of the plastic bag had been pulled inward toward the body and secured from the inside with a cord. The victim wore only a T-shirt, underwear, and socks. His penis was exposed. The bag also contained an aerosol spray can which was later determined to contain the propellants Dichlorodifluoromethane (Freon 12) and Trichlorofluoromethane (Freon 11). The toxicology report stated that the presence of both of these fluorocarbons was confirmed by electron-capture-gas chromatography and noted that studies have shown that fluorocarbons in high concentrations are capable of sensitizing the heart to epinephrine (adrenaline), resulting in severe cardiac arrhythmias.

Case #10

A girlfriend of a thirty-three-year-old man discovered his naked body face down on his bed. Believing him to be asleep, she turned him on his back and noted that the corner of a plastic bag was secured to his nose and mouth with black tape. An erotic magazine had been lying beneath him and it was opened to pictures of a woman fellating a nude man and a man ejaculating on a woman's breasts. Beside the bed were a metal tank containing Freon and a hose leading from the tank to a five-gallon plastic container. The container was covered with a plastic bag that had been taped to its top. One corner of the bag was cut, and this was the portion that was attached to the victim's face. It was observed that he had ejaculated onto his thigh. The room also contained a movie projector, and near the machine was an empty cannister for a pornographic film.

Case #11

A twenty-year-old married man was found sitting upright on a sofa by his father-in-law. The young man wore only a shirt. A plastic bread wrapper was on the sofa near his left hand, and his right hand held a can of Pam. An 8-mm movie projector was nearby, with a pornographic film in place. Toxicologic analysis disclosed toxic levels of fluorocarbons #11 and #12 in his blood and lungs, and no other cause of death was discernible at autopsy. His death was attributed to cardiac arrhythmia due to Freon inhalation.

In 1970 Bass published a summary report of a study said to show that a U.S. solvent-sniffing epidemic first observed in California in the late 1950s had had national impact by the mid-1960s, that fluorocarbon propellants in aerosol containers were the principal source of the rising incidence, and that severe cardiac arrhythmia appeared the most likely explanation for the deaths. Soon thereafter, Taylor and Harris (1970) confirmed through animal experimentation that fluorocarbon propellants did, indeed, sensitize the heart to asphyxia-induced changes in heart function capable of causing death through arrhythmia. Subsequent studies by chemical manufacturers reported that they were unable to demonstrate the cardiotoxicity of fluorocarbon propellants, while Harris (1973) had continued to demonstrate their toxicity. In 1975 the Consumer Product Safety Commission (CPSC) denied a request to ban Pam because as a food, Pam fell under the jurisdiction of the Food and Drug Administration (FDA). The CPSC announced plans for a nationwide information-and-education campaign; the FDA proposed warning labels on the product. Deaths from inhalation of Pam and other aerosol sprays containing fluorocarbon propellants continued to be reported in the United States (Crawford 1976) and Canada (Fagan and Forrest 1977). Subsequently, environmental concerns achieved what concern for direct loss of human life could not: substantial reductions in the use of fluorocarbon propellants in aerosol sprays.

Nitrites

Amyl nitrite, like nitroglycerin, has been in medical use for more than a century, primarily for the treatment of angina pectoris. The physiological actions of amyl nitrite and similar agents are complex but derive from their principal pharmacologic action of relaxing smooth muscles (the type of muscle that controls the size of blood vessels, thereby altering blood pressure). The administration of pharmacologically active but not toxic doses of the nitrites is accompanied by a transient fall in blood pressure that produces syncope (lightheadedness). Depending on the individual's physical status, mental set, and social setting, this syncope may be perceived as an unpleasant side effect of a medically necessary drug or as a pleasant "head rush."

Case #12

A thirty-nine-year-old single man was found prone beside his bed. He had obviously rolled off the bed, as the covers were pulled down around him. He was nude and there were indications that he had been masturbating prior to death. There was no trauma to the body, and the investigators were unable to arrive at a preliminary conclusion as to the cause of death. A search of the room revealed the following items of interest: a bottle of Dilantin (later determined to be for treatment of a seizure disorder), two containers of Rush, one of which was empty, and on a shelf above the bed, a small bottle labeled Locker Room Essence, several magazines of homosexual orientation, many articles of feminine attire, a photograph of the victim dressed as a female, and a device sold as a penis enlarger. Autopsy disclosed marked congestion of the lungs, liver, and kidney. The heart evidenced bilateral ventricular dilatation. Death was ruled to be due to methemoglobinemia resulting from the ingestion of isobutylnitrites.

The summary of the autopsy report read, in pertinent part:

> No specific anatomic cause of death was evident, but toxicology demonstrated a methemoglobin level of 113%. It is presumed that the deceased ingested isobutylnitrite which is a chief ingredient of "Rush." . . . It is highly unlikely that lethal levels of methemoglobinemia [sic] could be obtained by inhaling nitrite compounds. However, oral ingestion of highly concentrated isobutylnitrite could produce lethal levels of methemoglobinemia [sic]. Methemoglobinemia is a rare cause of death since levels in excess of 20% must be obtained. In this case the methemoglobin level of 113% is great enough to cause death. Theoretically, it is impossible to obtain a methemoglobin level in excess of 100%, and the level of 113% indicates a margin of error in the determination.

The contributor of this case interviewed an acknowledged homosexual about the use of isobutylnitrite as a sexual stimulant and was told that "butyl nitrite provides the same euphoric state as does choking."

Rush and Locker Room are among the better-known commercially produced compounds containing volatile nitrites which are not regulated by the FDA. They are marketed by mail order, with advertisements in major men's magazines, and through direct sales in "head shops," record stores, sexual-paraphernalia boutiques, pornographic bookstores, and leather-clothing stores in the homosexual districts of major cities. These agents are intended for inhalation (despite the manufacturers' disclaimers to the contrary), not oral ingestion.

Some of the nitrites readily oxidize hemoglobin to methemoglobin. This is particularly likely to result in serious toxicity or death when large doses have been orally ingested and in individuals with a preexisting anemia. Some years ago an outbreak of cyanosis (blue skin due to oxygen deficiency), shock, and coma was traced to the inadvertent substitution of sodium nitrite for sodium chloride (table salt) at a restaurant (Roueché 1947). Inhalation of volatile nitrites in a healthy individual who is not simultaneously using other drugs is highly unlikely to result in death.

The use of volatile nitrites had been well known in the drug subculture and the sexual underground for many years. This use attained wide recognition among physicians during the 1970s (Everett 1972; Sigell et al. 1978). Volatile nitrites became known as poppers because the first nitrites were packaged in small ampules that made a popping noise when crushed. Nonmedical marketing has been chiefly in the form of small vials, sometimes with warnings that the vapors are not to be directly inhaled, though this is precisely the way they are used (Kramer 1977). Special inhalers to be worn on a chain around the neck have been sold in specialty shops for over a decade (Everett 1972).

Users of volatile nitrites report that inhalation of these agents increases sexual excitement and prolongs orgasm (Everett 1972). In 1978, the manufacturer of Rush was quoted in *Time* (Anonymous 1978) as forecasting a 15 to 20 percent increase in the previous year's retail sales of some $20 million. The *Time* article also stated that manufacturers estimated that 5 million Americans regularly inhaled isobutyl nitrite on the dance floor and in bed. Despite the widespread use of volatile nitrites for sexual purposes, we are unaware of any reports of autoerotic fatalities or other sexual fatalities stemming from the *inhalation* of volatile nitrites. Indeed, none of the forty-seven forensic pathologists responding to a mailed questionnaire survey had ever seen a case of fatal isobutyl or amyl nitrite toxicity (Lowry 1979).

Exposure

The diagnosis of death by exposure is largely a diagnosis of exclusion, taking account of environmental conditions under which death occurred.

Although some specific pathologic findings have been said to be associated with death due to exposure to cold (Simpson 1965; Benz 1980), none of the associated findings is so specific as to prove that death was caused by a lowering of body temperature. It is well known that lowering of body temperature results in a slowing of metabolic processes. Prolonged lowering of body temperature eventually causes circulatory failure and cardiac fibrillation. Alterations in the capacity of hemoglobin to take up and release oxygen play an important part in this process (Mant 1968), causing hypoxia to the tissues and, eventually, alterations in the functioning of the vital centers in the brain (Simpson 1965). Exhaustion may speed the onset of hypothermia and hasten death (Simpson 1965).

Case #13

The victim, in his early fifties, was a white male, married and the father of three. He was educated beyond the master's level and owned a small business. He was discovered in a forest, suspended by his knees in a bowed position. Only his feet, shoulders, and head touched the ground. He wore a white-net shirt, blue bikini-type underwear, and ankle-length socks. His ankles were bound with cord. A separate piece of cord bound his legs together with five individual wraps from just below the knees to the upper part of his thighs. Another length of cord went around his waist, between his legs on each side of his scrotum, back around the uppermost part of his thighs, and was then interconnected to each of the leg wraps. A snap hook was attached to the cord above his knees, and a separate length of cord suspended the victim from a tree limb via this snap hook. His wrists were bound beneath his buttocks by pieces of nylon strap that were connected to a second snap hook, which in turn was attached to the cord encircling the legs. He had wrapped each wrist in heavy cloth to prevent chafing by the nylon strap. His penis was held down between his thighs by the nylon strap used to secure his wrists. Investigation determined the presence of ejaculate on his thighs. At the base of the penis, he had tightly tied a short piece of nylon rope. Near his body were his clothing and a carrying bag. The bag contained erotic books, magazines, and photographs of women and men. He had pasted facial photographs of his family and friends over the faces of models appearing in the erotica. His death was attributed to exposure.

In this case, the individual had engaged in extensive, nonasphyxial bondage behavior. His death was originally reported as a homicide. His inability to extricate himself by means of the snap hook near his hands led to his prolonged exposure to the elements. It is likely that at some point he struggled to release himself, hastening his death through fatigue. In the absence of any other demonstrable cause of death, and in view of the weather at the time, his death was attributed to exposure. We are aware of no other autoerotic fatalities in which the cause of death was exposure.

Cardiovascular Disease

Cardiovascular disease is among the leading causes of death in all industrial nations and is the subject of one of the most advanced medical specialities. The reader may therefore be surprised to learn that many types of cardiovascular disease cannot be definitively shown to have caused death, even after careful autopsy (Adelson and Hirsch 1980; Buja and Petty 1980). The term *cardiovascular disease* encompasses cerebrovascular accidents (strokes), coronary artery disease (heart attacks), and a host of less-familiar conditions. Cerebrovascular accidents are usually readily identified at autopsy, whereas coronary artery disease and other types of heart disease often cannot be shown to have caused death and sometimes cannot even be shown to have been present in the absence of a medical history documenting signs, symptoms, or laboratory findings prior to death. Sudden, unexpected death due to cardiovascular disease may occur at any time or place, and therefore it expectedly occurs during autoerotic or other sexual activity on occasion. Death is commonly attributed to cardiovascular disease when no other cause of death can be shown and there is either pathologic evidence of preexisting cardiovascular disease or the decedent is known to have had a sufficient number of recognized risk factors (for example, smoking, obesity, high cholesterol, and advanced age). The reader interested in learning more about the medicolegal investigation of death due to cardiovascular disease will find material on that subject in any textbook of forensic pathology.

Case #14

A sixty-year-old married man was at home alone as his wife was in the hospital. One of his children stopped by the residence to pick him up for a hospital visit and found him dead on his bedroom floor. He was lying on his back in an outstretched position. Frothy mucus emitted from his nose and mouth. The decedent's head was encased in a black, leather "discipline mask," from which only his nose was visible. Around each wrist was a leather cuff. The wrists were interconnected with a chain which encircled the waist and was secured with a lock in front. A second chain entered the front of a black, leather half-slip he wore and exited the slip just above his knees, where it was attached to two ankle cuffs and secured with a second lock. He also wore pajama tops and black, calf-length stockings. His death was attributed to cardiac failure during autoerotic activities and was ruled to be natural in manner.

Case #15

A sixty-five-year-old man was found dead in a public park by children at play. His body was lying face down and was protected from view by large bushes. He was dressed in female clothing, including a dress, brassiere, panties, pantyhose, and high-heeled shoes. The body was somewhat decomposed, and it was obvious that the death had occurred several days previously. To the immediate front of the body was an erotic magazine opened to photographs of couples engaged in heterosexual acts. Toxicology disclosed no trace of alcohol or other drugs. The cause of death was documented as a massive coronary.

Case #16

A seventy-year-old man was found dead in his home. He was lying on the floor wearing a shirt and sweater with his pants around his knees. A catheter tube protruded from his penis, and a bucket containing water was nearby. A piece of cord was tied around his waist. Tied to the cord behind him were two separate pieces of cloth that went through his gluteal fold, passed to both sides of his scrotum, and were tied to the cord in front of him. When the pieces of cloth were removed, it was learned that their purpose had been to secure a dildo in his rectum. Investigation determined that the decedent was known to fill his bladder with water through the catheter, insert the dildo in his rectum, and then masturbate with these in place. Death was ruled to be from "cardiac seizure."

Case #17

The wife of the deceased notified the sheriff's department that she had discovered her husband dead upon returning home from church. The officers arrived to find the seventy-seven-year-old victim lying on his bed. He was nude and had a bath towel beneath him. Cradled in his left arm was a vacuum cleaner. The bedclothes beneath the vacuum were scorched, indicating that the cleaner had been running for quite some time. A plastic bottle, approximately eight inches in length, was inserted in his rectum. The vacuum-cleaner attachment had been disconnected and removed be-

fore the officers arrived. Nonetheless, his penis was quite swollen, indicating that he had been using the vacuum cleaner to masturbate just prior to death. Following autopsy, his death was attributed to natural causes, that is, a heart attack.

These four cases of death attributed to cardiovascular disease during autoerotic activity are probably not at all representative of the majority of cases of natural death during masturbation. It is likely they were submitted because of the features of bondage, cross-dressing, insertion of items into the rectum, catheterization, and masturbation with a vacuum cleaner. Although it might appear that these activities are potentially lethal at advanced age, since the decedents were aged sixty to seventy-seven, this inference would be unwarranted. It would be more accurate to observe that advanced age, while potentially lethal, is consistent with the continuation of many types of sexual practices. It is nonetheless noteworthy that in each of these four cases, the autoerotic activity was one that would not in itself be likely to cause death.

The decedent in Case #14 was wearing a "discipline mask" from which only his nose was visible. A great variety of such devices is commercially manufactured, and some have flaps that may be snapped to occlude the nose or mouth. Catalogs of such devices available by mail order are sold in pornographic bookstores, and the masks and helmets themselves are sold in bondage-supply stores. It should also be noted that frothy mucus emitted from the decedent's nose in the same case. Frothy mucus stemming from the mouth and nostrils is a long-recognized sign of asphyxia (Webster 1930), particularly asphyxia through strangulation (Simpson 1965). Such mucus froth is a mixture of pulmonary edema fluid, mucus, and sometimes blood. Although Fatteh points out that the presence of pulmonary edema is not helpful in diagnosing asphyxia because it occurs in organic disease and other conditions as well, he also states that the presence of pulmonary edema "indicates struggle for survival for a time" (1973, p. 137).

Many deaths during manual masturbation doubtless go unrecognized, which is just as well. People may be naked at the time of death for any number of reasons (Rupp 1980), and nudity cannot be assumed to represent sexual activity. Although none of the deaths in this study was the result of stroke, deaths during sexual intercourse (Rupp 1980) or masturbation (Tomita and Uchida 1972) occasionally are due to stroke. More commonly, deaths during sexual intercourse, known as "la mort d'amour" (Johnson 1976) or "death in the saddle" (Massie et al. 1969; Rupp 1980) are due to coronary-artery disease (Ueno 1963; Trimble 1970). The same is true of natural deaths occurring during masturbation, whether or not the sorts of features that led to submission of the previous four cases were present.

Undetermined

In all medicolegal jurisdictions, a certain number of cases will be encountered in which the cause of death cannot be determined despite the most dogged efforts through investigation, autopsy, microscopic examination of the tissues, and toxicology (Petty and Curran 1980). Although the number of negative-autopsy cases has been estimated at 2 to 10 percent of all cases autopsied in the best of medicolegal centers (Fatteh 1973), one office recorded only 0.14 percent of cases as due to undetermined causes and another 0.53 percent as due to violence of undetermined origin (Adelson and Hirsch 1980). The cause of death was recorded as undetermined in only one case in our sample.

Case #18

A black woman in her early twenties was discovered in a severely decomposed condition. She was found on a bed in her locked apartment, where she had resided alone. She was nude and lay face down with a pillow under her abdomen and her buttocks in the air. Her right hand was beneath her, near her vagina. Her face was turned to one side, and a knife was beneath her cheek. On the bed immediately below her vagina lay a long sausage which, in all probability, fell from her vagina after death. On the kitchen counter a package of similar sausages, once frozen, had since thawed. The apartment door had been locked from within, and no other person was known to possess a key.

    A careful autopsy performed by a well-respected forensic pathologist failed to disclose a cause of death. The cause of death was listed as undetermined. It remains the only such case in the sample.
    In a Japanese case superficially similar to this one, a woman who died while masturbating with a carrot was found at autopsy to have suffered a subarachnoid hemorrhage (a form of stroke) (Tomita and Uchida 1972).

Conclusions

The preceding cases illustrate the complex relationships between the nature of the self-injurious autoerotic activity and the cause of death in autoerotic fatalities. The term *autoerotic asphyxia* should be reserved for cases in which the asphyxial mechanism employed for sexual purposes is the direct cause of fatal asphyxiation. Among atypical autoerotic fatalities, only the electrocution cases in which electric current was used for sexual purposes can currently be defined with sufficient precision to merit an independent label. We suggest that these be referred to as *autoerotic electrocutions*. Although the examples presented earlier include only a limited range of injurious agents, it is well to bear in mind that the dynamics of sexual masochism and erotic risk-taking are such that any injurious agent imaginable may be used for sexual purposes, potentially resulting in an autoerotic fatality.

Rupp (1980) mentioned cases in which gas-station attendants are found collapsed or dead on the floor following injury or rupture of the bowel from a grease-gun enema. According to Rupp, if the subject survives, he may tell a story of having been robbed by men who inserted the grease gun into his rectum and pulled the trigger, but in fact the grease-gun enema was probably self-administered. The sexual use of enemas, though only described in the psychiatric literature in English during the past decade (Denko 1973; Dietz 1974; Denko 1976), has been recognized for centuries (Institut für Sexualforschung, 1928) and is the subject of several specialized pornographic magazines.

We are aware of one case in which a man is said to have fatally shot himself during masturbation while wearing women's clothes. Another man survived an incident at age fifteen in which he shot himself with a gun inserted in his rectum while masturbating. His subsequent autoerotic activities included sticking pins into his urethra, infibulation of his nipples, cutting his nipples and buttocks with a razor, and forcing a chisel in his left breast to a depth of three inches. He had sadistic fantasies as well and was eventually convicted of an offense involving stabbing a female stranger.

Stekel's classic work, *Sadism and Masochism* (1929), contains many examples of sexual masochists whose fantasies or behaviors involved potentially lethal activities. We suspect that many autoerotic fatalities among sexual masochists go unrecognized as such. Cases in which death results from genital self-mutilation are typically ascribed to a psychotic disorder on the part of the decedent. At least some such deaths are probably a reflection of sexual masochism in the absence of psychotic disorder. Sexual masochism should be considered in the postmortem differential diagnosis of all cases in which self-inflicted injuries of an unusual nature result in death.

7

Investigation of Autoerotic Fatalities

*Robert R. Hazelwood,
Park Elliott Dietz,* and
Ann Wolbert Burgess

The majority of autoerotic fatalities involving injurious agents are accidental, but their features sometimes lead to mistaken impressions of suicide or homicide. The fact that many autoerotic fatalities share common characteristics with suicide, such as a finding that the victim was alone in a locked room or that he died by hanging, has led many investigators to initially classify an autoerotic death as a suicide. Other features, such as a blindfold, a gag, or physical restraints, have led to mistaken suspicions of homicide. In this chapter we review the most important features of the autoerotic-death scene and the principal sources of information regarding the victim's previous experience with the activity that led to his death.

The Autoerotic-Death Scene

The autoerotic-death scene and its contents vary according to the victim's age, resources, and sexual interests. Not all of the features presented next will be found in every case, but they are suggested to the investigator as details to be observed and, if present, documented. As in all death investigations, the scene should be preserved through photographs and sketches which compliment the written record. Deaths of this nature are well documented historically as early as the eighteenth century (discussed in chapter 2), yet the law-enforcement, medical, and social-science disciplines are naive about such occurrences. Even in those jurisdictions where knowledge is available, certain cases remain equivocal (covered in chapter 8) and require expert consultation.

The possibility of a victim's parent or spouse legally challenging the cause or manner of death listed on the death certificate should be anticipated. In one case, the parents of a victim litigated their son's death for two years, contending that he was murdered. In another case, the father

---

Adapted from: The investigation of autoerotic fatalities. *Journal of Police Science and Administration* 9:404–411, 1981.

brought such pressure on the local coroner, who had ruled the death to be accidental, that the coroner changed his ruling from accident during autoerotic acts to accident due to physical exertion. The decedent's insurance company may also contest the manner of death when accidental-death benefits are at stake, as discussed in chapter 9.

Although we stress scene preservation at several points in this chapter, we wish to emphasize that in some circumstances the investigator's first duty would be to attempt resuscitation. More frequently, however, the victim will have been dead for hours before being discovered, and that discovery will have been made by someone other than the investigator.

Location

As in many suicides, the individual preparing to act out his sexual fantasies typically selects a secluded or isolated location. The locations involved in the population studied included locked rooms; isolated areas of the victim's residence such as attics, basements, garages, or workshops; motel rooms; places of employment during nonbusiness hours; summer residences; and wooded areas. The victim's desire for privacy is paramount in the selection of location. Such acts require concentration on the fantasy scenario and, depending on the use of props, may require considerable preparation time. Thus the individual takes precautions to avoid disruption. The investigator should be alert to the possibility that the location itself may play a role in the victim's fantasy.

Case #1

The victim, a twenty-eight-year-old telephone-company employee was discovered dead by co-workers after he had failed to return to work from repair-service calls. His repair truck was located on a rural road approximately two miles from his last service call. The body was located in a heavily wooded area 250 feet from the roadway. The victim was lying face down with the upper portion of his body resting on his forearms. Around his neck was a ⅜-inch hemp rope secured by a slip knot. The rope extended from his neck to a tree limb approximately 6 feet overhead. To the left front of the victim were four magazines depicting nude females. The victim's pants were undone and his underwear had been lowered sufficiently to expose the penis and scrotum. Medical authorities recorded the cause of death as asphyxiation due to constricted carotid arteries.

Victim Position

Most commonly, the victim's body is partially supported by the ground, floor, or other surface. Occasionally, the victim is totally suspended. The most common position noted in our series was one in which the deceased was suspended upright with only the feet touching the surface. In most such cases, some type of ligature was around the neck and affixed to a suspension point within reach of the victim. The investigator should not be unduly influenced in deciding whether a death is accidental or homicidal by the fact that the body position seemingly indicates the involvement of a second party. Accidental-death victims have been found sitting, kneeling, lying face upward or downward, or suspended by their hands.

Case #2

On their arrival at the scene, the police found the thirty-two-year-old fully clothed victim lying on his stomach on the living-room floor. A handkerchief was over his mouth and tied behind his head. A length of rope wound around his neck and was tied with a slip knot. The rope ran down his back and was attached to a brown, leather belt which held his ankles together. His feet were pulled toward the head by the rope connecting his neck and feet. Blood had trickled from his nose and ears. The responding officers initially believed the death to be a homicide, but the investigating detectives fortunately recognized features characteristic of autoerotic asphyxia and were not swayed by the position of the body. An examination of the decedent's head revealed no blunt-force trauma, and the ear-and-nose bleeding was properly attributed to asphyxiation. They also noted that the victim's arms were free: had he not lost consciousness, he could have released the ligature by the slip knot at his neck or by cutting the rope with a serrated steak knife found on the floor nearby. On a coffee table beside the body were two similar pieces of rope that had been tied with slip knots. He had practiced with those two pieces of rope before engaging in the lethal act.

The Injurious Agent

The investigator at any death scene is charged with the responsibility of gathering information that will allow determination of any action or lack thereof that contributed to the victim's death. We recommend that the injurious agent be studied in great detail, including a careful search for and analysis of possible malfunctioning.

In our series, the most common injurious agent was a ligature of some sort that compressed the neck. Other injurious agents identified in this study included devices for passing electrical current through the body; restrictive containers; obstruction of the breathing passages with gags; and the inhalation of toxic gases or chemicals through masks, hoses, and plastic bags.

In the construction or use of these devices, the individual risks miscalculation. Depending on the mechanism used, he may misjudge the amount of time, substance, pressure, or current. The agent or apparatus that has been used demands scrutiny by the investigator to determine whether or not a malfunction has occurred.

Case #3

A twenty-three-year-old single white male college student was discovered in an apartment he shared with another male. At the time of his death he was wearing only a pair of athletic shorts. His hands were secured in a pillory which rested across his shoulders. This restraining device consisted of two pieces of 1½ × 4½ × 37-inch wood secured at one extreme by a springload hinge. Two holes, each measuring 2¾ inches in diameter, had been cut to accommodate the wrists. These holes were lined with gray rubber stapled to the wood. A 6-inch hole had been cut to fit the neck and was similarly lined. Situated between the neck and one wrist aperture was a padlock. Approximately 2½ feet from the victim's body was a set of keys, one of which fit the padlock securing the pillory. He was wearing a full-face gas mask with a hose leading from the mask to a metal cannister. The bottom of the cannister had been taken off and its original contents removed. In the cannister, he had placed thirteen cotton balls saturated with chloroform, a wadded wash cloth, two sheets of toilet paper, and a small bottle containing chloroform. He had then replaced the bottom, using masking tape to secure it. He apparently dropped the keys, was unable to retrieve them, and lost consciousness. He died from chloroform inhalation.

The Self-Rescue Mechanism

The self-rescue mechanism is any provision that the victim had made to reduce or remove the effects of the injurious agent. The self-rescue mechanism may be nothing more than the victim's ability to stand erect, thereby lessening the pressure about his neck, or it may be as involved as an interconnection between ligatures on the extremities and a ligature around the neck, thereby allowing the victim to control pressure on his neck by moving his body in a particular way or pulling on a key point. Any of a wide variety of items or potential actions that the practitioner had available may have been intended as a self-rescue mechanism. If the injurious agent is a ligature, a slip knot or knife may be involved; if locks are involved, a key might be present; if chains are involved, a pair of pliers may be nearby. As with the injurious agent itself, the possibility of a malfunction of the self-rescue mechanism must be carefully considered. The following case illustrates the necessity for identifying and closely examining the self-rescue mechanism. (This case is reported in greater detail as Case #5 in chapter 8.)

Case #4

A twenty-three-year-old white female died as a result of ligature strangulation. The woman had used an extension cord to interconnect her ankles with her neck. She had used a slip knot as a self-rescue mechanism. Examination of the slip knot revealed that in tying it, her hair had become entangled in the knot, thereby preventing her from disengaging it.

Bondage

The phrase *bondage and domination* is used to describe a range of sexual behaviors closely related to the features commonly associated with autoerotic deaths. (See chapter 5 for further information on bondage and cordophilia.) Bondage refers to the use of physically restraining materials or devices that have sexual significance for the user. The importance of this characteristic cannot be overemphasized, for its involvement is most often responsible for the misinterpretation of these deaths as homicidal rather than accidental. In those cases in which the authors have been called on to provide an opinion as to whether a death was autoerotic or not, it was usually the involvement of bondage that created a question as to whether the victim alone was responsible. Each case must be judged on its own merit.

Physical restraints noted in this study included ropes, chains, handcuffs, and other similar devices that restricted the victim's movement. Even in obvious cases, it is incumbent on the investigator to prove that it was physically possible for the victim to have placed the restraints as they were discovered. It may be necessary to duplicate bindings or knots, and for that reason, the knots should not be cut or undone prior to scrutiny. Failure to be thorough in this aspect of the case may create additional problems in dealing with the deceased's family. Even when the investigation is particularly thorough and well documented (as in the case described next), the involvement of bondage may preclude familial satisfaction with the death being ruled accidental and sexually related.

Case #5

A forty-year-old married man was discovered dead by his wife in the basement of their home. He was totally suspended by a rope that had been wrapped several times around an overhead beam. Around his neck was a hangman's noose that had been meticulously prepared. The body was dressed in a white T-shirt, a white panty girdle with nylons, and a pair of women's open-toed shoes. His hands were bound in handcuff fashion with the wrists approximately 10 inches apart. Over his head was another girdle, and his ankles were bound with a brown-leather belt. On discovering the body, the victim's spouse assumed her husband had been murdered. The investigators correctly assessed the death as accidental and attributed the bound wrists, ankles, and covered head to sexual bondage.

The investigating officers in Case #5 were astute in recognizing that the girdle covering his head was a bondage-related feature. Bodily restraint through bondage includes not only restrictions in the movement of the body but also constriction of the body and restrictions of the organs of sensation and expression. Constrictive materials identified in this study included elastic garments (for example, girdles, support hose, and tight underwear) and other materials such as ace bandages. In one case, a man covered himself entirely with mud prior to placing a ligature around his neck. As the mud dried, it caked and constricted the skin (Case #3, chapter 4). Examples of restrictions on the organs of sensation and expression that were identified in this study include hoods, blindfolds, and gags. In addition, belts, decorative chains, and other features have been observed that we presume to have been elements of symbolic bondage for the victim, as they often are for individuals who engage in other forms of sexual bondage behavior.

Sexually Masochistic Behavior

The investigator will sometimes find that the decedent had inflicted pain upon his genitals, nipples, or other areas of the body (see chapter 5). In addition to whatever pain may be associated with bondage restraints or constrictive materials, pain may have been induced mechanically, electrically, or through self-induced burns, piercing, or frank mutilation. Cases in our series have included a belt tightened around the scrotum, clothespins affixed to the nipples, electrical wire inserted in the penis or anus, an electrified brassiere, and cigarette burns of the scrotum. The term *infibulation* is used to describe the passing of needles or pins through the body, most often through the scrotum, penis, or nipples, but sometimes through an earlobe or the nose. In one case in our series, pins had been passed through each of the decedent's nipples. The self-mutilation may be more extreme, as in the following case.

Case #6

This thirty-one-year-old white male was found suspended from a beam by a hangman's noose around his neck. His feet were touching the floor. He was nude except for a black-leather belt about his waist. Handcuffs secured his wrists in front, and a key to the handcuffs was found in his right hand. Examination of his penis revealed a surgical-like incision around the circumference of the shaft. Inserted and tightened into the incision was a metal washer. The outer edge of the washer was flush with the penis shaft (see Case #3, chapter 8).

Attire

Sometimes the victim is attired in one or more articles of female clothing, especially undergarments. Nylon, lace, leather, rubber, or other materials that held sexual significance for the victim are commonly part of his attire. The investigator should be alert to the possibility that the victim's attire has been adjusted, altered, or completely changed by family members or others prior to the investigator's arrival. Although such an occurrence was not commonly reported to the authors, the police contributing cases reported added difficulty in resolving the manner of death when such alterations had occurred. Although the individuals responsible for altering the scene were technically interfering with a death investigation (a punishable offense), none was charged. In each instance in which the victim's attire had been altered, this had been done by family members. They attributed their alterations to shame, embarrassment, or impulse.

Case #7

A sixteen-year-old white male was found dead in his room by his father. When the police arrived, they found the victim lying on his back and wearing blue jeans, a T-shirt, jockey shorts, and wool socks. A belt, looped on one end, was near his head, as were his glasses. His father informed the officers that when originally found, his son was wearing only his socks and T-shirt. The victim's underwear and pants were on the floor at the end of the bed. The father said that he did not know why his son had been undressed when first found and that he had dressed his son without thinking.

As illustrated by Case #7, the investigator cannot assume that the scene has remained unchanged since its discovery. Had the adjustment in attire not been discovered, the death might have been ruled a suicide. Close examination of the body and its lividity may reveal that attire or restraints have been adjusted, altered, or completely changed, or that the body has been moved since death.

Protective Padding

Frequently the victim will be found with soft material between a ligature and the adjacent body surface. The purpose of this protective padding is to prevent abrasions or discoloration that might prompt inquiries from friends or family. In Case #7 the parents had no idea their son was involved in such dangerous activities. His mother, however, recalled that some months prior to her son's death she had noticed burn marks on both sides of his neck. When she inquired as to their cause, he had explained the marks as having occurred when he had been grabbed by his jersey while playing football. When he was discovered dead, there was no protective padding in evidence. (Contrast this with the case mentioned by Miller (1981), referred to in chapter 1.)

Commercially available bondage equipment includes leather and satin-like restraints lined with lamb's wool, fur, or other soft materials, and these are sometimes found in use or among the possessions of autoerotic-death victims. In several cases in our series the victims had displayed considerable ingenuity in permanently affixing protective padding to homemade apparatus.

Case #8

An older, white male victim was discovered dead in his residence. He had interconnected his neck and feet with rope and belts that were arranged over a hook installed on the inner wall of his closet. The interconnecting ligature caused his body to arch. He had attached rubber-foam insulation to that portion of the ligature around his neck. The rubber foam was held in place with duct tape.

Sexual Paraphernalia

Sexual paraphernalia was found on or near the victim in many cases in our series. These paraphernalia included vibrators, dildos, and fetish items such as female garments, leather, and rubber items.

Often, materials that are present are not recognized as having a sexual meaning for the victim because they do not appeal sexually to the investigator and are dismissed as inconsequential. All items at the scene and their proximity to the body should be noted and photographed in their original positions for later interpretation. The following case involved such items and, fortunately, was well documented in writing and photographs.

Case #9

The victim, a seventeen-year-old white male, was found partially suspended by the neck (feet touching the floor) by a rope attached to a pipe positioned across an opening to his attic. His body was nude, and his hands were loosely bound behind his back. The police searched the room in which he had died and found an expensive 35-mm camera containing a roll of undeveloped film. The film, developed by the police, depicted the victim in several sexual poses and in one previous asphyxial episode. A photographic negative found in the room documented yet another previous hanging episode and had been altered by the victim by piercings through the nipples. The police also discovered sketches depicting females in poses approximating the victim's position at death and in his previously photographed episodes and showing piercing of the nipples. In searching the attic over the victim's room, the police discovered the following items: six socks that had been cut, several lengths of rope with knots in them, a bicycle tube with a sock tied to it, one pair of black-rubber gloves, several pieces of black bicycle innertube, one pair of blue knee pads, one pair of underwear attached to a T-shirt with silver duct tape and cut from the neck of the shirt to the crotch of the underwear, one 2 × 4, and a segment of 1-inch electrical conduit bent in the middle.

Much of the material documented in Case #9 might have gone unnoticed by an untrained investigator, for the sexual significance of the items is obscure. It is also noteworthy that in Case #9, as in many others in the series, the victim's erotic materials may be in locations other than the immediate scene. Materials found in other cases have included diaries and special-interest publications (see the following). In some instances an overwhelming number of materials is found, as in Case #10, an extremely well-documented case submitted by the Royal Canadian Mounted Police.

Case #10

A fifty-one-year-old single male was discovered suspended by a rope around his neck and attached to a tree limb. His feet were touching the ground. He was attired in normal clothing except that he had on two leather jackets, one of which belonged to a teenage neighbor. The subsequent investigation revealed that he was a homosexual and had sexually solicited the neighbor boy on the day of his death and had been rejected. He was able to talk the young man into leaving his leather jacket overnight.

A search of the victim's residence revealed large quantities of sexual photographs, bondage material, and fetish items. Included in the inventory of items were over 50 leather jackets and coats, ropes, chains, handcuffs, leg irons, a penis vice, scrotum weights, electrical-shock devices, a variety of leather discipline masks and helmets, traffic cones with fecal matter on them, 107 pair of leather gloves of which 29 were determined to have seminal stains inside, a mace with chain and spiked ball, canes, whips, and assorted padlocks.

Props

The investigator should be alert to items located at the scene that may have been used as fantasy props. Items identified as props in this study included mirrors, commercial erotica, photographs, films, and fetish items (discussed in chapter 5).

Mirrors. In eleven cases (ten men and one woman), mirrors had been positioned to allow the victim to view him or herself. Ten of these were asphyxial deaths and one was atypical (see Case #8, chapter 6). Four of the ten men were both cross-dressed and bound.

Commercial Erotica and Special-Interest Publications. The presence of commercial erotica was mentioned in forty-four of the cases. Erotica was either found at the death scene or at the victim's home. Reported titles reflected a diversity of interests and included: *Penthouse, Playboy, Oui, Forum, Hustler, Drummer, Male Lovers, Gay Stud, Boy Friends, Gay Orgy, Bound Beauties, Bondage Beavers, Hog Tie, Knotty, Oralism, Hot Tongues, Hardened Leather,* and *Master and Slave.* One wife volunteered that the bondage magazine found by her husband's body was open to his favorite bondage picture. She said he would replicate to exact detail every knot and tie in the picture (see Case #1, chapter 5). Magazines about women's fashions and hairstyles were also found in the possession of some cross-dressers.

Books found included writings on knot tying, escapology, the occult, witchcraft, transcendentalism, parapsychology, masochism, sadism, and sadomasochism. In the room of one eighteen-year-old college student, an encyclopedia was opened to an entry on telepathy that described how one could transfer feelings of pain to another person through ESP. Also found were marriage manuals and books on human sexuality (for example, *Our Bodies Ourselves, The Sensuous Man, The Sensuous Society, The Rogue*).

Photographs and Films. Photographs found at the death scene included those of the victim as well as those of others. A search of one victim's bedroom (see Case #9) revealed several photos of the victim engaging in various autoerotic activities. Another victim had taken photographs of friends and relatives and superimposed them on nudes in magazines (see Case #13, chapter 6).

In one case (Case #11, chapter 6), a movie projector threaded with a pornographic film was found, indicating that the victim had been watching the film prior to or during his final autoerotic act. One man found bound and hanging, with mirrors arranged such that he could view himself, had been watching an explicitly sexual movie on cable television.

Masturbatory Activity

The victim may or may not have engaged in manual masturbation during the fatal autoerotic activity. The presence of seminal discharge is not a useful clue in determining whether a death is due to sexual misadventure. Seminal discharge frequently occurs at death, irrespective of the cause or manner of death (see chapter 2). The authors have noted that some investigative personnel rely heavily on this single factor as evidence that an autoerotic death has occurred. To be sure, the existence of seminal stains on the victim or nearby surfaces should be noted, photographed, and collected for possible blood-type determination and comparison to the victim, but the mere presence of seminal staining is not evidence of sexual activity.

Manual masturbation may be suggested by finding the victim's hand on or near his genitals, but the investigator should remember that the extremities may twitch or move in the final movements of life. Other indicators of sexual activity include such findings as a dildo or vibrator in or near the body, the penis wrapped in cloth to prevent staining of garments, or exposure of the genitals of a victim who is otherwise dressed. Individuals committing suicide by hanging avoid nudity (except for prisoners). Complete nudity in death by hanging is presumptive evidence of an autoerotic death.

Frequently no direct evidence of manual masturbation exists. Indeed, some living practitioners of autoerotic asphyxia have reported that they did not manually masturbate while asphyxiating themselves but rather used asphyxiation to arouse themselves sexually, after which they would manually masturbate.

Evidence of Previous Experience

Although an important element in understanding what occurred in a particular case is knowledge of the victim's previous experience with the activity that led to his death, surprisingly few of the routine medical or police reports we have seen have addressed the issue of previous experience. We have found five types of information useful in judging the extent of the victim's prior experience: information from relatives and associates, permanently affixed protective padding, suspension-point abrasions, complexity of the injurious agent, and collected materials.

Information from Relatives and Associates

Although family members, sexual partners, and friends sometimes have no awareness of the victim's dangerous autoerotic practices, they may nonetheless have observed behavior that gains meaning in retrospect. One father noted that his son was always tying knots. Another father knew that his son occasionally put a belt around his neck and tightened it until becoming weak.

In another case a victim passed electrical current to his body by wires and a rotisserie (Case #8, chapter 6). Interviews with the parents and siblings of the thirty-year-old victim resulted in a wealth of information that not only indicated similar prior activities but also provided insight into his development. His sister said that their father constantly reminded the deceased to "be a man in everything he did." At age four, he had been spanked repeatedly until he learned how to drive the farm tractor. During his childhood, increasing amounts of responsibility were thrust upon him, and he gradually withdrew from others. When he was twelve, his father suffered a heart attack and he assumed control and operation of the farm. He despised his father and would become quiet or leave when his father approached. A brother said that the victim had been fascinated with fire since the age of nine when "he would stand and stare at the fires and sometimes would cry when watching them." In the twenty-one years preceding the death, the farm experienced six major fires, occurring between midnight and 2:00 A.M., and totalling $65,000 in damages. These fires were attributed to faulty wiring (installed by the victim), an overheated stove, an unexplained explosion, and, in three instances, to unknown causes. Several other fires also occurred that were not reported to the authorities at the time. Each of these was discovered by the victim. In addition, a number of mysterious fires occurred within walking distance of the farm between midnight and 3:00 A.M. Another brother stated that he and the deceased would rig chairs to conduct electrical current and would arrange for each other to sit on the chairs, experiencing minor shocks. The victim also made firebombs and electrical bombs. His parents reported that it was not unusual for him to remain in his locked room for long periods of time. They said that he was an expert in electricity and performed all the electrical work on the farm. They had observed devices similar to the one that caused his death in his room during the preceding four or five years.

In other instances, a relative or associate may be aware of the victim's prior activities. The wife of a twenty-six-year-old victim had discovered her husband suspended from an exercise bar on two occasions prior to the fatal episode. Another wife had known that her husband was in the habit of placing a belt around his neck, attaching it to the bedroom doorknob, and leaning away from the door while masturbating (see Case #3 in chapter 5).

Permanently Affixed Protective Padding

As mentioned previously, the investigator should note protective padding and its placement. One factor indicative of prior practice is the permanent affixing of such padding to ligatures or devices used in the activity. This suggests both that the victim had engaged in similar acts in the past and that he intended to do so in the future. The padding indicates the victim's intent to prevent leaving marks on his body.

Suspension-Point Abrasions

If the victim's death involved the use of ligatures over or around suspension points, the investigator should examine those areas and others like them for abrasions or grooves caused by similar use in the past.

Case #11

A young white male died while suspended from a braided, leather whip that went around his neck and over the top of a closet door. The whip was secured to a wheel and tire on the opposite side of the door. His hands were free, but his ankles were loosely bound with leather thongs. The door top revealed several grooves and abrasions from previous use.

Complexity of the Injurious Agent

When the injurious agent is highly complex, it is likely that the apparatus became complex through repetitive experience and elaboration over time.

Case #12

The victim, a twenty-six-year-old white male, died while suspended by leather wrist restraints from a hook in the ceiling. When found, he was wearing a commercially produced "discipline mask" and had a bit in his mouth. A length of rope was attached to each end of the bit and ran over his shoulders, going through an eyelet at the back of a specially designed belt he was wearing. The pieces of rope ran to eyelets on both sides of the body and were connected to wooden dowels that extended the length of his legs. The ropes were attached to two plastic water bottles, one on each ankle. The bottles were filled with water and each weighed 7 pounds. The victim's ankles had leather restraints about them. A clothespin was affixed to each of the victim's nipples. The victim's belt had a leather device that ran between his buttocks and was attached to the rear and front of the belt. This belt device included a dildo that was inserted in his anus and an aperture through which his penis protruded. His penis was encased in a piece of pantyhose and a toilet-paper cylinder. A small red ribbon was tied in a bow at the base of his penis.

Collected Materials

The type, quantity, complexity, and cost of sexual materials collected by the victim provide indirect evidence of the duration of his activities (see Case #10). While in most instances the victim will be found in close proximity to his collection of sexual materials, the investigator should search other areas known to be under the control of the victim for additional materials.

Investigation of Autoerotic Fatalities 135

Investigative Challenges

Investigating the death of a human being is never easy. The task becomes even more difficult when the manner of death is questionable and there are misgivings about the circumstances in which the victim died. In deaths involving dangerous autoeroticism, the question of whether the death was accidental or intentional is inevitable. Occasionally, however, another aspect presents itself: the possible involvement of a second party. The investigator must satisfy himself about whether another person was involved in the death. The following cases address this issue.

Case #13

Fire-department personnel responded to a residential fire and were directed to a second-floor bedroom where they found the body of a black male lying in bed. His wrists were handcuffed and his ankles were bound with handcuffs; the keyholes of both pairs of handcuffs faced away from his hands. There was a band of material around his neck and the victim wore the remnants of pajamas. Near the body lay a magazine containing photographs of nude women. The body was that of a sixty-one-year-old black male who had lived there with his wife and three sons. At autopsy he was noted to have suffered burns of 80 percent of his body surface, and this was the cause of his death. The manner of death was initially listed as undetermined. The possibility was entertained that he had been engaged in an autoerotic ritual involving bondage and fire, though at the time the body was discovered handcuff keys were not found near the body and the cause of the fire was not immediately discernible. A very thorough investigation ensued, and it was learned from the victim's spouse how this occurred.

On the evening of the fire, the victim and his wife had retired to bed where he initiated sexual contact. They engaged in oral intercourse, but he was unable to achieve orgasm and directed his wife to handcuff his wrists and ankles and to place her nightgown around his mouth as a gag. She then used a towel to flagellate him. Unable to bring about ejaculation, she used a belt, still to no avail. He then moved the nightgown above his mouth and placed a cigar in his mouth. His wife lit it for him and went downstairs to attend to the wash. As she was doing so, the phone rang and she conversed for 15 to 20 minutes. When she returned upstairs to "try to get him to climax," she discovered the fire.

When questioned as to previous similar acts, she replied that her husband had used the handcuffs only once before and that prior to that he had used elastic bandages to secure his wrists and ankles. She also said that during oral intercourse that evening he had been looking at the magazine found near his body. She stated that he was known "to play with himself while watching women on TV or while he was riding in a car" and that "he would have an erection, we would have sex, then he would get up and go to the bathroom and fondle himself until he reached a climax. He would do this every morning and night. He liked for me to put my finger in his rectum. He used to bite me pretty hard on my back and in the area of my rectum and my vagina. On other occasions he has had me tie him to the bed with the elastic bandages, his hands and arms spread eagle, on his back." She went on to say that on previous occasions he had set fire to the bed after falling asleep, but she had never had to call the fire department. The victim's sons reported that they had discovered and played with the handcuffs in the week preceding the death.

Although this death was not due to autoerotic activity (and was not included in the sample), it presented certain factors characteristic of such deaths (for example, bondage and nudity). Thorough investigation proved otherwise. The death was ruled to be accidental, and no charges were lodged against the spouse.

In the following case, the question was somewhat more complex in that the possibilities of accident, suicide, or murder were all salient.

Case #14

A twenty-three-year-old black woman was found dead in her bathroom. The victim's upper torso rested on the edge of the bathtub, her face was in the water, and her knees were on the floor. The faucets were turned on, and water had filled the tub, spilled onto the floor, and run throughout the house. There was vomitus in the tub water. A piece of rope had been doubled, looped around her on the left side of her neck with the loose ends coming across and over her right shoulder. Her wrists were wrapped together in front of her body and the end of the rope securing them rested in her right hand. The decedent was nude, and a 9½-inch bolt was on the floor beside the body. There was a bruise on the left side of her forehead and drops of blood were found on the edge and side of the tub. At autopsy it was learned that the left side of her neck exhibited a superficial incision 3 to 4 inches in length. There was no water found in the lungs, eliminating the possibility of drowning. Aspiration of vomitus was determined to be the cause of death. (See chapter 6, where this case is briefly mentioned, for a discussion of aspiration.)

In the initial stage of the investigation, officers were informed by a relative and a friend of the deceased that she had often talked of suicide and had made statements such as "I wish God would go ahead and take me, I'm tired of living in this world." The relative related that as recently as the previous week, the victim had expressed a desire to die. Her physician said that when he had last seen her, she had complained of being "uptight," and he had prescribed Valium. In the four days preceding her death, she had missed one day of work and had gone home twice complaining of illness.

In this case, the investigator is initially confronted with three possibilities as to the manner of death. There are suicidal indicators: the superficial incision on the left side of her neck suggests a "hesitation mark" as sometimes found in suicides; the statements of a relative and a friend indicating that the victim was depressed and desired to die; the statement attributed to the victim by her physician about being "uptight"; and the fact that she had missed one day of work and had come home early on two other days during the four days prior to her death.

There are also factors in her death that are consistent with sexually related homicide: the fact that she is bound and is found with her face submerged in water; the bruise on her head with blood on the edge of the tub; and the fact that she is nude.

However, there are behavioral and environmental features that contradict suicidal intent. A former fiancé said the victim had never talked of taking her life, and a current boyfriend substantiated this. A close female acquaintance spoke on the telephone with the decedent on the evening prior to her death and noted no indications of depression. Another close friend advised that she knew of no problems the victim was experiencing and that she was typically in a good mood and "bounced back quickly from any depression." This friend could recall no instance in which the deceased had spoken of suicide or of a wish to die. She further stated that she and the victim had made plans for the weekend of the victim's death. Another interview of the physician revealed that the victim had attributed her being "uptight" to the fact that she worked in sales and the post-Christmas rush was overwhelming. Her father, who was vacationing in Hawaii with his wife, said that he had spoken with his daughter three days prior to her death and that everything seemed normal. He said that he and his daughter were quite close and that she frequently discussed her problems with him. He had invited her to accompany his wife and him to Hawaii, but she had declined because she had just begun her job and felt she would be fired if she were absent during the Christmas rush. She had recently purchased a car with a loan that he had cosigned, and she expressed concern that if she were fired, he would have to make the payments. She indicated plans to travel to Hawaii the following summer. It was also learned that the victim had made a dental appointment for the day of her death and had confirmed the appointment on the preceding day. Environmentally, there were factors contradicting suicidal intent: the victim's bedroom was in disarray (for example, her purse was on the floor and the bed was unmade); the television set was on; Christmas tree lights were left on; and the front and rear porchlights were on.

As for homicide, the boyfriend who discovered her body after admitting himself to the residence with a personal key was given and passed a polygraph examination and was able to document his status at the presumed time of death. There were no indications of forced entry to the residence, and nothing was missing. The scene exhibited no signs of a struggle, and the body evidenced no defense wounds or broken nails. As mentioned, the only signs of trauma to the body were the superficial incision on the neck, the bruised forehead, and the marks from the ligature.

A theory that accounts for all of the facts in this case is that the victim had been drawing a bath while asphyxiating herself with the rope, intending to use the bolt for manual masturbation, or already having done so. Through asphyxiation, she lost consciousness, struck her head on the bathtub, and aspirated vomitus. This theory leaves some doubt concerning the superficial incision of the neck, which can only be assumed to have been self-inflicted through a masochistic desire to feel pain. Although it is our opinion that this case represents an accidental autoerotic fatality, it is not possible on the basis of existing information to definitively exclude the less-probable possibility of homicide or the remote possibility of suicide.

Chapter 8 gives in-depth consideration to equivocal cases, along with certain techniques for arriving at an opinion as to the manner of death.

8

Equivocal Deaths: Accident, Suicide, or Homicide?

*Robert R. Hazelwood,
Park Elliott Dietz,* and
Ann Wolbert Burgess

Thus far, we have focused largely on autoerotic fatalities. Autoerotic fatalities, however, are only a subset of the broader class of sexual fatalities, that is, deaths that occur as a result of or in association with sexual activity. Sexual fatalities span a broad range, which also includes deaths due to natural causes during coitus (Ueno 1963; Massie et al. 1969; Trimble 1970; Johnson 1976) or masturbation (Massie et al. 1969; Tomita and Uchida 1972) and lust murder (Podolsky 1965; Hazelwood and Douglas 1980). In the majority of sexual fatalities, manner of death can be ascertained with a high degree of certainty through customary investigative techniques, assuming that the personnel involved are knowledgeable and experienced with these cases. In a small proportion of cases, however, manner of death is more elusive, making it difficult to determine whether an autoerotic fatality has occurred.

Knowing of our research on autoerotic fatalities and work with other types of sexual fatalities, investigative agencies have submitted equivocal deaths to us for evaluation and have solicited opinions as to the manner of death and/or the possibility of second-party involvement. In each instance, the requesting agency provided well-documented reports including photographs, autopsy findings, and information about the victim's history.

The most frequent question that arises in the investigation of sexual fatalities is whether an individual who was alone committed suicide or died accidentally. Less often, the question posed is whether another person had been present, and if so, whether the death was intended or not. These questions involve complex issues of fact, behavior, and intent and are not always answerable. Opinions should not be rendered in such cases without detailed information about both the death scene and the victim's history.

Adapted from: Sexual fatalities: Behavioral reconstruction in equivocal cases. *Journal of Forensic Sciences* 27:763–773, October 1982. Copyright American Society for Testing and Materials, 1916 Race Street, Philadelphia, Penn. 19103. Reprinted with permission.

In this chapter, we present several cases that were submitted for an opinion. The reader will note that as the chapter progresses, the complexity of the cases increases. Cases #1 to 4 revolved around the question of whether the death was an accident or a suicide, and Cases #5 to 7, in which evidence suggested or indicated the presence of a second party, added the possibility of murder.

Accident or Suicide?

Case #1

A forty-three-year-old married man was discovered dead by his wife when she returned home from work and found the residence locked. He was partially suspended by a leather belt fastened around his neck and secured over the top of the closed bedroom door. He was attired in white panties, pantyhose, a bra containing water-filled balloons, slip, sweater, skirt, calf-length boots, earrings, and feminine wig. His wrists were loosely bound with a terrycloth towel, and separate belts secured his ankles and thighs. The hair had been shaved from his arms and legs. Tape held his penis against his scrotum and between his legs.

Analysis of Case #1

This case exhibits several of the characteristics commonly found in accidental asphyxial autoerotic deaths and would present little difficulty for an investigator educated or experienced in the subject.

The decedent wore female clothing, and additional feminine garments were found among his possessions. Cross-dressing, complete or partial, was the most common costume observed in the study. The victim had used a belt to suspend himself. The overwhelming majority of such deaths are caused by a ligature encompassing the neck. Also to be noted is the fact that the suspension point (the top of the door) was within reach of the deceased, a common characteristic in asphyxial autoerotic deaths. The additional elements of bondage (restraint of his wrists and ankles and binding of his penis) serve to create the illusion of helplessness and contribute to the realism of a masochistic fantasy. Such bondage (apart from the asphyxial mechanism) is also common among autoerotic fatalities.

Typically, there was no eyewitness confirmation of the victim's participation in autoerotic asphyxia. Of the cases studied, fewer than 10 percent documented that family members or friends knew of the victim's autoerotic practices prior to the death. In this case, inspection of the upper edge of the bedroom door revealed several indentations suggesting its prior use as a suspension point.

The victim's wife reported no knowledge of neck-compression activities, but she did know that her husband had been cross-dressing for eighteen years. She said that prior to a door being installed in their bedroom, he had practiced transvestism in the attic. In the three months preceding his death, he had accepted his paraphilia and had begun shaving his arms and legs, had his earlobes pierced, and wore feminine attire in her presence. A photograph of him wearing female clothing was also found. His transvestism is related to his use of tape to hold his penis between his legs, allowing him to more closely resemble a woman. His wife did not object to his transvestite practices and reported that he had seemed happier than ever before. The fact that the victim was in good spirits is important in that this is characteristic of individuals who die in this manner.

Case #2

A thirty-year-old married man had been left alone for three hours while his wife, who was eight months' pregnant, and their two children went to a church-related activity. Upon her return, she discovered him dead in an upstairs bedroom that he was converting to a nursery. The victim was suspended from a rope that encompassed his neck and was attached to a pulley. A second rope passed over the pulley and ended in his left hand. The pulley was hooked to a metal bar which extended between two beams in the roof. His feet were touching the floor, his pants were around his ankles, his underwear was semen-stained in front, and his shirt had been rolled up to expose his chest. The cause of death, as determined by the medical examiner, was asphyxiation due to hanging. The victim was described as having been in excellent spirits, eagerly anticipating the birth of his third child. He was also elated over the fact that he had successfully followed a diet-and-exercise program, resulting in a 40-pound weight loss.

Analysis of Case #2

This case was submitted for opinion by the attorney for the executrix of the deceased's estate. His widow was involved in litigation with her husband's insurance company concerning the accidental-death-benefits clause of his life-insurance policy (see chapter 9).

The evidence in this case is consistent with accidental death. The victim used a pulley apparatus with two ropes. One rope went over the pulley and attached to his neck with a hangman's noose; the second rope served a control or braking function. By maintaining pressure on a braking rope, he could prevent the pulley from turning. This in turn would allow the noose to compress his neck and alter the flow of blood to his brain, producing a transient hypoxia, the extent of which he could control, at least while conscious. He could then loosen the ligature by allowing the control rope to slip or, should he lose consciousness, the control rope would slip from his grasp, automatically slackening the rope attached to his neck: a dead man's release. On this occasion, one rope had slipped off the track and jammed the pulley, preventing its rotation and resulting in his body weight being suspended from the rope, thereby causing his death.

The victim hid this sexual activity from his family and friends. At the time he died, his family had been at church, and he had removed the telephone from its cradle to prevent calls from interrupting his autoerotic ritual. The condition of his clothing is indicative of masturbatory activity.

The hangman's noose used for the ligature had symbolic value to the victim, who probably had an execution fantasy. His history also suggested a fascination with bondage activities in that he collected handcuffs, ropes, and locks and was very knowledgeable about the various types of knots.

The complexity of the apparatus he used strongly suggests prior practice. Rather than simply hanging himself, he used a sophisticated pulley system as part of his autoerotic ritual. On prior occasions, he was apparently able to engage in this activity without serious consequences.

The victim was described as being in excellent spirits, oriented toward the future, enjoying good physical health, and being interested in his work and family. His recent weight reduction was said to have improved his self-image. There were no precipitating stresses identified and no history of psychiatric disorder. His wife reported their life together as being at its highest point, with good prospects both financially and personally. If he had intended suicide, he would not have required an elaborate pulley system to achieve this aim.

Case #3

A thirty-three-year-old man was discovered dead in an unfinished room on the second floor of a warehouse where he was employed as a security guard at night. He was in an upright position with his feet on the floor. A rope attached to a wall behind him passed over a beam approximately 6 feet above him and ended in a hangman's noose which encircled his neck. He was nude except for a black, leather belt around his waist and a pair of handcuffs which were passed through the belt and secured his wrists in front. A handcuff key was found in his right hand, and his left hand held his penis. Around his left ankle was a shipping tag secured by wire, and on the tag was the notation, "77–0130 5/11/77." About the circumference of his penis was a surgical-like incision which accommodated a washer. Beneath him, two cinderblocks rested on newspapers. A cigarette butt of the type smoked by the victim was located 1½ feet in front of him. Against a wall, to the rear of the victim and neatly stacked, were a pair of men's trousers, a shirt, and a pair of ankle boots. His service revolver and holster were also in the room. The large room was otherwise empty, with barren, cinderblock walls.

The victim's automobile was parked outside the warehouse. Its interior was in disarray and contained several empty cans, snack cartons, and wrappers, and several magazines, including Forum and Oui.

He had made a career as a peace officer and worked in this capacity during the day. Five days after discovery of the body, a box containing his badge, credentials, undershorts, and uniform was found behind some boxes on the floor below the death scene.

He had lived in a one-bedroom efficiency apartment, a search of which revealed bondage magazines. Although not unkempt, there had been no attempt to tidy up the apartment (for example, there were dirty dishes in the sink).

He sometimes stayed with his wife of ten years, from whom he had been separated for six months. On the evening preceding his death, he had visited his wife and made arrangements to take their son (with whom he enjoyed a very close relationship) to the zoo the next day. According to his wife, he had appeared to be in normal spirits during the visit. His wife was the beneficiary of his life-insurance policy.

In the hours preceding his death, he had called a female acquaintance at 1:30 A.M. and again at 4:30 A.M., requesting that she visit him at the warehouse, but she had refused.

At the time of his death, he was experiencing financial difficulties, was working at a second job, and was said to have been occupationally dissatisfied. His co-workers described him as having changed from a relatively outgoing individual to one who seemed depressed and overworked (he worked an excessive amount of overtime to obtain additional salary). On at least two occasions during the week preceding his death, he had made suicidal statements, for example, "I ought to put a .38 in my mouth," and "I can understand why someone would kill themselves."

His wife said that approximately two years previously he had begun practicing sexual bondage at home and had requested that she tie him *up and whip him and that she allow him to reciprocate. She said that she had declined to participate.*

Analysis of Case #3

This case presents the examiner with multiple contradictory features. The death scene had many features commonly found in autoerotic fatalities: secluded location, nontotal suspension, bondage, the use of a hangman's noose, nudity, and the presence of ejaculate. When further investigation uncovered the victim's history, however, manner of death became uncertain because indicators of suicide were also present.

The victim had experienced some of the stressors and exhibited some of the behaviors commonly found among persons with suicidal intent. He was experiencing marital, financial, and occupational problems; his co-workers described him as being overworked and depressed; he had been rejected by his female acquaintance on two occasions on the very morning of his death; his possessions had been neatly placed at the scene; and he had made two suicidal statements in the week preceding his death. These are highly suggestive that the victim intended to end his life.

We believe, however, that the victim did not intend to die on this occasion but expired accidentally during autoerotic activity. This opinion was derived through several considerations.

The victim's interest and involvement in sexual bondage and sadomasochistic activities are well documented by his wife's verification of his interest in bondage and flagellation for at least two years before his death. Bondage materials were found in his apartment, and at the time of his death he was handcuffed and held the key in his right hand. Handcuffs are a common bondage device, and the key serves as a self release mechanism. The washer fixed around his penis is a masochistic feature. At the time of death, he was totally nude except for the belt and was holding his penis in his left hand. While nudity is consistent with autoerotic fatalities, it is rare in suicides among nonprisoners. The black, leather belt suggests symbolic bondage or a leather fetish.

Had he intended to take his life by hanging, it would not have been necessary to fashion so exotic a ligature as a hangman's noose; a simple loop would have sufficed. Having previously stated, "I ought to put a .38 in my mouth," he might have used his .38 revolver, which was found in the room where he died. It is probable that he kept the weapon in close proximity in the event someone entered the building. Had he intended to die by hanging, he would have had no need for this weapon. He had affixed a tag to his ankle. While it may be argued that the numerals "0130" represent the time (in military hours) of the first call to his friend, there are thirteen wraps in a hangman's noose, and the middle digits in the notation are also 13. In our opinion, the tag was a prop used by the victim in his ritualistic fantasy (see the following). In our opinion, if he had intended to die, he would not have hidden his uniform and identification but would have placed them where they could readily be found.

Typically, a person with suicidal intent makes plans for death but not plans for the future. In this instance, the victim visited his son on the evening preceding his death and arranged to take him to the zoo the following day. The victim's automobile and residence were extremely cluttered and contained sexual materials and bondage paraphernalia. It is unlikely that an individual would intend for such materials to be found.

Despite his separation from his wife, he had made no changes in the beneficiary of his life-insurance policy. Considering the close father-son relationship, it seems likely that if he had planned to die, he would have taken steps to ensure that his preadolescent son would be financially secure.

Our reconstruction of the death scenario is that the victim was acting out an execution fantasy when he accidentally expired (such fantasies are not uncommon and are documented in several cases in our study). This is evidenced by the hangman's noose, the secured wrists, the body tag on the ankle, and the cigarette butt immediately in front of him, representing "the last smoke."

Case #4

A twenty-seven-year-old white man had been living for three years in a common-law situation with a woman two years his junior. On the day of his death, she had left him alone in their home while she went shopping. On her return, she went to the kitchen to put away her purchases and found a hand-written note on the kitchen table: "Sharon, the obvious solution to the problem finds me hanging in the bathroom. But it won't be so awful cause in my own kinky way I'll have enjoyed the method of my demise (as will be evident by the unusual attire). Loved you. Sorry. Bill." On reading the note, the woman at first thought it was a joke and went to the bathroom. When she attempted to open the door, she found it blocked by the victim's body. After forcing the door open, she found him partially suspended by a ligature around his neck. He was clad in a pink sweater, pantyhose, panties, a brassiere, and high-heeled boots, all of which belonged to her.

She denied any knowledge of his desire to cross-dress and reported that she had never had any reason to suspect transvestism. She said they had had a normal sexual relationship for three years, during which he had never suggested sexual bondage or asphyxiation. The paper on which the note was written had deep and worn creases, suggesting that it had been repeatedly folded, opened, and refolded.

Analysis of Case #4

The facts that the victim acted alone, was not totally suspended, and was cross-dressed indicated that his death was an autoerotic fatality. In labeling his own behavior kinky, he indicated his awareness of the deviant nature of this sexual activity. In stating that he would enjoy the hanging, he reveals that he previously had similar experiences and found them pleasurable. These facts create a strong presumption that his death was accidental.

This presumption is overcome by the fact that the content of his note clearly implies suicidal intent. The investigating authorities properly ruled this death as a suicide. Nonetheless, the fact that the note appeared to have been repeatedly folded creates a question as to whether he may have used this note repeatedly as a prop for a suicide fantasy or as a farewell to his lover in the event he should die during a self-hanging episode. In any event, his note indicates that he was aware that his self-hanging created a substantial risk of death.

A Question of Murder

Case #5

A twenty-two-year-old single woman was discovered dead by her sister, who had been staying with the victim temporarily. The sister had been away for two days and returned on a Sunday at 9:00 P.M. to discover a note on the front door requesting that she be as quiet as possible as a man was sleeping on the kitchen floor. She went directly to her bedroom and did not discover the victim until the following morning.

The deceased was found in an arched position with an electrical cord attached to her neck by a slip knot, passing over a doorknob, and wrapped around her ankles. Her abdomen, thighs, and forearms rested on the floor, and her feet were pulled back toward her head. The right side of her head was against the door's edge, and her hair was entangled in the slip knot. She was clothed only in a blouse that she normally wore for sleeping. Commercial lubrication cream was found in the victim's vagina, and a battery-operated vibrator was found 4 feet from her body. The only trauma exhibited was a 1½-inch contusion above and behind her right ear. The scene was not disturbed, and there was no sign of a struggle. On her bed were a series of drafted letters she had written in response to an advertisement seeking a possible sexual liaison.

Autopsy revealed no evidence of recent intercourse, and no alcohol or other drugs were detected in the body. The cause of death was determined to be asphyxia due to laryngeal compression.

The victim had been in excellent physical condition, had made plans for a canoe trip on the day following her death, and had recently been in good spirits. She was sexually active but was reportedly disappointed in her sexual relationships as she had difficulty attaining orgasm. She used contraceptive cream and a diaphragm to prevent pregnancy, and these items were located in her car. Although her sister found the note at 9:00 P.M. Sunday, a neighbor reported having seen the note early that morning. (Also reported as Case #4, chapter 7.)

Analysis of Case #5

The victim's position illustrates features found in a number of autoerotic asphyxias, including interconnection of the neck with the limbs and the arching and binding of the body. Her state of undress and the presence of lubrication cream and a battery-operated vibrator indicate sexual activity.

A critical element in the resolution of this case was the fact that examination of the slip knot (self-rescue mechanism) revealed that the victim's hair was entangled in it and would have precluded its release. This observation, coupled with the contusion above her right ear and the fact that her head was adjacent to the door's edge, suggests that the victim attempted to disengage the ligature by pulling the slip knot. Not being able to do so, she thrashed about, striking her head on the edge of the door, thereby causing the contusion. The autopsy surgeon reported that the contusion would have been insufficient to render her unconscious and that it is not likely that the victim could have been forced into such a position without being unconscious or leaving evidence of a defensive struggle.

The question of the note on the door was never resolved. Its presence since early Sunday morning suggests that a male visitor had been there on Saturday evening. The victim's drafted letters to a male, whom she had not yet met, further suggest that she was alone at the time of her death as it is unlikely that she would have had such letters on her bed had she been entertaining a male friend there. The death was officially ruled accidental, and the matter was closed.

Case #6

A thirty-year-old single woman was found dead in her locked apartment. She was nude and lying supine on a blanket on the bedroom floor. A pillow beneath her buttocks elevated them. Her legs were slightly spread, and her arms were by her sides. A blouse was lodged in her mouth and covered her face. Next to the body was a dental plate belonging to the victim. Near her left foot were an empty beer can, an ashtray, and a drinking glass. Neither the body nor the scene exhibited signs of a struggle. The victim's clothes and purse (containing her keys) were on her bed. A vibrator and leather-bondage materials were found in her closet. The door was locked with a spring bolt. The autopsy report indicated that she had choked to death.

Analysis of Case #6

While the body condition was consistent with either masturbation or sexual activity with a partner, the victim's sexual paraphernalia were found in her closet, not near her body. The leather-bondage items in the closet suggest previous sexual bondage activity. Although we are familiar with several confirmed autoerotic fatalities involving mechanical airway obstruction, none involves the insertion of a gag to such a depth in the oropharynx. Consultation with forensic pathologists confirmed our suspicions that it would be next to impossible for one to asphyxiate oneself in such a manner. Although the door was locked and the victim's keys were in her purse, the lock was spring-activated and would have locked on closing. The victim's willing participation is suggested but not proved by the absence of defense injuries, signs of a struggle, or alcohol or drugs in her body. In sexual acts involving bondage or manual restraint between consenting partners, one partner depends on the other for release, thereby allowing that person wide latitude in the act. We concluded that the death occurred during sexual activity that included use of the gag and at least one other person. It is not possible to determine whether the other person(s) intended to kill the victim. Thus in our opinion the manner of death was homicide, but we are unable to determine whether this was murder or manslaughter.

Case #7

A sixty-five-year-old single man was found dead in his one-bedroom apartment, while his stereo blasted hard-rock music.

His abdomen was in contact with the floor next to the bed, and his arms were pulled onto the bed behind him. His wrists were tied with a short length of rope. A black, leather belt tied to a telephone cord extended from his wrists to the bed headboard. The belt was too small to have been worn by the victim, and three additional belts of varying sizes were also found in the room. The telephone cord had been pulled from the wall.

The victim's feet were tied to the footboard by another piece of rope. He wore only an undershirt and an athletic supporter. A jacket covered his head, which was lying on a dresser drawer. Beneath the jacket, two knit shirts were wrapped around his head, and a white T-shirt, which had been used as a gag, was tied tightly around his head.

Resting on an air conditioner above the victim's headboard was Penthouse *magazine, opened to a page depicting two women fondling one another. The room had been ransacked, and some personal items (for example, his watch and some clothes) were missing, though expensive stereo equipment and over $600 in cash were found in the room. He had a collection of tapes of classical music, and his friends confirmed that he preferred such music.*

He had been seeking information on homosexuality, and examination of a homosexual pornographic magazine found in his bedroom revealed his fingerprints on the corona of a penis pictured in the magazine as well as several smudged prints on other penises in the book.

He had a history of heart disease, and his death was attributed to airway obstruction and coronary thrombosis. During the autopsy, the victim's anus was found to be enlarged, a condition commonly present in individuals who repeatedly act as the receptive partner in anal intercourse. As noted by the medical examiner, however, this is also common in nonhomosexual individuals of the victim's age.

Analysis of Case #7

The question in this instance was whether the deceased had been murdered or had died while engaging in sexual bondage activities, either alone or with another person. The complexity and tightness of the bindings were such as to have precluded his being able to tie them himself. The fact that the telephone cord had been torn from the wall strongly suggests the presence of a second person, as it is unlikely that an individual would disable his own telephone to obtain bondage materials. The T-shirt used to gag the victim was tied so tightly that it caused the victim's lower jaw to recede far behind the upper jaw. These observations, coupled with the fact that his radio was tuned to a hard-rock station, though he preferred classical music, leave little doubt that a second party was present when he died.

As mentioned, the room had been ransacked, but valuables were left undisturbed. Drawers were pulled out, tables overturned, and the scene littered with clothing. Even though the victim was bound and gagged, two shirts and a jacket had been placed over his head unnecessarily.

In our opinion, the victim had brought a person to his room for the purpose of engaging in sexual bondage activities. He was lying supine on the bed, allowing himself to be bound at the wrists and ankles with the small lengths of rope and to be gagged with the T-shirt. He suffered a heart attack, and his partner, thinking him dead, panicked and attempted to make it appear to be a robbery by ransacking the apartment. The dresser drawer beneath the victim's head indicates that the room had been ransacked while the victim was still on the bed. Frightened, remorseful, and unable to look at the victim's face, his partner wrapped the shirts around the victim's head. After the unidentified person left the room, the victim began struggling against his bonds and rolled off the bed.

After arriving at this conclusion, Robert Hazelwood provided the requesting agency with a criminal-personality profile of the unidentified sexual partner.

> The offender is a Hispanic male between the ages of nineteen and twenty-five years. He is a high-school dropout and is either unemployed or employed in a menial job requiring little or no contact with the public. It is believed that the subject was associated with the victim in some capacity. While having little education, he has average or better social intelligence. He frequents adult bookstores, purchasing heterosexually oriented bondage literature. At the time of the offense, he resided alone or with his family and lived within walking distance of the scene. He is from an upper-lower socioeconomic environment and has either moved or joined the military since the death. He would be described by friends and family as a quiet, passive type of person who is an "underachiever." It is possible that he has a history of juvenile offenses. He is single and his social life is restricted to a few male friends.

The police later developed a suspect who was a twenty-year-old Hispanic male who had resided with his family within three blocks of the death scene. He knew the victim and had joined the military shortly after the victim's death. The young man had gone AWOL and had sent a letter to his commanding officer advising that he was contemplating suicide and had been depressed for the "last three months." The letter was written in April. The victim had died in January. Although we believe the victim's death was unintended and that this is a case of manslaughter, we cannot be certain that it was not murder.

Discussion

Suicidal sexual fatalities are extremely rare. To our knowledge, the only unequivocal autoerotic suicide case that has been published is Case B in the paper by Litman and Swearingen (1972). Knight (1979) records a case with a suicide note which, like the preceding Case #4, compels the conclusion that the death was an intentional suicide. Our own case files include only one unequivocal sexual suicide, and that case involved a partner who assisted the man's suicide at his direction and was therefore not autoerotic in the strictest sense (though her sexual arousal was not an issue and she did leave him alone to die, as he requested).

We believe there should be a strong presumption that the manner of death in an autoerotic fatality is accident. This view contrasts sharply with that of Richardson and Breyfogle (1946) who wrote that mere proof of hanging should overcome the legal presumption against suicide, should eliminate the need for proof of motive, and should "cast the burden of going forward with the evidence upon the party claiming that death was accidental." In our view, if a hanging is accompanied by clear indications of sexual activity (not merely the presence of ejaculate), it should be presumed accidental in the absence of evidence to the contrary. This is not to say that the decedent was unaware of the risk, for there is a substantial body of opinion and some very suggestive evidence that those who engage in autoerotic asphyxia are indeed aware of the risk to their lives. A better way to pose the question is whether their knowledge of the risk should be viewed as similar to that of motorcyclists who ride without helmets, skydivers, men who habitually inject heroin, or men who play Russian roulette. As shown in chapter 9, medicolegal determination of the manner of death as accidental is not determinative of the payment of accidental-death benefits, for which purpose policy language and applicable law are important.

Cases #1 to 4 illustrate many pertinent factors in considering whether an autoerotic fatality might be a suicide. A suicide note in the handwriting of the decedent, left where it would certainly be found, is the best single indicator that an autoerotic fatality was suicidal. Yet even when this is present, as in Case #4, one must consider whether the note is a prop for a suicide fantasy that has been enacted repeatedly.

As illustrated by Cases #5 and 6, behavioral reconstruction is complicated considerably when there is suggestive but inconclusive evidence of the presence of a second party. Case #5 apparently did not involve a second party, despite preliminary indications to the contrary. Cases #6 and 7 probably represent an unusual group of sexual-manslaughter cases.

Usher (1975) mentions an English case in which a prostitute was suffocated with a pillow by a client who subsequently said that he frequently used suffocation as foreplay. A woman he had picked up shortly before the prostitute's death confirmed this by saying that he had almost suffocated her. Usher refers to the death as a murder but does not indicate how manslaughter was ruled out. Case #6 may be analogous to the one Usher mentions, though the victim's possession of bondage equipment and the indications that she was a willing participant weight the evidence toward unintended death.

Two of the earliest documented fatalities from sexual asphyxia—those of the musician Kotzwarra in London in 1791 and that of the Reverend Parson Manacle of Newgate Prison—involved second persons (discussed in chapter 2). We think it likely that Case #7 is analogous to the cases of Kotzwarra and Reverend Manacle in two respects: (1) the decedent probably requested bondage and asphyxia for his sexual pleasure, and (2) it is unlikely that either the decedent or his partner intended his death.

The possibility remains, however, that Cases #6 or 7, or both, were in fact murders in the course of sexual activity. In addition to the evidence set forth in the case analyses, it should be noted that asphyxia, although a frequent mechanism in sexual murders, is far more often accomplished in murders through manual or ligature strangulation or through suffocation with an external object (such as a pillow) than through the use of gag materials.

A novelist with forensic-science experience, P.D. James (1972), has written a fictional account of a murder camouflaged as an autoerotic fatality and subsequently altered to appear like a suicide. A colleague has told us of one case in which a murder is believed to have been committed by a police officer who attempted to conceal it as an autoerotic fatality but neglected to arrange an escape mechanism. The case reported by Wright and Davis (1976), in which two prostitutes left an intoxicated client tied up after robbing him, resembled an autoerotic asphyxia in a few respects but did not appear to have been intentionally camouflaged.

Conclusions

In the United States, sexual murders outnumber autoerotic fatalities, which in turn outnumber cases of sexual manslaughter. Even for the most experienced medical examiners and law-enforcement investigators, a small number of these deaths remain equivocal after all efforts at resolution. In the preceding examples we have attempted to illustrate the importance of careful investigation (a subject developed at greater length in chapter 7) and detailed behavioral analysis and reconstruction in resolving equivocal sexual fatalities. The practical importance of these distinctions lies in the responses of family members and friends to sexual fatalities, in the life-insurance benefits that may in some instances be awarded according to the certified manner of death (Curvey 1974) and legal presumptions of intent (chapter 9), and in the potential prosecution of living persons in possible homicides.

We are familiar with several fatalities during sexual bondage between partners in which subsequent information from the partner facilitated the determination with reasonable certainty that the death constituted murder, manslaughter, or suicide. In the absence of such an informant, however, the intent of the deceased or of a missing partner can only be inferred from their behavior. Postmortem behavioral analysis requires not only historical information about the victim elicited through interviews with third parties, such as mates, co-workers, and acquaintances, as others have shown (Litman et al. 1963) but also detailed knowledge of the physical evidence from the scene and elsewhere, including those locations where the victim's personal possessions are kept.

The caseload of sexual fatalities in a jurisdiction is likely to be considerably lower than the caseload of vehicular, gunshot, poisoning, drowning, and other deaths. For this reason most investigators, regardless of discipline, do not have the opportunity to acquire experience with many sexual fatalities in the course of their careers. Yet even where the best-equipped laboratories and interdisciplinary teams are available, final determination of the intent of the participants remains a matter of judgment. Whether the legal authority to render such judgment rests with a law-enforcement officer, a medical examiner, a coroner, a coroner's jury, or a court, a small proportion of sexual fatalities involves misleading or ambiguous clues. For these equivocal cases, we recommend consultation with specialists who have experience in both sexual fatalities and postmortem behavioral analysis. In such cases, consultation is most useful when sought early in the investigation so that investigative leads can be pursued before evidence is altered or destroyed and before memories are lost, blurred, or otherwise become inaccessible.

9

Judicial Decisions Regarding Insurance Benefits in Autoerotic Fatalities

Park Elliott Dietz and
Robert R. Hazelwood

Many of the physicians who have written about autoerotic fatalities have ventured opinions as to whether a specific death was an accident or a suicide or as to which of these manner of death categories the class as a whole ought to be assigned. These authors generally have not provided a detailed analysis of their reasoning so their many opinions will not be reviewed here (see chapter 2 for references to these writings).

Today, forensic pathologists are unanimous in their opinion that such deaths should be classified as accidents (see the survey by Curvey, 1974, described in chapter 2). For example, pathologists in the United States have written that "the manner of death is *always* accidental, unless absolutely proven otherwise" (Chapman and Matthews 1970) and that in recent years "there has been general agreement that these deaths are accidental" (Rupp 1980).

In contrast, psychiatrists in the United States, emphasizing unconscious dynamics and evidence for depression in some of the few individuals engaging in autoerotic asphyxia who had been interviewed by psychiatrists (see chapter 2), have written that "Bondage can be fatal, a mix of suicide and accident" (Litman and Swearingen 1972) and that "it would seem appropriate to consider this a suicidal syndrome of life threatening behavior, involving erotization of dying brought about in order to escape overwhelming anxiety, rather than 'accidental death' " (Resnik 1972).

Such general opinions as these should not determine the medicolegal ruling of manner of death in an individual case, regardless of the view one adopts. Rather, careful investigation (see chapter 7) and behavioral reconstruction (see chapter 8) must form the basis of opinion in each case.

The varied and still-unstandardized techniques known as the psychological autopsy (see generally Farberow and Shneidman 1961; Litman et al. 1963; Tabachnick et al. 1966), the psychiatric autopsy (Bendheim 1979), and behavioral reconstruction (Hazelwood et al. 1982) all involve efforts to deduce the behavioral elements of an event in the absence of the critical informant. Courts are said to be admitting opinion evidence based on such techniques with increasing frequency in both civil and criminal cases (Lichter 1981; Dregne 1982). Despite this fact, and despite the consistency with which autoerotic fatalities are now ruled accidental by medical examiners and coroners, accidental-death benefits are not always paid to seemingly eligible beneficiaries.

Decisions regarding the payment of death benefits on insurance policies initially are made by the insurance companies themselves. Only in contested cases do these decisions fall within the purview of the courts. The opinions of public officials charged with the responsibility of investigating death and certifying the cause and manner of death, though sometimes accorded weight, are not determinative of the payment of death benefits. (For general information on insurance law, see Keeton 1977.)

Each of the authors has provided consultation in a disputed-death-benefits claim in which the beneficiary of a life-insurance policy contested the insurer's payment of benefits. From these and kindred experiences, we know that the judicial determination of facts may be substantially different from the scientific determination of facts in method, evidentiary concerns, and conclusion. This is more than amply demonstrated in the judicial opinions reprinted in this chapter. In each case, death was certified as accidental in manner, yet the insurer did not honor the accidental-death-benefits clause of the decedent's life-insurance policy. One case was litigated at a state court, the others in federal courts. Each court opinion[a] is followed by an analysis of the judicial opinion in light of the findings set forth in the preceding chapters.

Runge v. Metropolitan Life Ins. Co.[b]

CRAVEN, Circuit Judge.

This is a suit on double indemnity clauses of two insurance policies. On the date of his death, plaintiff's husband, Wilbur L. Runge, Jr., was insured by Metropolitan under two policies with a total face value of $19,000. Metropolitan paid the face amounts but declined to pay double on plaintiff's contention that death resulted from injuries sustained "solely

---

[a]In the tradition of legal casebooks, the decisions are reprinted without quotation marks. They were authored by the Courts and are in the public domain. The Comment section following each case is, of course, ours. Ellipses either indicate the site of deletions within a paragraph or were part of the original opinion. Other text deletions are indicated with three asterisks, except for deleted citations, which, like deleted footnotes, are not indicated.

[b]537 F. 2d 1157 (4th Cir. 1976).

through violent, external and accidental means" within the meaning of the double indemnity clauses of the policies. The district court entered summary judgment in favor of Metropolitan. We affirm.

Sandra Trusty Runge is the widow of Wilbur L. Runge, Jr., and is the beneficiary named in both policies issued by Metropolitan. Runge died under very bizarre circumstances. Briefly stated, Runge hung himself in the course of engaging, as the district court found:

> [I]n an unusual autoerotic practice in which he was seeking to heighten the experience of masturbation by stimulation of certain nerve centers in the brain through the asphyxial process. The decedent had tied the electrical extension cord in such a fashion that when hanging from it the balls of his feet would rest on the floor, and by standing on his toes he would be able to vary the pressure on his neck. The decedent placed the noose formed in the electrical cord around his neck and stepped from the chair or the stool to the floor, and then proceeded to masturbate. At the time he reached orgasm the asphyxia was accentuated to the degree that the decedent lost consciousness, his body relaxed, and he was hanged to death.

It is agreed that the insured's death was not suicide, that he was not murdered, and that he did not die of natural causes. Metropolitan has stipulated that the insured's death was "violent" and "external" within the meaning of the double indemnity clauses, but denies that death resulted from "accidental means." Thus the sole issue is whether or not Runge died by "accidental means." We are inclined to think he did not—as that phrase has been construed by the Virginia Supreme Court.

In *Smith v. Combined Insurance Co. of America,* 202 Va. 758, 120 S.E. 2d 267 (1961), the insured was a fugitive who had taken refuge in a barn. The deceased fired upon law enforcement officers and seriously wounded at least one policeman. After refusing to surrender, tear gas grenades accidentally set the barn on fire, and the deceased was burned to death. In denying recovery upon the deceased's accidental death policy, the Virginia Supreme Court held that:

> Where the policy insures against loss of life through accidental means, the principle seems generally upheld that if the death of the insured, although in a sense unforeseen and unexpected, results directly from the insured's voluntary act and aggressive misconduct, or where the insured culpably provokes the act which causes the injury and death, it is not death by accidental means, even though the result may be such as to constitute an accidental injury.

202 Va. at 761, 120 S.E. 2d at 269.

In this case, the court concluded, the insured had "voluntarily put himself in a position where he knew or should have known that death or serious bodily injury would be the probable consequence of his acts. In such a situation his death was not effected by an 'accident' within the meaning of the policy." 202 Va. at 762, 120 S.E. 2d at 269.

In *Wooden* v. *John Hancock Mutual Life Insurance Co.*, 205 Va. 750, 139 S.E. 2d 801 (1965), the deceased insured provoked an argument with another which precipitated a struggle for a pistol. During the struggle, the gun discharged accidentally, and the insured was shot to death. Again, the Virginia Supreme Court ruled that the death had not been the result of "accidental means." The court noted:

> [D]eath or injury does not result from accident or accidental means within the terms of an accident policy where it is the natural result of the insured's voluntary act, unaccompanied by anything unforeseen except the death or injury. . . . In accord with this principle it is generally held that if the insured voluntarily provokes or is the aggressor in an encounter, and knows, or under the circumstances should reasonably anticipate, that he will be in danger of death or great bodily harm as the natural or probable consequence of his act or course of action, his death or injury is not caused by an accident within the meaning of such a policy.

205 Va. at 755, 139 S.E. 2d at 804-05.

On the basis of the district court's findings of fact, which are supported by the record and are not clearly erroneous, we hold that Wilbur L. Runge, Jr., did not die as a result of "accidental means." Runge deliberately placed his neck into a noose which he himself had designed and constructed, having first locked the doors to his house to prevent intrusion, and at a time when interruption was unlikely. He then intentionally and deliberately self-induced asphyxia by hanging himself in the noose, lost consciousness, and died. Death, under these circumstances, was a natural and foreseeable, though unintended, consequence of Runge's activity. The decision of the district court will be
AFFIRMED.

Comment

Runge is apparently the first reported judicial opinion on the payment of accidental-death benefits for an autoerotic fatality. In neither *Runge* nor subsequent cases did any party argue that death was natural or the result of suicide or homicide. Nonetheless, dispute centers on whether the death was accidental within the meaning of the insurance agreement and applicable law.

In *Runge,* the court focused solely on the issues of whether death had resulted from "accidental means" (a key phrase in the insurance policy) and drew upon two Virginia cases for precedent in the interpretation of this phrase. One quoted passage of the *Smith* opinion spoke of death resulting "from the insured's voluntary act and aggressive misconduct" as an exclusion from the meaning of accidental death. Although Runge's death clearly resulted from his voluntary acts, it is arguable whether he was engaging in "aggressive misconduct." With respect to the word *aggressive,* one side of the argument would be that the usual and ordinary meaning of aggression is limited to outwardly directed attacks. On the other side, the argument would be that all self-injurious behavior represents aggression turned inward. Whether Runge's behavior represented misconduct is even more hotly contestable as part of the broader debate as to what should be the law's business (Geis 1979).

In any case, the Court in *Runge* placed greater emphasis on another quotation from the *Smith* opinion as to whether the insured "knew or should have known that death or serious bodily injury would be the probable consequence of his acts." How probable a consequence should injury or death be in order to meet this threshold? The usual and ordinary understanding of accident includes injuries and deaths among car drivers, swimmers, general aviation pilots, and even motorcyclists, skiers, and skydivers. If the proportion of autoerotic hangings resulting in death were lower than the proportion of parachute jumps resulting in death, and the Court had received evidence to this effect, would the *Smith* opinion support a finding that Runge's death was accidental? More to the point, if evidence had been received that Runge had engaged in similar behavior on hundreds of prior occasions without injury, could the Court have relied on *Smith?*

The language relied on from *Wooden* differed in one important respect from that relied on from *Smith.* The Court in *Wooden* used the words "natural or probable consequence of his act." Even if death is not, in fact, a probable consequence of autoerotic hanging, it is surely a natural consequence. What would be an example of an unnatural consequence? All consequences in nature are natural. The Court in *Wooden* used natural to mean probable or foreseeable. (See Prosser 1971, p. 252, for a general statement of this usage.)

A portion of the *Smith* opinion not quoted in *Runge* actually put forward the language quoted from *Wooden* that a death is not accidental if "it is the natural result of the insured's voluntary act, unaccompanied by anything unforeseen except the death or injury" (quoted in the Court of Appeals decision in *International Underwriters, Inc.* v. *Home Ins. Co.*). Thus whether death or injury is unforeseen is not a decisive point. Instead some other intervening occurrence must be unforeseen if a death under these circumstances is to be considered a result of accidental means. Could Runge's loss of consciousness have been such an unforeseen intervening occurrence, or does asphyxial loss of consciousness in and of itself constitute an injury?

Note that the Court in *Runge* determined certain facts that could not have been scientifically established. For example, the Court found that the asphyxial process heightens "the experience of masturbation by stimulation of certain nerve centers in the brain." Although this is no doubt true in some sense, it has never been scientifically demonstrated. The Court also determined as a matter of fact the sequence of events in which the decedent stepped to the floor, masturbated, reached orgasm, and lost consciousness. Yet as emphasized in earlier chapters, many individuals engaging in autoerotic asphyxiation do not manually masturbate; antemortem masturbation is often not demonstrable postmortem; and ejaculation is a common postmortem phenomenon regardless of antemortem sexual activity. The Court feels able to determine facts that science cannot determine because the Court may rely on the opinion testimony of expert witnesses. When such opinions are believed, they become facts. One of the justifications for this arrangement—which is so foreign to scientists—is that courts must resolve cases on the evidence presented and cannot put them aside until science has matured.

Some of the preceding questions are dealt with in the following cases. In reading these cases, note in particular the use of the terms *accidental, probable, natural, foreseeable,* and *injury.*

Cannon v. Metropolitan Life Ins. Co.[c]

CALLISTER, District Judge.

Plaintiff, Bonnie Given Cannon, brings this action against defendant, Metropolitan Life Insurance Company, seeking enforcement of a double-indemnity provision contained in a life insurance policy insuring the life of plaintiff's former husband.

* * *

Mr. Given's death was the result of hanging by the neck. Essentially, the deceased had bound himself by ropes, including a noose around his neck, which were designed to cut down the blood flow to his brain, all of which was intended to sexually stimulate him and heighten the autoerotic activity in which he was engaged at the time of his death.

Plaintiff received over $4,000.00 in death benefits under the policy within three months after Mr. Given's death. Although the face amount

---

[c]Civ. no. 77-4044 (D. Idaho, March 23, 1979).

of the insurance policy was $2,000.00, the date of Mr. Given's death occurred before the tenth anniversary of the policy, which entitled the plaintiff to the payment of an additional $2,000.00.

* * *

Plaintiff, believing her former husband's death was accidental, felt the double-indemnity provisions should apply. She based her determination that Mr. Given's death was accidental on a single conversation with a friend, Mr. Roby Oliphant, and a single call to the Pocatello Police Department wherein she was informed that the police report listed the death as "accidental."

When Metropolitan refused to pay more money under the policy, plaintiff filed her suit for an additional $8,000.00 upon the basis that the circumstances of her former husband's death were "accidental" within the terms of the "Additional Indemnity Benefit" section of the policy. Upon defendant's motion for summary judgment, the Court ruled that any recovery upon the policy by plaintiff herein could not exceed $4,000.00 rather than the $8,000.00 originally claimed.

* * *

Policies of insurance are, of course, contracts and their terms must be given their plain and conventional meaning.

Ambiguities in policies of insurance should be interpreted in a manner most favorable to the insured.

Where the terms of a contract of insurance are clear and unambiguous, they are accorded their clear and literal meaning irrespective of the result for the insured.

The "Additional Indemnity Benefit" section of the policy in question reads as follows:

> The Company [defendant] will pay to the Beneficiary [plaintiff], subject to the provisions of this policy, an additional sum equal to twice the amount shown as the "Face Amount of Insurance" on page 3, unless the Insured's death occurs while in any armed forces in which case the additional sum will be an amount equal to such "Face Amount of Insurance", upon receipt of due proof that the death of the Insured occurred as the result, directly and independently of all other causes, of bodily injury caused solely by external, violent, and accidental means.

Two schools of thought have emerged in interpreting the phrase "as the result, directly and independently of all other causes, of bodily injury caused solely by external, violent, and accidental means." The first school is that to be accidental, the means, that is, the actual physical circumstances or devices inflicting death, must be accidental in the sense that they have not been chosen, selected or voluntarily used by the deceased. These cases inquire only into whether the act which caused death was voluntarily undertaken; if it was, the death is not considered accidental. *Hayden* v. *Insurance Company of North America,* 490 P. 2d 454 (Wash., 1971).

The second school of thought, to which Idaho subscribes and which is binding upon this Court, tries to determine whether or not death was an unforeseeable consequence of the device, act or circumstances undertaken by a deceased.

> We conclude . . . that if the result of an act was not natural and probable and should not reasonably, under all the circumstances, have been foreseen, and is tragically out of proportion to a trivial cause, it is an accident within the meaning of the above-quoted provisions of the insurance contracts in question herein. *O'Neil* v. *New York Life Insurance Company,* 65 Idaho 722, 152 P. 2d 707, 711 (1944).

Plaintiff argues that the certified death certificate classification of the cause of death is binding upon the Court. In support of her argument, plaintiff refers to G. Bell, *Handbook of Evidence for the Idaho Lawyer* (2nd ed. 1972), which reads as follows:

> A copy of a death certificate certified by the state registrar is prima facie evidence of the facts stated therein. This includes not only the fact of death but the cause of death stated in the death certificate. *Corey* v. *Wilson,* 93 Idaho 54, 454 P. 2d 951 (1969). *Id.* at 185.

The court would have been inclined to accept plaintiff's argument if the death certificate were the sole evidence before the Court on the issue of the cause of death. But, once the coroner testified as to the basis of his decision that Mr. Given's death was accidental, any *prima facie* presumption arising from the death certificate was dispelled. The coroner testified that he based his conclusion or [sic] the cause of death primarily on the expert literature dealing with deaths arising from conduct similar to Mr. Given's, rather than a close inspection of the apparatus used by the deceased. According to plaintiff's expert witness, Dr. Charles O. Garrison, people who participate in auto-erotic conduct, such as the conduct which led to Mr. Given's death, do not intend to die. He explained that participants in this conduct usually design a fail-safe mechanism which releases the pressure around the neck if they lose consciousness. And, since death does not occur by natural means, disease or intentionally, the literature classifies the death as accidental. Mr. Garrison, the coroner and the plaintiff defined "accidental" as not intentional.

It was upon the same literature that the coroner relied in forming his conclusion as to the cause of Mr. Given's death. However, neither the coroner's testimony nor the photographic evidence convinces the Court that the specific knot wrapped and tied around decedent's wrist was a fail-safe procedure. There is no evidence before the Court suggesting that the decedent had a long history of successful auto-erotic experiences using this same procedure. Since there is no evidence that Mr. Given used a reasonably planned release mechanism which normally functioned properly, the Court cannot accept the death certificate classification of the cause of death.

Therefore, in order to carry her burden, plaintiff had to establish that the death was by "accidental means" within the standards set by common law. As noted earlier, Idaho classifies death as by "accidental means" "if the result of an act was not natural and probable and should not reasonably, under all the circumstances, have been foreseen, and is tragically out of proportion to a trivial cause. . . ." *O'Neil* v. *New York Life, supra*.

There is no dispute that the decedent was involved in an auto-erotic process wherein he tied himself with a rope in such a manner that when he put his weight on the rope a noose would tighten around his neck. The tightened noose would restrict the flow of blood to the brain, bringing about a partial asphyxia. If the noose were not released, the natural result would be unconsciousness and then death.

As indicated in the evidence, the decedent could have released the pressure around his neck by standing up. Obviously, only he had the ability to control to what degree of asphyxia he would induce in the auto-erotic process. It is also obvious that he chose not to release the noose by standing and subsequently lost consciousness. Therefore, the natural and probable result of his failure to stand would be death in the absence of a fail-safe release mechanism.

The Court has no evidence before it concerning the nature of the knot around Mr. Given's wrist. Although the coroner testified that it looked like it could have been some sort of slip knot, he testified that he neither examined it closely nor tested it in order to determine that it was, in fact, a slip knot that had merely failed to operate properly. Plaintiff had the burden of proving that a reasonably planned fail-safe mechanism failed to operate properly. Therefore, the Court concludes that plaintiff has failed to establish that death was caused by "accidental means" as defined by Idaho law.

Comment

The interpretation of accidental means binding upon the Court in *Cannon* derives from *O'Neil* and specifies that "if the result of an act was not natural and probable and should not reasonably . . . have been foreseen, and is tragically out of proportion to a trivial cause, it is an accident. . . ." In order for a death to be considered accidental, the *O'Neil* language requires that a two-pronged test be satisfied. The first prong is that the result of the act must not be natural *or* probable *or* such as to reasonably have been foreseen. According to this language, whether death was or should have been foreseen may be decisive (compare this to our comment on *Runge*). The concept of foreseeability allows great latitude of interpretation since many different consequences of an act may all be foreseeable even though only one of them is voluntarily sought. The second prong is that the result must be "tragically out of proportion to a trivial cause." It is doubtful that self-hanging or self-strangulation would be regarded by any court as a trivial cause of resulting injury or death.

Noteworthy features of the decision in *Cannon* are the coroner's reliance on expert literature, the importance attributed to a fail-safe mechanism, and the judicial finding that the decedent "had the ability to control to what degree of asphyxia he would induce in the auto-erotic process." The Court found that the coroner had relied on expert literature rather than on his own inspection of the apparatus used by the decedent in reaching his opinion regarding the *cause of death*. The plaintiff's argument that the cause of death listed on the death certificate is binding on the Court was rejected on the grounds that the coroner's testimony dispelled any prima facie presumption arising from the death certificate. The distinction between cause of death and manner of death is nowhere raised in this opinion. Surely the cause of death was asphyxiation, and the dispute concerned the *manner of death*.

The importance of investigation is further underscored by the Court's finding that "neither the coroner's testimony nor the photographic evidence convinces the Court that the specific knot wrapped and tied around the decedent's wrist was a fail-safe procedure" and that "There is no evidence before the Court suggesting that the decedent had a long history of successful autoerotic experiences using the same procedure." Evidence for each of these points—a fail-safe device and a long history of previous success—can often be ascertained through thorough investigation and should be investigated in every case. It would appear that in this case the coroner's failure to demonstrate these two features to the satisfaction of the Court was among the bases on which the plaintiff's claim was denied.

In holding that the death could not be considered accidental "since there is no evidence that Mr. Given used a reasonably planned release mechanism which normally functioned properly," the Court suggests that had there been such evidence, the ruling might have been in plaintiff's favor. (For an example of such a case, see Case #2 in chapter 8 in which the decedent had an elaborate pulley system and died when a rope jammed the pulley, or the following *International Underwriters, Inc.* v. *Home Ins. Co.*) Thus the Court in *Cannon* left open the possibility that some asphyxial autoerotic fatalities would be considered accidental by that Court.

This Court, we believe, expressed an inappropriate degree of certainty in stating that the decedent obviously had the ability to control the degree of asphyxia and that "he chose not to release the noose by standing." This view does not take account of the carotid baroreceptor response (see chapter 4) through which an individual may unexpectedly lose the capacity to voluntarily relieve the asphyxia. An individual accustomed to autoerotic asphyxiation may fail to escape for any of a variety of reasons. Precipitous loss of consciousness through a previously unexperienced carotid baroreceptor response is every bit as unforeseeable as the jamming of a pulley that normally functions properly. If the latter would be regarded as a basis for awarding accidental-death benefits, as this Court implied, the former should be as well. In any case, this Court might have found that no evidence suggested that consciousness had been lost through the carotid baroreceptor response and that the burden of proof on this point rested with the plaintiff.

The Court wrote that plaintiff's expert, Dr. Garrison, had "explained that participants in this conduct usually design a fail-safe mechanism which releases the pressure around the neck if they lose consciousness." Although a self-rescue mechanism is always or almost always present, fail-safe mechanisms are actually uncommon. Would the Court have devoted so much attention to the absence of proof of a fail-safe mechanism if expert testimony had not mistakenly claimed that the specific knot tied about the decedent's wrist was a fail-safe mechanism? Note that expert testimony was given credence in determining some, but not all, of the facts and that expert testimony was not given credence in defining *accidental* or determining the ultimate issue.

Sigler v. Mutual Benefit Life Ins. Co.[d]

STUART, Chief Judge.

. . . Plaintiff, Diane Lee Sigler ("Mrs. Sigler"), initiated this action against defendant Mutual Benefit Life Insurance Company ("Mutual") seeking to recover the proceeds of a $50,000 accidental death group insurance plan under which her husband was covered . . .

The facts before the Court are not in dispute. On or about August

---

[d]506 F. Supp. 542 (S.D. Iowa, 1981).

16, 1979, plaintiff's husband was found dead in the bathroom of his hotel room in Denver, Colorado where he was attending a seminar. Both parties concede that plaintiff's husband's death was not the result of suicide or foul play; instead, it is agreed that his death resulted from an autoerotic experience. It is agreed that Mr. Sigler died by asphyxiation while attempting to increase sexual gratification from masturbation. The autoerotic practice involves the participant "hanging" himself by the neck, creating an asphyxial state, in an attempt to stimulate nerve centers in the brain and heighten the masturbation experience.

* * *

The Court first will address plaintiff's claim for benefits under the accidental death provision of the insurance agreement. The issue to be resolved in considering this claim is whether death resulting from such autoerotic experience is an accidental death under the terms of the insurance agreement and Iowa law.

The relevant portions of the insurance agreement provide:

> ACCIDENTAL DEATH BENEFIT: If accidental bodily injury sustained by a person insured under the Policy results, directly and independently of all other causes, in his death within ninety days after the date of such injury, the amount of insurance otherwise payable upon the death of the person insured under the Policy will be increased by the applicable Accidental Death and Dismemberment Benefit Principal Sum referred to in the Schedule of Insurance of this Certificate, subject to the further provisions and limitations hereafter stated. RISKS NOT ASSUMED: Accidental death or dismemberment is not a risk assumed under the Accidental Death or Dismemberment provisions of the Policy if it results directly or indirectly from: (f) intentionally, self-inflicted injury of any kind, while sane or insane.

Under the law of the State of Iowa, it is clear that the meaning of "accident" or "accidental" for purposes of accidental death insurance benefits is to be determined in the context of the terms' common sense or ordinary usage.

> One thing, at least is well settled: the words "accident" and "accidental" have never acquired any technical meaning in law, and when used in an insurance contract, they are to be construed and considered according to the common speech and common usage of the people generally.

Lickleider v. *Iowa State Traveling Mens' Ass'n,* 184 Iowa 423, 428, 166 N.W. 363, 365, as mod'f 168 N.W. 884 (1918). The Supreme Court of Iowa, in defining these terms in light of their common meaning, stated ". . . if the insured does a voluntary act, the natural, usual, and to be expected result of which is to bring injury upon himself, then a death so occurring is not an accident in any sense of the word, legal or colloquial, . . ." *Lickleider,* 166 N.W. at 366. In the same year, the Supreme Court of Iowa again faced the issue of defining "accident" or "accidental" and held:

> [H]e must have known and appreciated the danger, or the risk must have been so apparent that, as an ordinarily reasonable man, he must be held to have known and appreciated it, and with the knowledge have intentionally taken the risk.
>
> *Rowe* v. *United Commercial Travelers Ass'n,* 186 Iowa 454, 464, 172 N.W. 454, 458 (1919).

The Eighth Circuit Court of Appeals has also considered the definition of "accident" for purposes of accidental death insurance policies under Iowa law. Most recently in *Estate of Wade* v. *Continental Insurance Co.,* 514 F. 2d 304, 307 (1975), the Circuit Court stated:

> Iowa follows the general rule that the determination of whether an injury is accidental must be made from the point of view of the insured and what he intended or should reasonably have expected.
>
> > The word "accident" . . . means happening by chance, unexpectedly taking place, not according to the usual course of things.
> >
> > . . . [I]f the insured does a voluntary act, the natural and usual, and to be expected result of which is to bring injury upon himself, then a death so occurring is not an accident. But if the insured does a voluntary act, without knowledge or reasonable expectation that the result thereof will be to bring injury upon himself from which death may follow, then a bodily injury resulting in death is caused by an accident.
>
> *Continental Cas. Co.* v. *Jackson,* 400 F. 2d 285, 288 (8th Cir. 1968).

Applying these principles to the undisputed facts, the Court is of the opinion that plaintiff's husband's death was not an accident since a reasonable person would have recognized that his actions could result in his death. The Court finds that a reasonable person would comprehend and forsee [sic] that placing a noose around his neck and subsequently hanging himself with the noose for the purpose of inducing asphyxia could result in his death. Certainly, the record indicates that plaintiff's husband did not intend to cause his own death, but, under the circumstances, he reasonably should have expected that his actions could be fatal.

This Court's conclusion is consistent with the Fourth Circuit Court of Appeal's decision in *Runge* v. *Metropolitan Life Insurance Company,* 537 F. 2d 1157 (1976). In *Runge,* the court had before it facts and circumstances nearly identical to those presently in issue. The plaintiff therein initiated suit against an insurance company to recover accidental death benefits upon the death of her husband that resulted from an autoerotic practice in which he sought to increase sexual gratification from masturbation by hanging himself to induce asphyxia. The circuit court affirmed the district court's granting of the insurance company's motion for summary judgment, concluding that the person's death was not accidental:

> Runge deliberately placed his neck into a noose which he himself had designed and constructed, having first locked the doors to his house to prevent intrusion, and at a time when interruption was unlikely. He then intentionally and deliberately self-induced asphyxia by hanging himself in the noose, lost consciousness, and died. Death, under these circumstances, was a natural and foreseeable, though unintended, consequence of Runge's activity.

Runge 537 F. 2d at 1159.

Based upon the foregoing discussion, the Court must find that plaintiff's husband's death was not accidental under the terms of the applicable insurance agreement and the law of the State of Iowa.

Even if Mr. Sigler's death was found to be accidental within the meaning of the policy, recovery would be barred by the clause excluding from coverage an "intentionally, self-inflicted injury of any kind". Although Mr. Sigler did not intend to produce the unconsciousness that resulted in his death, his voluntary acts were intended to temporarily restrict his air supply to heighten the sensations of masturbation. Therefore, the elements of "intentionally, self-inflicted" are satisfied. The only question remaining is whether self-inflicted hanging is an "injury of any kind". The Court believes that it is. If someone else had placed Mr. Sigler in the same position as he placed himself to temporarily restrict his ability to breathe, it would have been an injury. In the Court's opinion, it continues to be an injury even when it is self-inflicted.

Therefore, plaintiff's motion for summary judgment is denied, and defendant's motion is granted insofar as it requests judgment on plaintiff's claim for insurance benefits.

* * *

Comment

In *Sigler,* the Court based its ruling on the interpretation that a death is not an accident if a reasonable person would have recognized that his actions could result in his death. Under this interpretation, would a driver's death be accidental if he lost control of his car while speeding on a wet road? Could any self-inflicted gunshot fatality of an adult be accidental under this interpretation? Has any accidental death ever resulted from an activity that *could not* result in death? If not, did the Court succeed in adhering to its own statement that under Iowa law, the meaning of accident is to be determined in the context of the term's "common sense or ordinary usage"?

Note that the Court found that self-inflicted hanging does constitute an injury, even in the absence of resulting unconsciousness or death. The Court mistakenly regarded diminished ability to breathe or diminished air flow as the mechanism through which asphyxia develops in hanging. As discussed in chapter 4, compression of blood vessels in the neck is an earlier and more certain effect of hanging than reduction in air flow, which occurs only with extreme pressure. Would the court have ruled differently had it understood the physiology of hanging, or would the compression of blood vessels be regarded as an injury? Blood vessels are compressed whenever a tourniquet is applied to the arm before drawing blood, whenever a wristwatch band is tightened, and whenever one wears elastic hosiery. Are all of these injuries?

Connecticut General Life Ins. Co. v. Tommie[e]

CORNELIUS, Chief Justice.

This is a suit upon a group insurance policy to recover accidental death benefits. Jerry Lee Tommie was insured under a Connecticut General group policy . . . Jerry's wife and mother . . . were named joint beneficiaries, and upon his death they demanded the $120,000.00 accidental death benefit provided by the policy. The insurer refused to pay on the grounds that Mr. Tommie's death was not an accident and further was the result of either self-inflicted injury or disease.

The insurance policy provided that accidental death benefits would be payable if the insured ". . . has received an accidental bodily injury, and as a result of the injury, directly and independently of all other causes, has suffered . . . Loss of Life." The policy specifically excludes from coverage any loss which results directly or indirectly from ". . . suicide or intentionally self-inflicted injury, . . ." and infection or disease.

The circumstances surrounding Mr. Tommie's death were as follows: While Mrs. Tommie was out of the house shopping for groceries, Mr. Tommie dressed himself in her wig, bra, nightie and panties. He went into a bedroom and placed the end of a nylon exercise rope in a noose

---

[e]619 S.W. 2d 199 (Tex. Civ. App. 1981).

around his neck. He placed a pad around his neck under the rope. Standing with his back to the door he ran the other end of the rope over the top of the door and down the opposite side of the door around the outside doorknob, and then tied that end around his left foot. The exercise rope was equipped with pulleys so that with his left foot he could increase or decrease the pressure of the rope around his neck. The purpose of the preparations made by Mr. Tommie, according to the medical testimony, was to heighten sexual pleasure during masturbation by reducing the supply of blood, and therefore the supply of oxygen, to the brain by gradually tightening the rope around his neck. The reduced oxygen to the brain produces a state of hypercapnia, or an increase of carbon dioxide in the blood, and a state of hypoxia, or a decrease in oxygen in the blood, which is supposed to increase the intensity of orgasm. When Mrs. Tommie returned she went to the bedroom and found the exercise rope looped over the top of the door and around the doornob [sic]. The door was open about 2½ to 3 inches. She could not push the door open so she got a kitchen knife and cut the rope. At that time she heard her husband's foot hit the floor. She called the police and they found him dead with the rope tight around his neck. The medical testimony was that Mr. Tommie had died from anoxic brain damage secondary to the ligature around his neck. From the position of the body and the other circumstances, it appeared that Mr. Tommie had blacked out or had otherwise lost his balance and fell, placing the full weight of his 200 pound body on the rope around his neck.

The jury found that Mr. Tommie's death was an accident and was not the result of either an intentionally self-inflicted injury or disease, and the trial court rendered judgment accordingly. Connecticut General contends by its first four points of error that there is no evidence or insufficient evidence that Mr. Tommie's death was the result of an accident independent of all other causes, and that the jury's finding of accidental death is against the great weight and preponderance of the evidence.

In *Freeman* v. *Crown Life Ins. Co.*, 580 S.W. 2d 897 (Tex. Civ. App.—Texarkana 1979, writ ref'd n.r.e.), this Court analyzed and summarized the many decisions concerning death arising from dangerous or negligent activities and concluded that:

> ". . . The mere fact that a person's death may have occurred because of his negligence, even gross negligence, does not prevent that death from being an accident within the meaning of an accident insurance policy. It is only when the consequences of the act are so natural and probable as to be expected by any reasonable person that it can be said that the victim, in effect, intended the result and it was therefore not accidental. . . . More is required than a simple showing that the in-

sured could have reasonably foreseen that injury or death might result. As Justice Doughty said in *Republic Nat. Life Ins. Co. v. Heyward,* supra, the insured must have acted in such a way that he should have reasonably *known* his actions would *probably result in his death.* . . ."

The beneficiaries here had the burden to establish that Mr. Tommie's death was due to an accident. Their evidence revealed that his death was by violent and external means, thus raising a presumption that the death was accidental. *Republic Nat. Life Ins. Co. v. Heyward,* 536 S.W. 2d 549 (Tex. 1976); *International Travelers Association v. Marshall,* 131 Tex. 258, 114 S.W. 2d 851 (1938); *Freeman v. Crown Life Ins. Co.,* supra. They also produced other evidence that the death was an accident when tested by the rules announced in *Freeman.* Dr. Norton testified that she encountered from time to time in her medical practice the same type of auto-erotic activity as Mr. Tommie was engaged in, and that while some forty deaths per year were reported in the United States as a result of such activity, death is not the normal expected result of that behavior, but would be considered unusual or unexpected. Dr. Montgomery also agreed that death in those circumstances would not be reasonably expected. Dr. Norton further testified that it was likely that Mr. Tommie had engaged in the practice for several years, considering his age and the fact that such behavior generally begins in young men during pubescence or shortly thereafter. From that testimony and all the other evidence, it can reasonably be concluded that, although the type of activity in which Mr. Tommie was engaged was foolish and fraught with substantial risk of injury or death, it was not of such a nature that the insured should have reasonably known that it would probably result in his death. The finding of the jury that the death was accidental was supported by sufficient evidence and was not so against the great weight of the evidence as to be manifestly wrong.

The appeal also urges that there was no evidence that Mr. Tommie's death was not caused by an intentionally self-inflicted injury, and therefore the beneficiaries failed to carry their burden to show that the death was not caused by one of the policy's excluded risks. The jury found that the death was not the result of a self-inflicted injury. If there is any probative evidence to support that finding, we must uphold the verdict in that respect.

The evidence reveals that Mr. Tommie put a rope around his neck with the intent to tighten it to a degree necessary to reduce the amount of oxygen to the brain. Connecticut General argues that this conclusively shows that Mr. Tommie intentionally injured himself, and that it was only the extent of the injury that was unintentional.

The term injury is not defined in the policy. In that situation it must be given the usual and normal meaning which would be ascribed to it by ordinary persons. Inasmuch as Mr. Tommie placed a pad between the rope and his neck and there is no evidence that the rope inflicted any external injury to his body, we must determine from the record if a reduction of the supply of oxygen to the brain in order to produce a state of hypercapnia is an injury within the normal and usual meaning of that term.

There is abundant evidence that Mr. Tommie, aside from his propensity to unusual sexual practices, was a well-adjusted, happy individual who was looking forward to the future, and that he did not intend to commit suicide. There is also evidence that a state of hypercapnia simply alters the amount of oxygen in the brain, thus heightening or intensifying certain body sensations, and that it may be accomplished by various drugs as well as by other means. We believe this evidence and the reasonable inferences which may be drawn therefrom constitute some probative evidence that Mr. Tommie did not intentionally inflict upon himself bodily injury in the normal and usual meaning of that term, and that the jury finding must be upheld.

There was also sufficient evidence that the death was not caused by disease. The medical testimony was that Mr. Tommie had transvestite tendencies and that his sexual practices and fantasies were unusual, but that they were not such as would constitute a disease in either the medical or the ordinary sense of the word.

* * *

The judgment of the trial court is affirmed.

Comment

To our knowledge, *Tommie* is the only reported appellate-court opinion upholding a lower-court finding that an autoerotic fatality was accidental under state law and the terms of the insurance agreement. In *Tommie*, the Court reached two opinions that differ from those in the preceding cases.

The first divergent opinion was that Tommie's death was accidental. The Court pointed out that the evidence showing death to have been by violent and external means raised a presumption that death was accidental and then considered whether this presumption had been overcome. The language relied on from *Freeman* specified that to overcome a presumption of accidental death requires more than a "showing that the insured could have reasonably foreseen that injury or death might result." This goes beyond the requirement in the two preceding cases of a showing that the insured *should* have foreseen the result *(Cannon)* or that he would have recognized that his actions *could* result in death *(Sigler)*. Moreover, the *Freeman* opinion underscored that to overcome a presumption that death was accidental, "the insured must have acted in such a way that he should have reasonably *known* his actions would *probably result in his death*. . . ." Expert testimony apparently convinced the jury that Mr. Tommie knew from experience that his actions would *probably not* result in his death.

The testimony referred to by the Court was not testimony about whether Mr. Tommie knew the probability that his actions would result in death. Rather, it was testimony about whether other people expect to die when engaging in similar behavior and about the age at which other people begin such behavior. Should the trial court have admitted such testimony? If most drivers in car crashes are intoxicated, should that fact be admissible to prove that a particular driver was intoxicated when his car crashed? How did Dr. Norton know that "such behavior generally begins in young men during pubescence or shortly thereafter"? Does the evidence presented in earlier chapters compel this conclusion?

The second divergent opinion in *Tommie* is the Court's finding that Mr. Tommie "did not intentionally inflict upon himself bodily injury in the normal and usual meaning of that term . . . ." In order to reach this conclusion, all that was required of the Court was to find some evidence from the trial record on which the jury might have based its finding that "death was not the result of a self-inflicted injury." The Court found two lines of evidence that it regarded as probative of this issue. The first was the evidence that Mr. Tommie was well-adjusted, happy, and looking forward to the future and that he did not intend to commit suicide. Does the Court appear to understand that otherwise well-adjusted, happy, nonsuicidal sexual masochists are known to whip, pierce, cut, and burn themselves, too? Is mental state relevant to a determination of whether an injury occurred?

The second line of probative evidence relied on in upholding the jury finding was that "a state of hypercapnia simply alters the amount of oxygen in the brain, thus heightening or intensifying certain body sensations, and that it may be accomplished by various drugs as well as by other means." This statement obviously derives from expert testimony. Assuming the testimony was accurate, something substantial was lost in the translation. It is not accurate to say that hypercapnia alters the amount of oxygen in the brain. Hypercapnia is the state of increased carbon dioxide in the blood and tissue; hypoxia is the state of decreased oxygen in the blood and tissue; and in hangings both occur, but not as a result of one another. More importantly, neither hypercapnia nor hypoxia *simply* heightens or intensifies body sensations. This is one effect of mild hypercapnia or hypoxia, but as either progresses it results in the entire chain of pathophysiology described in chapter 4, eventuating in death.

If the jury had heard testimony about the predictable sequence of events in hanging, would it have found that death was not the result of self-inflicted injury? In any case, it should be noted that the Court did not *find* that Mr. Tommie did not intentionally inflict bodily injury on himself, but rather *upheld* the jury finding to that effect based on *some* probative evidence.

International Underwriters, Inc. v. Home Ins. Co.[f]

(District Court Opinion)

LEWIS, Senior District Judge.

These consolidated suits were brought by . . . beneficiaries to collect the accidental death benefits under two insurance policies issued by The Home Insurance Company.

The insured died while performing an autoerotic act.

The defendant denied liability and moved for summary judgment, relying on *Runge v. Metropolitan Life Ins. Co.*, 537 F. 2d 1157 (4th Cir. 1976).

Perceiving a conflict in the evidence as to the cause of death, the Court allowed the parties time to complete their discovery, and set the matter for hearing on the merits.

Instead of calling live witnesses, the plaintiff, by agreement with counsel for the defendant, filed written statements from:

> the decedent's wife—two Fairfax County emergency medical technicians—three Fairfax County Police Officers—three close friends and neighbors—the doctor who performed the autopsy—an article entitled, ''Autoerotic Asphyxial Death'', a medical/legal analysis of 43 cases—a certificate of analysis from the Bureau of Forensic Sciences—30 photographs of the scene surrounding the insured's death—the death certificate, and the reports and resumes of two expert witnesses. The defendant offered no counter-statements or exhibits.

From the record thus made, the Court finds:

> That the insured was a happily married man with two children, with another soon expected;
>
> He was quite excited about the prospective birth of his third child and was working in the room in which he died, fixing it up to be the nursery;
>
> His finances were in better shape than they had ever been;

---

[f]500 F. Supp. 637 (E.D. Va. 1980).

Insurance Benefits in Autoerotic Fatalities 175

He had recently gotten involved in blacksmithing and had established a blacksmith's guild, and had purchased a number of antique blacksmithing tools;

He was interested in, and considered an expert, as regards pulleys, ropes and knots, and had an extensive lock collection, including leg irons and handcuffs; He left no notes nor memoranda of any kind indicating suicide.

On the morning of his death, his wife had taken the children to attend church and to work in the nursery—and then to do some shopping.

When she left home around ten o'clock, a.m., her husband was dressed and eating breakfast—he indicated he was going to be working on the upstairs bedroom that he was converting into a nursery.

When she returned home some three hours later, she went upstairs to the nursery and found her husband just hanging there. The Fairfax authorities were called.

They observed an elaborate pulley apparatus mounted on two exposed beams in the ceiling.

When nothing could be done to revive the insured, the emergency medical technicians left.

The room in question was apparently being rebuilt—there was no ceiling in the room so that several roof beams and rafters were exposed.

There was a pulley transfixed by an axle attached to the top of one such exposed ceiling beam. The pulley consisted of a clothesline rope inside the wheel portion and a nylon rope attached to the axles by a six-inch piece of strap. The nylon rope had a noose attached to its end which could be raised by pulling the clothesline rope attached to the pulley which, in turn, rotated the axle. The axle was 85 inches from the floor. There was a notch cut into the beam in which the axle was resting.

The insured's trousers were in a position somewhat below his hips and his undershorts were on—there were wet stains on his undershorts and on his legs.

The police took a series of photographs of the insured's body and of the room in which he was found—these photographs accurately portrayed the scene as found by the police upon their arrival.

In describing an autoerotic asphyxial death, Dr. James C. Beyer, who performed the autopsy, stated:

What happens when an accident occurs is that something goes wrong in the suspension system. The person may be on a chair or a ladder and they fall with their full body into the suspension system and they hang themselves. They frequently use a pulley-type system which becomes jammed and the same result ensues. The idea of the pulley system is that one uses two ropes; the first rope is attached to the neck and the second controls the pulley system itself. By pulling on the one rope, pressure is increased on the second rope. In addition, this system has a "fail safe" mechanism; *i.e.* as one pulls himself up, he may reach a point where he loses consciousness which, in turn, causes him to release his hold on the control rope, thereby permitting his body to fall to the floor.

As regards the insured, Dr. Beyer's findings disclosed that his death was caused by asphyxiation, secondary to accidental hanging.

Dr. Beyer testified that in his professional opinion, the insured's death was a result of this autoerotic practice. His conclusion was based principally on the following facts:

The existence of this pulley system which permitted regulation of pressure on the neck.

There was no known use for this pulley system in the room in which it was found.

When the insured was found, the pulley system was jammed.

In order to commit suicide by hanging, you have to have some means of maintaining constant steady pressure on the neck. You cannot do that by holding something in your hand.

The insured's clothing was found in such a manner so as to suggest masturbation.

The deceased was found with a hangman's type noose. People engaging in this type of deviant sexual practice often do not use just a simple device but rather go in for something which, in their mind, has some significance. The use of the hangman-type noose is not too uncommon.

There was no apparent motive for suicide.

A ladder was found nearby the body and the body was found with the toes barely touching the ground.

The experts called by the plaintiff stated:

The complexity of the apparatus to alter the physiological state can be viewed as an indicator of prior autoerotic practice.

In this case, rather than just using a rope, the insured used a sophisticated pulley system as part of his autoerotic ritual.

On prior occasions he was apparently able to engage in this activity without serious consequences; but, on this occasion, the victim may have failed to take into account his recent and significant 40-pound weight loss in judging his response to the effect of the apparatus on him. In other words, he may have lost consciousness more rapidly on previous experiences, and this unanticipated turn of events proved fatal.

The experts found the circumstances surrounding the insured's death to be far more consistent with accidental asphyxiation associated with autoerotic hanging than with any alternative expectation [sic], such as suicide, homicide, or death by natural causes.

The preponderance of the evidence indicated, in their opinion, that the insured died an unnatural and unintentional death.

The Court concludes from the evidence that the insured's death was caused by the malfunctioning of the pulley system while performing an autoerotic act resulting in death by asphyxiation.

The pulley system in this case was designed to allow the pressure on the neck to be regulated—had not the pulley system jammed, the insured's hand-hold on the control rope would have collapsed, dropping him to the floor.

The insurance policy in this case covered "loss from injury."

> "Injury," as defined in the policy, means accidental bodily injury sustained by the covered person, . . . which results directly and independently of all other causes, in a loss arising out of the hazard defined in the description of hazards.

"Loss of life" is one of the losses provided for in the policy.

Having found that the insured's death was the accidental result of his autoerotic activities on the day in question, the insurance carrier must honor its coverage against "accidental death," and

IT IS SO ORDERED.

The defendant's reliance on *Runge, supra,* is misplaced—the insurance policy in *Runge* covered injuries sustained solely through violent external and accidental means.

The insurance policy in this case is an accidental-result policy.

Virginia has long recognized the difference between accidental means and accidental-result policies.

The Court, in *Runge,* relied heavily on two Virginia cases. *Smith* v. *Combined Insurance Company of America,* 120 S.E. 2d 267 (1961), and *Wooden* v. *John Hancock Mutual Life Ins. Co.,* 139 S.E. 2d 801 (1965), wherein the Virginia Supreme Court held:

> In this case [Smith], the court concluded, the insured had voluntarily put himself in a position where he knew, or should have known, that death or serious bodily injury would be the probable consequence of his acts.

In such a situation, death was not effected by an accident within the meaning of the policy.

In *Wooden,* the Virginia Supreme Court noted:

Death or injury does not result from accident or accidental means within the terms of an accident policy where it is the natural result of the insured's voluntary act, unaccompanied by anything unforeseen, except the death or injury.

The facts in *Runge* are materially different from the facts in this case:

The decedent [Runge] had tied the electrical cord in such a fashion that when hanging from it, the balls of his feet would rest on the floor and by standing on his toes he would be able to vary the pressure on his neck. The decedent placed the noose formed in the electrical cord around his neck and stepped from the chair or stool to the floor, and then proceeded to masturbate. At the time he reached orgasm the asphyxia was accentuated to the degree that the decedent lost consciousness, his body relaxed, and he hanged to death.

The Court held that death under these circumstances was a natural and forseeable, though unintended, consequence of Runge's activity.

In contrast, the insured's pulley system in this case was designed to preclude the risk of death—should unconsciousness approach, the failsafe feature was designed to release the pressure on his neck and drop him to the floor.

Under these conditions, death was neither intended, natural nor foreseeable.

Autoerotic acts, such as this, are not uncommon in this day and age—death seldom occurs—unless one is fully aware of all the circumstances associated with the death scene, and the attendant ropes, belts and other physical paraphernalia are thoroughly examined, the true nature of the case may be missed. Therefore, it is extremely important that the forensic pathologist completely comprehend and properly diagnose these tragic cases and label them correctly insofar as cause and manner of death are concerned.

In this case, the examining pathologist has so done and has concluded that the cause of death was accidental—the defendant insurance carrier offered no evidence to the contrary.

Finally, the defendant contends, its insurance policy expressly excludes coverage for any death "caused by, contributed to or resulting from . . . intentional self-inflicted injuries."

They argue that the placing of a hangman's noose around one's neck and strangulation to the point of partial asphyxia was certainly an intentionally self-inflicted injury which caused, contributed to, or resulted in the insured's death.

The fallacy of this argument is that it is not supported by the uncontradicted evidence in this case. The insurance company conceded that the insured's death was not intentional—and there was no evidence of strangulation:

> "Injury" resulting in the insured's death, as defined in the policy, was not the voluntary placing of the hangman's noose around the insured's neck nor the self-inflicted partial asphyxia—neither of which caused harm or death—the "injury" was the loss of consciousness caused by the malfunction of the pulley system.

Insurance policies under Virginia law are to be construed according to their terms, and the plain meaning of such terms must be given effect. . . . [T]hus, where the policy is susceptible to two constructions—one which would effectuate coverage and the other would not, it is the Court's duty to adopt that construction which would effectuate coverage.

Had the insurance carrier in this case intended to exclude coverage for accidental death resulting from voluntary autoerotic acts, it could and should have plainly so stated.

It has not so done, and judgment will be entered for the plaintiff . . .

* * *

Comment

The facts in this case are unique among those resulting in reported court opinions. The unique feature is that a workable fail-safe mechanism (not to be confused with a self-rescue mechanism) was in place but failed to function. In the language of *Smith,* the decedent neither knew nor should have known that the pulley would jam, and he therefore neither knew nor should have known that death or serious bodily injury would be the probable consequence of his acts. Indeed, because of the fail-safe mechanism, death or serious bodily injury was an improbable consequence of his acts. In the language of *Wooden,* something unforeseen did occur—namely, the jamming of the pulley. The Court stressed the fail-safe feature in reaching its conclusion that death was accidental.

The Court's logic in finding that this accidental death should not be excluded from payment of death benefits under the clause of the policy excluding coverage for "intentional self-inflicted injuries" is less comprehensible. It is not clear from the opinion who it was who argued or concluded that "the 'injury' was the loss of consciousness caused by the malfunction of the pulley system." The insurer would have been wiser to argue that the injury was the self-induced asphyxia; the plaintiff would have been wiser to argue that the injury was the sustained asphyxia that resulted from pulley malfunction and caused death. If loss of consciousness was the injury, it may well have been self-inflicted, since some persons who engage in autoerotic asphyxia purposely carry it to the point of unconsciousness. Indeed, the fact that the decedent had designed a fail-safe mechanism would be probative of the issue that he was such a person. The insurance company apparently lost its case in the District Court by conceding too much and by failing to offer evidence in support of its position.

It is noteworthy that several unfounded bits of expert opinion and puzzling interpretations of medical issues found their way into the judicial opinion. The first unfounded opinion was an expert's statement that "what happens when an accident occurs is that something goes wrong in the suspension system." Although true in this case, this is most uncommon among autoerotic fatalities. As illustrated by the cases in the preceding chapters, equipment failure is the exception rather than the rule. The second unfounded opinion was an expert's statement that "they frequently use a pulley-type system which becomes jammed and the same result ensues." Although pulleys might be used in a sufficient number or proportion of cases to be called frequent, jamming of a pulley system is a rare cause of an asphyxial autoerotic fatality.

The first puzzling interpretation of a medical issue was the Court's statement that the pathologist concluded that the *cause* of death was accidental, even though the Court had in the preceding sentence recognized that cause and manner of death are two distinct issues. The second puzzling interpretation is the Court's statement that "there was no evidence of strangulation." The context of this statement is such that the Court may have meant to say that the insurance company somehow conceded that there was no evidence of strangulation; if so, the writing is merely imprecise. Whomever it was who thought there was no evidence of strangulation was either recognizing the distinction between hanging and ligature strangulation (discussed in chapter 4), in which case the lack of evidence of strangulation is immaterial or else was entirely off the mark. If what was meant by strangulation was compression of the neck, reducing blood flow and causing asphyxia, it is difficult to see how the Court found no strangulation while praising the pathologist for his thorough investigation, from which he concluded that asphyxiation was the cause of death.

International Underwriters, Inc. v. Home Ins. Co.[g]

(Court of Appeals Opinion)

WIDENER, Circuit Judge.

This case arises from the unfortunate death by asphyxiation of plain-

---

[g]662 F. 2d 1084 (4th Cir. 1981).

tiff's decedent. The insurance company carrying two accident policies on the decedent refused to pay the policies' beneficiaries after concluding that the death was not an accident. The beneficiaries sued in a Virginia Circuit Court, and the cases were removed under diversity jurisdiction to the district court, which held that the death was accidental under Virginia law. *International Underwriters, Inc.* v. *Home Insurance Co.*, 500 F. Supp. 637 (E.D. Va. 1980). The insurance company appealed, and we reverse.

Decedent's wife found his body hanging from a rope and noose suspended from the ceiling of an upstairs room of their home. 500 F. Supp. at 638. Neither party disputes the following description of events that led up to the death:

> ". . . was attempting, while masturbating, to induce partial asphyxia by means of a hangmen's [sic] noose attached to a pulley which he could control by means of a separate rope. It is well documented that partial loss of oxygen intensifies the sensations of orgasm. The pulley system was designed . . . to protect him from asphyxiation if he lost consciousness since he would then lose his grip on the separate rope and the pressure on the noose would abate, allowing his autonomous [sic] nervous system to restore his breathing. Apparently the pulley system jammed when . . . [the decedent] lost consciousness and failed to release pressure from his neck."

There is no claim that the death was caused by suicide, homicide or natural causes.

Accident policies issued by Home Insurance Company and owned by the deceased and his employer, International Underwriters, Inc., provided for payment:

> for loss from injury, to the extent herein provided. "Injury" means accidental bodily injury sustained by a Covered Person during the term of this Policy, which results directly and independently of all other causes in a loss arising out of the hazards defined in "Description of Hazards." [Injury includes death under the policies.]

The policy also provided, under the label "Exclusions," that:

> This policy does not cover any loss caused by, contributed to or resulting from: (1) intentionally self-inflicted injuries . . .

The district court concluded that the death resulted from the malfunctioning of the pulley system and thus the death was an accident, making Home liable under the terms of the policies. We believe the district court misinterpreted Virginia law with respect to the definition of accident.

The Virginia Court has considered on several occasions whether particular injuries were accidents for insurance purposes. In *Smith* v. *Com-*

bined Insurance Company of America, 202 Va. 758, 120 S.E. 2d 267 (1961), the insured died when the barn in which he was hiding from police caught fire after tear gas cannisters were hurled into the barn. Faced with the question of whether the insured's death was by accident, the court said:

> In *Ocean Accident & Guarantee Corp.* v. *Glover,* 165 Va. 283, 285, 182 S.E. 2d 221, 222, we adopted this definition:
>
>> Accident: An event that takes place without one's foresight or expectation; an undesigned, sudden, and unexpected event; chance; contingency, often; and undesigned and unforeseen occurrence of an afflicted or unfortunate character; casualty, mishap; as, to die by accident.
>
> The generally accepted rule is that death or injury does not result of an accident or accidental means within the terms of an accident policy where it is the natural result of the insured's voluntary act, unaccompanied by anything unforeseen except the death or injury.

202 Va. at 760-61, 120 S.E. 2d at 268. The court ruled that the insured knew or should have known that death or serious injury was a probable consequence of his action and thus his death was not an accident within the meaning of the policy. Id. at 762, 120 S.E. 2d at 269.

The Virginia Court has followed the above quoted language from *Smith* in *Wooden* v. *John Hancock Mutual Life Insurance Co.,* 205 Va. 750, 139 S.E. 2d 801 (1965) (not an accident when insured visited home of estranged wife and was shot following argument), and *Byrd* v. *Life Insurance Co. of Virginia,* 219 Va. 824, 252 S.E. 2d 307 (1979) (insured could have foreseen possibility of injury when he visited home of girlfriend's ex-boyfriend); see also *Harris v. Dunkers Life & Casualty Co.,* 222 Va. 45, 278 S.E. 2d 809 (1981) (remanding to determine whether insured should have reasonably foreseen that his actions would put him in danger of death or serious bodily injury).

While the Virginia Supreme Court has not considered whether a victim would foresee that death could result from commission of an autoerotic sexual act utilizing a noose, this court has considered the question under a virtually identical factual situation, also under Virginia law. In *Runge* v. *Metropolitan Life Insurance Co.,* 537 F. 2d 1157 (4th Cir. 1976), the victim unintentionally hanged himself with an electric cord while attempting to produce the same effect as the insured sought in the instant case. Id. at 1158. After discussing *Smith* and *Wooden,* the *Runge* court said:

> Runge deliberately placed his neck into a noose which he himself had designed and constructed, having first locked the doors to prevent in-

trusion, and at a time when interruption was unlikely. He then intentionally and deliberately self-induced asphyxia by hanging himself in the noose, lost consciousness, and died. Death, under these circumstances, was a natural and foreseeable, though unintended, consequence of Runge's activity.

Id. 537 F. 2d at 1159. Furthermore, we note that in what is apparently the only other reported case dealing with this factual pattern, a federal district court in Iowa, applying similar state law, denied recovery because a reasonable man would have recognized that death could result from his actions. *Sigler* v. *Mutual Benefit Life,* 506 F. Supp. 542 (S.D. Iowa 1981).

The district court in the instant case noted the Virginia Supreme Court decisions in *Smith* and *Wooden* but neither applied nor distinguished them. 500 F. Supp. at 639-40. The district court distinguished *Runge* because it said *Runge* concerned an accidental means policy, while the policy here covers accidental results. As well it distinguished *Runge* on its facts, noting that the *Runge* victim's system for restricting air flow did not have sufficient safeguards in case he should lose consciousness, while:

> In contrast, the insured's pulley system in this case was designed to preclude the risk of death—should unconsciousness approach, the fail-safe feature was designed to release the pressure on his neck and drop him to the floor.

500 F. Supp. at 640. We think these distinctions are not sufficient reasons for failing to find *Runge* quite persuasive. The overriding similarity in the two cases is that the insured in each case voluntarily placed his head in a noose with the intention of restricting the air flow to the point of asphyxia, loss of consciousness. Neither victim intended that his noose system would cause death, but it cannot be said that either failed to realize the risk of death or serious bodily injury naturally resulting from voluntarily induced unconsciousness with a noose around the neck, restricting blood and air flow.

The district court relied upon, and the plaintiffs base a principal argument on, differences between the policy language in *Runge* and that here. The *Runge* opinion involved a policy that would pay for fatal injuries sustained "solely through violent, external and accidental means." 537 F. 2d at 1158. Plaintiffs contrast this accidental means policy with what they characterize as an accidental results policy in the instant case. And it does appear that Virginia may recognize a difference between accidental means and accidental results policies, the former being more restrictive. While Home argues that this distinction is no longer valid, it is unnecessary for us to reach the question. Rather, we note that the part of the *Smith* opinion we have quoted above applies to injuries that result from "accident *or* accidental means." 202 Va. at 761, 120 S.E. 2d at 268 (emphasis added). The fact that the *Smith* opinion did not differentiate between the types of policies at this point, and the lack of significant dissimilarity between the policy in *Smith* and the instant case, persuades us that the *Smith* opinion should apply here. In *Runge* we applied the law as stated in *Smith* to the particular facts of that case. The facts here are the same with the insignificant addition of the fail safe feature of the noose. We think the same result should obtain.

Because the decedent voluntarily placed his neck in the noose and tightened the same to the point where he lost consciousness, we think his death was the natural result of a voluntary act unaccompanied by anything unforeseen except death or injury. *Smith,* 120 S.E. 2d at 268. He is bound to have foreseen that death or serious bodily injury could have resulted when he voluntarily induced unconsciousness with a noose around his neck. We are thus of opinion that his death was not an accident under Virginia law and that judgment should be for the defendant.

* * *

The judgment of the district court is accordingly
REVERSED.

Comment

The Court of Appeals overturned the District Court's finding because it considered malfunctioning of a fail-safe mechanism to be an insignificant difference from the facts in *Runge*, which it cited as the controlling law in Virginia. Apparently the Court of Appeals did not regard the jamming of the pulley as a significant unforeseen event. This is particularly ironic in view of a judicial opinion rendered in another circuit after this opinion was filed but before it was published. The beneficiary in *Sigler* appealed the District Court's decision, arguing that the District Court's decision in *International Underwriters* undermined the decision of the District Court in *Sigler*. The Court of Appeals disagreed and affirmed the summary judgment against *Sigler,* noting in a footnote: "The present case is easily distinguishable from *International Underwriters* because that case involved the failure of a system of ropes and pulleys designed to protect the insured from death as he engaged in autoerotic acts." *Sigler v. Mutual Ben. Life Ins. Co.,* 663 F. 2d 49 (8th Cir. 1981). Thus what the 4th Circuit Court of Appeals regarded as "the insignificant addition of the fail safe feature" was regarded by the 8th Circuit Court of Appeals as a feature that easily distinguishes the cases.

The rationale expressed for overturning the District Court's opinion does not appear to us to be based on a logical interpretation of the case law cited. The Court seems to be denying the obvious factual distinction between cases in order to give the appearance of moral consistency with its earlier opinion in *Runge*. As suggested by our Comment on the District Court opinion, we would have found reversal on the self-inflicted-injury issue more consistent with our understanding of autoerotic fatalities and this series of judicial opinions than this reversal on the accidental-death issue.

Conclusions

The small number of cases available for analysis and the variations among cases in policy language, applicable law, and trial records are such that it would be premature and presumptuous of us to attempt to discern the principles on which these cases have been decided with any expectation of assisting future judicial decisions.[1] We do, however, wish to make two general observations in concluding this chapter.

The first of these is that neither the parties to these cases nor the courts rendering these opinions have had before them the full body of current information regarding autoerotic asphyxia. In the absence of complete information, the courts have rendered decisions that in some instances reflect inadequate or incorrect expert evidence and erroneous legal presumptions, as noted in our specific comments on the cases.

Each of the cases reviewed previously involved some determination as to the intent, mental state, or behavior of the insured, yet there are three areas in which scientific evidence was developed in none of the cases: the mental disorder[2] of the insured (see chapter 5), the temporal sequence of subjective[3] and physiological effects in ongoing asphyxia (see chapter 4), and the precipitous loss of consciousness that may occur through the carotid baroreceptor response (see chapter 4). We expect each of these areas to become a focus of expert evidence in future litigation, resulting in requests for psychiatric consultation in such cases (as occurred in the litigation described in Note 1). It should be noted, however, that few psychiatrists are experts in the medicolegal investigation of death, just as few forensic pathologists are experts in psychopathology and mental processes.

The second general observation concerns the social-policy implications of judicial decisions in these cases. The fact that accidental-death benefits were ultimately denied in four of the five cases detailed earlier (the sole exception being the affirmation of a Texas jury verdict, in *Tommie*), despite a diversity of policy language, state law, and trial records, may reflect a reluctance on the part of the courts to allow beneficiaries to gain from what is perceived as the insured's misconduct. If the courts seek to deter[4] autoerotic asphyxia, the denial of monetary benefits might indeed be a more powerful deterrent than would overt moral pronouncements, which are conspicuously absent from these judicial opinions. But like the doomsday machine in *Dr. Strangelove,* neither the threat of benefits denial nor the threat of death can be hoped to deter unless communicated to those whose conduct one hopes to influence.

Notes

1. For suggested statutory language designed to standardize legal consideration of a victim's contribution to his injury, see O'Connell (1979), who proposes abolition of contributory and comparative fault from tort systems.

2. Mental disorder was a central issue in an unreported Florida case (described by Miller and Milbrath, in press), defended on the basis of policy language excluding recovery for "death caused or contributed to, directly or indirectly, by disease or bodily or mental infirmity . . ." Both the plaintiff and the defendant insurance company offered expert testimony as to whether the insured suffered from a "mental infirmity." The defendant's expert testified that "death was due to or the product of a long standing masochistic—sadomasochistic—bondage—sexual perversion," and the plaintiff's experts emphasized indications of the decedent's positive mental health and lack of mental impairment. The finding was for the plaintiff (Miller and Milbrath, in press).

3. A German commentator has argued that the insured's state of consciousness at the time an accident is triggered should be decisive in forming medicolegal opinions of the manner of death in autoerotic fatalities (Naeve 1975). Although efforts to ascertain the insured's state of consciousness are desirable, neither that nor any other single factor should be decisive.

4. See Calabresi (1970) for an authoritative analysis of the presumed deterrent function of accident compensation through the system of imposing tort liability. Theoretically, the more expensive accidents are to the defendant, the greater the incentive to reduce the number and severity of accidents. For the victim, however, nonfinancial risks may be more powerful deterrents than financial liability. O'Connell (1979) emphasizes that for the individual victim "the desire to avoid injury will almost invariably be stronger than the desire to avoid financial loss." In a note, O'Connell goes on to say that such financial concerns as victims may have are diminished when personal safety is at stake because "the desire

to avoid bodily pain and physical injury is paramount for the individual.'' Obvious exceptions to this general principle include instances in which the potential financial losses are great and the potential bodily injury is slight (for example, risking abrasions to retrieve a diamond necklace from a drainpipe) and instances in which the financial loss is highly probable but there is a low probability of suffering bodily injury in the course of averting the financial loss (for example, gathering one's valuables as a building fire appears to be thirty minutes away from one's property). Thus the rational decision maker will weigh the perceived probability and severity of financial losses against the perceived probability and severity of bodily injury. A less-obvious exception, but more pertinent to our concerns here, is the potential victim for whom bodily pain is pleasurable, namely, the sexual masochist.

References

Adelson, L. *The Pathology of Homicide: A Vade Mecum for Pathologist, Prosecutor and Defense Counsel.* Springfield, Ill.: Charles C Thomas, 1974.

Adelson, L., and Hirsch, C.S. Sudden and unexpected death from natural causes in adults. In Spitz, W.U., and Fisher, R.S. (eds.). *Medicolegal Investigation of Death: Guidelines for the Application of Pathology to Crime Investigation,* 2nd ed. Springfield, Ill.: Charles C Thomas, 1980, pp. 88–117.

Adjutantis, G., Coutselinis, A., and Dritsas, C. Suicidal strangulation. *Forensic Science* 3:283–284, 1974.

Alexander, H.B. Latin-American. In Gray, L.H. (ed.). *The Mythology of All Races in 13 Volumes.* Vol. 11. New York: Cooper Square, 1964.

American Psychiatric Association. *Diagnostic and Statistical Manual of Mental Disorders,* 3rd ed. Washington, D.C.: American Psychiatric Association, 1980.

Anders, F. *Das Pantheon Der Maya.* Graz, Austria: Akademische Druck-u. Verlagsanstalt, 1963.

Anonymous. Carotid bodies. *Lancet* 1:80–81, 1978.

Anonymous. *Modern Propensities: Or, an Essay on the Art of Strangling &c, Illustrated with Several Anecdotes.* London: J. Dawson, n.d.

Anonymous. Rushing to a new high. *Time* 112:16, July 17, 1978.

Associated Press. Hanging game proves headlong rush to death. *Colorado Springs Gazette Telegraph* (Colorado Springs, Colo.), April 3, 1981.

Auden, G.A. An unusual form of suicide. *Journal of Mental Science* 73:428–430, 1927.

Bass, M. Sudden sniffing death. *Journal of the American Medical Association* 212:2075–2079, 1970.

Beckett, S. *Waiting for Godot.* New York: Grove Press, 1954.

Bell, A.P., Weinberg, M.S., and Hammersmith, S.K. *Sexual Preference: Its Development in Men and Women.* Bloomington, Ind.: Indiana University Press, 1981.

Bendheim, O.L. The psychiatric autopsy: Its legal application. *Bulletin of the American Academy of Psychiatry and the Law* 7:400–410, 1979.

Bennett, E. *The Maya Epic.* Madison, Wisc.: University of Wisconsin-River Falls Press, 1974.

Benz, J.A. Thermal deaths. In Curran, W.J., McGarry, A.L., and Petty, C.S. (eds.). *Modern Legal Medicine, Psychiatry, and Forensic Science.* Philadelphia: F.A. Davis, 1980, pp. 269–304.

Berlyne, N., and Strachan, M. Neuropsychiatric sequelae of attempted hanging. *British Journal of Psychiatry* 114:411–422, 1968.

Bloch, I. *Anthropological and Ethnological Studies in the Strangest Sex Acts in Modes of Love of All Races Illustrated*. New York: Falstaff Press, 1935.

Bloch, I. *Marquis de Sade: His Life and Works*. New York: Castle Books, 1931.

Bloch, I. *The Sexual Extremities of the World*. New York: Book Awards, 1964.

Boss, M. (Abell, L.L., trans.). *Meaning and Content of Sexual Perversions: A Daseinsanalytic Approach to the Psychopathology of the Phenomenon of Love*. New York: Grune & Stratton, 1949.

Bourke, J.G. *Scatalogic Rites of All Nations: A Dissertation upon the Employment of Excrementitious Remedial Agents in Religion, Therapeutics, Divination, Witchcraft, Love-Philters, etc., in All Parts of the Globe*. New York: American Anthropological Society, 1934.

Boy Scouts of America. *Handbook for Boys*, 21st printing. New York: Boy Scouts of America, 1935.

Boy Scouts of America. *Handbook for Boys*, 37th printing. New York: Boy Scouts of America, 1944.

Brittain, R. The sexual asphyxias. In Camps, F.E. (ed.). *Gradwohl's Legal Medicine*, 2nd ed. Baltimore: Williams & Wilkins, 1968, pp. 549–552.

Buja, L.M., and Petty, C.S. Heart disease, trauma, and death. In Curran, W.J., McGarry, A.L., and Petty, C.S. (eds.). *Modern Legal Medicine, Psychiatry, and Forensic Science*. Philadelphia: F.A. Davis, 1980, pp. 187–206.

Burchell, H.B. Editorial. Electroshock hazards (and urine as an electrolyte). *Circulation* 41:17–19, 1970.

Burroughs, W.S. *Cities of the Red Night*. New York: Holt, Rinehart and Winston, 1981.

Burroughs, W.S. *Naked Lunch*. New York: Grove Press, 1966.

Burton, J.F. Adolescent sex hangings. In Fisher, R.S., and Petty, C.S. (eds.). *Forensic Pathology: A Handbook for Pathologists*. Washington, D.C.: U.S. Government Printing Office, 1977, pp. 133–135.

Cairns, F.J., and Rainer, S.P. Death from electrocution during autoerotic procedures. *New Zealand Medical Journal* 94:259–260, 1981.

Calabresi, G. *The Cost of Accidents: A Legal and Economic Analysis*. New Haven: Yale University Press, 1970.

Chapman, A.J., and Matthews, R.E. Accidental death during unusual sexual perversion: A case report. *Journal of Forensic Medicine* 17:65–68, 1970.

Coe, J.I. Sexual asphyxias. *Life-Threatening Behavior* 4:171–175, 1974.

Comfort, A. (ed.). *The Joy of Sex: A Cordon Bleu Guide to Lovemaking.* New York: Crown, 1972.

Crawford, W.V. Death due to fluorocarbon inhalation. *Southern Medical Journal* 69:506–507, 1976.

Curran, W.J. History and development. In Curran, W.J., McGarry, A.L., and Petty, C.S. (eds.). *Modern Legal Medicine, Psychiatry, and Forensic Science.* Philadelphia: F.A. Davis, 1980, pp. 1–26.

Curvey, C.E. Effect of the manner of death in medicolegal cases on insurance settlements involving double indemnity. *Journal of Forensic Sciences* 19:390–397, 1974.

Danto, B.L. A case of female autoerotic death. *American Journal of Forensic Medicine and Pathology* 1:117–121, 1980.

Davis, J.H. Asphyxial deaths. In Curran, W.J., McGarry, A.L., and Petty, C.S. (eds.). *Modern Legal Medicine, Psychiatry, and Forensic Science.* Philadelphia: F.A. Davis, 1980, pp. 249–266.

Dearborn, L.W. Masturbation. In DeMartino, M.F. (ed.). *Sexual Behavior and Personality Characteristics.* New York: Citadel Press, 1963, pp. 239–254.

DeMartino, M.F. (ed.). *Human Autoerotic Practices.* New York: Human Sciences Press, 1979.

Denko, J.D. Klismaphilia: Amplification of the erotic enema deviance. *American Journal of Psychotherapy* 30:236–255, 1976.

Denko, J.D. Klismaphilia: Enema as a sexual preference: Report of two cases. *American Journal of Psychotherapy* 27:232–250, 1973.

Dietz, P.E. Clinical approaches to teaching legal medicine to physicians: Medicolegal emergencies and consultations. *American Journal of Law & Medicine* 2:133–145, 1976.

Dietz, P.E. Crime and sexuality. *Bulletin of the American Academy of Psychiatry and the Law* 6:vi, 1978a.

Dietz, P.E. Kotzwarraism: Sexual induction of cerebral hypoxia. Unpublished manuscript, Medical Criminology Research Center, McLean Hospital, Belmont, Mass., 1978b. (Presented at Grand Rounds, Royal Ottawa Hospital, University of Ottawa, Ottawa, Ontario, Canada, February 6, 1979.)

Dietz, P.E. Letter to the editor (on klismaphilia). *American Journal of Psychotherapy* 28:322–323, 1974.

Dietz, P.E. Sampling bias and the case report: The example of postmortem cesarian section. Paper presented at the Annual Meeting of the Robert Wood Johnson Foundation Clinical Scholars Program, Scottsdale, Ariz., November 16, 1979.

Dietz, P.E. Sexual bondage behavior. *Bulletin of the American Academy of Psychiatry and the Law,* in press.

Dietz, P.E. Social factors in rapist behavior. In Rada, R.T. (ed.). *Clin-*

ical Aspects of the Rapist. New York: Grune & Stratton, 1978c, pp. 59–115.

Dietz, P.E. Toward a scientific forensic psychiatry. *Journal of Forensic Sciences* 22:774–780, 1977.

Dietz, P.E., and Evans, B. Pornographic imagery and prevalence of paraphilia. *American Journal of Psychiatry* 139:1493–1495, 1982.

Dietz, P.E., and Hazelwood, R.R. Atypical autoerotic fatalities. *Medicine and Law* 1:307–319, 1982.

Disch, T.M. Pleasures of hanging (Review of *Cities of the Red Night*). *New York Times Book Review*, March 15, 1981, pp. 14–15.

Dregne, N.M. Psychological autopsy: A new tool for criminal defense attorneys? *Arizona Law Review* 24:421–439, 1982.

Edmondson, J.S. A case of sexual asphyxia without fatal termination. *British Journal of Psychiatry* 121:437–438, 1972.

Ellis, H. *Studies in the Psychology of Sex* (4 vols.). New York: Random House, 1936.

Enos, W.F., and Beyer, J.C. Sex crimes. In Spitz, W.U., and Fisher, R.S. (eds.). *Medicolegal Investigation of Death: Guidelines for the Application of Pathology to Crime Investigation.* Springfield, Ill.: Charles C Thomas, 1973, pp. 373–384. (Pp. 511–526 in 2nd ed., 1980.)

Everett, G.M. Effects of amyl nitrite ("poppers") on sexual experience. *Medical Aspects of Human Sexuality* 6:146–151 passim, December 1972.

Fagan, D.G., and Forrest, J.B. "Sudden sniffing death" after inhalation of domestic lipid-aerosol. *Lancet* 2:361, 1977.

Farberow, N.L., and Shneidman, E.S. (eds.). *The Cry for Help*. New York: McGraw Hill, 1961.

Fatteh, A. Artefacts in forensic pathology. In Wecht, C.H. (ed.). *Legal Medicine Annual: 1972*. New York: Appleton-Century-Crofts, 1972, pp. 49–74.

Fatteh, A. *Handbook of Forensic Pathology*. Philadelphia: J.B. Lippincott, 1973.

Fisher, R.S. Electrical and lightning injuries. In Spitz, W.U., and Fisher, R.S. (eds.). *Medicolegal Investigation of Death: Guidelines for the Application of Pathology to Crime Investigation,* 2nd ed. Springfield, Ill.: Charles C Thomas, 1980, pp. 367–376.

Ford, R. Death by hanging of adolescent and young adult males. *Journal of Forensic Sciences* 2:171–176, 1957.

Francis, J.J., and Marcus, I.M. Masturbation: A developmental view. In Marcus, I.M., and Francis, J.J. (eds.). *Masturbation from Infancy to Senescence*. New York: International Universities Press, 1975, pp. 9–51.

Frazer, J.G. (Gaster, T.H., ed.). *The New Golden Bough*. New York: Criterion Books, 1959.

Freuchen, P. *Book of the Eskimos*. Cleveland: World, 1961.

Gardner, E. Mechanism of certain forms of sudden death in medico-legal practice. *Medico-Legal Review* 10:120–133, 1942.

Geddes, L.A., and Baker, L.E. Response to passage of electric current through the body. *Journal of the Association for the Advancement of Medical Instrumentation* 5:13–18, 1971.

Geis, G. *Not the Law's Business: An Examination of Homosexuality, Abortion, Prostitution, Narcotics and Gambling in the United States*. New York: Schocken Books, 1979.

Gonzales, T.A., Vance, M., and Helpern, M. *Legal Medicine and Toxicology*. New York: D. Appleton-Century, 1940.

Gonzales, T.A., Vance, M., Helpern, M., and Umberger, C.J. *Legal Medicine: Pathology and Toxicology*, 2nd ed. New York: Appleton-Century-Crofts, 1954.

Gosselin, C., and Wilson, G. *Sexual Variations: Fetishism, Sadomasochism and Transvestism*. New York: Simon & Schuster, 1980.

Groth, A.N. *Men Who Rape: The Psychology of the Offender*. New York: Plenum Press, 1979.

Gutheil, E.A. The psychologic background of transsexualism and transvestism. *American Journal of Psychotherapy* 8:231–239, 1954.

Guthkelch, A.C., and Smith, D.N. (eds.). *A Tale of a Tub. To which is added the battle of the books and the mechanical operation of the spirit. By Jonathan Swift*, 2nd ed. New York: Oxford University Press, 1958.

Gwozdz, F. The sexual asphyxias: Review of current concepts and presentation of seven cases. *Forensic Science Gazette* 1:2–4, 1970.

Harris, W.S. Aerosol propellants are toxic to the heart (letter). *Journal of the American Medical Association* 223:1508–1509, 1973.

Hayden, J.W., and Comstock, E.G. The clinical toxicology of solvent abuse. *Clinical Toxicology* 9:169–184, 1976.

Hazelwood, R.R., Burgess, A.W., and Groth, A.N. Death during dangerous autoerotic practice. *Social Science and Medicine* 15E:129–133, 1981a.

Hazelwood, R.R., Dietz, P.E., and Burgess, A.W. The investigation of autoerotic fatalities. *Journal of Police Science and Administration* 9:404–411, 1981b.

Hazelwood, R.R., Dietz, P.E., and Burgess, A.W. Sexual fatalities: Behavioral reconstruction in equivocal cases. *Journal of Forensic Sciences* 27:763–773, 1982.

Hazelwood, R.R., and Douglas, J.E. The lust murderer. *FBI Law Enforcement Bulletin* 49:18–22, April 1980.

Henry, R.C. "Sex" hangings in the female. *Medico-Legal Bulletin* (Richmond) 20:1–5, February 1971.

Herrick, R. Upon love. In *Hesperides: or, The Works Both Humane &*

Divine of Robert Herrick Esq. London: John Williams and Francis Eglesfield, 1648.

Hirschfeld, M. *Sexual Anomalies: The Origins, Nature, and Treatment of Sexual Disorders.* New York: Emerson Books, 1948.

Hohman, L.B., and Schaffner, B. The sex lives of unmarried men. *American Journal of Sociology* 52:501–507, 1947.

Holzhausen, G., and Hunger, H. Unfälle mit Todesfolge bei autoerotischer Betätigung. *Archiv für Kriminologie* 125:164–167, 1960.

Honick, B. State prison inmate found hanged at farm. *The Nashville Banner* (Nashville, Tenn.), June 21, 1976.

Hudgel, D.W., and Weil, J.V. Asthma associated with decreased hypoxic ventilatory drive: A family study. *Annals of Internal Medicine* 80:622–625, 1974.

Hunt, A.C. Unnatural death due to asphyxia. In Camps, F.E. (ed.). *Gradwohl's Legal Medicine*, 2nd ed. Baltimore: Williams & Wilkins, 1968, pp. 335–344.

Institut für Sexualforschung. *Bilder-Lexikon: Kulturgeschichte*, Vol. 1. Vienna: Verlag für Kulturforschung, 1928.

Institut für Sexualforschung. *Ergänzungsband zum Bilder-Lexikon: Kulturgeschichte-Literatur und Kunst Sexualwissenschaft*, Vol. 4. Vienna: Verlag für Kulturforschung, 1931.

Jablonski, S. *Illustrated Dictionary of Eponymic Syndromes and Diseases and Their Synonyms.* Philadelphia: W.B. Saunders, 1969.

James, P.D. *An Unsuitable Job for a Woman.* New York: Charles Scribner's Sons, 1972.

Johnson, C.D. The heart and la mort d'amour: Sex, sudden death and the heart. *Boletin Asociacion Medica de Puerto Rico* 68:118–121, 1976.

Johnstone, J.M., Hunt, A.C., and Ward, E.M. Plastic-bag asphyxia in adults. *British Medical Journal* 2:1714–1715, 1960.

Kaplan, H.I., Freedman, A.M., and Sadock, B.J. (eds.). *Comprehensive Textbook of Psychiatry/III*, 3rd ed. (3 vols.). Baltimore: Williams & Wilkins, 1980.

Keeton, R.E. *Cases and Materials on Basic Insurance Law*, 2nd ed. St. Paul, Minn.: West, 1977.

Kerr, D.J.A. *Forensic Medicine: A Text-Book for Students and a Guide for the Practitioner*, 6th ed. London: Adam & Charles Black, 1957.

Kinsey, A.C., Pomeroy, W.B., and Martin, C.E. *Sexual Behavior in the Human Male.* Philadelphia: W.B. Saunders, 1948.

Kinsey, A.C., Pomeroy, W.B., Martin, C.E., and Gebhard, P.H. *Sexual Behavior in the Human Female.* Philadelphia: W.B. Saunders, 1953.

Knight, B. Fatal masochism—accident or suicide? *Medicine, Science and the Law* 19:118–120, 1979.

Knight, B. Forensic problems in practice: VII.—Asphyxia. *The Practitioner* 217:139–144, 1976.
Kohout, P. (Ckova-Henley, K.P., trans.). *The Hangwoman*. New York: Putnam, 1980.
Kramer, N.D. Availability of volatile nitrites. *Journal of the American Medical Association* 237:1693, 1977.
Leonard, J. Review of *The Hangwoman*. *Books of the Times* 4:256–257, 1981.
Lester, G., and Lester, D. *Suicide: The Gamble With Death*. Englewood Cliffs, N.J.: Prentice-Hall, 1971.
Lichter, D.H. Note: Diagnosing the dead: The admissibility of the psychiatric autopsy. *American Criminal Law Review* 18:617–635, 1981.
Lindenberg, R. Systemic oxygen deficiencies. In Minckler, J. (ed.). *Pathology of the Nervous System* (3 vols.). New York: McGraw-Hill, 1968, pp. 1583–1617.
Litman, R.E., Curphey, T., Shneidman, E.S., Faberow, N.L., and Tabachnick, N. Investigations of equivocal suicides. *Journal of the American Medical Association* 184:924–929, 1963.
Litman, R.E., and Swearingen, C. Bondage and suicide. *Archives of General Psychiatry* 27:80–85, 1972.
Lowry, T.P. Amyl nitrite: A toxicology survey: A national survey of emergency room physicians and forensic pathologists. In Nickerson, M., Parker, J.O., Lowry, T.P., and Swenson, E.W. *Isobutyl Nitrite and Related Compounds*. San Francisco: Pharmex, 1979, pp. 89–91.
Luke, J.L. Asphyxial deaths by hanging in New York City, 1964–1965. *Journal of Forensic Sciences* 12:359–369, 1967.
McCormick, D. *The Unseen Killer: A Study of Suicide, Its History, Causes and Cures*. London: Frederick Muller, 1964.
McDowell, C.P. Death investigation: Sexual asphyxia. *Forensic Science Digest* 4:162–169, 1978.
Mant, A.K. Heat, cold, and electricity. In Camps, F.E. (ed.). *Gradwohl's Legal Medicine*, 2nd ed. Baltimore: Williams & Wilkins, 1968, pp. 379–390.
Mant, A.K. The significance of spermatozoa in the penile urethra at post-mortem. *Journal of the Forensic Science Society* 2:125–130, 1962.
Marti-Ibañez, F. *A Prelude to Medical History*. New York: MD Publications, 1961.
Massie, E., Rose, E.F., Rupp, J.C., and Whelton, R.W. Sudden death during coitus—Fact or fiction? *Medical Aspects of Human Sexuality* 3:22–26 passim, June 1969.

Masters, W.H., and Johnson, V.E. *Human Sexual Response*. Boston: Little, Brown, 1966.

Merkley, D.K. *The Investigation of Death*. Springfield, Ill.: Charles C Thomas, 1957.

Mendelson, J.H., Dietz, P.E., and Ellingboe, J. Postmortem plasma luteinizing hormone levels and antemortem violence. *Pharmacology Biochemistry & Behavior* 17:171–173, 1982.

Meyer, J.K. Paraphilias. In Kaplan, H.I., Freedman, A.M., and Sadock, B.J. (eds.). *Comprehensive Textbook of Psychiatry*, 3rd ed., Vol. 2. Baltimore: Williams & Wilkins, 1980, pp. 1770–1783.

Miller, E.C., and Milbrath, S.D. Medical-legal ramifications of an autoerotic asphyxial death. *Bulletin of the American Academy of Psychiatry and the Law*, in press.

Miller, J. A deadly experiment. *Chronicle-Tribune* (Marion, Ind.), April 26, 1981.

Milner, R. Orgasm of death. *Hustler* 8:33–34, August 1981.

Money, J. Paraphilias. In Money, J., and Musaph, H. (eds.). *Handbook of Sexology*. New York: Elsevier/North-Holland Biomedical Press, 1977, pp. 917–928.

Money, J. Paraphilias: Phyletic origins of erotosexual dysfunction. *International Journal of Mental Health* 10:75–109, 1981.

Money, J., and Ehrhardt, A.A. *Man & Woman, Boy & Girl: The Differentiation and Dimorphism of Gender Identity from Conception to Maturity*. Baltimore: Johns Hopkins University Press, 1972.

Moore, G.C., Zwillich, C.W., Battaglia, J., et al. Respiratory failure associated with familial depression of ventilatory response to hypoxia and hypercapnia. *New England Journal of Medicine* 295:861–865, 1976.

Moritz, A.R. *The Pathology of Trauma*. Philadelphia: Lea & Febiger, 1954.

Mountain, R., Zwillich, C.W., and Weil, J.V. Hypoventilation in obstructive lung disease. *New England Journal of Medicine* 298:521–525, 1978.

Naeve, W. Versicherungsmedizinische Beurteilung tödlicher autoerotischer Unfälle. *Zeitschrift für Rechtsmedizin* 75:299–309, 1975.

Newman, W.S. *The Sonata in the Classic Era: The Second Volume of a History of the Sonata Idea*. Chapel Hill, N.C.: University of North Carolina Press, 1963.

O'Connell, J. A proposal to abolish contributory and comparative fault, with compensatory savings by also abolishing the collateral source rule. *University of Illinois Law Forum* 1979:591–607, 1979.

Parke, W.T. *Musical memoirs; Comprising an Account of the General State of Music in England*, Vol. 1. London: Henry Colburn and Richard Bentley, 1830.

References

Paulos, M.A., and Tessel, R.E. Excretion of β-phenethylamine is elevated in humans after profound stress. *Science* 215:1127–1129, 1982.

Petit, G.J., Petit, A.G., Geille, A., and Chambat, J.B. Strangulation, suffocation, and auto-eroticism. *International Criminal Police Review* 322:262–264, 1974.

Petty, C.S., and Curran, W.J. Operational aspects of public medicolegal death investigation. In Curran, W.J., McGarry, A.L., and Petty, C.S. (eds.). *Modern Legal Medicine, Psychiatry, and Forensic Science*. Philadelphia: F.A. Davis, 1980, pp. 51–94.

Podolsky, E. The lust murderer. *Medico-Legal Journal* 33:174–178, 1965.

Polson, C.J. Electrocution. *Medico-Legal Journal* 27:121–135, 1959.

Polson, C.J. *The Essentials of Forensic Medicine*, 2nd ed. Springfield, Ill.: Charles C Thomas, 1965.

Polson, C.J., and Gee, D.J. *The Essentials of Forensic Medicine*, 3rd ed. Oxford: Pergamon Press, 1973.

Polson, C.J. Strangulation—Accident, suicide or homicide. *Journal of the Forensic Science Society* 1:79–83, 1961.

Prosser, W.L. *Handbook of the Law of Torts*, 4th ed. St. Paul, Minn.: West, 1971.

Quiroz-Cuaron, A., and Reyes-Castillo, R. Auto-eroticism and accidental strangulation. *International Criminal Police Review* 250:171–178, 1971.

Rada, R.T. Psychological factors in rapist behavior. In Rada, R.T. (ed.). *Clinical Aspects of the Rapist*. New York: Grune & Stratton, 1978, pp. 21–58.

Ramsey, G.V. The sexual development of boys. *American Journal of Psychology* 56:217–234, 1943.

Reese, J.J. *Text-Book of Medical Jurisprudence and Toxicology*, 7th ed. Philadelphia: P. Blakiston's Son, 1906.

Reinhardt, J.M. *Sex Perversions and Sex Crimes*. Springfield, Ill.: Charles C Thomas, 1957.

Resnik, H.L.P. Erotized repetitive hangings: A form of self-destructive behavior. *American Journal of Psychotherapy* 26:4–21, 1972.

Richardson, O., and Breyfogle, H.S. Medicolegal problems in distinguishing accident from suicide. *Annals of Internal Medicine* 25:22–65, 1946.

Robertson, W.G.A. *Manual of Medical Jurisprudence and Toxicology*, 5th ed. London: A. & C. Black, 1925.

Rogers, J.H. Some Australian cases of accidental hanging as a result of auto-erotic practices. *International Criminal Police Review* 202:272–274, 1966.

Rosenblum, S., and Faber, M.M. The adolescent sexual asphyxia syndrome. *Journal of the American Academy of Child Psychiatry* 18:546–558, 1979.

Roueché, B. *Eleven Blue Men and Other Narratives of Medical Detection.* Boston: Little, Brown, 1947.
Rupp, J.C. The love bug. *Journal of Forensic Sciences* 18:259–262, 1973.
Rupp, J.C. Sex-related deaths. In Curran, W.J., McGarry, A.L., and Petty, C.S. (eds.). *Modern Legal Medicine, Psychiatry, and Forensic Science.* Philadelphia: F.A. Davis, 1980, pp. 575–587.
Sade. *Justine, or Good Conduct Well Chastised (1791).* In Seaver, R., and Wainhouse, A. (comps. and trans.). *The Marquis de Sade: The Complete Justine, Philosophy in the Bedroom, and other writings.* New York: Grove Press, 1965.
Sade. *Justine, or the Misfortunes of Virtue.* New York: Castle Books, 1964.
Sass, F.A. Sexual asphyxia in the female. *Journal of Forensic Sciences* 20:181–185, 1975.
Schechter, M.D. The recognition and treatment of suicide in children. In Shneidman, E.S., and Farberow, L. (eds.). *Clues to Suicide.* New York: McGraw-Hill, 1957, pp. 131–142.
Schneider, J. Macabre experiment led to teen's death. *The State Journal* (Lansing, Mich.), October 11, 1978.
Shankel, L.W., and Carr, A.C. Transvestism and hanging episodes in a male adolescent. *Psychiatric Quarterly* 30:478–493, 1956.
Sigell, L.T., Kapp, F.T., Fusaro, G.A., Nelson, E.D., and Falck, R.S. Popping and snorting volatile nitrites: A current fad for getting high. *American Journal of Psychiatry* 135:1216–1218, 1978.
Simpson, K. *Taylor's Principles and Practice of Medical Jurisprudence* (2 vols.), 12th ed. London: J & A Churchill, 1965.
Sivaloganathan, S. Curiosum eroticum: A case of fatal electrocution during auto-erotic practice. *Medicine, Science and the Law* 21:47–50, 1981.
Smith, S.M., and Braun, C. Necrophilia and lust murder: Report of a rare occurrence. *Bulletin of the American Academy of Psychiatry and the Law* 6:259–268, 1978.
Snyder, L. *Homicide Investigation,* 2nd ed. Springfield, Ill.: Charles C Thomas, 1967.
Spitz, R.A. Authority and masturbation: Some remarks on a bibliographic investigation. *Psychoanalytic Quarterly* 21:490–527, 1952.
Spitz, W.U. Asphyxia. In Spitz, W.U., and Fisher, R.S. (eds.). *Medicolegal Investigation of Death: Guidelines for the Application of Pathology to Crime Investigation.* Springfield, Ill.: Charles C Thomas, 1973, pp. 270–295. (Pp. 320–350 in 2nd ed., 1980.)
Stearns, A.W. Cases of probable suicide in young persons without ob-

vious motivation. *Journal of the Maine Medical Association* 44:16–23, 1953.

Stearns, A.W. Accident or suicide? *Journal of the Maine Medical Association* 46:313–337 passim, 1955.

Stekel, W. (Brink, L., trans.). *Sadism and Masochism: The Psychology of Hatred and Cruelty* (2 vols.). New York: Liveright, 1929.

Stoller, R.J. *Perversion: The Erotic Form of Hatred.* New York: Pantheon Books, 1975.

Stoller, R.J. *Sexual Excitement: Dynamics of Erotic Life.* New York: Pantheon Books, 1979.

Strassmann, G. Mechanical asphyxia. In Gradwohl, R.B.H. (ed.). *Legal Medicine.* St. Louis: C.V. Mosby, 1954, pp. 260–284.

Strauss, A.F., and Mann, G.T. Forensic pathology seminar. *Journal of Forensic Sciences* 5:169–216, 1960.

Svensson, A., Wendell, O., and Fisher, B.A.J. *Techniques of Crime Scene Investigation,* 3rd ed. New York: Elsevier, 1981.

Swift, J. A discourse concerning the mechanical operation of the spirit. In a letter to a friend. A fragment. In Guthkelch, A.C., and Smith, D.N. (eds.). *A Tale of a Tub,* 2nd ed. New York: Oxford University Press, 1958.

Tabachnick, N., Litman, R.E., Osman, M., Jones, W.L., Cohn, J., Kasper, A., and Moffat, J. Comparative psychiatric study of accidental and suicidal death. *Archives of General Psychiatry* 14:60–68, 1966.

Taylor, G.J. IV, and Harris, W.S. Cardiac toxicity of aerosol propellants. *Journal of the American Medical Association* 214:81–85, 1970.

Thomas, F., and Van Hecke, W. Hanging as a cause of accidental death in a rare form of sexual perversion. An instructive case. *International Criminal Police Review* 129:173–177, 1959.

Tomita, K., and Uchida, M. On a case of sudden death while masturbating. *Japanese Journal of Legal Medicine* 26:42–45, 1972.

Trimble, G.X. The coital coronary. *Medical Aspects of Human Sexuality* 4:64–72 passim, May 1970.

Ueno, M. The so-called coition death. *Japanese Journal of Legal Medicine* 17:330–340, 1963.

United Press. Sex-hanging insurance. *San Francisco Chronicle* (San Francisco, Calif.), October 29, 1981.

Usher, A. Accidental hanging in relation to abnormal sexual practices. *Newcastle Medical Journal* 27:234–237, 1963.

Usher, A. Sexual violence. *Forensic Science* 5:243–255, 1975.

Walsh, F.M., Stahl, C.J. III, Unger, H.T., Lilienstern, O.C., and Stephens, R.G. III. Autoerotic asphyxial deaths: A medicolegal analysis of forty-three cases. In Wecht, C.H. (ed.). *Legal Medicine Annual: 1977.* New York: Appleton-Century-Crofts, 1977, pp. 157–182.

Webster, R.W. *Legal Medicine and Toxicology.* Philadelphia: W.B. Saunders, 1930.

Wecht, C.H. [Chapter introduction]. In Wecht, C.H. *Legal Medicine Annual: 1977.* New York: Appleton-Century-Crofts, 1977, pp. 155–156.

Wecht, C.H. The role of the forensic pathologist in criminal cases. *Tennessee Law Review* 37:669–687, 1970.

Weisman, A.D. Self-destruction and sexual perversion. In Shneidman, E.S. (ed.). *Essays in Self-Destruction.* New York: Science House, 1965, pp. 265–299.

Willey, G.R. Maya archaeology. *Science* 215:260–267, 1982.

Wolfe, R.J. The hang-up of Franz Kotzwara and its relationship to sexual quackery in late 18th century London. Paper presented as the 11th Annual Janus Foundation Lecture on the History of Medicine, San Francisco, Calif., January 15, 1980.

Wright, R.K., and Davis, J. Homicidal hanging masquerading as sexual asphyxia. *Journal of Forensic Sciences,* 21:387–389, 1976.

Index

Accidental deaths: autoerotic fatalities misclassified as, 22–23, 28, 38–39, 121–122; equivocal cases, 140–146, 151; and insurance companies, 37, 122, 141, 151, 155–187; and position of body, 123
Adelson, L., 61, 66, 114, 117
Adjutantis, G., 36
Adolescents, 10–11, 30, 40–41, 56
Age of victims, 36, 42, 50, 51, 93–94
Airway, obstruction of, 6, 48, 49, 71–73; incidence, 66; pathophysiology, 62; by vomitus, 67, 73, 101, 102–104, 138; *see also* Aspiration; Choking; Suffocation
Alcohol, 38, 103
Alexander, H.B., 14–15
American Psychiatric Association, 77, 79–80, 85
Amphetamine, 6
Amyl nitrite, 110–112; *see also* Nitrites
Anesthetics, 6, 25, 30, 73–74, 102, 109; incidence of fatalities, 67; pathophysiology, 62–63
Anders, F., 15
Armed Forces Institute of Pathology, 38
Arts, autoerotic asphyxia in, 7–9, 15
Asphyxia, 6–7, 8–9, 15, 105; *see also* Autoerotic asphyxia; Hypoxia
Aspiration, 67, 73, 101, 102–104, 136, 138
Associated Press, 10, 11
Auden, G.A., 23
Autoeroticism, 2–6; *see also* Masturbation
Autoerotic asphyxia: age of victims, 50, 51, 93–94; in ancient civilizations, 14–15; and aspiration, 103; and bondage, 25, 27, 33, 34–36, 71–72, 73, 81–85, 114–115; and cross-dressing, 27, 28–29, 30, 34–35, 70, 72, 93; and homosexuality, 30, 39, 78–79, 86, 100, 130, 149; incidence, 48–49, 58–59; individual discovery of, 55–57; marital status of victims, 50; and masochism, 23, 27, 38, 80, 85–86, 97–98, 99; mechanisms of, 59–60; newspaper reports, 10–11; and paraphilias, 79–96, 99–100; pathophysiology, 49, 59–63, 66; psychodynamics, 97–99; and sadism, 32, 39, 86–90, 91–92; and sexual advice literature, 9–10, 57, 131; sex of victims, 31, 33, 36, 41, 42, 49–51, 66; social class of victims, 50–51; subjective effects, 63–66; types, 66–76
Autopsy. *See* Behavioral autopsy; Psychological autopsy

Baker, L.E., 104
Bass, M., 110
Beckett, S., 8
Behavioral autopsy, 53, 152–153, 155–156
Belgium, 30, 58
Bell, A.P., 2
Bell, G., 162
Bendheim, O.L., 155–156
Bennett, E., 14
Benz, J.A., 113
Berlyne, N., 66
Beyer, James C., 36, 175–176
Birdlime, Mrs., 19–21
Bloch, I., 8, 19, 25, 56, 104
Bode, Vaughn, 9–10
Bondage: and autoerotic asphyxia, 25, 27, 33, 34–36, 71–72, 73, 81–85, 114–115; and cross-dressing, 30, 126; and discovery of autoerotic asphyxia, 56–57; equipment, 128; and fetishism, 92; and homosexuals, 79; incidence of fatalities, 47, 51, 58–59; and investigation of fatalities, 125–126, 140; and masochism, 85; and pornography, 56–57, 67, 130–131, 143; and suicide, 155
Bon Ton Magazine, 22
Boss, M., 26, 32, 98
Bourke, J.G., 5
Boy Scouts of America, 4–5
Brain, 66, 105
Brassieres, 90–91, 93, 103, 106, 107
Braun, C., 39
Breast fetishism, 91
Breyfogle, H.S., 151
Brittain, R., 32, 42, 43, 107
Buja, L.M., 114
Burchell, H.B., 108
Burns, 38, 72, 86, 126, 135–136
Burroughs, W.A., 8, 64–66
Burton, J.F., 36
Butyl nitrite, 10, 111–112; *see also* Nitrites
Byrd v. Life Insurance Co. of Virginia, 182

Cairns, F.J., 108
Calabresi, G., 186

201

Cannon v. *Metropolitan Life Insurance Co.*, 160–165, 172
Cardiovascular disease. *See* Heart attacks; Strokes
Carotid artery, compression of, 23, 24–25, 26, 60–61
Carotid baroreceptor, 60–61, 165, 185
Carr, A.C., 28–29, 32, 55–56, 64
Catholicism, 4
Chains, 35, 36, 92, 93, 114–115, 125
Chapman, A.J., 32, 62, 155
Chemicals and gases, 48, 124
Chest, compression of, 6, 48, 49, 74–76; and children, 34; incidence of fatalities, 67; pathophysiology, 63
Children, 29, 30, 31, 34, 38
Chloroform, 25, 30, 63, 67, 73, 124
Choking, 49; *see also* Airway, obstruction of
Cities of the Red Night (Burroughs), 8, 64–66
Coe, J.I., 36–37
Comfort, A., 9, 57, 107
Comstock, E.G., 109
Connecticut General Life Ins. Co. v. *Tommie*, 10, 169–174
Consumer Product Safety Commission, 110
Continental Gas Co. v. *Jackson*, 167
Control, sense of, 26–27
Coprophilia, 29, 69, 95, 100
Cordophilia, 40, 41, 81–85, 99; *see also* Bondage
Corey v. *Wilson*, 162
Crawford, W.V., 110
Criminal behavior of victims, 97
Cross dressing, 103, 106–107, 115; and autoerotic asphyxia, 27, 28–29, 30, 34–35, 70, 72, 93; and bondage, 30, 126; and investigation of fatalities, 127–128, 140, 145–146; and masochism, 29, 34–35, 99–100; *see also* Transvestism
Curvey, C.E., 37, 153, 155
Cyanosis, 6, 66, 112

Damned, The, 8–9
Danto, B.L., 41–42
Davis, J.H., 38, 52, 59
Dearborn, L.W., 5
DeMartino, M.F., 4
Denko, J.D., 118
Depression, 36, 40–41, 97, 137, 155; and risk-taking, 77
Diagnostic and Statistical Manual of Mental Disorders (DSM-III), 77, 78, 79–80, 81, 86

Diaries. *See* Writings of victims
Dietz, P.E., 4, 19, 26, 43, 56, 57, 64, 81–82, 98, 118
Dildos, 95, 115, 129, 131, 134
Disch, T.M., 8
Discipline masks, 114, 116, 130, 134
Diving gear, 31, 56
Domination. *See* Bondage
Double indemnity, 37, 156–160, 161
Douglas, J.E., 139
Dregne, N.M., 156
Dürer, A., 15

Edmondson, J.S., 36
Effigies, 90
Ehrhardt, A.A., 2
Electrocution, 48, 51, 104–108, 132–133; incidence of fatalities, 101
Ellis, H., 25
Enemas, 118
Enos, W.F., 36
Epilepsy, hanging induced, 23
Equivocal cases, 137–138, 140–153
Erotica. *See* Pornography
Escape mechanisms, 42; *see also* Fail-safe mechanism; Slipknots
Eskimos, 27
Estate of Wade v. *Continental Insurance Co.*, 167
Ether, 30, 63, 109
Evans, B., 57
Everett, G.M., 112
Evidence, removal of, 32, 52–53, 71, 127–128
Exhibitionism, 39, 40
Exposure, death from, 49, 51, 101, 112–114

Faber, M.M., 9, 42, 56, 64
Fagan, D.G., 110
Fail-safe mechanism, 179
Fantasy, sexual, 2
Farberow, N.L., 155
Fatteh, A., 36, 104, 116
Federal Bureau of Investigation, 37, 45
Fetishism, 40, 90–93, 99, 100, 129; and bondage, 82
Films, 110, 131
Fisher, B.A.J., 105
Flagellation, 15, 33, 135
Fluorocarbons. *See* Freon inhalation
Food and Drug Administration, 110, 112
Foot fetishism, 65–66, 91, 92
Ford, R., 27, 29, 90
Forrest, J.B., 110
Fort Collins, Colorado, 10–11
Francis, J.J., 3, 4

Index

Francis A. Countway Library of Medicine, 22
Frazer, J.G., 15
Freeman v. Crown Life Ins. Co., 170–171
Freon inhalation, 101, 108–110
Freuchen, P., 27
Frotteurism, 95

Gags, 71–72, 82, 84, 102, 124
Games, 34, 51, 56
Gardner, E., 26, 61
Garrison, Charles O., 162, 165
Gas masks, 124
Geddes, L.A., 104
Gee, D.J., 60, 107
Geis, G., 159
Genital masochism. *See* Self-mutilation
Germany, 31, 43
Gonzales, T.A., 25–26
Gosselin, C., 40
Gould, Judge, 16, 22
Gradwohl's Legal Medicine, 27–28, 36
Graham, James, 104
Greeks, 15
Groth, A.N., 26
Gunshot wounds, 118
Gutheil, E.A., 28, 29
Guthkelch, A.C., 7
Gwozdz, F., 33, 58

Halothane, 63
Handbook of Evidence for the Idaho Lawyer (Bell), 162
Handcuffs, 143, 144
Hanging, 6, 67–68; incidence, 66; pathophysiology, 60–61; *see also* Judicial hangings
Hangman's noose, 72–73, 127, 144, 176
Hangwoman, The (Kohout), 8
Harris, W.S., 110
Harris v. Bankers Life & Casualty Co., 182
Hayden, J.W., 109
Hayden v. Insurance Company of North America, 162
Hazelwood, R.R., 45, 59, 107, 139, 150, 155–156
"Head rushing," 10–11
Heart attacks, 49, 51, 102, 114–117, 149–150; and electrocution, 105–106, 108; and fluorocarbons, 109, 110; and vagal inhibition, 61, 62
Hennepin County, Minnesota, 37, 58
Henry, R.C., 33, 36, 102
Herrick, R., 7
Hill, Susannah, 15–18, 22

Hirsch, C.S., 114, 117
Hirschfeld, M., 18
Hohman, L.B., 5
Holzhausen, G., 30
H.O.M., Inc., 57
Homicide: autoerotic asphyxia misclassified as, 38, 121–125, 137–138; disguised as autoerotic fatalities, 52, 152; equivocal cases, 137–138, 146–150, 152
Homosexuality: and autoerotic asphyxia, 30, 39, 78–79, 86, 100, 130, 149; and bondage, 79; ego-dystonic, 79; and fantasy, 2; incidence of autoerotic fatalities, 47; and masochism, 86; and nitrites, 111–112; pornography, 78; and transvestism, 93, 111
Honick, B., 10
Hormones, 6
Houston, Texas, 58
Hudgel, D.W., 61
Hunger, H., 30
Hunt, A.C., 32
Hustler, 9–10, 41
Hypercapnia, 170, 172, 173
Hypoxia, 13, 173; physiology of, 61, 66; subjective effects, 63–66, 97–98
Hypoxyphilia, 81, 99; *see also* Kotzwarraism

Incest, 39
Infibulation, 33, 51, 86, 118; and investigation of fatalities, 126–127
Inhibition, sexual, 4
Institut für Sexualforschung, 25, 118
Insurance companies, 37, 122, 141, 151, 155–187
Intelligence of victims, 32, 36
International Travelers Association v. Marshall, 171
International Underwriters, Inc. v. Home Ins. Co., 159, 165, 174–185
In the Realm of the Senses, 9, 33
Investigation of autoerotic fatalities, 121–153
Ixtab, 8, 13–15, 65

Jablonski, S., 43
James, P.D., 8, 52, 152
Johnson, C.D., 116, 139
Johnson, V.E., 1, 5
Johnstone, J.M., 30, 98
Joy of Sex, The (Comfort), 9, 57
Judicial hangings, 14, 15, 23, 24, 57
Judicial opinions and autoerotic fatalities, 10, 53, 155–187
Jujitsu, 61

Justine (Sade), 7–8

Kaplan, H.I., 77
Keeton, R.E., 156
Kerr, D.J.A., 30
Kinsey, A.C., 1, 5
Klismaphilia, 95, 118
Knight, B., 38, 39–40, 62, 151
Knots, interest in, 75, 92, 142
Kohout, P., 8
Kotzwarra, Francis, 15–18, 22, 56, 80–81, 152
Kotzwarraism, 13, 19, 80–81, 85
Kramer, N.D., 112

Leather, 72–73, 82, 87, 90, 91, 114, 127, 130, 148
Leonard, J., 8
Lester, D., 33
Lester, G., 33
Lichter, D.H., 156
Lickleider v. *Iowa State Traveling Mens' Ass'n.*, 166–167
Ligottism, 81–85; *see also* Bondage; Cordophilia
Lindenberg, R., 66
Litman, R.E., 9, 30, 34–36, 41, 42, 43, 53, 58–59, 77, 79, 151, 153, 155
Location of victim's body, 122
Locker Room Essence, 111, 112
Locks, 35, 124, 125
London, 59
Los Angeles, 58–59
Los Angeles Free Press, 35
Lowry, T.P., 112
Luke, J.L., 58
Lust murder, 27, 29, 32, 39

McCormick, D., 31
McDowell, C.P., 39
Mackintosh fetishism, 40
Manacle, Parson, 19–21, 152
Mann, G.T., 30
Manslaughter, negligent, 51
Mant, A.K., 30–31, 105, 113
Marcus, I.M., 3, 4
Marital status of victims, 50, 51
Marsyas, 15
Marti-Ibanez, F., 104
Masochism, 187; and autoerotic asphyxia, 23, 27, 85–86, 97–98, 99; and bondage, 85; and cross-dressing, 29, 34–35, 99–100; and electrocution, 108; and investigation of fatalities, 125–127, 140; and religion, 33; and self-mutilation, 86, 118–119; term, 19; and transvestism, 27, 29, 99–100

Massachusetts, suicides in, 27
Massie, E., 116, 139
Masters, W.H., 1, 5
Masturbation, 1, 2–6; guilt, 36; and hanging, 28; and household appliances, 107, 115–116; and hypoxia, 64; and investigation of fatalities, 131–132
Matthews, R.E., 32, 62, 155
Mayans, 14–15
Medek, Peter, 8
Men: autoerotic fatalities, 49–50, 51, 66; cordophilia, 82–83; masturbation, 5
Mendelson, J.H., 6
Merkley, D.K., 30
Methemoglobinemia, 111
Mexico, 33
Meyer, J.K., 80
Milbraith, S.D., 186
Miller, E.C., 186
Miller, J.A., 10, 11, 128
Milner, R., 10
Mirrors, 27, 29–30, 36, 41, 91, 130
Modern Propensities, 15–22
Money, J., 2, 80
Moore, G.C., 61
Moritz, A.R., 14, 102
Mountain, R., 61
Mud, 69, 95, 126
Museo de Antropológica (Mexico City), 14
Mysophilia, 69, 95, 100

Naeve, W., 186
Naked Lunch (Burroughs), 8, 64
Narcissism, 29–30, 41–42
Necrophilia, 39, 95
Newman, W.S., 15
Newspaper reports of autoerotic fatalities, 10–11
New York City, 58
Nipples, mutilation of, 86, 89, 118, 126–127, 129
Nitrites, 59, 101, 110–112
Nitrous oxide, 25, 56, 63, 67, 73, 94, 109
Nudity, 69; as evidence of autoerotic fatality, 27, 132, 144

Ocean Accident & Guarantee Corp. v. *Glover*, 182
O'Connell, J., 186–187
Onanism, 4; *see also* Masturbation
O'Neil v. *New York Life Insurance Company*, 162, 163–164
Ontario, Canada, 59
Orgasm, 1–2, 64
Oriental societies, 33

Oshima, Nagisha, 9
O'Toole, Peter, 8
Outdoor autoerotic fatalities, 61–68, 89–90

Pam, 110
Panties, 90, 92–93
Paraphernalia. *See* Dildos; Fetishism; Leather; Locks; Rubber; Vibrators
Paraphilias, 13, 79–96, 99–100
Parents. *See* Relatives of victim
Parke, W.T., 15
Partners, 51, 79, 135, 153
Paul, D., 59
Paulos, M.A., 6
Pedophilia, 56, 94
Penis: mutilation of, 86, 143; strangulation, 24, 29; taping of, 93, 140
Petit, G.J., 37
Petty, C.S., 114
Photographs, 83, 86, 89, 129, 131
Plastic bags, 6, 28, 30, 32, 39, 70–71, 124; and anesthetics, 73; and Freon inhalation, 109–110; incidence of fatalities, 58, 66; pathophysiology, 62; transvestism, 70–71
Podolsky, E., 139
Poisonings, 51
Polson, C.J., 30, 31, 60, 62, 105, 107
Poppers, 112; *see also* Nitrites
Pornography, 36, 42, 109, 113, 115; bondage, 56–57, 67, 130–131, 143; and discovery of autoerotic asphyxia, 56–57; films, 110, 131; and investigation of fatalities, 130–131, 143–144
Position of victim's body, 122–123
Props, 122, 130–131
Prosser, W.L., 159
Prostitutes, 3, 25, 151–152
Protective padding, 11, 27, 36, 67; as evidence of autoerotic asphyxia, 27, 30, 97, 128, 133;
Psychological autopsies, 77–78, 155–156
Pulmonary edema, 116

Quiroz-Cuaron, A., 33, 37, 62

Race and autoerotic fatalities, 32, 50, 51
Rada, R.T., 26
Rainer, S.P., 108
Ramsey, G.V., 5
Rapists, 26–27
Rectum, insertions in, 36, 38, 51, 69, 95, 115, 118, 126; and electrocution, 106, 108

Reese, J.J., 23
Reinhardt, J.M., 29–30
Relatives of victim: alteration of evidence, 32, 52–53, 71, 127–128; challenge of verdict, 121–122, 125, 153; information about victim, 132–133
Religion, 4, 33, 37
Republic Nat. Life Ins. Co. v. Heyward, 171
Resnik, H.L.P., 33–34, 43, 98, 155
Reyes-Castillo, R., 33, 37, 62
Risk-taking, 1, 35, 37–38, 53, 97, 98; and depression, 77; and discovery of autoerotic asphyxia, 56
Robertson, W.G.A., 23, 151
Rogers, J.H., 32, 58
Rope fetishism, 92; *see also* Bondage; Cordophilia
Rosenblum, S., 9, 40–41, 42, 56, 64
Roueché, B., 112
Rowe v. United Commercial Travelers Ass'n., 167
Rubber fetishism, 10, 29, 90, 127, 128
Ruling Class, The, 8
Runge v. Metropolitan Life Insurance Co., 156–160, 167–168, 174, 177, 178, 182–185
Rupp, J.C., 36, 42, 57, 70, 98, 102, 116, 118, 155
Rush, 111, 112

Sacher-Masoch, Leopold von, 19
Sade, Marquis de, 7–8, 18–19, 56
Sadism: and autoerotic asphyxia, 32, 39, 86–90, 91–92; oral, 98; term, 18–19
Sadism and Masochism (Stekel), 23–24, 118–119
Sadomasochism, 26–27, 38, 90; *see also* Masochism; Sadism
Sass, F.A., 37
Scarves, 91, 92
Schaffner, B., 5
Schechter, M.D., 29
Schizophrenia, 96–97
Schneider, J., 10, 11, 56–57
Self-mutilation, 33, 38, 42, 72; and masochism, 86, 118–119, 126–127
Self-rescue mechanism, 124–125, 142; *see also* Slipknots
Semen, mythology of, 5
Sexual advice literature, 9–10, 57, 131
Sexual arousal, 1–2
Shankel, L.W., 28–29, 32, 55–56, 64
Shneidman, E.S., 155
Shoe fetishism, 23, 91
Shoshone-Bannock, 34

Sigell, L.T., 112
Sigler v. *Mutual Life Ins. Co.*, 165–169, 172, 183, 184
Silk, J.W., 25
Simpson, K., 14, 27, 30, 31, 56, 62, 102, 108, 113, 116
Sivaloganathan, S., 107–108
Sketches by victims, 87
Slipknots, 72, 75, 123, 125, 146, 147
Smith, D.N., 7
Smith, S.M., 39
Smith v. *Combined Insurance Co. of America*, 157–158, 159, 177, 181–182, 183–184
Snyder, L., 31–32
Spermatozoa, presence after death, 30–31
Spiders, 98
Spilsbury, B., 26
Spitz, R.A., 36, 60, 102
Spitz, W., 3
Sterns, A.W., 27, 28, 33, 70
Stein, Robert, 9
Stekel, W., 23–24, 25, 29, 32, 41, 55–56, 64, 89, 118–119
Stoller, R.J., 2, 37–38, 99
Strachan, M., 66
Strangulation, 6, 24–27, 36, 49, 180; incidence, 66; ligature, 68–69; psychophysiology, 60–61
Strassman, G., 27–28, 102
Strauss, A.F., 30
Strokes, 49, 116, 117
Suicide, 39–40, 41; autoerotic, 52–53, 151; autoerotic asphyxia misclassified as, 4, 26, 27, 28, 29, 31, 33, 36, 38; and bondage, 155; discovery of autoerotic asphyxia during attempt, 55–56; equivocal cases, 137–138, 140–146; notes, 34–35, 53, 145–146, 151; and transvestism, 57
Suffocation, 49, 102, 151–152; and pathophysiology, 61–62
Suspension-point abrasions, 133–134
Svensson, A., 42
Swearingen, C., 9, 30, 34–36, 41, 42, 43, 53, 58–59, 77, 79, 151, 155
Sweater fetishism, 91, 92–93
Swift, J., 7
Sydney, Australia, 32, 58

Tabachnik, N., 155
Taylor, G.J., 110
Telephone scatologia, 95
Temple of Health, 104
Tessel, R.E., 6
Thomas, F., 30, 58
Tomita, K., 116, 117, 139

Transsexualism, 96
Transvestism: and autoerotic asphyxia, 93–94, 98, 100; and fetishism, 93; and homicide, 52; and homosexuality, 93, 111; incidence, 47, 99, 100; and sadomasochism, 27, 99–100; and suicide, 57; *see also* Cross-dressing
Traumatic asphyxia. *See* Chest, compression of
Trimble, G.X., 116, 139
Tsiminaki's sign, 23

Uchida, M., 116, 117, 139
Ueno, M., 116, 139
Undetermined fatalities, 51, 62, 101, 117
Unsuitable Job for a Woman, An (James) 8, 52
"Upon Love" (Herrick), 7
Urethra, insertion in, 51, 106, 108, 118, 126
Urophilia, 95
Usher, A., 31, 151–152

Vagina, insertion in, 51, 61, 117
Vagus nerve, 26, 62
Vanbutchell, Martin, 22, 56
Van Hecke, W., 30, 58
Vibrators, 37, 86, 129, 131, 146, 147, 148
Vomitus, aspiration of, 67, 73, 101, 102–104, 136, 138
Voyeurism, 39, 95

Waiting for Godot (Beckett), 8
Walsh, F.M., 38–39
Webster, R.W., 116
Wecht, C.H., 33, 38
Weil, J.V., 61
Weisman, A.D., 31, 55–56, 64
Wendell, O., 42
Willey, G.R., 14
Wilson, G., 40
Wolfe, R.J., 19, 22, 56
Womb, return to, 98–99
Women: and autoerotic asphyxia, 31, 33, 36, 41, 42, 50, 66; and cordophilia, 82–83; and masochism, 25; and masturbation, 5; and paraphilias, 85
Wooden v. *John Hancock Mutual Life Insurance Co.*, 158, 159, 177–178, 182, 183
Wright, R.K., 38, 52, 152
Writings of victims, 34–35, 65–66, 70, 86, 87, 91–92, 129–130

Yahgan, 27

Zoophilia, 95

About the Authors

Robert R. Hazelwood is a Supervisory Special Agent of the Federal Bureau of Investigation. He is a faculty member of the FBI Academy's Behavioral Science Unit and an adjunct faculty member of the University of Virginia. He received his undergraduate degree from Sam Houston State Teacher's College and the M.S. from Nova University. Mr. Hazelwood also served a one-year fellowship in Forensic Medicine at the Armed Forces Institute of Pathology. Prior to entering the FBI in 1971, he served eleven years in the U.S. Army's Military Police Corps, attaining the rank of Major, and received many awards and decorations including the Bronze Star in Vietnam. His works have been published by the *Journal of Police Science and Administration, Social Science and Medicine, American Registry of Pathology, Journal of Forensic Sciences, FBI Law Enforcement Bulletin*, and other professional journals. Mr. Hazelwood has lectured extensively throughout the United States, Canada, and the Caribbean. He has taught over 10,000 law-enforcement officers and criminal justice personnel about interpersonal violence and has been consulted by agencies throughout North America in the investigation of sexual assaults and homicides.

Park Elliott Dietz, M.D., M.P.H., Ph.D., is associate professor of law and of behavioral medicine and psychiatry at the University of Virginia Schools of Law and Medicine and medical director of the University's Institute of Law, Psychiatry and Public Policy in Charlottesville, Virginia. He studied psychology and genetics (A.B.) at Cornell and medicine (M.D.), public health (M.P.H.), and sociology (Ph.D.) at Johns Hopkins. He was a Robert Wood Johnson Foundation Clinical Scholar during psychiatric residencies at Johns Hopkins and the University of Pennsylvania. While assistant professor of psychiatry at the Harvard Medical School he worked with the criminally insane and testified for the government in the trial of John Hinckley, Jr., on charges arising from the attempted assassination of President Reagan. Currently he chairs the Committee on Abuse and Misuse of Psychiatry in the U.S. of the American Psychiatric Association and is a member of the Committee on Federal Trauma Research of the National Academy of Sciences, the Executive Committees of the American Academy of Psychiatry and the Law and the American Academy of Forensic Sciences, the Committee on Psychiatry and Law of the Group for the Advancement of Psychiatry, and the editorial boards of the *Bulletin of the American Academy of Psychiatry and the Law,* the *Journal of Forensic Sciences, Behavioral Sciences & The Law,* and *Legal Aspects* *of Psychiatric Practice*. He is a consultant to the Behavioral Science Unit of the FBI Academy and principal investigator for a National Institute of Justice study of threats and attacks against public figures.

Ann Wolbert Burgess, R.N., D.N.Sc., F.A.A.N., is associate director of nursing research of the Department of Health and Hospitals of Boston and van Ameringen Professor of Psychiatric Mental Health Nursing at the University of Pennsylvania School of Nursing. She studied at Boston University and the University of Maryland and received the Doctor of Nursing Science in psychiatric-mental-health nursing at Boston University. She is principal investigator on a research project studying the use of children in pornography, funded by the National Center on Child Abuse and Neglect; on a demonstration project of a randomized clinical trial to increase rate of return to work for heart-attack victims, funded by the Robert Wood Johnson Foundation; and on a joint research project with the Behavioral Science Unit of the FBI Academy studying sexual-homicide crime scenes and patterns of behavior, funded by the National Institute of Justice. Dr. Burgess has held faculty appointments at Boston College and Boston University. She has written textbooks in the field of nursing and crisis intervention; coauthored articles in the field of victimology; and coauthored the clinical textbook, *Sexual Assault of Children and Adolescents*.